SILENCE

SILENCE

ARISYAN VIOLET 1

Pola Pane

Paperback ISBN: 978-1-7348606-2-7
Epub ISBN: 978-1-3933605-2-0

***

Written By Pola Pane
Published By Royal Hawaiian Press
Cover Art By Tyrone Roshantha
Translated By Rafal Stachowsky
Publishing Assistance: Dorota Reszke

***

For More Works By This Author, Please Visit:
www.royalhawaiianpress.com

***

Version Number 1.00

PROLOGUE

Silence
Do not think about what it was,
which always tired you.
Because this will not come back.
Don't ever count again
Days from the loss of strength.
Another stanza of life.
You are afraid of your own shadow,
because someone always walking behind you.
When a new day gets up,
you are convinced that
it's another one
the worst in your life.
Do not think about what it was,
which always tired you
because this will not come back.
Don't ever count again
days from the loss of strengthAnother stanza of life.
Days have passed, months,
thoughts bear hard on your head.
This life, fate makes so, that
You want to live one moment,
it comes back every day.

CHAPTER I

If despair is without illusions, you have to act like hoping or killing yourself.
ALBERT CAMUS

Diffused orange light shone through the dense cloud cover, adding horror to the desert landscape. Endless plain, dry lonely tree and I - Emily Walker - lost and so lonely. For some time, I stood still, unsuccessfully trying to catch my breath. Strangely enough, I was sure I hadn't been breathing for a good few minutes, but death wasn't coming. Instead, fear appeared - ruthless, persistent, slowly filling every cell of my body.

I closed my eyelids. I waited.

For what? I had no idea...

opened my eyes and stared into the darkness. A familiar smell of moisture and mold struck my nostrils. I came back to reality.

"Dream," I repeated in my mind, "it's just a bad dream, the one I've been dreaming of for two weeks since I decided to go outside."

Maybe it is a promise from a near end?

Maybe... but it doesn't matter anymore.

There was a murmur of my mother, Megan, heavy but steady breathing from the next bed, and the muffled groan of springs indicated that she had turned to the other side. She will wake up soon and we will have to talk. About us, our future and my desperate decision. For several days I have been gathering the courage to tell her about my decision - right or wrong, it doesn't matter. In the face of time that is inexorably shrinking, it really doesn't matter.

I would like to end this nightmare. It's a life without a normal life, a week without days of the week, a day without daylight, one like the other, the same as yesterday and the day before yesterday.

Carefully, so as not to make noise, I sat on the mattress. I reached out under the bed, where I hid an old, faded backpack. I pulled it to me. It had everything that could ensure survival on the surface: a dirty, worn blanket, a jacket of brown nylon, some worn mummy clothes, a pack of hard military biscuits and a metal battered mug. To a bulky backpack I pocket things that - as I thought - I should have on hand: compass, map of the area, a bottle of muddy water, a folding knife and cardboard box with a few matches in the it.

It had to be enough.

I bent down and started tying my shoes. When I tied the other one, the adjoining bed creaked in a characteristic way. Instinctively, I turned my face that way. Although neither the outline of the Earthling figure, nor even the vague shadow distracted the dense night, I knew that my mother was awake and had just sat on her bed.

"Are you awake?" I heard a sleepy voice.

"Yes."

I took a deep breath and regretted it. In addition to the air, an intense, unpleasant musty smell entered my nostrils. I hated the scent that had been with me since I was a child, filling my whole body, irritating my throat, sticking my tongue, confusing my mind.

It's time to say: enough!

I swallowed hard.

"Mom, we need to talk." I tried to make it sound resolutely, but I couldn't hide the trembling voice.

She didn't speak, but if I could look through the darkness around us, I would certainly see fear in her eyes. She had been watching me with growing concern for several days. She knew I was planning something, and I knew she wouldn't like it. Despite this, no force was unable to alter the meters of my decision. To encourage myself, I clenched my hands on the backpack straps.

"I decided to go outside," I said.

She was still silent, so I repeated a little louder:

"I'm going outside."

Silence.

"Do you hear what I'm saying?!"

"I hear and think you are crazy," she said in a strangled voice. "I don't understand what came to your mind, Emily? There is only death outside."

"We don't know for sure. Anyway, here only death is waiting for us, so what's the difference." I shrugged. "It doesn't matter where I die. In the shelter or on the surface. I don't want to live like that.

"Don't say that," she rebuked me. "You're only eighteen years old and your whole life ahead of you."

"Yeah, for sure..." I came to her word, "rather all my life behind me. I don't feel anything ahead of me - I murmured grimly. Besides, I'm an adult, so I can decide for myself."

She didn't answer, so I continued:

"I thought about everything and I think somebody survived. I want to find other people."

"Do you really believe that? I don't think anyone survives," she said with resignation.

I got angry.

"And what with us? Freak of nature? Statistical error? Come on, I will never believe it. Logically speaking, if we survived up to ten years, so probably others also did.

"We survived because your grandfather had quite an original hobby and built a fully equipped shelter in his garden," she laughed nervously. "I never thought I'd ever be grateful to him for this weirdness."

"I don't understand what you want to wait for here? For salvation? After all the water we have is enough to us at most a week, and food for two, maybe three days," I argued. "I'm serious, I'm not going to stay here an hour longer."

She sighed.

"Emily... you're right. We should at least try. Just don't think I will let you go alone. I will go with you, and this is not subject to discussion," she stated categorically.

I expected such an answer. Just a few days ago I thought we would go together, but lately my mother has completely lost strength. She was denying herself food and water that it would be enough for me as long as possible. I realized too late. And now... Now, she wouldn't have gone half a kilometer. Together we had no chance, separately our chances were not much

higher, but I wanted to take a chance, even if my trip would end a few steps from the shelter.

"Mommy, please. Don't complicate..." I said pleadingly.

She was silent. I almost heard running thoughts through her head, and their mad gallop seemed to resound in my head also. I felt that she analyzed something intensely. She saw my determination, recognized it in my voice and breathing. She knew perfectly well that I would not give up, that it was too late to change my mind. Still, she tried to find a different solution. Better for both of us.

The match's crack broke the silence. My mother lit candle burned to the middle, the last one, which we had. A slightly yellow light brightened the room. She sat next to me and put her arm around tenderly.

"Emily, listen to me. We go together, whether you like it or not."

„But..." I tried to interrupt her, but she covered her hand over my mouth, not allowing to speak.

"Listen to the end. Just don't interrupt me, I'm asking you so much."

I nodded my head.

"We'll do it like that: we will go out together and if the outside conditions are bearable, we will go to grandfather's house, after all it is only a hundred meters. There is a good chance that the house is still standing. We would have shelter for the next night or even for a few days," she explained calmly. "We will gather strength, maybe we will find some food and we will decide what to do next. If the air is still deprived of enough amount of oxygen... Well, we can't

do anything. Just like you said, no matter where we die, whether here or there. I'm sick of this stinking hole too."

Frankly speaking, I didn't think about house of grandfather as a temporary shelter. There was some logic in it, and reluctant I agreed.

"When we go?" I asked.

Mom smiled.

"Even now. Well... maybe not immediately." She looked pointedly at my packed backpack. "I'd like to take some things too. Give me a few minutes."

It cost US A lot of effort to break through two heavy hatches securing the exit. We did quite well with the first one. We got to the vestibule, which almost immediately turned into a concrete tunnel with a low ceiling of several meters. I could feel a slight slope under my feet. The corridor led slightly upwards, with each step increasing the impression that the ceiling was falling more and more. We walked the rest of the distance bent in half, almost sliding our noses on the ground. Finally, the tunnel turned right and we stopped in a spacious chamber, directly in front of the second hatch. We had an unpleasant surprise here. The metal handle acting as a handle did not want to move even by a millimeter. Mom cursed badly.

"I'm sorry..." she muttered. "I think we're stuck here for good."

"Calm down, I'll bring something heavy from the shelter.

I threw my backpack to the ground and headed back. It seemed shorter now. I came back

armed with a large hammer. A few bumps were enough for the door to let go.

We make it.

We were free.

Mom squeezed tight my hand and with firmly gesture pulled behind. Into the dark. We were outside now, afraid to draw air into our lungs. I felt a gentle breeze on my face. With the influence of this unexpected caresses I took a deep breath, and I felt something strange in my head - not from lack of oxygen, but of the excess.

We could breathe, and it was amazing.

None of us spoke. We just stood in silence and breathed steadily, savoring every portion of the fresh air. As time passed, some hope crept into my heart, not so much for the better tomorrow, but in general for some tomorrow.

The feeling of joy did not last long, it was destroyed by my mother.

"Let's go quickly to the building," she whispered at some point. "Something is probably wrong."

"How's that? It is better, than we thought." I was surprised at her unreasonable anxiety, but I began to listen up and look nervously, trying to see something in the dark.

"It's suspiciously quiet," she whispered in my ear. "It is abnormal."

She was right, why I did not pay for it attention. The silence was so overwhelming that my ears hurt.

We headed towards grandfather's house. My mother went first, firmly put up the steps, and I was so close, as I could, clinging tightly to her arm. Soon we reached the door at the back of the house.

I was afraid.

Although it was quite cold, sweat trickled down my back. For the first time I realized that this is a completely new, alien world to me, and even if it preserved such a form, as before the disaster, still would not be my world. The truth is I didn't know anything about life. My knowledge was limited only to what I read from books or what I learned from my mother. How much it was to be useful to me, the future will show.

Mom put her hand carefully on the door handle. The door gave way quite reluctantly, and the metal hinges creaked loudly. We walked over the threshold fearfully and stopped in the lobby, listening.

"I don't think there is anyone here," she said with relief. "I panicked unnecessarily, but this silence... this silence is so... strange, as if all nature has died."

"Because it died." Now I fully realized it.

"We'll worry about that tomorrow," my mother said cheerfully.

She dug out a match from her pocket and lit the kerosene lamp on the dresser, then with a heavy sigh she sank into a nearby dusty chair. She looked tired and a few years older.

I looked around the house distrustfully, unable to get rid of the feeling of internal anxiety. The building looked unoccupied for years. Floors, furniture and other equipment were covered with long-lasting rusty brown dust, and its particles floating in the air uncomfortably scratched the throat. I stood

motionless and did not have the courage to go further. I glanced at my mother. She looked as the air had escaped out of her, and even worse... as if the life had escaped out of her. When she realized I was looking at her, she gathered herself and got up from the chair, effortlessly straightening her back. She grabbed the lamp with one hand and, holding onto the wall with the other, walked deeper into the house.

"We'd better look for something to eat," she ordered.

I followed her into the kitchen. She set the lamp in the middle of the kitchen table and set about opening the next cabinets, scooping all their contents on the floor. Cans, jars, noodle bags, rice... there was even a lot of it.

"Well, we're rich," she said contentedly, regaining strength in second, as if new life had entered her with hope.

„It's possible." I looked suspiciously stacks on lightly rusted cans and dusty food packaging. "It is not known if they are still suitable for eating."

"I think that most of them are fine. And anyway, we'll find out soon. How about a warm dish?" She ignited the stove burner and gave me a triumphant smile. "There is still a lot of gas left in the gas bottle. Check if there is tap water."

I turned on the tap. It hissed, the faucet spat out a few small, dried grains of rust and fell silent.

"Unfortunately." I folded my hands helplessly.

"It's nothing. There is nothing to complain about, and still it is not bad."

We were finishing eating warm canned soup and I had the impression that the last hours were the best thing that happened to me in my life when the sky began to shine in the east and the dawn of the morning appeared to our eyes. For all the years spent in the shelter, the sun became such an abstract concept for me that the sight of light seeping from the sky, not from the fluorescent lamp, surprised me a little. I totally forgot, how that is, when the day wakes up.

I approached the window and stuck my face at the light. Rays penetrating the dirty windows gently warmed my face. I closed my eyelids.

"Incredible..." I whispered.

I stayed there for some time and only when I opened my eyes I could take a closer look at the landscape outside the window. The view was depressing. Stumps of trees, brown, bleak, dead... An abandoned car in front of the house, next to a falling shed. All covered with a layer of volcanic dust. A shiver ran down my back when I realized that my world was dead. Although... not really. In places of the ocean of dust emerged islets of lush greenery contrasting with still life, arousing in me a spark of hope that maybe not all was lost.

"You look terrible." Some groan rescued me from thoughtfulness.

I changed my gaze from post-apocalyptic scenery to my mother.

"You too," I said and started giggling. I could not resist.

We were both dirty, tousled and terribly emaciated, the light of day highlighted this. For nine years life in

the shelter was quite bearable. Only last year has hit us hard. The generator failure deprived us of electricity and running water, and the storage tank only allowed us to quench our thirst.

I went to the large standing mirror, rubbed it roughly with the sleeve of my sweatshirt and looked at my reflection. Under the layer of sticky dirt, I could barely see my own features.

"Great," I murmured. "I do not know, how I look like."

"We could use a good bath," my mother sighed.

"Uhm... you can always dream."

"Come on." She grabbed my hand and led me into the kitchen. „We have to do something with it."

She took a bottle of vegetable oil and a relatively clean roll of paper towels from one of the cupboards.

"This isn't the same, as the water, but that effect should be satisfactory."

We used almost all the oil and indeed our skin - except that it got sticky - got a lighter shade.

I came back to the mirror to look at myself again. I saw a slim girl's face with a small, slightly upturned nose and large green eyes surrounded by a range of long, dark lashes. I smiled.

"It's not so bad, but what about it?" I pointed a dirty tangled head on my head.

"I'm afraid it needs to be cut down," my mother decided. She opened one of the kitchen drawers and took out scissors. "Sit down!" She ordered, offering me a chair.

Then efficiently cut off my hair, leaving several centimeters strands.

"Finished, now you." She handed me the scissors.

I started cutting with some fear. I methodically cut her brown hair glued together in large pods. After the moment she had a hairstyle such as mine. Only now I could see, how much we are alike - the same delicate features, the same color of eyes, the same nose, the same shape of the lips. Only the hair color I had after my dad - blond in a shade of ripe grain. And if it wasn't for our mother's wrinkles, mainly around the eyes and lips, we could pass for sisters.

"So, what's the plan we're making?" She asked when she finished watching the effect of my hairdressing actions in the mirror.

"I have no idea." I shrugged. "At first, it would be good to look around for water, and then look for some living things, preferably people."

"From what I remember, the nearest town is in the north, twenty kilometers away. We can leave tomorrow at dawn."

"You got to be kidding me." I looked at her mockingly. "You're too weak. You're not gaining strength until tomorrow morning, who do you want to fool? I have to go alone. We won't go far together."

She shook her head for a long time.

"We should not be separated," she said finally. "We can wait a few days."

"This will not change anything. The sooner we will find out, what's going on here, the better. Mom don't worry. I can handle myself," I assured.

"Well, we can try," she agreed reluctantly. "All in all, we had luck so far, it remains to have hope that it will not leave us. Give me a map."

I took the map from my backpack and laid it out on the kitchen table. We leaned over it both.

"We're here." She marked the place with no name by a cross, from which she led up a line along road 34, up to the town of Creston. "You must reach Creston."

Dressed in a slightly loose khaki t-shirt and short shorts revealing skinny, extremely pale legs with black sneakers above the ankle, I headed north. I didn't know that at the time, but I was heading toward destiny.

The sun rose over an hour ago. Despite the dark glasses my mother provided me with, I narrowed my eyes in pain. I wasn't used to such harsh daylight.

It was going to be a warm April day. The weather is just perfect for such a trip, but the awareness that this is not a sightseeing trip, actually a game for life, spoiled the pleasure a bit. Still, I couldn't stop to smiling. Each breath containing a portion of real air was unique. Even dry taste of roadside dust on the tongue did not seem unpleasant. It remains me I'm alive, that I breathe, and that the joy of life consists of just such a little thing, not a great thing.

Slowly I rid of the fear, replaced it with curiosity, and it was pushing me forward. I walked more and more confidently leading to Creston. The road, like everything else, was also covered in a thin layer of rusty dust. From time to time, individual wind flies blew it up, revealing deep cracks on the asphalt surface. The forest was beginning to the left, though it was more like a cemetery of dead trees. I wanted to touch one of them, I wanted to find out if it was really

dead. I went to the nearest tree and put my palm to the rough bark. With the other hand, I tried to push the branch hanging above my head, but it fell apart when touched. I followed the falling particles and saw something colorful among the layers of plant debris. I squatted down and carefully broke broken branches and dried needles. I saw tiny green leaves, among which small, purple flower heads protruded. Violet - the first form of life I came across.

I do not know what guided me, but without hesitation I took a bottle from the backpack and spilled half the amount on the parched earth around the plant. After a while I realized that it was stupid and irresponsible. I used up almost all the water, and do not come even half of the way.

"I'm a moron," I muttered under my breath. I brushed off my hands and returned to the road.

After about an hour of walking, I stopped to rest. I didn't feel well. My body was very weak, and years of malnutrition and a poor diet have done their job. The air acted strangely at me, causing dizziness, and an excess of free space around made that I felt a strong anxiety. I began to seriously consider returning. I was slowly losing faith that I would meet someone in Creston, someone alive.

I sat on the side of the road. Chewing on the biscuit and sipping it with the remaining water, I wondered what to do next. I still had my mother's tearful face when she said goodbye to me this morning. It wasn't long after all, and I already missed her.

Suddenly my thoughts of the further journey were

interrupted by silent noise in the distance. I got up and strained my hearing. Initially, I had trouble determining if I really heard something or if it was just a hallucination caused by fatigue and an excess of sensations. However, from second to second the sound grew stronger and reminded me of something.

Is the engine purr?

I did not manage to analyze it, because the answer to the question asked in my mind was just around the corner. A dark green, large car was rushing towards me. With horror I watched it stops a few meters away from me. Fear gripped my throat, at the same time taking away the ability to move. I stood so stunned, mindlessly staring at the cab from which the tall young man had left. Black, straight, short-cut hair with a slightly longer, frayed bangs falling on the forehead, thick dark eyebrows and a surprised look at his eyes, strange eyes... with intensely purple irises. Although there was something stranger in his appearance - skin. It was orange! I feverishly searched my thoughts, trying to match his peculiar appearance to any race I knew, but my efforts failed.

We stood in front of us, measuring our eyes, and the boy looked no less surprised than me. I was about to speak when my attention was caught by the object in his left hand. I had no doubt he was holding a gun in his hand and it seemed like he was going to use it.

It sobered me up. Immediately, I regained my power over my body, all muscles tightened, and the brain suggested one word: "run". In a split of second, I turned back, leaped over the roadside ditch and ran into the dead forest. I rushed blindly, not looking under my feet, as far as possible from the road, from this place, from him...

I raced with death.

Dry branches of the trees lapped my face, these eruptive bushes ripped off my clothes, their spikes dug into bare forearms, but I felt no pain.

"Wait a second!" I heard behind my back.

I didn't mean to. Driven by fear and adrenaline, I accelerated. And then a piercing whistle reached my ears. The image of the forest suddenly blurred, like tears in my eyes, and my body stilled. I lay limply on hard ground. I was losing my consciousness.

Death.

I was so afraid of it... And dying is like falling into fluff, it doesn't hurt... maybe later... Later there was only darkness.

CHAPTER II

We can't predict the most important. Each of us experienced the greatest joys in life then, when nothing announced them.
ANTOINE DE SAINT-EXUPÉRY

I stretched slowly. What a stupid dream. Stupid, though disturbingly realistic. I have never dreamed like that before. I barely lifted my heavy eyelids, but I closed them again. Damn... what's going on? Why can't I wake up?!

I lay still for a moment, trying to gather my thoughts. I called in the last memory: a dead forest, escape, frightening and unpleasant whistling nothingness.

Am I dead?

I slowly took air in my lungs, then let it out slowly. And so, a few times. I'm breathing so I didn't die. Another control inhalation, after which I realized that the smell reaching my nostrils is completely foreign to me. I did not recognize in it the familiar musty smell, mold and choking dust. In fact, the air had no smell. I opened my eyes again. I looked carefully. No change. I could still see a small, clean room. White, diffused light filtered from the ceiling. Frightened, I sat up abruptly on the bed. I felt a slight jerk in my left elbow flexion. I looked at my hand. A needle stuck in a vein connected me to a plastic bottle suspended on a telescope standing next to the bed with a rubber tube.

Drip?!

The clear liquid seeped lazily straight into my bloodstream, drop by drop. Everything seemed so real that it was not able to be a dream, but if it was not a dream, so in that case what is it?

"Focus, Emily," I reminded myself.

It was hard to take my thoughts. In my memory the scene appeared as clear as if it took place a moment before. I shuddered. The last image recorded by my brain is a strange orange individual.

Wait, wait. After all, I should be hurt, sore... I leaned back and started to examine my body in a hurry for more severe injuries, but I found nothing but a few yellowing bruises and a few scratches. I was surprised by the appearance of my skin. It was white, delicate and fragrant, as if it belonged to someone else. Apparently, someone bathed me and changed into a clean T-shirt. But who?

At the same time, my ears caught bits of conversation. Sounds came from behind blue glass doors. I strained my hearing. Two people spoke in low voices. I could clearly hear the nice alt belonging to the woman and the calm male voice with a slight hoarseness.

"Is she awake long ago?" The woman asked.

"About five minutes ago," the man replied.

"So why didn't you go to her?"

"That's probably not the best idea, Sofie. You should talk to her first. A lot of things happened to her, I wouldn't want to scare her. Try to prepare her properly."

"Prepare?"

"Prepare for what?"

I didn't understand anything.

"Well. I'll talk to her first."

"Try to do it quite gently," he added.

The door opened slowly, and a medium-tall woman dressed in a white apron entered the room. She could have been my mother's age. Her red, slightly wavy hair was brushed back and tied up in a ponytail. She was smiling at me uncertainly.

"Good morning. My name is Sofie," she introduced herself, "I am a doctor. How are you?" She looked at me with concern.

Startled by the sight of a man, I crouched my legs under me and involuntarily moved back, leaning my back against the cool, smooth wall. I shuddered, more out of fear than out of cold.

"What's your name?" Undaunted by my reaction she repeated attempt to contact. "You have a name, right?"

I looked at her, confused, eyes wide open, trying hard to suppress the irrational feeling of fear that first overwhelmed my body and was now sneaking into my mind. I did not understand my subconscious fear.

That's what I wanted, that was my goal - to find other people. In addition, the woman looked kind and more civilized than I might have expected.

What the hell is the going on with me?!

What's wrong with me?

I still could not utter a word, and Sofie's face get the expression of growing dismay. As if the woman did not know how to behave in the absence of any reaction on my part.

"Do you understand what I'm saying?" She asked, clearly worried.

She must have taken me for a savage and I couldn't blame her, because now I looked like that - like a small, curled, frightened animal. I cleared my throat quickly, but the dry throat made me utter a hoarse whisper:

"Emily... I'm Emily Walker."

She breathed a sigh of relief when I finally spoke.

"And me, Sofie," she introduced herself again. "You can call me by my name."

I nodded slightly.

She came to the table by the door in silence and, without taking her eyes off me, poured half a glass of water from the bottle standing there. She gave me it. I grabbed the vessel eagerly, clinging back to the wall. I drunk the whole content greedily.

"Thank you. I gave her back the glass and then embraced my arms. I folded my hands into fists to hide that they were trembling. It didn't work out, she noted.

"Are you afraid?"

"Yes... no... I don't know..." I mumbled incoherently. I could not give a definite answer. For now, nothing bad happened to me, and the woman looked kind, I was not afraid of her. Still, the new surroundings gave me goose bumps.

"You don't have to worry about anything," she assured calmly. "You are safe here."

Here that is where?

"What is this place?" I dared to ask.

"Hospital in Exira, Iowa.""Exira, Exira in Iowa, Exira... " I repeated several times, trying to match the name to some point on the map. Nothing of that.

"Korin found you near Creston four days ago," she added.

I paled.

"Four days?! I've been here for four days?!" I jumped out of bed. Maybe a little too sharply, because I felt spin in my head. If it weren't for Sofie, I'd have fall to the ground. She took me with the one hand, and with the other one she catches the frame with drip at the last minute.

"Relax, where are you in such a hurry?" She said, putting me back on the bed.

"I can't stay here," I groaned. "I have to go back for my mother. She stayed at grandfather's house. She was too weak to come with me." Tears came to my eyes.

"It's okay." She stroked my back soothingly. "Your mother is fine, she lies in the next room.

"But how... How did she come here? It is impossible." I shook my head in disbelief. Everything was becoming more and more unreal. "I want to see my mother, I want to talk to her," I finally demanded.

Without a word, she took off the drip, gripped my arm and led me towards the blue door.

"You will soon find out that she is okay."

We went out into the empty corridor. Its blue, unadorned walls contrasted strongly with the white of the shiny marble floor. Here, too, diffused white light filtered from ceiling. Sofie gently directed me towards the ajar neighboring door. I took my steps uncertainly. I felt, as if someone stuck thousands of thin needles in all my muscles. We entered a room almost identical to the one we had just left. It was only an extra bed. My mother took the one closer to the door. I barely recognize her. The lower part of her face was obscured by a transparent silicone mask that supplied oxygen, and a tangle of tubes and colored cables connected her body to some complicated apparatus. One of the devices made short, rhythmic beeps.

I walked slowly to the bed with shaky legs. I sat on the edge of the mattress and gently stroked the top of my mother's hand. She didn't even flinch. If it wasn't for the warmth of the skin and steady rise and fall of the chest, I would think she was dead.

"You lied to me." I looked at the doctor reproachfully. "You said she was okay."

"Because she's not. We were leading her into a pharmacological coma so that the body would recover faster," she explained patiently. "We'll wake her up in two, maybe three days."

She said it in such a tone that I believed her. I calmed down a bit.

"You didn't explain me; how did you know where to look her?" I asked in an undertone.

"When Korin brought you here, we looked at your things and..." She went to the bedside table, pulled out a drawer. "We found this." She handed me a carefully folded piece of paper.

"My map?" I recognized it immediately, but still did not see relation.

I looked at Sofa questioningly."The route of your journey is marked on it, so just in case we checked the place marked with a cross. In this way we found your mother. She came here the day after you.

"Thank you... for everything," I whispered. I couldn't find better words to express my gratitude. I should still ask who is Korin, but I could not, Sofie first peppered me with question.

"Will you tell me what you did in such a wilderness?"

"We lived in a shelter."

"How long?"

"Almost ten years."

"Do you want to tell me about it?"

I did not want. But I had no choice. I appreciated what Sofie had done for me and my mother. I was slowly starting to trust her, now I had to earn my trust by describing the not very interesting story of my life.

We sat on a free bed. The doctor squeezed my hand encouragingly. I hesitated a moment. I wasn't sure if I could tell everything calmly and without tears. I started with the moment when my dad, a well-respected astrophysicist, was urgently called to a secret military base somewhere near the Canadian border.

"We didn't even think he would come back again." I could hardly put these events into words. "Dad call to us the day before the catastrophe, warning my mother about the approaching comet, the threat of destruction and its consequences. My mother became hysterical, she cried and laughed alternately, laughing which scared me. I started crying, seeing her like this. I was only eight years old, I did not understand what happened, I knew only that something was wrong. My crying made my mother shake off her first shock and act. She packed the most necessary things and went to a public shelter. The news of the upcoming disaster spread at lightning speed. Panic broke out. Before entering the shelter, there were Dante scenes. Many people lost their lives trying to get inside. A lonely woman with a small child had no chance. Then my mother remembered about the bunker built by her father. My grandfather a few years before his death completely fortified, sold his family estate, moved to a remote area south of Creston and prepared for the coming of the end of the world. My mother decided that we would look for shelter there. The murderous race against time has begun. We had to go over a thousand kilometers and probably only a miracle made we reached the place before the crash. The shelter was quite modern, powered by geothermal energy and well supplied with food, mainly with military rations with an extended expiry date. Grandpa thought about almost everything, except... the radio. My mother didn't think about it either, so we lost the opportunity to contact other people, but at least we survived..." I stopped, it was getting harder to talk about it.

Sofie squeezed my hand tightly, comforting me with a simple gesture. I took a deep breath and continued:

"The day on which the hatch of shelter slammed behind us etched in my memory forever. It was then that I realized that nothing would ever be the same. Not only I lose my father, but also my childhood."

"If you didn't know what the world was like outside, why did you leave the shelter?" She asked.

I looked at Sofie with glassy eyes.

"Honestly? We didn't care. Less than a year ago our generator processing energy from the interior of the Earth to electricity screwed up. This deprived us of electricity and running water, the submersible pump stopped working. It's good that the ventilation and oxygen regeneration system had a separate power source, at least we had the air," I sighed heavily. "Life was terrible there, but last year... last year..." I fell silent. At this memory in front of my eyes stood the dark, dingy interior of the shelter. The picture was so clear that I felt the unpleasant, sticky taste of the smell of rot and mold air on my tongue. It's like I'm back there. I felt sick. With effort, I swallowed, hid my face in my hands and cried.

"Shhh... It's okay, now it can only be better." Sofie hugged me tightly and didn't let go until I calmed down. " You'll see, everything will work out fine," she said with conviction.

I wanted nothing more than to believe it. Actually, the future was already in brighter colors. After ten years of non-existence, I was born again.

And in this way the question I had to ask earlier returned.

„Who is Korin? You said: Korin found you. Who is this... Korin?"

"Dr. Almar's son."

"What did he do around Creston?" I drilled.

"Two times a month we conduct routine tests in the field. Korin was then on his way to one of our experimental bases. He was supposed to bring samples of plants and soil, instead he brought... you."

I acknowledged her explanation, it seemed quite logical. However, my curiosity aroused for good. Samples, research, experimental bases... everything sounded foreign and a bit exotic. I wanted to know more.

"Will you tell me what the situation on Earth looks like? How many people survived? Do we have a chance to survive? What about nature? How..."

"Emily," she interrupted, "that's enough. I understand you have a lot of questions, but it's the middle of the night. This is not the right time for such conversations. I promise I will answer all your questions tomorrow, but now you should sleep. If you want, you can sleep in this room, it will be better for you with your mother by the side."

"Please..." I looked at Sofie, pleading. I'm not sleepy."

She sighed in resignation.

"Fine. Let me briefly outline our situation because I can see that you won't sleep without it."

I nodded and want to hear anything.

"Let's get straight to the effects of the disaster," she said without unnecessary introductions. "The comet was not large, it did not hit any of the continents, but it fell into the ocean at enormous speed, which caused a slight displacement of the tectonic plates. Almost all over the world, the earth shook, in some regions of the world seismographs registered shocks of up to eight degrees on the Richter scale. Western Europe suffered the most. Chaos reigned. Volcanoes erupted. Unbelievable amounts of volcanic dust stopped the flow of sunlight. A whole bunch of toxic compounds leaked into the atmosphere, and the oxygen content shrank from almost twenty-one to three percent. No living organism could survive in such conditions. Plants, animals and people were dying..." her voice broke. She cleared her throat to hide it.

"But I think everything is back to normal, right?" I asked hopefully.

"Almost," she said slowly, "but it's not due to Earthlings."

„Earthlings?!"

What a strange word for people.

So, there are some non-Earthlings?

Someone has colonized us?!

"So, whose?" I said not knowing what's going on.

Sofie was silent for a long time.

"I think you're ready," she finally began. "When it turned out that the collision with the comet was inevitable, scientists working for the government decided to take a chance. They sent an SOS radio signal into space, more like a miracle than real help. We were lucky. Six years ago, the signal was received by residents of Aris, planet around four light-years from us. Shortly thereafter, the Arisyans came to Earth with a research-rescue mission.

There are strangers on Earth! I shivered, moving away from Sofie. She didn't make any attention for my reaction, she continued:

"They brought a lot of specialized equipment and modern technologies unknown to us. Restoring of the composition of air took them about a year and a half, now we jointly working on the restoration of fauna and flora."

"We work," I groaned in horror. "So, you're one of them? Did you go to their site?" I moved away a little more.

"No, silly," she said quickly. "We only have a common goal."

I shook my head disapprovingly. Something was wrong about all of this, there had to be a catch somewhere. I was so stupid to believe that someone flew from another planet to save a group of people, without expecting anything in return.

"And you just believed in their selflessness?" I assumed with an ironic tone.

"I assure you, Emily that the Arisyans also benefit from this situation."

"Oh, sure," I snorted.

"You'll see, you change your mind when you knew them a bit closer. They are really good, valuable people, but they are a little different from us, not only mentally, but also with appearance."

"I mean, what...? They have green skin and an antenna on top of their heads?" My brain maliciously gave me the image of a Martian from a comic book.

"You hit the skin."

"Are they green?!"

She laughed, my amazement apparently made her laugh.

"No, orange," she corrected.

I was pale. Fear and uncertainty returned, and the images of events four days ago were moving slowly in my head. Everything inside me was boiling when I knew who was shooting at me.And she treated strangers like good friends!

Sofie's smile disappeared.

"Emily, what happened?" She was clearly worried.

"This orange wanted to kill me!"

"You're wrong," she said emphatically.

"He shot me!"

"I know," she sighed, "but he did not want you did get hurt. Korin has never used an infra-paralyzer without a need."

"Does this orange even have a name?" I snorted dismissively.

"Stop it!" She raised her voice for the first time. „Arisyans are this same people crumpled like us and skin color has nothing to do with it! Do not spend judges in cases which you do not know! Earthlings or Arisyans, who nowadays cares about this division? We - People, that's all that counts."

She paused. She stared at me, waiting for a reaction. There was silence in the room, interrupted only by the sounds of medical equipment. I did not speak for a long time, I tried to sort it out, analyze it. I seem to say too much. I should not judge anyone, the more that so far, I didn't feel any harm. On the contrary, I am sitting here now, safe and sound, my mother comes to health in the next bed, and I behave like an ungrateful moron. I was ashamed. I went out to be a racist, and I wasn't like that, my mother taught me since childhood that everyone is equal regardless of skin color and origin.

"I'm sorry," I whispered in remorse. "I don't know what got into me."

The doctor breathed a sigh of relief and smiled wanly. She looked at me closely for a long moment, frowning. It was like she was considering something.

"I think it's time you met someone."

She touched the bracelet fastened on her wrist. A red diode flickered on it. When it went out, Sofie got up and walked to the door. She lifted them. A strange anxiety swept over me. I went back instinctively, adhering to the cold wall. I was shaking again.

"You can come in now," she said to someone who was waiting outside the door.

An exceptionally tall, slim man entered the room. A few wrinkles marked his forehead and the corners of his mouth, his hair was black, cut short, slightly gray on the temples. If it wasn't for the orange skin tone and purple eyes, I would never say that he was alien. I was expecting someone more different, meanwhile this... man? he seemed amazingly Earthling. His character exuded a hypnotic calmness that gradually began to spread on me. I felt the earlier fear of the newcomer slowly fading away. I relaxed. He must have noticed, because he smiled shyly, a little apologetically. I returned the smile automatically.

"I'm Almar," he introduced himself briefly, but he didn't reach out hand to greet me, he didn't even come closer. Apparently, he was afraid all the time that he would scare me.

"Emily, " I managed to say.

I no longer felt panic, but I couldn't get rid of the impression that the peace that had prevailed in the room was unnatural and its source was this man. I focused on his face. It was trustworthy. It expressed patience, kindness, nobility and... goodness. Goodness first and foremost. Perhaps Sofie is really not mistaken about the Arisyan people?

"How are you feeling?" He asked carefully. "Nothing hurts you, don't you feel lost?"

„I'm a little dazed, but except of this I feel pretty good," I said a little shakily. "Are you a doctor?"

He hesitated.

"Actually... you can put it like that."

I raised an eyebrow.

"From an earthly point of view, I'm a doctor, although everyone on Arisa has several specialties. Professionally I deal with the chemistry and biology, especially genetics."

"Almar is the head of the Arisyans research expedition on Earth," interjected Sofie.

"I see... I wonder why you do it? Why are you helping us?" I directed the question directly to Almar.

"Contrary to appearances, we also benefit from it," he explained. "Thanks to the experience acquired on Earth, we will be able to save our planet when the need arises. In fact, we've been expecting tragedy on Arisa for centuries. And that's nothing bad happened, it is just happy coincidence of circumstances."

"What tragedy do you mean?" I asked boldly. I was so intrigued that I forgot about my earlier fears.

"It's a topic for a longer conversation," he said wearily. "It's late. I think you should sleep now, and tomorrow I invite you to my office, I will try to answer the questions that bother you."I wanted to protest when Sofie interrupted:

"Almar is right, Emily. You have to postpone this conversation until morning."

"It's okay," I agreed reluctantly. "Let it be in the morning."

"Let's get up, SWEETIE!" A big, black woman pulled the comforter off me vigorously.

I jumped out of bed scared. I looked at her half-conscious, trying to remember where I was. She sent me a wide, happy smile.

"We're getting up, we're getting up!" she rushed me. „Don't waste the day. Eat the breakfast quickly, as it cools down, during this time I will change the drip to your mother."

Slowly I came to myself. I remembered the night talk with Sofie and Almar, and the doctor's promise of explanation. I glanced at the next bed. The nurse was correcting my mother's pillow.

"What about her?" I asked, concealing my concern.

"Don't worry, she'll be like newborn. Dr. Sofie says we'll wake her up tomorrow."

"When can I see Sofie?" The doctor's absence disturbed me.

"Not soon. Doctor went home, she'll come tomorrow. She must rest. She was sitting here, darling, on duty for almost four days without a break. She was terribly worried about what it would be with you. She deserves a rest."

"Sure, I understand," I said without conviction. I felt a slight disappointment that Sofie had left me alone. Although I shouldn't blame her, because last night she introduced me to a new reality with a special feeling. It's hard, I will have to face Almar alone.

"Okay, we're talking here, and the scrambled eggs are getting cold." The nurse's determined voice made me clear.

Only now my sense of smell noted the appetizing smell coming from a plate set on the table.

"Scrambled eggs? From real eggs?" I was surprised. "From the hen?"

"No, from a rooster," she murmured, giving me a menacing look.

I sat down to breakfast without a murmur. For a moment I lost touch with reality, focusing only on food. I almost forgotten, which means a real meal. I pleased every bite, trying to remember the last time I ate something equally tasty. I was barely done; the woman began to conduct me again.

"Take your clothes," she pointed to a pile of evenly folded clothing lying on the edge of the bed, "and hurry up to the bathroom! I will handle with the bed at the time."

Still sleepy, I dragged myself obediently toward the door she pointed out. I was just about to splash roughly, but the sight of a clean, glass shower enclosed me like a magnet. I could not resist. I dreamed of bathing for a very long time. With delight I went under a pleasantly warm stream of water, rinsing off the remains of sleep and unpleasant memories. I felt so good that I lost track of time. I do not know, how long I stood under the shower, but certainly a good few minutes. I was sobered up by the impatient voice of the nurse, ruthlessly breaking through the sound of water.

"Emily! Did you drown there?"

"I'm going!" I turned off the tap reluctantly. I wiped myself off at an express pace. I pulled on black, narrow jeans and a red T-shirt, pushed my fingers with short, frayed hair and fell out of the bathroom.

"Finally!" She stood by the door leading to the corridor, arms folded and a stern expression. "For a penny of respect for someone's time. Do you think I have nothing better to do than babysitting some kid?!"

"I'm sorry," I muttered.

"I still have a lot of work to do. I will only walk you to the elevator, you will go to Almar's office alone."

I shrugged with feigned nonchalance.

"No problem, I'll manage somehow."

We went out into the corridor. This time it wasn't empty, lots of people hurried through it. Maybe I exaggerated. A few people, but after many years in the shelter, three people meant a crowd to me. Earthlings and Arisyans looked friendly. Everyone wore the same bracelet on their wrists as Sofie and Almar had. I was sure it was somehow used for communication, but maybe it had other uses as well.

The sight of so many people and the clearly perceptible, friendly atmosphere gave me a shocking effect. From the beginning I was bothered by how many people survived the cataclysm and only now could I see that quite a lot. I felt warm around my heart, everything was undeniably better.

The promise accompanying me accelerated. I almost had to run to keep up with her. We came to the end of the corridor, which here expanded into the shape of the letter T and stopped in front of the wall with a string of five blue metal doors.

„Elevators In," she explained. "The middle one will get you to the doctor's office. You should not get lost, he is on the top floor."

I got into the middle elevator and, according to the nurse's instructions, pressed the number fifteen. The cabin moved slowly upwards with a slight jerk. I stuck my back to the smooth wall, trying to ignore the growing tingling of fear under my skin.

CHAPTER III

It is important to never stop asking. Curiosity does not exist without a reason. It is enough if we try to understand even a little bit of this secret every day. Never lose your holy curiosity. Who can't ask, can't live.

ALBERT EINSTEIN

The elevator door slid open quietly. I took in a huge gulp of air and filled with fears entered the spacious, bright study. In front of me, behind the large nut-brown desk sat Dr. Almar. He was bent at the sizeable stack of documents and had not even noticed my arrival.

"Good morning," I said shyly.

He raised his head.

"Oh... it's you, Emily. Welcome." He smiled.

I don't know if it was a calm tone of the voice, a smile or a gentle look, but again my fears were suppressed.

"I see Doris guided you well," he said.

"You mean that overbearing nurse?" I chained the elevator to my chin.

"Oh, I think she wasn't nice to you." He shook his head laughing.

"Maybe a bit," I admitted.

"Don't judge her too harshly, she is a good woman. Sometimes she manages people too much, but

she already has that nature and you have to accept it. And you know what... as a consolation I will tell you a secret," he lowered his voice almost to a whisper," there are times that even I am afraid of her."

"You?" I raised my eyebrows in surprise.

We laughed at the same time.

"Will you give me five minutes?" He glanced at the desk. "I have to finish something."

"Of course, please don't disturb yourself."

"In the meantime, you can look around a bit."

Now I had time to look closely at the study and sort out the questions I wanted to ask Almar. And there were thousands of them. They were anxiously in my head, literally bumping into its interior. In addition, there were more and more new ones. I wanted to know so many things. About the world, about the new reality, about the Arisyans... Impatient curiosity grew in me every minute.

I stepped nervously from foot to foot and looked am expectantly toward the desk. Almar was still browsing the documents in full concentration. My portion of questions will have to wait.

I looked around the room. Cabinet decorated exceptional so modestly, even ascetically. To the right of the desk was a long sofa upholstered in dark brown leather, and a mysterious cylinder-shaped object in the left corner of the room. I puzzled it for a long moment. It could have been a table, though intuition told me that it had a completely different function. I quickly annotated my mind to ask Almar about it and turned my eyes to unadorned smooth, shiny walls. They looked as made with brown, slightly

smoky glass. On their even surface I could not see the window openings, which surprised me a little, because the interior was extremely bright. I raised my head and looked up, searching for a source of light. And I opened my mouth in silent admiration. Above my head was a gigantic glass dome, and the rays of the morning sun reflected from it formed light reflections on the surface. I wasn't standing in an ordinary room, actually it wasn't a room! I was directly on the roof of the building.

"Do you like it?"

I moved at the sound of the doctor's voice. I didn't notice when he finished browsing the documents and joined me, standing behind my back.

"It's beautiful..." I said, not hiding delight.

"Arisyans like it when it's bright. Probably because the planet receives light from two stars."

At the same time, he pressed a button on a small, elongated device that he clutched in his hand. Unexpectedly, the previously brown walls began to brighten, until they became almost completely transparent. Enchanted, I slowly approached the glass pane and looked down. The tower surrounded a real, inhabited city! I froze. The low, single-family housing was cut by neat asphalt streets, people walked in traffic, cars flashed past them, and everything was in a vast sea of greenery.

"I thought almost all the vegetation was extinct. It is true that I saw on the way little grass and a few feeble producing plants, but it is nothing compared to this!" I pointed the view outside the window.

"At the moment, restoring terrestrial fauna and

flora is a priority for us," he said matter-of-factly. "We will not maintain proper air composition."

"Sofie said the atmosphere was all right."

„Yes and no. The composition of the air is not yet stable, although we are in control of the situation. Immediately upon arrival, we placed a system of chemical filters in the Earth's atmosphere that worked at full speed for the first two years. Now they are set to thirty percent power and they will have to keep working until we restore the old order." He paused for a moment. "I think we'll have a longer chat. Maybe we will sit down." He suggested and started toward the brown couch.

I followed him obediently. Almar did not sit back in the middle, but took his place on the very edge, as if he deliberately left me free space. I appreciated this gesture. I sat on the other side uncertainly.

"I guess you have a lot of questions," he began. "If possible, I'll try to answer them."

Yes, I had a lot of questions, though doubts came first. I didn't hide with them at all.

"I admit that something is wrong to me. Are you helping us, bringing life back to the planet, recreating ancient Earth... Am I to understand that you are some kind of space Earthlingtarian institution? Help for Earth or something?" I asked.

"Help for Earth, you are saying? Hmm... interesting observation," he said, stroking his chin thoughtfully. „You are exceptionally bright for your age, but probably more accurate name for it would be Aris for Earth - Earth for Aris."

I frowned. Again, he suggested mutual benefit. It

was hard to believe in it. For what kind of benefit could the Arisyans have if they did not take over our planet?"

Almar must have seen the disbelief on my face because he hurried to explain:

"See, Emily. Aris is very similar to Earth in many respects but is more exposed to a collision with a comet or asteroid than Earth. Most of the comets that appear in your sky come from the cloud of icy bodies far beyond the orbit of Neptune, called by Earthlings Clouds of Oort. There are several similar objects in our system, and thus the probability of a catastrophe is several times higher. As I mentioned yesterday, we have been expecting the worst for centuries, developing various scenarios, conducting computer simulations and, in fact, we are prepared for the worst. But... only theoretically."

"I still don't understand the reason for your presence on Earth." I was getting a bigger headache.

"I will now use words that I do not like, but in part they best reflect what we do here. Testing ground. Earth is our testing ground."

I made big eyes.

"Do you experiment on people?!" I raised my voice.

"Absolutely not," he said quickly. "We're just trying out the methods we've developed to save our planet. On Aris, we had no way to test them. Here we have the opportunity and for now the results are satisfactory. It means a lot to us - he added and fixed his eyes on me.

He was waiting for me to say something. I was

silent for a long time. I had trouble deciding if I should trust Almar. I studied his face carefully, it was wise and honest, in its own way charismatic. It couldn't belong to a liar. Anyway, he just gave me a reason for the Arisyan's reasoning, I believed him. Still, my inquisitive mind kept multiplying questions.

"Sounds sensible, but I'm thinking about another thing. Since Aris is four light years away from Earth, and it only took you two years to get here, so you had to vary at a speed greater than the speed of light. And that's impossible, right?"

„It's possible." He smiled. "However, not with the use of Earthling technologies. We use tachyons to propel our spaceships. They allow you to reach twice the speed of light."

Tachyons... I've heard that name before. I rubbed my forehead with my hand as if it could affect my brain. I tried to concentrate simultaneously fever word searching the recesses of memory. My thoughts shifted in my head, just like a slow-motion movie, frame by frame, until they stopped at the right one.

I got it!

I knew that this concept is not foreign to me. This and one more thing - neutrino. Dad once hypothesized that a neutrino is a tachyon, but it seems to be wrong.

"Do you use tachyons? Do they really exist?"

"Have you heard of tachyons?" Almar seemed no less surprised than me.

"Of course! These are hypothetical elementary particles moving at a faster speed than light," I recited. "Dad was a physicist," I added quickly.

"I see, young lady, that you will probably surprise

us many more times," he said honestly.

"I will try to."

"I have a question for you. Actually, I should ask it to your mother, but I think it won't make much difference if I ask you. Would you like to live in a town, do you have any other plans?"

Plans? We didn't go that far into the future. The only plan was to leave the shelter and, even in my wildest dreams, I never thought that life could change so radically for the better. Everything now has a new meaning. In addition, I received a unique gift from fate - the ability to decide about my future. A wonderful gift.

But... wait, wait. I think there must be more places where life is reborn, otherwise Almar would not ask if we want to stay.

"What alternative do we have?"

"In addition to Exira, we also occupy four more villages: Manning, Harlan, Perry and Panora. In total, they are inhabited by over fifty-thousand people, including five hundred Arisyans. In the north of the country, as far as we know, life is also slowly returning to normal. People are rebuilding cities and new settlements are emerging, but life is far more dangerous there than here. Apparently, residents regularly harass armed gangs, robbing mainly of food, fuel and medicine."

I needed a moment to think. Sure, my mother would prefer to go back to our home in the North, but since we had to lose our lives, only regaining it, I made the only right decision in this situation:

"We stay, at least for now."

At the same moment, I heard the characteristic murmur of the sliding door. I turned my head in that direction and... froze. A tall, black-haired boy entered the office. I recognized him right away - Korin.

52

"Hi," he said freely.

I pressed myself deeper into the back of the couch. The memory of the meeting on the road came back with a vengeance. Surprise, fear, panic. I wrapped my arms around myself, gripping my elbows tightly. I had the feeling that the room was out of oxygen.

Korin approached slowly without taking his eyes off me. He stopped maybe two steps from the couch.

"You look a little better, than at the day I last saw you," he said, looking me in the eye. The corners of his mouth rose in a mocking smile.

The voice and meaning of these words caused me to be overwhelmed by an incomprehensible wave of anger. I wanted to get up and kick him in the ankle. I barely stopped myself. Instead, I gave him an angry look and pouted contemptuously, then looked at Almar, who didn't seem to notice my hostile reaction. He was looking thoughtfully at the wrist, where the red color pulsated on the bracelet.

"Unfortunately, I have to leave you. Duty calls me on a branch," he announced unexpectedly, springing from the site.

"Replace me," he said to Korin. "Show Emily, where we come from, and later take her to house, which we have prepared for her and her mother," he said and headed toward the elevator.

We were alone.

Our eyes met and in Korin's eyes I noticed the same kind of peace as I had before in Almar's eyes. Although my mind constantly offered me a meeting scene on the road, I stopped feeling anxiety, although I was still tense. And probably a little angry. Seconds passed. We measured each other and... we were silent. I shuddered when he spoke first.

"You don't like me much." More stated than asked.

Yes, I do not like you, I wanted to say at first reflex, fortunately I bit my tongue in time. I had no right to speak to him like that, the boy saved my life and the only feeling that I should have to him is gratitude.

"Honestly, I'm a little afraid of you." I got the diplomatic answer.

„No need to. No one ever found any signs of aggression in me."

"And that says someone who shoots defenseless Earthling without warning," I said defiantly.

He was confused. Something like embarrassment appeared in his purple eyes.

"Then, in the forest..." he began uncertainly, "I shot because... I was surprised by this meeting, maybe even more than you. I wasn't sure you were Earthling at all. You looked terrible, like some forest spooky. I was afraid that when escaping, you will kill any of the trees. That's why I used the infra-paralyzer."

"Good one. Forest spooky," I muttered under my breath.

He annoyed me. Again.

Frightened, he ran his hand through his hair, and his face was so scared that I almost laughed. All my

agitation evaporated, giving way to common sense. I decided that speaking of this matter was pointless. I should treat it like something that just had to happen to lead me to where I am now. Destiny? Perhaps. In any case, the matter at road was a thing of the past.

"I think we should start again," I said, getting up. I reached out my hand. "I'm Emily Walker, Earthling," I introduced myself.

"Korin. Arisyan." With some hesitation he took my hand, holding down a bit longer in a strong embrace.

I touched the Arisyan for the first time. Weird feeling. I was most surprised by the texture of his orange skin, it was soft and smooth, completely devoid of coarse hair typical of earthly men. I also didn't see any stubble on his face. I noticed similar features earlier at Almar. Is this what their race characterized? No facial hair, orange skin, purple iris and unnatural calmest? I wonder how else they differ from people? I did not ask, I felt it was too early to ask questions. Anyway, Korin intimidated me, and not because he was a stranger. He intimidated me for some other, unspecified reason.

Now that he stood so close, I could look at him more closely. I analyzed every, even the smallest detail of his face. A triangular chin, a prominent but extremely shapely nose, full lips parted in a warm half smile, and those eyes, purple with darker rims around the irises. Exactly then I came to the conclusion that Korin is just pretty and this insight embarrassed me very much.

„Do you want to see our planet, or we skip it?" He asked unexpectedly.

"Of course, I want to."

He grabbed my hand and led me towards the peculiar waltz I initially thought was a table. From a distance, the shiny countertop looked like it was made of black, polished glass. Only when we came closer it turns out that it was not glass, but some dark, liquid substance resembling the surface of a forest pond on a moonless night. Korin switched the button on the same remote control that Almar had previously used. The glass dome of the roof began to take on the color of the night sky until the room was completely dark. However, not for long because after a while the surface of the pond became slightly cloudy, and several luminous balls of different sizes emerged from its interior. Fascinated by this unusual view, I was waiting with bated breath what next. The two largest and brightest balls emitting a bright yellow light broke away from the rest and whirled up. They moved away once and once came close together, making elliptical circles. Soon a third ball joined them, much smaller. It glowed faintly red. Immediately after it rose five more start dancing around the largest object. It hit me in the end that the roller is a kind of holographic planetarium, and all that seems to my eyes, it is not a

Solar System, but some other, in a way very similar to it. I circled the "table", watching this extraordinary spectacle with delight.

"I see you like it." Korin's voice brought me back to reality.

"Amazing! Are you from there? Where it is?"

"On a cosmic scale quite close, just over four light-years from the Sun. You, Earthman, at these two stars," he pointed to the brightest spheres, "you say Alfa Centauri A and Alfa Centauri B. The smaller, red one is Proxima Centauri. Our planet is one of five circling Alfa Centauri A. Second, counting from the star, is Aris."

Look at the indicated planet more closely. It reminded me of Earth once seen in photos taken from space. It was also blue, though with a slightly purple shade, only the continent distribution was different.

"You miss it?" I asked, glancing at Korin.

"What?" He frowned. I don't think he really understood what I was asking him.

"Your planet." I explained.

He shrugged.

"I never thought about it, but I didn't think so."

"Don't you miss your friends, family, home...?!" I was surprised.

"No."

Short and to the point. A raw "no" chilled me until I flinched. I looked at Korin for the first time as an alien, as an alien being whose otherness I had just started to discover. He must have noticed a change in my face because he hurried to explain:

"Unlike you, we don't get attached to people or places. This is one of the fundamental differences between our races."

"One of the differences..." I repeated thoughtfully. "There is a lot of them? These... differences."

"Not much, although quite significant."

"Will you tell about them?"

"Above all, emotions. Instead of being guided by

logic and reason, you trust your feelings too often. It's a bad choice. Feelings limit and slow down the development of civilization.

"Korin, I think you exaggerated now. What have emotions to develop civilization?"

"Contrary to appearances, a lot. Just analyze the history of the Earth."

"Sure. And you are an outstanding expert in the knowledge of our history," I mocked.

"I had it in training," he replied calmly. "And I know one thing, people have always created to destroy. Greed, lust for power, unreasonable hatred, aggression... are a straight path to conflicts and unnecessary wars. Do you know what your world would look like without all this, how far could you go?" He blurted out and fell silent.

At first, I didn't know what to say. Korin just made me realize the sad truth - we were only creating to destroy. Because it was wars and preparations for them that fueled technological progress on Earth. But wouldn't the progress be smaller without wars? It's hard to say unequivocally. I decided not to go further in this discussion. Subconsciously, I felt that a peaceful approach to the life of Arisyans is definitely a better solution.

"It's all right. Only that it is impossible to influence the nature of man, we are like this and it must be accepted."

"Not necessarily, we succeeded in this change."

"How? Have you manipulated in your brains?" I ironized.

"Not directly. We have removed the gene

responsible for nerve connections with this brain center in which higher feelings arise, among others aggression and hate."

Korin's answer explained a lot. It was impossible not to notice that the Arisyans were different in their own way, but until now I could not determine what these differences are. Each of them was the epitome of calmness and self-control, and these were not the characteristics of the average person. I didn't know if it was good or bad. I only felt indefinite anxiety.

I shook my head disapprovingly.

"You know what, I don't know much about genetics, but it seems to me that what you did is against nature. It is hard to believe that this genetic interference did not cause any side effects."

"We didn't have trouble on Aris, but..." he hesitated.

"However, there is a "but"." I laughed with satisfaction.

"We encountered a small problem only here on Earth. You are too complicated for us."

"Complicated?" I frowned. "In what sense?"

"Each of you reacts quite differently to the same problem, in many cases acting against the elementary principles of logic. We're lost in this."

"No wonder you're getting lost," I said coldly. "Social perfection probably killed your personality effectively, and your behavior depends on your personality."

"It is better to kill personality than people because of an excess of negative emotions. Don't you think."

"So, from your point of view we are emotionally and maybe even mentally unbalanced?"

"Something like that."

"Thanks a lot," I snorted. And yet he still teased me.

"Hey, do not be offended, I just say what I think. I always say what I think. The Arisyans don't know lies, it's simpler."

"Depends to who. Didn't you think that people don't always want to hear the truth?"

"Of course, a typical Earthling approach. Think wisely, if it were to say so directly, wouldn't it be easier to communicate? Without unnecessary lying, guesses, understatements, finding tricks by force... Why waste time on it? Why complicate everything? Every civilization should be based on trust."

I was pondering. In this, what I heard from Korin was quite right. Ten years of isolation deprived me of experience, so I had a really vague idea about Earthling behavior. I was never forced to lie, at best conceal the truth, but perhaps only because I did not have for this opportunity?"

"You're probably right," I finally admitted. "Take the correction that your methods worked on Aris. We are at the "complicated" Earth here and not necessarily white is white, black and black. Anyway, the truth is not always pleasant and sometimes something better left unsaid, then to let be sincere. You may unwittingly hurt someone. Sometimes it's better to say an innocent lie, believe me..." I interrupted.

I realized that he did not completely understand my reasoning, or almost nothing. He was still looked at

me with his violet eyes, as if he wanted to read everything on my face that the words couldn't explain. Under this perspective, I felt, as my cheeks blush and appear the second time that day wave of shame flooded me. I couldn't let him notice that something was happening to me, the more that I didn't know why I was reacting like that on him.

"Let it be," I sighed resignedly. "I may be complicated, but you... you're weird."

He narrowed his eyes and smirked at me.

"Come, I'd better take you home."

A few minutes later we stood in front of the hospital building. Behind my back I had a glass, automatic door, and before me was a view that I didn't shout at and I was slowly beginning to doubt if I would ever get used to it - the view of normality. Transparent air, gentle spring sun, light breeze in the hair, wonderful juiciness of grass... Maybe for most people it is not worth paying attention, but for me a wonderful phenomenon, daydream, personification of beauty and the essence of real life. For a moment I feel like a child run up to the extending spinning skyscraper equally cut lawn and just lay on it, savor the stunning scent of the earth, or at least take a walk after it barefoot, to feel, like blades of grass weaves shots in the toes. I could not afford such a freedom. In the corner of eye, I saw that Korin already turned toward the parking lot and I had to run to catch up with him.

He walked quickly toward the dark green car parked at the very end. I got to know the car right away,

the same came out few days ago from behind the corner. Land rover, I read the inscription on the hood. Korin opened the passenger door, he waited until I got in the car and then walked around the car and sat down on the spot for the driver. Without a word, he started the engine and we went straight onto the asphalt road.

"How far is this house?" I asked.

"A few blocks away. It's a small town, so it's not far away."

I didn't want to talk, views caught my eye too much. I still couldn't believe that this stunning beauty was real, and I hoped it wouldn't go away when we turn the corner of the next street. I felt like I used to, as in my childhood. Memories from before the disaster began to flow from the recesses of the mind. Initially quite blurry and foggy, but from minute to minute more and more taking shape. Apparently, my brain needed a catalyst in the form of a normal world for the distant past to come back to my head. The suburbs of Fargo looked very similar, where I used to live with my parents. And I thought that this picture would never come back, that those less pleasant memories erased it. I thought about those times. Mum, dad and me. A real loving family. We were so happy. And... I realized that nothing would ever be the same. A wave of sadness flooded over me, which I couldn't control. Although I clenched my teeth so as not to fall apart, tears leaked from my eyes. I tried to discreetly wipe them with a hand, but he noticed it.

He looked at me a little frightened. From his face I knew that he didn't understand what was happening to me again. He stopped the car.

"Do you want to get off?" He asked anxiously.

"No, keep going."

"Will you tell me what's wrong with you?"

There was no point in explaining it to him.

"Nothing, I just felt sad, but don't make me explain why... you won't understand anyway."

"I said you were complicated," he muttered under his breath and put the car in gear.

We drove on in silence. Finally, Korin turned off the road into the gravel driveway, stopping in front of the light-painted house. I got out of the car, but I didn't dare step through the threshold, even though I knew it was my home now. I waited, until Korin come first. I followed him with some hesitation, but all the time I could not get rid of the impression that the house is not empty, as if I expected to find previous residents.

The interior was very much like a grandfather's house. From the small hall one entered a guest room connected to the kitchen, and the border between these rooms was marked by a four-person table. The middle of the living room was occupied by a dark red sofa with green leaves, two bulky armchairs with identical upholstery and a rectangular bench. A large library filled to the brim with books stood by the window. A double-glazed door led through a stone terrace to a small but well-kept garden. In addition, the house had two bedrooms, a wardrobe and a large bathroom. But the most important thing for me was the fact that here is cozy and clean, you could not say about the shelter or a grandfather's house covered with dust. I was glad to finally live in civilized conditions.

„To who this house belongs to?" I asked Korin.

"I have no idea. In any case, it stood empty for years. We packed the owners' personal belongings in cardboard boxes and placed them in the attic. If they accidentally came back, we'll take you to another place. But no one will come forward. If anyone survives, they should already be here, so either dead or living somewhere else. You have some new clothes in your wardrobe, there is food in the fridge for a few days, and we left quite a few of your frivolous books on the shelf." He pointed bookcase with chin.

"Frivolous books?" I was surprised by the word.

I went to the bookcase, tilted my head to the side and began to look at the backs of the covers: Steinbeck, Hemingway, Sienkiewicz, Márquez, Shaw, Cortazar... almost only Noble prize winners.

"They are classics!" I shouted.

"Classic intellectual garbage can for the brain."

"You're telling some nonsense again."

He went to the shelf, picked up one of the books, and flipped through.

"That's bullshit here. You will not learn anything from it and you will only lose time reading this paper. Maybe you can explain to me, why is it worth to read them?"

"You didn't think it was for pleasure?"

"For pleasure, you can do completely different things, in addition to being pleasant, are they also useful? For example, sport." He glared at me critically, gently took my arm above the elbow, squeezing slightly non-existent biceps. "You could also use some work on fitness.

I gave him a murderous look. I knew I was fragile, but he didn't have to point out to me right away. Moron.

"So maybe you will explain me, what else do you think littering the brain, takes up disk space or what else would you call it?!"

"Actually, everything that does not lead to knowledge of a particular topic, it is a waste of time for us. We are surprised by your interest in fine literature, art, painting, music, sculpture, cinema, film... we simply cannot understand it, but since it amuses you..." He shrugged. "We are able to accept a lot, we respect your difference and we would like you to respect ours."

"I get the impression that you treat your brain like some damn device, and your personality comes down to the personality of a robot. It is sick."

He was teasing me again. I could not understand, how is it possible that once he seemed a great guy, and once a madman loving too much the science.

I think he realized that I was nervous again because he decided to change the topic. He was clearly starting to learn my reactions, more accurately reading my mood from the tone of voice and body language. He definitely tried to avoid situations that could lead to conflict. Or is this something wrong with me? Maybe I criticize too much? Maybe I'm not tolerant enough? I need to control myself more.

He put down the book he had in his hand for a long time and walked over to the kitchen table.

"If something was missing, at the end of the street is a small shop belonging to a Chinese. Everyone calls him Mr. Cheng. There you can replenish your supplies."

"But, Korin..." I started with some embarrassment, "there is a minor problem. I don't know what currency is currently in force, in any case neither my mother nor I have any money."

"There is no currency, there are points," he said, placing a kind of credit card on the counter.

I went to the table, picked up the card and began to watch it carefully. It was silver, and its surface was covered with grooves of varying width. They looked a bit like a bar code from food products, only that they were cut out and not painted. I took my eyes away from the card and glowered at Korin.

"Points? Where do we get hmm... points?"

"Your mother will get them when she starts working, but you can also get them in the form of a scholarship, of course, if you want to study,"

"Can I go to school?" I was surprised. Somehow, I had not thought that a return to normal life also includes so-obvious things, like an ordinary science in a real school.

"Sure! My father didn't mention you?"

"No."

"I thought he gave you more information about the rules in the current world. He was called to the ward too quickly, which is probably why he did not have time to say about the school and the scholarship system."

"I've always dreamed of going to school!" I was terribly excited about it that awaits me in real science school building, where the rooms, table, benches, and above all other students. I didn't care about any scholarships. "Which class will I go to?" I asked him.

"It depends how you do the placement tests. Earthlings did not have equal access to knowledge, which is why the groups vary greatly in age. Each subject can be taught at three levels: basic, intermediate and advanced."

"And what level are you at?"

"In every subject at advanced, apart from terrestrial biology, I am at intermediate here."

Sure, how else. I thought I'd like to attend some classes with him because in a sense he was my only friend. And despite everything, I managed to like him. Although I thought it was impossible to get into the advanced group with anything.

„I'll go now," he said. "I'll come for you tomorrow morning and drop you off at school."

I paled when I saw him heading towards the door.

„Why you want to go? Should I stay here? Alone?!"

He stopped, turned back and carefully looked at me.

"Something's wrong?" He asked surprised.

"Everything is not okay!" I shouted. „It will be better when you will take me back to the hospital," I said, and walked resolutely to the exit.

„No way." He shook his head. "Doris will not let us in one hundred percent, and I do not intend to convince her, because it will do nothing, and I will be at her black list. Even my father would have no effect on this matter."

"Don't leave me here alone," I groaned.

I knew that I was safe, but I could not get rid of the subconscious fear that began to accompany

me since I came to the surface. I looked at Korin pleadingly, he stopped teasing me.

"Stay... please."

He studied me for a long time. I think he found my emotional state poor, although not willingly, but he agreed.

"Okay," he sighed, resigned. "But I have to agree a few things with my father."

He took a cell phone from his trouser pocket and dialed the number. Almar picked up after a few rings.

"Hi, Dad," he said into the phone and went straight to the point. "Emily is afraid to sleep here alone. Should I stay with her?"

Almar didn't mind, but he still asked about school issues. I deduced this from Korin's reply:

"I'm almost done. I have all the materials in my car, so I'll work on it tonight."

Again, a moment of silence as Korin listened intently to his father. At the end he smiled, saying:

"That's great. I won't mention about it... I'll bring her back tomorrow. Bye." He hung up.

"It's done," he said to me, putting the cell phone back in his pocket.

"Thanks." I felt relieve that today I will not be alone, because loneliness was a thing what I think I feared the most.

"You're welcome." He shrugged.

After Korin's call to Almar, one thing did not leave me peace and I could not resist not asking about it:

"Why did you speak English to your father? You don't have any language?"

My observation surprised him.

"We have our own language, but it will be a bad idea, you will not understand the conversation," he said that in that tone, as if it was obvious.

"Well... I did not expect the Arisyans to comply with the standards of good manners so much."

"Don't get excited, I acted only as instructed." He brought me down straight away.

"What instruction now?!"

"I have received training on how to communicate with your civilization."

"And what, you have modified the textbook entitled Earthlings User Manual?" I looked at him from under raised eyebrows.

"Something like that," he confirmed.

I shook my head in disbelief.

"Well, there's nothing like a scientific approach," I said. "Anyway, I'm glad you could stay."

"It's not a problem. I have one condition."

"Only one?" I asked, frowning."

"I need at least two hours of peace to finish my biology report."

"No problem, I will try not to disturb you," I assured. "Can I have a condition too?"

"Depends on what condition."

"I don't know about you, but I'm hungry, I haven't had anything in my mouth since breakfast. I can make dinner, unless you differ from us and you don't eat normal meals."

"No, we have this common," he laughed. "And what did you suspect us of?"

"Well... maybe you drink engine oil to make your brain work better or the battery electrolyte. You know, it is different with aliens."

He looked at me with an indulgent smile.

"This is the effects of reading this nonsense, your literature looks like that. This is just a pseudoscience."

"Okay, write what you have to write, and I will see what I can do to eat," I finished the topic. I did not want to start a discussion again about the advantages of literature and the need for reading inscribed in Earthling nature. Even relying on sensible arguments was pointless, because it would not lead us to anything. It was enough for me that Korin is here now, that he agreed to stay the night and that I would not be alone in this strange house.

When he went out to the car for a moment for his things, I looked through the kitchen cabinets and fridge. I found flour, eggs, milk and jam, so I decided to make pancakes. Quite risky venture. I knew how to do them in theory, the practice could be different.

The front door slammed and Korin brought what looked like a tablet under his arm, holding a device resembling headphones. He spread everything on the kitchen table.

"What is it?" I asked with interest.

"Thought recorder," he explained briefly.

„Oh," I nodded, even though we still do not know what it was. I decided not to ask any more, and he still consider me as someone with not too much knowledge.

I took care of the pancakes, though I watched the corner of my eye with interest. He put on his headphones, not on his ears, but on his temples. After a while, the text quickly appeared on the screen. I glanced at Korin, he looked very concentrated, and his

purple eyes seemed absent. Well, now everything is clear, the thought recorder. I was so absorbed and the device, and Korin, who looked good in these headphones that I did not notice when burnt pancake. In an instant the kitchen was filled with clouds of gray smoke. Korin immediately jumped from the chair, pulled the headphones off his head and ran to the stove, putting out the burner under the pan. I felt stupid. I opened the window a little, grabbed the cloth and began to remove the smoke. The boy looked at me reproachfully.

"Sit down better. Just don't touch anything," he added as soon as he saw that I was sitting in the chair he had just occupied. "I'll make dinner because you obviously don't have culinary talent."

"And you have?" I asked skeptically.

"Of course." He grinned. "Culinary art is one of the things pleasant and useful. You have to eat something."

This culinary defeat spoiled my mood for the rest of the evening, and I wanted to show off before him. In addition, he behaved as if he had spent half his life in the kitchen. He did real miracles with the pan. He turned pancakes, rejecting the pan with one hand. I had nothing to impress him.

"You're good," I expressed my appreciation, though unnecessarily, because he still seemed too satisfied with his skills.

"I know."

"Asshole," I murmured so that he wouldn't hear, but at least I felt relieve.

After the meal, Korin returned to his report, and I started cleaning up the dishes. When I finished, I didn't know what to do with myself. It tempted me to talk with the boy, but I do not think he was delighted that I will bother him again. I was trying to find a job. First, I visited the house thoroughly, looked in every corner, into every wardrobe, cupboard or drawer, then I went around the small garden, admired the colorful, spring flowers on the flower beds along the house, sat for a while on the stone steps, warming my face in the warm rays of the setting sun. However, the new reality did not taste as good as it did this morning. I couldn't understand why? And suddenly I was dazzled. Korin. It's because of him. In the company of an Arisyan I felt lost, as if I wasn't myself, as if my mind and body were not functioning properly. I didn't like it at all.

I had to think about something else.

I went to the bookcase, closed my eyes and pulled out a random book. I looked at the title - A class game. I opened on the eighth page, where the first chapter began, and settled comfortably on the couch. Whether I would be able to meet Maga? I read the first sentence mindlessly, which overflowed through my mind like water through a sieve, not leaving behind even a bit of content. I made a second attempt. Could I... and third... None sense. I closed the book and, unable to resist, looked surreptitiously at Korin. I liked to look at him. He fascinated me. Although he seemed arrogant, he had the full right to do so. He was tall, handsome, well-built, and in addition intelligent. There was no indication for him to have any complexes. One thing I didn't like about him - he didn't have a good opinion about Earthlings. Sometimes I had the impression that he treated us like some inferior species. Although maybe not so much worse, as somehow defective. And at some point, during these considerations I fell asleep.

I don't know, I slept for a long time. A scream woke me up. It was already dark in the room, and only a pale moonlight penetrated the interior, lazily leaking from behind a blindly closed blind. I lay on the couch in the living room, where I fell asleep over the book, and Korin was leaning over me a little scared.

"Emily, what happened? You were screaming."

"I screamed?" I asked half consciously.

He nodded.

"I think I dreamed something," I said in a sleepy voice, rubbing my forehead with my hand.

"Dreams," he murmured. "I could never understand what it meant."

"Don't you dream about anything?" I was surprised.

"No. Our sleep is deep, almost like hibernation. It is important to properly regenerate the body at night. It has been clearly proven that an adult needs seven to nine hours of sleep to be able to function efficiently during the day," he explained. "So, what did you dream about?"

"The usual, but different."

„You didn't explain a lot," he said sarcastically. "So, what do you usually dream about?"

"A great void with the smell of loneliness and a dead tree in the middle of an endless plain. This time a big black crow was sitting on the tree and looking at me with empty eye sockets."

"You woke up screaming because some black blind

bird was staring at you?! Emily, you should listen to yourself, it's absurd."

"I know," I admitted, embarrassed. Korin just made me aware of the lack of logic in what I said. But do dreams have to make sense? "Could you sit here for a while until I fall asleep?" I asked, I still felt uncomfortable.

He sighed.

"Okay."

He sat on the floor with his head placed on the couch a few centimeters from mine. I reached for his hand and sheltered mine in it, cuddling my cheek in Korin's hand. I needed someone close to me now.

He looked at me strangely but did not withdraw his hand.

"I know many Earthlings, but you are probably the most unusual of all."

I smiled to myself. Hugged by his smooth hand, I closed my eyes, and I decided to think of something pleasant. Imagine, how it would be to go to school, meet peers, meet new people, have friends... I always dreamed about this. It is not known when I fell asleep.

I was woken by the rays of the rising sun wandering my face. I felt something warm and soft under my cheek. He sat down slowly and stared at the place where my head was resting a moment ago. I slept all night in Korin's hand, and he slept sitting on the floor, his left cheek against the couch. Apparently, he hasn't changed position since last night.

Why he didn't go to the bedroom to sleep?

Did he do it for me?

He was afraid that if I stay alone again I will wake up screaming?

In any case, without regard to his own convenience, he stayed here, and I felt it was very nice. I pushed the fringe away from his forehead, he didn't move, he slept like a stone. I felt remorse that he had spent the night on the floor because of me.

I glanced at the electronic clock hanging on the wall, it was almost seven. At least I will try to prepare breakfast, cereal with milk I should rather not screw up. Carefully I got up from the couch and went as quiet as I could to the bathroom. When I looked in the mirror, the morning good humor splashed like a soap bubble. I tried to bring order somehow, but not much could be done. All because of these frayed short hair without gloss, pale complexion and little feminine clothes. I winced at my reflection.

I've never cared about my appearance until now. And now I wanted to look nice, not for myself, but for him, I wanted to please him. It didn't make the slightest sense. Am I in love? Is this what love looks like? Is it even possible? I don't even know him well! Anyway, the common sense told me that Korin is not the right person to locate feelings.

I wonder if Arisyan women are pretty?

"Stop it" I scolded myself.

Breakfast - this is a safe topic. Although not necessarily in my case.

A bit depressed I dragged myself into the kitchen. When I was pouring milk over the cereal, Korin woke up.

"I hope you do not plan to poison us," he made a joke, seeing my actions.

„Me too."

We sat at the kitchen table and we started to eat our portion.

„Korin," I looked him in the eye. "Thanks... thanks for not laughing at me last night. By the way, thanks for everything."

"No problem, admittedly, I don't know why there was so much noise at night, but most importantly that it helped you."

"Thank you again."

"But I would not recommend myself for the future, the floor is not a very comfortable space to sleep. Everything numbs," he said, ostentatiously massaging his neck.

I got up to clean up after breakfast. At that time, Korin dressed and packed his things.

"Ready to tests?" He asked cheerfully.

"I think so. Are they difficult?"

„It depends... I don't know, how much you know. You may need some compensatory classes."

"You could be surprised." He was teasing me again, and he was so sweet at night.

CHAPTER IV

Love is full of traps. When it wants to make known about itself -blinds with light and does not let you see the shadows [...]

PAULO COELHO

The closer we got to school, the more courage left me to leave a barely vague memory under the president's office.

"You'd better take me home," I said grimly to Korin.

"Don't kid me."

"I'm serious, I can't make it," I murmured and turned back with the intention of escaping, but Korin immediately sensed my intentions. He grabbed my arm tightly and simply pushed me through the door. He did it so quickly that I could barely read the names on the metal plates attached to the door. Professor Lorena and Professor David Holix. I heard 'good luck' quickly and a heavy door slammed shut behind me with a soft click.

There were two solid desks facing each other in the office. Behind one sat an older, dignified-looking Arisyan woman with traces of an old, original beauty on her face, and on the other a small, balding man with a big belly, giving an extremely nice impression.

"Good morning," I stammered nervously.

"Good morning," they replied almost simultaneously.

I cleared my throat.

"My name is Emily Walker, I was supposed to take tests today."

"Of course, Dr. Almar informed us that you would show up." The man jumped up from the swivel chair, came up to me and grabbed my hand, shaking it vigorously. "I am Professor Holix, director of Earth Affairs, and this is Professor Lorena for Arisyan Affairs." He pointed at the Arisyan woman.

Lorena was not so effusive, she just nodded and immediately returned to her affairs. Professor Holix looked at me closely from behind the small round glasses in a wire frame, then asked:

"How do you feel before the test?"

"Not special," I said truthfully.

He patted my shoulder kindly.

"There is nothing to be afraid of. You can do it."

He brought a chair to his desk.

"Sit down," he commanded.

When I took the place indicated, he put a large stack of translucent, black printed film in front of me and handed me a navy-blue marker pen.

"You enter the solutions in the free places. The tasks have different levels of difficulty, so you should write something there," he said as a consolation.

I flipped through the test, the films rustled softly. I noticed a lot of free space between the commands, probably for typing solutions. However, I preferred to make sure I could write on the film like that.

"You enter the solutions in the free places," the director explained, noticing my hesitation. "We

don't use paper. Firstly, in the current situation it is the product I scarce meters, and secondly, films are much more economical, can be used repeatedly, removing the letter in a dedicated plate setter.

"I understand..."

"Well, let's do it," he encouraged me. "I think three hours should be enough for you," he said, glancing at his watch.

I took the test. Initially, I was a bit nervous, so I couldn't focus enough, but when I solved the first task without major problems, getting a fairly reasonable result, I relaxed a little. Maybe I'm not as stupid as I was afraid before. The questions came from various fields. I had the slightest problem with mathematics, but the others did not cause me much difficulty. I filled the empty fields under the instructions with a quick, small text so that I didn't even notice when I reached the last page. And not only that fits in time, a provision which I was, was up hour.

"I'm done," I said.

"So fast?" Professor Holix did not hide his surprise.

I noticed that even Professor Lorena looked astonished. Just as she hadn't paid me the slightest attention before, probably thinking that another blunt man had come to the tests, now she carefully appraised me with her eyes as if I were some kind of paranormal phenomenon. Under the influence of her gaze made me an uncomfortable feeling until I had to look in different place.

Professor Holix took from me a pile of foil with solutions.

"Wait a few minutes outside the door," he said. "We will check your work and determine which groups to assign you to."

I left the office, letting out a small sigh of relief.

"Phew... and it's over."

I thought it will be worse. Actually, I was unnecessarily afraid of this test.

I sat on one of the benches in the corridor. Now I had to be patient and wait for the results. I looked at the clock on the wall, focusing my attention on the minute hand, which seemed to be moving much slower than it should have been. I felt a bit like a criminal before the sentence was pronounced.

Finally, the door opened, and I was asked inside. I entered the office and the first thing that struck me in the doorway was their smiles. They were smiling at me. Both. I think I did really well, but I still didn't know if it was good or not.

"It is inconceivable to me, but your mathematical knowledge is at the level of Arisyan knowledge," Lorena said to me with a distinct note of recognition in her voice. "This is the first time I've come across here on Earth." She shook her head in disbelief. "Anyone teach you?"

"Yes, mom. She is a mathematician."

"I can see that she is an exceptionally good... mathematician." She frowned for a moment, as if considering something. Or maybe it just seemed to me.

"I will help you choose the subjects you will attend at school. She said after a short silence. "Most of them you probably know are ordinary earthly lessons. In some cases, only the name was changed while the essence of the item was preserved, but there were also a few new Arisyan ones and you can also sign up if you feel like it."

She showed me the foil with a long list of courses run at school. After a series of questions and answers, doubts and detailed explanations, after a stormy and educational discussion, my schedule was created. To my surprise, Lorena saw no obstacles to me attending most subjects along with the advanced group. She made me a great joy with this, which meant that the search without any excuses, I could see more of Korin.

In this way I came to the advanced group on mathematics, chemistry, physics, history and geography. I had a choice of Arisyan geography, but I forgave myself this subject by placing it in the category of completely useless knowledge. The average level fell on world literature, because unfortunately I did not read the right number of books, which was the main marker of the level of literary knowledge, and on biology. In the middle group there was also an object called "art", which covered all artistic activities, from painting, through sculpture, drawing, music, to acting. I do not quite know, as such a course would look like, do I have the appropriate abilities, or rather a knack for each of these, or it is enough to be good in one direction only. Or maybe I have a sincere desire?

In the shelter, one of my few pastimes was playing the guitar, I liked spending time like that. My mother taught me the basic grips, and the rest came up with the same chords. After a year, I knew the instrument well enough that I just felt it with my whole body. In principle, I had the impression that I and the guitar are one organism. The music sounded in my head, it flowed straight from my heart and I was able to easily translate it into appropriate sounds. Unfortunately, not for long. Like everything in life, the instrument was not long-lived, and the strings even more so, so my musical career lasted quite a short time. For a long time, I missed it. The guitar was a kind of addiction for me - when I was playing, there was no pain for me, loneliness or suffering caused by isolation, or a sense of meaninglessness in my life, only me and the music were important. I told Lorena about it and that is why she decided that I should develop my skills in this direction.

"But there is a problem," I said worriedly. "I don't have a guitar."

She waved her hand.

"It doesn't matter. In the houses we took, there are a lot of different things left by previous owners, so probably the guitar will also be found at some place. You should ask in a circle, maybe one of the students has it."

Unfortunately, I had to study other subjects from scratch. There was no typical Arisyan subject, but it did not occur previously in the curriculum ordinary earthly school. These included: genetics, history of the universe, astronomy enriched with extensive knowledge of Arisyan and medical training, which is something like a doctor's course. In addition, I signed up for Arisyan. Idiotic idea, I know, another superfluous skill. I hoped that thanks to my knowledge of the language I would get to know not only Korin but also Arisyans.

Obligatory classes, but without division into levels of advancement, also included sport and experimental work in the field. Finally, my timetable took shape, and Professor Holix, who hadn't spoken at all for some time, asked:

"Do you have a printout of the timetable with an accurate map of the school building?"

"I will be very grateful, I hardly know anyone here, so it will definitely be useful to me, especially in the first days."

With a freshly printed plan in hand, I look around the deserted school yard. The lessons were still going on. I sat on the steps leading to school, casting a quick glance toward the parking lot. Korin's car was in the same place where we left it this morning, so I decided to wait for him here, he was supposed to take me to the hospital. Finally, I could meet with my mother for the first time, since we found ourselves in a completely new reality. I could not wait.

After a few minutes, the sound of a bell ringing for a break reached my ears, and a moment later a crowd of smiling and talking young lands spilled out of the building, among which Earthlings predominated. However, not the advantage of Earthlings most striking, but the fact that they stayed away from the Arisyans. It worried me a bit. Couldn't they get along? Or maybe they didn't like each other? When I was in the hospital, I noticed full tolerance and acceptance between our races, and here there was a clear division into two separate worlds.

No, I have been too long to deliberate over this, because I recognized the Korin's slender figure. He was handsome, a lot... In fact, all the Arisyans had a kind of disturbing beauty in them, but Korin just had more of it than others, or it was only my feeling. He was now standing at the top of the stairs, looking around anxiously, apparently looking for someone. I waved to him. In response, he gave me such a wonderful smile that all anger for unceremonious thrust into the director's office completely evaporated from me. I felt a pleasant warmth spreading through my stomach. Were those famous butterflies in the stomach?

To mask my joy somehow, I decided to act a bit inaccessible.

"Hey, little one," he said freely, sitting down next to me on the step. "How did it go?"

I decided to keep silent.

"Very bad?" He tried to guess when he heard no answer.

"Why bad?" I couldn't stand it, his question irritated me. I don't think he really thought about my state of mind.

"I don't know," he muttered in confusion. "You say nothing, so I thought..."

"Then you better not think," I said, maybe a little too sharply. I didn't understand why I speak to him in such a way, after all, I like him, but I could not help it that his insinuations irritate me.

"Okay, I turn my thinking off." He laughed at me wickedly. "Why don't you tell me how it went?"

That smile disarmed me. Anyway, I couldn't sulk for a long time, not at Korin. It was simply impossible not to like him."I came to the advanced level from science subjects, and differently to the others."

"Wow, I see I underestimated you," he said with genuine appreciation.

"And I didn't say you'd be surprised?"

„You did, but I thought you were overestimating your possibilities again."

"Again?" I snorted. "Well... when it comes about my person, not really thinking is your strong side." I joked.

"Because you're more complicated than the average person."

He stood up and took my arm.

"Come on, you probably can't wait to see your mom."

"Yes, let's go now," I said, feeling myself blushing. And it's not because that he just squeezed my hand. I just felt a shame that by yesterday day, and almost all of today's I didn't thought even once about Mom. Only now Korin made me realize that this should be the most important thing for me, and I was terrified that it wasn't. For the last 24 hours my thoughts stubbornly revolved around Korin. He intrigued me. I was annoyed. But I liked him, I think I liked him too much, which was worrying me. Am I in love? Or maybe it's just a crush? Or a storm of youthful hormones that had been dormant so far, now making itself felt with doubled strength? I'll think about it later. At the moment, only my mother and her health mattered.

We got into the car and went off from the school.

"Is Arisyan difficult?" I asked unexpectedly.

"Why do you ask?" He glared at me briefly and frowned. "Well, no..." he groaned. "Have you signed up for Arisyan?!"

I nodded eagerly.

"Why?" He asked.

"Curiosity." And what I had to tell him that for him? „So, it is difficult or not, because you did not answer?"

"It's hard to say... It's a little throaty from English, and with some sounds you have to set the language to get the correct wording."

"What other languages ??do you have on Arisa?"

"Only Arisyan. Another element differentiating our civilizations. We have unified the language on our planet, it greatly facilitates the flow of information between distant regions. You should follow our example, meanwhile you have absolutely no respect for the capacity of minds, another proof of waste. In addition, language differences make communication difficult.

"But you learned English." I noticed.

"I had to. Without knowledge of the language, it would be difficult for us to do anything on Earth."

"You could have forced people to learn Arisyan."

He looked at me with obvious indignation.

"Never. Nobody. To nothing. We don't force anyone." He said, carefully accentuating each word. "And we're not going to force you," he added. "We know from experience that this often has the opposite effect."

I did not comment on his speech, I did not make it. My attention was caught by the view behind the

windshield. I realized that we were not going to the hospital at all. Tower, which housed the clinic, was the only tall building in the town, and now I had it behind, not in front of me. We were going in the opposite direction.

"We're not going to the hospital?" I was surprised.

"A small change of plans," he replied enigmatically.

I looked at him suspiciously.

"How is that?"

"You'll see in a moment." He laughed. "Surprise."

I didn't even have to ask what the surprise was because we had just arrived at my house. My home... I was slowly starting to get used to calling this place. Suddenly the front door opened, and my mother stood on the threshold, smiling happily. Now, I knew for sure that I was at home and that this is where I belong. Because after all, home is always where are the people you love. I ran to her, we fell into each other's arms and for a moment neither of us could say a word. When the first emotions subsided, she saw Korin behind me, who was standing by his car and was just rummaging with his shoe in a gravel driveway. He obviously didn't know what to do with himself.

"You must be Korin." Mother gave him a warm smile. "Megan, Megan Walker, mother of Emily."

"Nice to meet you." They shake their hands.

"I wanted to thank you for taking care of my daughter, for finding her, for... for everything..." It was hard for her to choose words because of her emotions. "I will never forget it, I hope that one day I will be able to pay my debt of gratitude."

"There really is nothing to talk about," he said, slightly embarrassed.

"Let's drink something warm." Suggested my mother. "I just put in water."

"Thank you, maybe another time. I'll go to my place, I haven't been home for a long time. He gave me an eloquent look that apparently did not escape my mother's attention, and I blushed again.

She looked at me first, then at him and sighed.

„I will make coffee," she said as she entered the house. I was sure she wanted to leave us alone.

„What is your first lesson on Monday?" Asked Korin as my mother disappeared behind the door.

I looked at the plan.

"World literature," I replied.

He rolled his eyes.

„Another unnecessary subject," he muttered. "I don't think I'll ever comprehend your bizarre tendency to useless things in life. Can you tell me what other brain-trashing subjects you have chosen besides literature and Arisyan?"

"Art," I said softly.

"Do you want to splash paint?"

"No, I'm not interested in painting, I will play the guitar."

"So, you focused on making noise?"

"Not noise but music," I was indignant.

"Noise is noise, and no matter whether you call it music. For me, every sound that does not occur naturally in nature is associated with noise."

"This Arisyan philosophy of life is just sick. Denying yourself all pleasure doesn't lead to

anything good. Maybe you should take the opportunity that you now live on Earth and revise your views on certain matters?"

He shook his head disapprovingly.

"I do not feel such a need," he interrupted my argument, returning to the topic of music. "And how are you doing with your guitar, do you usually make a big noise or a small one?"

"You don't have to worry if you mean whether I'm falsifying. I used to play quite well. Anyway, it's a problem because I don't have a guitar anyway. Professor Lorena advised me to ask students if they had one, but I don't know anyone here beside you."

"I think... well, I think you know the right person. I see what I can do. He grumbled at me and hopped into the car."

"See you on Monday at school," he said, away.

"Bye."

I waved goodbye to him and when the car disappeared around the corner, I entered the house. I was overcome by sadness. It was only Friday afternoon, and I got so used to the company of Korin that I knew one thing - I will miss him. Despite all the features that irritated me in him, he became close to me in his own way. Although, I felt through my skin that the emotional chaos that had been inside me from this morning could only mean trouble in the future.

I found my mother in the kitchen and she was putting two steaming cups on the table. The pleasant aroma of coffee hovered in the air, reminiscent of the word home, which has now become completely new

to me, because it ceased to be just an image, and finally became something real and tangible.

"Come on, Emily, we need to discuss a few things." My mother patted the seat adjacent chairs.

We sat next to each other. She gave me sugar.

"How did the tests go?" She asked first.

"Supposedly great." I grinned happily. "I surprised everyone with my knowledge of science."

"And the others?" she demanded up.

"A little worse," I shouted. "But not bad."

"And how are you feeling?" I quickly changed the subject before it occurred to her to ask about Korin. "And what exactly happened that you woke up the day before?"

"Minor complications have occurred, arrhythmias plus low blood pressure. All in all, nothing serious, but Sofie immediately decided to get me out of coma."

I got angry.

"Why didn't anyone inform me? They should tell me!"

"You were at a conversation with Almar. And believe me, you better not know. You wouldn't want to watch me like this. For the first few hours I felt confused. Hysterical. I needed a little more time than you to get used to the new reality."

The telephone ringing interrupted us. To tell the truth, I was surprised by the strange sound coming from the room, but my mother immediately explained that it was a cell phone and that she got it from Almar."

She jumped up from her chair and ran to pick up, and I followed her out of curiosity.

"Megan Walker, hallo?" She said into the handset.

The person on the other side spoke for some time. I tried to read from my mother's face what the conversation was about, but none of that. I couldn't read in mind, so I could wait patiently for it to finish.

"I think I can handle it. When can I start?" My mother asked the interlocutor and I immediately gave her a questioning look. She gestured that she would tell me later. But she looked pleased, so I calmed down a bit.

"Well, I'll be there on Monday morning. See you later," she added finally, then hung up.

Putting the phone on the bench, she took a deep breath.

"Lorena, the school principal called. She just offered me a mathematics position. I accepted this job," she said, looking at me with a glint of satisfaction in her eyes.

"Great!" I was happy. "So, we'll stay here longer?"

"Almar told me you wanted to stay."

„Very much." The tone of my voice spoke for itself. "But when..."

She interrupted me.

"We're staying, Emily. For a time. Outside the cities of Arisyan is too dangerous, I prefer not to risk traveling to Fargo now. But someday everything will normalize, then we will come back home."

"Do you think there is something to come back to?" I asked.

"I don't know if there is anything to go back to, but there is definitely something to come back to. At least I have what for."

"I do not understand."

"See, Emily. I made an appointment with your father that if any of us survives, we will leave a message at home where we are. I have a feeling your dad is still alive and if I don't go there and check it out, hope will still be on me. If it were possible, I would leave today." Tears appeared in her eyes. "But it's too dangerous. Also, I'd like to give you a childhood you never had. You also deserve something from life, and my affairs have already been waiting so long, so they can wait a little longer. Anyway, school is a nice thing."

"I miss dad too, but I remember him like through the fog. I'm afraid I won't meet him, even if we pass each other on the street." I confessed sadly.

She put her arm around me.

"I assure you that you will recognize him, your heart will tell you that he is he." She said with conviction. She let me out of her arms. "Okay, we're changing the subject, because I will completely break up. What do you think about them, what do you think about Arisyans?"

Until she asked, I didn't think more about it. I just accepted the fact that they are here, that they are an integral part of the new life in our world, and I didn't mind. They did not arouse negative emotions or give the impression of invaders from space, and most importantly, they aroused sympathy.

"I think they are fine, a little specific, but fine," I said after a moment's thought.

"I think so too," my mother admitted. "Although... I think something is wrong with them, I find it difficult to say what. I may be wrong, but..." she sighed, "I

don't know anymore. I think maybe it is nothing."

"You don't fool yourself. Theoretically, they're on Earth, hmm... sort of like a fourth race, at least physically. They are different... Psyche? Mind? I don't know how to put it. It's because of genes. They have modified genes."

"But how... What do they have?" She was surprised.

So, I told her my conversation with Korin and told her everything I had learned about the Arisyans. My mother listened carefully, and her face slowly showed understanding, as if only now she was able to match the missing pieces of the puzzle.

"Now I understand... almost. And what is all this Korin like?" She asked finally.

"Nice," I answered, trying to keep my voice flat.

She looked into my eyes. She noticed that I was hiding something, that I didn't want to tell her something.

"Just nice?" She drilled.

I hesitated for a moment with the answer.

"Well... I like him," I said finally.

The rest I added already in the mind "and he is handsome, intelligent, sympathetic, cheerful, saved my life, slept on the floor when I felt scared and lonely, and cooks well, and I like to look at him, and I love the feel of the soft, orange skin and most I like his violet eyes." So, I could list goes on, not only in thought, but the voice, but I did not want to, at least for now. I couldn't predict how she would react to the news that her only daughter liked a stranger. Anyway, these feelings were also something new to me, I was lost in

them myself, I often didn't know how I really felt. After all, Korin is the first guy I met, and I can suddenly change my mind when I meet others. But I wasn't surprised by the fact that my mother noticed that I was different, she knew me inside out. I don't know if this kind of fascination with other people can be read from my face, but apparently it was possible to mine.

"Does it seem to me or is something going on?" She asked with a hint of suspicion.

"What?" - I shrugged, as if I did not care about Korin.

She knew that I could say nothing more, so she stopped exploring the subject. From time to time, she looked at me with concern, but never once asked anything. I was extremely grateful for that because I would have to lie to her for the first time in my life and I didn't want to do it.

All Saturday I wandered around the house aimlessly, unable to find a place for me. I even tried to read some romance, but the fate of its heroes completely did not interest me. Saturday seemed to go on forever, and finally the evening came, followed by an almost sleepless night. The time seemed to stand still. Fidgeting anxiously in the strange half-sleep, I barely lived to see Sunday morning. On Sunday afternoon mother found me at the mirror, when I tried to do something with my hair, or rather with what has left. All attempts to style a decent haircut brought me aggression. I looked at my mother with tears of anger in eyes.

"Let me handle this." She grabbed my hand and

dragged me into the bathroom.

I put together my blond hair in unruly, disheveled haircut, using for this purpose a special gel.

"I will show you how to use makeup cosmetics," she suggested.

"Do you think I should do that?"

"I think it's time to start."

She showed me how to make the right makeup. It turned out that the Arisyans took care of all our Earthling needs, including cosmetics. Only after these beautifying procedures she led me in front of the mirror. Shades of beige and black crayon advantageously stressed my big, green eyes, and highlighted the delicate lipstick shaped lip contour. With staggering, how little interference can advantageously change a woman's appearance. I must say that now, despite the short hair, I was pretty, I could even like to others. Not only could, I just wanted to be considered as beautiful girl and I think my mom was perfectly aware to who.

CHAPTER V

I used to have too much respect for nature. I faced things and landscapes, let them act. Now it's over, I will intervene.

HENRI MICHAUX

On Monday I woke up extremely early and could not fall asleep. Behind the window came the monotonous hum of rain, and the drops of water played a loud rhythm on the windows. However, this did not spoil my humor, it was such trifles that enjoyed the most, gave life meaning. I've longed for rainfall, like the sun, for a long time. I didn't even worry about getting wet on my way to school. Actually, nothing could stifle my excitement on the first day of school and the certainty that I would like it. I jumped happily out from under the covers and humming a cheerful tune under my breath, I walked to the closet with a dancing step.

I wondered for a moment what to wear. Finally, my choice fell on light blue jeans. Actually, I also want to wear short green skirt, but at my pale, lean and practically devoid of muscular legs it was not the best idea. It also rained. In a small backpack unearthed from the bottom of the closet, I put a class schedule, which I got on Friday from Professor Holix and a few felt-tip pens. Just a gentle make-up and, before my mother got up, I was already dressed and ready to go.

I pulled up the blind and looked out of the window. The downpour intensified.

Hmm... in total, an umbrella or a raincoat could be useful. So, I started to search the wardrobes, storage compartments and drawers, looking for something to protect against rain. My mother caught me on this.

"Emily, what are you doing?" She asked reproachfully.

"I'm looking for an umbrella."

"We won't need it."

"How is that? It's raining." I sent her questioning look.

She didn't answer right away. She went to the dresser standing just by the front door, opened the top drawer, took something out of it, and shook her hand. The object in her hand made a characteristic metallic sound.

"The keys?" I was surprised.

"Car keys," she added. „It's in the garage."

"Do we have a car? Seriously?!" I enjoyed it. "What car is this?"

"Old, red Ford Forbes, but in good condition."

"And your license is still valid?"

"This is not required. It's enough for me that I know how to ride."

I have to admit that my mother was quite good at the wheel. Driving a car was one of the skills you simply don't forget. We arrived at the school half an hour before the start of the lesson, because my mother had to agree with the management of the employment conditions. There were already a few cars in the parking

lot, but I didn't see a green Land Rover among them, so Korin wasn't there yet. We ran into the school building, escaping from the rain.

"How do I look?" My mother asked, ruffling her hair with her hand to shake off the drops of water.

I looked at her with appraising eyes. In a navy-blue suit and red top under the jacket she looked pretty good, though she looked a bit nervous.

"Pretty, but come on," I urged her.

I showed her where the management's office was. She hesitated for a long time whether to come inside. I had no other choice, so I did the same as Korin did with me on Friday - I just pushed her through the door. I walked around the corridor for a while, then headed back to the second floor.

First lesson - world literature, room D-201. I stood in front of the classroom door with a feeling of strange squeezing in my stomach, I didn't have the courage to go inside again. What do I have with this entering the room? Maybe it's some kind of unnamed phobia? I have no problem leaving but entering... well. In the end I decided to wait for the teacher under the room. I leaned my back against the wall, surreptitiously watching the students passing the corridor. I would give a lot to disappear now. Several people gave me a curious look, thankfully no one stopped to talk.

Almost flush with the doorbell, Professor Holix appeared.

"Good morning," I said with relief, finally seeing a familiar face.

"Hello, Emily. Why didn't you enter the class?"

"I'm just getting courage."

"Head up, girl."

He opened the door with an inviting gesture.

"Meet the new student. Emily Walker," he introduced me loudly.

"Hello everyone." I smiled wanly.

"Hi," answered a dozen or so voices.

I looked around the class with interest. Almost all Earthlings, of different races, sat in two rows of three-seater benches. Almost, because the last one was occupied by Arisyans and some fair-haired boy, who at first glance seemed a little older than the other students. Only next to the two stood a free chair, so the professor told me to sit there. I walked slowly to the indicated table and took a seat next to the girl absorbed in reading a book.

"Hey, I'm Emily," I said shyly.

She raised her head, giving me a warm smile.

"Kori."

After a while, a fair-haired boy leaned out from behind Arisyan girl.

"Tom," he introduced himself briefly.

„Nice to meet you."

Kori closed the book and put it in front of her. I read the title: Gone with the wind. Hmm... intriguing. Arisyan woman with a book? And apparently, they are not interested in literary bullshit, would I misunderstand something? I looked at her again, this time more closely. Black, straight shoulder-length hair with an evenly trimmed fringe, orange skin... The girl did not stand out with anything special, she looked like other Arisyans. She apparently sensed that I was watching her because she looked at

me, smiling shyly. How do I know this smile? Those eyes, lips, nose, chin...? I think I'm insane, but I could bet I've seen that face somewhere. It is sick, I can see Korin everywhere, it has completely taken over me. Probably by the fact that I think so many times of him. Or maybe I am under illusion? They are similar to each other so alike. We took our eyes off each other because Professor Holix started the lesson. He wrote on the white, glass board topic:

"Lord of the flies" - a man against the mystery of evil.

"What is evil? Is man evil by nature?" He asked, encouraging the class to discuss.

I began to wonder what I could say about it and nothing came to my mind. Of course, I knew this book very well, but until now I didn't have to delve into the text so much. Considerations like: what the author meant and whether he had anything at all, never attracted me. Mainly interested in the story, judge, whether it is interesting or not. Apparently, the school was not enough, so I'll have to learn how to draw conclusions from read texts, although I do not know, if I can.

Hopelessness.

I watched more students join in the discussion. Almost everyone told a story about their lives that they associated with evil. Unfortunately, I couldn't draw on my own experience because I didn't have any. Nothing happened in my life, it was bland so far - neither good nor bad.

Professor Holix with amazing energy circled between the benches to finally stop by ours. I

swallowed with nervousness, I could still feel empty. I was hoping he wouldn't ask me anything.

"And maybe better prevent evil, rather than later to repair its effects?" Kori asked a little rhetorically.

"How?" Tom said unexpectedly.

"Genetics," the girl said.

He snorted, this word annoyed him.

"Genetics," he repeated contemptuously. "It's best to remove all genes from yourself and us. It will definitely be good for humanity. You've already deleted one gene too much."

"What do you mean?"

"You know well."

They would probably argue like that if the professor did not interrupt this peculiar exchange.

"Relax, my dear, control your emotions. Everyone has the right to their own opinion. Now I'd like to know what Emily thinks about it?"

"I think..." I cleared my throat. "I think that evil is different for every man."

"Well done, that's probably the most reasonable sentence I heard here today," he praised.

"Phew... Have I handled the situation?"

"I think," he continued, "that it is the perfect conclusion to this lesson. For the next class, in a week, you will prepare a paper on the topic: What is good? I suggest writing a job in pairs, then you will get to know another person's point of view, which will be a very valuable experience."

The professor left the room.

"Emily, would you like to write this paper with me?" Kori suggested unexpectedly. "Of course, if you

don't mind," she added quickly.

"Sure, I'll be very eager to do it," I was happy because I had already liked the girl.

"What subject do you have now?" She asked.

I glanced at the schedule.

"Two lessons of math in room D-102."

She seemed surprised.

"Impossible, I have math in D-102," she said.

"So, why I can't have one too?" I frowned. "After all, we had classes together now."

"The point is, our group is very advanced," she began to explain. "No Earthman has yet attended this level of the course."

"It's time to change that." I smirked.

"As you wish." She shrugged. "Come, I will lead you."

Who does she think I am? I thought. I didn't like that she considered me inferior to the Arisyans. Or maybe all the "orange" people had a similar opinion? Earlier, I observed almost identical reaction in Korin. Well, according to them, Earthlings were wasting time on unnecessary entertainment, instead of feeding the mind with a portion of additional information to help save the universe. Tom's voice snapped me out of my thoughts.

"See you in biology," he said without anger, more to Kori than me, and left the classroom.

"Bye," she answered quietly, follow him with her eyes to the door.

I suddenly remembered their strange quarrel at the end of the class, and now this goodbye. It was as if the two of them were connected by something other than ordinary camaraderie. By the way, what did Tom mean with such contempt for removing genes? After all, the Arisyans did it in good faith, in the name of a higher good, could something go wrong?

"What was about at literature, you know, between you and Tom?" I asked directly, immediately regretting my directness. I shouldn't be interested, I almost don't know the girl.

She was confused.

"He just has trouble accepting some of the Arisyan qualities. He perceives our otherness more than others. That's the way he is."

"He doesn't like you?"

"I didn't say that, he can't get used to us so quickly. He is also very distrustful of people. His parents died immediately after the disaster and he grew up in a shelter next to a foreign family. He wasn't treated well. Sometimes he was starving. It was a very difficult period for him. He did not think about science then. When the nightmare ended, he settled in town and wanted to help rebuild your world. My father convinced him that he should learn that proper knowledge is the only way. Reluctantly, but Tom agreed with him. He is a really talented boy, he quickly makes up for education gaps, although going to school with adolescents annoys him. He's twenty-three years old and thinks he's too old for that."

I was more prepared to hear complain about him than to the line of defense she served me. Either the famous

Arisyan forbearance prevailed, or some other consideration. I don't know why, but I had the impression that it was probably the latter. She also

mentioned age. I had not wondered before how old exactly are the Arisyans whom I met, how long do they live, how old can Korin be? Suddenly it started to interest me.

"And you, Kori, how old are you?" I asked.

"Earthly nineteen, and Arisyan slightly more than fourteen."

In surprise, I stopped in the middle of the corridor. Earth age, Arisyan age... it was too much for me. Kori stood in front of me.

"Arisa's circulation time around Alpha Centauri is exactly four hundred and seventy-six days," she said, seeing my face.

"Now I understand, I think." I thought about it for a moment. "So, I'm less than fourteen?"

"That's right."

"How long the Arisyans study?" I asked, because her answers ignited my curiosity. I wanted to get to know Arisyan better, by the way I would get to know Korin better.

"Sometimes, all life. It is very rare that Arisyans only performs one profession. Our minds are capacious, like a system of thousands of microprocessors, we can absorb a large amount of knowledge in a fairly short time. We learn while we are working. Practice perfectly ground the acquired knowledge, without it any knowledge is useless and easily flies from the head."

Absorbed in conversation, I didn't even notice when we entered the classroom. I only realized when Kori fell silent. The Arisyans stood in small groups of several, discussing fiercely. Hardly anyone paid us any attention. I strained to hear what they were talking about. I could not understand anything of this chatter, they spoke in a strange language with a throaty sound. It was the first time I came across Arisyan. I felt a little insecure.

Among the students standing by the window, I recognized Korin's figure. He stood with his back to us, but when one of his colleagues said something to him, he turned, smiled and headed towards us. My heart leaped into my throat.

"Hi, sister," he said to my companion.

It was only now that I understood why Kori's face seemed familiar to me from the very beginning. They were siblings. And I thought that again because of the excess of impressions and the flow of new information, the mind is playing tricks on me.

"Are you siblings?! Why didn't you say you had a sister?" I said reproachfully.

"Because you didn't ask." He smiled and mischievous flashes appeared in his eyes.

"Twin sister," Kori interjected.

"Come sit with me today." Before I could protest, he pulled me with him.

Out of the corner of my eye, I noticed that Kori took a seat on the penultimate bench, next to a girl. Korin and I sat in the first one, right at the teacher's desk. Around five minutes to the start of the lesson remained.

"You look quite nice today," he whispered, leaning into my ear. His warm breath touched my cheek. A pleasant shiver ran down my back. I almost groaned. Why is he doing this to me? I didn't know what to say

to this compliment, because I think I just heard the compliment. I preferred to direct the conversation to safer, emotion-free areas. The closer I got to know Arisyans, the more questions I had.

"You said you were not interested in books, meanwhile I meet your sister in literature class. Something doesn't suit me."

"Yes, my sister is unusual in this respect. I think she has a genetic defect, although they are very rare. For now, it manifests itself as a harmless quirk, but if it gets worse, you will have to do something about it," he said, kind of jokingly, but somewhere inside, some inner voice told me that it wasn't quite a joke.

I was a little scared, but I didn't show it. I wonder if I will ever understand him? Maybe, being in his company more often, I will get to know him better and find answers to the questions that bother me. So far, there was nothing to indicate it, it was getting worse, more and more question marks appeared, more and more secrets... Is something wrong with the Arisyans? Korin did not tell me everything, I had the impression that I did not know anything about them. But I'll find out. If not today, then tomorrow, if not tomorrow, then in a week, if not in a week, in a month, there will still be a lot of time and opportunity. I would ask directly, but I didn't quite know what to ask. Objectively, everyone was nice, so I shouldn't pick on, maybe it's my fault? Maybe something is wrong with me? After all, I didn't have much contact with people and now I expect from them what I should not.

Professor Lorena entered the room, the buzz of conversation ceased abruptly. She went to the desk,

looked around the classroom, finally stopped her gaze at me and announced with a studied smile:

"We have a new student, Emily Walker." I felt the curious glances of several pairs of eyes. "Therefore, from today classes will be held in English, not in Arisyan, as it has been until now. Also, try to use earthly symbols and names as you were taught in the course."

I did not hear the slightest murmur of dissatisfaction because of the change of the language of the lecture, so it was probably not unusual or burdensome for the Arisyans. Amazing how quickly they accepted the new rules.

Lorena took a bundle of foil from a green plastic folder and distributed one to each. I looked at my card. Two tasks printed with the small black font. I glanced over

Korin's shoulder, his foil looked similar, but the tasks were different.

"Please, choose one task for yourself, in a moment represent your solution on the board."

I delved into the content of the command and breathed a sigh of relief, I should not have major problems with solving not only one, but both tasks."

"And? You can do it?" Korin elbowed me gently.

"Worry about yourself," I grunted as I heard in his voice a doubt of my knowledge.

The students approached the board in turn, presenting their solutions. They used different methods, in some I couldn't quite understand. They used many foreign on Earth theories. This was the case with Korin's task. He based his reasoning on definitions and statements completely unknown to me to obtain the

correct solution after writing four tables. I was surprised that he chose this method.

"You didn't understand something, Emily?" Lorena asked. She must have noticed that I was frowning more and more.

"No, it's all right," I answered quietly. I didn't want to be smart one, not at the first lesson.

"For sure? If something is unclear to you, Korin will explain again."

I blushed, not out of shame, but out of anger. Who do they think they are?! I felt like a worse species again, as if I was by definition a human with a smaller brain and less intelligent.

"I would have done it differently," I said finally. "From my point of view, the easier way."

Startled, Lorena raised her eyebrows.

"Sit down, Korin. Please, Emily, the board is yours."

I got up from my seat. Korin handed the pen to me with astonished expression and returned to the bench. I wiped the board and started presenting my own version of the solution. I made it up quite quickly, without even writing down the entire board, I received exactly the same result as Korin just now.

"Pretty clever," Lorena said. "I didn't think anything would surprise me. I have to admit you are good."

"It's thanks to my mother, she taught me everything. She called such shorter methods the "smarter method"." I smiled with satisfaction and returned to the bench.

I glanced at Korin, he looked at me for a long

moment with a strange expression on his face. His expression expressed disbelief, admiration, recognition, bewilderment... It was a mixture of all these feelings at once.

"What?"

"Nothing, you're quite intelligent for a human," Korin said seriously.

"I hope it's a compliment."

"Of course, it's a compliment," he said uncertainly. "What? I said something wrong again?"

"I can't say I'm surprised." I snorted.

"But admit, I'm doing better and better."

"But what?"

"Understanding you."

Before the end of the lesson, two more people managed to present solutions to their tasks. Unlike Korin, I couldn't concentrate. He stared intently at the blackboard while I stared thoughtlessly at it. I considered how much Korin must try to understand me and how uncertain he is in dealing with me. Was his understanding of the world so different from mine? Or is it a natural need to avoid conflicts? He was very careful with every word so as not to offend me. I wonder if he was so careful with other Earthlings? Did he just not want to hurt me? In contrast, Kori stood out from the Arisyan pattern, she was specific. It was as if she had some secret. After all, I myself witnessed a sharp exchange of opinions of Arisyan girls with an Earthling, which probably did not happen often.

Two hours of biology before us. We went down to the ground floor, but not just us. Many Arisyans also

went to these classes. Certainly, other students will join us soon. I wondered how big the hall must be to accommodate everyone.

"Can we all fit in one room?" I asked doubtfully.

"We're not staying in the building, biology is in Eden," Kori said.

"In Eden?" I was surprised.

"That's what the Earthlings called it, you'll see why," Korin explained.

We left the school building through the back exit. Fortunately, it stopped raining and the sun was slowly breaking through the cloud cover. I looked away, squinting against the harsh light. On the left, behind the basketball court, there were gigantic greenhouses. On the right, behind the tennis court, there were lush plantations, meadows, freshly plowed fields and animal runs. The school was the last building of the town, and behind it, up to the horizon, was only paradise.

"Eden," I whispered with delight.

Juicy, fresh green, the color of flowering shrubs and this smell, above all the smell. A wonderful aroma filled my nostrils, a mixture of flowers, grass, earth, sun and colors. I've lived so many years without noticing that each color has its own unique fragrance. But to me, violet smelled the most beautiful - the color of Korin's eyes.

I noticed a lot of people at work. Dressed in colorful work overalls or white, blue or green aprons they hung around the plants. Some people in overalls had large spray tanks on their backs with a thick tube tapering at the end, just like the ghost busters from the

Ghostbusters movie. Others, in turn, looked like artists painting with brushes flowers, but I guessed that they pollinate them. On the other hand, people in their aprons noted something meticulously. Although they apparently performed different activities, they all meant the same thing - recreating species. Some detail caught my attention.

"Animals are not in the farms, are you not afraid of escaping?" I turned to siblings.

"There is a force field around the paddocks for animals, the same as the one that protects the town, maybe a little weaker. Without it," Korin showed me the left wrist on which he wore an unusual bracelet," even the mouse will not slip. This is "key" to the force field, by the way determines GPS coordinates, also acts as a pager."

When we passed both pitches, Tom caught up with us. He came straight to the three of us, as if he were permanently assigned to us.

"How's your math, egghead?" He joked.

"Emily cut Korin down to size," Kori said with satisfaction.

"Seriously?! I wish I had seen it. He deserved it."

"Some Earthlings have all one's marbles," Korin said, looking meaningfully at Tom, who only shrugged.

We entered, along with a group of other students, into one of the greenhouses. It was sultry and hot inside, a real tropical heat. Narrow path through the thicket of vegetation, until we reached a fairly large room inside the greenhouse. There were long tables here, on which a lot of small pots with tiny seedlings were placed. Each pot has a plate with a description of

the species, date of planting and other data.

At the top of one of the tables was a tall, wiry old man with a gray, thin beard and a sour expression on his face. He gave the impression of a man to be feared. I never liked people who couldn't smile, and he apparently had a problem with that.

"Professor Spite," Korin whispered in my ear. "You must be careful not to get into his black books, he is terribly memorable. Tom got into his black books in the first lesson and has been screwed up ever since."

"What have you done? Admit it, Tom."

"He killed the mosquito," Kori said with a smile.

"Because he wanted to bite my hand away," Tom defended.

"A thoughtless being has ruined the efforts of other beings to restore nature to its former order," Korin mocked in a shrill whisper.

"Spite is a psychopath," Tom murmured, dissatisfied that everyone was mocking him.

We laughed out loud. The professor looked critically at our amused four and then looked at me. I shuddered when I heard his voice. He spoke slowly, carefully sweeping every word through his teeth.

"The being is new."

"Me?" I asked, although I knew he meant me.

"Who else? I know the rest of the creatures." He nodded at me with a long, wrinkled finger. "You'll come over."

I took three small steps forward and stopped maybe half a meter from him, I was no longer laughing. He handed me a plastic notebook and some small black instrument, later I found out that it was a

laser measuring cup.

"Now you will go to another being and learns what to do. At the end of the class, I will check exactly how much you learned," he said.

I nodded, grabbed what he had given me, and quickly found myself next to Korin, only then relaxed.

"What with that?" I pointed at the objects in my hands.

"I'll show you in a moment," he whispered in my ear. "Come to that table."

We took the workplace furthest from the professor.

"Where did you get that guy from? Tom was right, he is a psychopath. In any case, he definitely is sick in the head," I said in a whisper.

"We had no choice, he is the only biologist who knows earthly nature so well."

"Maybe he also needs to modify his genes?"

"You know we don't do such things to people. Although he would have been useful," he said ironically. For the first time in my presence he joked and probably quite successfully, since he made me smile.

"Korin, what should I do with it?" I asked again, showing the black device.

"You need to measure these plants." He pointed to a long row of pots. "But precisely!" he noted. "Each sheet separately and write the measurements in the notebook along with the plate number."

"You must be kidding me," I said indignantly. I was completely indifferent to the length of leaves, stems or other parts of this herb. "Each one? Cannot be automated somehow?"

"It can be, but Professor Spite says that we also need to train patience."

"For two hours?!" I moaned.

"I will help you, but only today. I don't touch anything next time."

He picked up one of the pots, measured the whole plant with skillful movements, then recorded all the data. I watched with admiration how gently the muscles in his arms tighten. The orange skin harmonized perfectly with the black of the T-shirt, and I realized that instead of focusing on remembering all these activities that I will be forced to repeat in a moment, I remember the shape of his hand with details. In addition, I enjoyed it. I barely looked away from him, took the measuring tape and began the measurements. It took me a while before I got to a similar practice, but soon I could have a fairly casual conversation with Korin during these activities.

"I met your mother before math, she was just leaving the building."

"They didn't hire her?" I got scared. I thought she would run the classes right away.

"She is starting tomorrow. I said I'd take you back."

"You didn't have to," I said, but deep down I was happy.

"I didn't have to, but I wanted to. Besides, I have a surprise for you in the car."

"I hope it's pleasant."

"Depends on who." He made mysterious face. "Definitely yes for you."

"Beings don't talk, beings measure." I heard an

unpleasant voice behind me and, despite the heat, a cold shiver ran down my back.

Professor Spite appeared unexpectedly at our part of the table and stood by us until the end of the class. He clearly curved space-time with his presence, because the last ten minutes of the lesson lasted an hour.

"I tought that this nightmare would never end," I said with relief when the whole group spilled out in front of the greenhouse.

"Don't joke, it's my favorite class." Tom smiled mockingly.

"Mine not, although today they were quite bearable." Korin winked at me, and I blushed as usual, quickly turning my head in the other direction, hoping he wouldn't notice.

Everyone was in a good mood. Tom and Kori walked side by side, there was not even a trace left after the argument. Joking, we arrived at the parking lot.

"See you tomorrow," I said to Kori and Tom.

"See you," they replied.

However, before we left with Korin, I noticed something strange. Tom brushed Kori's hand with his hand and there would be nothing unnatural in this gesture if he were not so subtle and tender. I wasn't wrong, these two definitely have something in common. Just why are they hiding it?

We approached Korin's car. He opened the rear door wide.

"First a surprise. Especially for you," he said, stepping aside to reveal my view.

A guitar lay in the backseat. Lovely. Warm shaded brown with a characteristic white ornament on the box.

"Real acoustic Gibson," I shouted with delight. "How could you leave it in the back seat, it is worth a fortune?!"

He looked at me indulgently.

"Wasn't there a carrying case?" I asked without taking my eyes off the instrument.

"Why do you need a case?"

"It's a sensitive instrument. You have to handle the guitar gently, like a woman."

"Earthly woman, I think," he muttered, but I heard it.

"You're wrong with every woman."

I didn't feel like arguing, now my biggest desire was to pick it up. I ran my hand over the neck, stroked the box, sucking the smell of a mixture of wood and varnish mixed with dust in my nostrils.

"Thank you. You don't even know how much joy you gave me."

"I see," he smiled.

I sat in the back with a guitar. I hugged it tightly, just like a child who got a Christmas present and is afraid that it would give back for bad behavior. He didn't comment on this. We arrived at my house without a word.

"Will you come in?" I asked without conviction.

He looked at me, then at the guitar and again at me.

"Maybe not today."

"Korin, thanks." I climbed on my fingers quite spontaneously, kissed his cheek and ran home. He stood motionless for a moment, then got into the car and drove away.

I didn't think that it was possible, and yet... Korin lost with the guitar today. After returning home, I played for a few hours and couldn't finish, everything else didn't matter. When, after a few practices, I started to turn over the fingers weaned from the guitar, I played the first song that came to my mind. I don't know why this one. I remember that when I wrote it, I had a black dog, and my mother tried unsuccessfully to comfort me.

Insomnia
Nights come,
when you can't close your eyes,
you feel like time
stopped in place,
millions of thoughts in your head,
can you help yourself?

What is happening,
maybe it has some meaning,
better learn to live,
not counting the days, not counting the losses.

You know well,
that time is running out fast,
if you want to change something,
you have little time.
It's time to say no,
you know how it ends.

And you don't want to help yourself,
so how can I help you?
Nights come,
when you can't close your eyes.

You have no strength and fear in your eyes,
it won't let believe that
a better tomorrow will come,
and you will not stand aside,
watching the whole world laugh at you.

What is happening here,
maybe it has some meaning,
better learn to live,
not counting the days, not counting the losses.

You know that well,
time is running out fast,
if you want to change something,
you have little time.

CHAPTER VI

You are always responsible for what you tamed.
ANTOINE DE SAINT-EXUPÉRY

My mother insisted that we leave the house a little earlier, she didn't want to be late the first day of work. The second day of school was waiting for me. It was a bit difficult for me to get used to the new lifestyle, to get used to new situations, to assess people I met. Kori, Tom and above all Korin. Can I call them my friends? Is it too early for that? I wished that yesterday I did not insist harder Korin to come to us for a coffee. Today we didn't have any joint lessons in the plan, so I expected that I wouldn't meet him until tomorrow and I felt sad. On the other hand, it is better that he did not come in yesterday, he would certainly have bored. I had other job. I looked at the fingertips of my left hand. Corns. It will take some time for the skin on my fingers to harden and get used to the strings again. Well, passion requires sacrifice. I glanced over my shoulder at the back seat of our Ford, behind me was a guitar. It was really beautiful. I was looking forward to music classes.

We drove so fast that we arrived a lot ahead of time. Mom parked near the main entrance. I was surprised that Korin's car was already standing there. Why did he arrive so early?

"What time do you finish today?" My mother asked, getting out of the car.

"At two o'clock, but the last two hours will be in the hospital, medical training. I wonder what it might look like?" I wondered aloud. "I hope they don't make me cut a frog or autopsy because I think I'll vomit."

"There may be a problem with frogs, they probably all went extinct, I would bet for corpses," my mother grinned at me.

"You can comfort a man," I murmured.

"It won't be that bad, I will drop by the hospital at two o'clock."

She patted my shoulder tenderly and headed for the staff room. However, I stayed outside. Before class, I still wanted a sip of fresh air, I think I will never get bored of it.

"Emily Walker, I'm looking for you everywhere, I am circling around with this case like an idiot."

I started, hearing a familiar voice behind me. Korin. He had a black guitar case in his hand.

"You couldn't bring it right away with the guitar?" I asked mockingly.

"I didn't think it was that important, so I picked up only the guitar yesterday. Besides, it was dusty, hmm... terribly dusty.

"You had to vacuum or wipe with a damp cloth," I laughed. I was amused by his weasel word.

"I came across this later."

"Oh, I see that thinking is your weak spot again," I shook my head.

"Don't complain anymore."

He put the case on the top step, took the guitar from me, carefully put it inside and closed the lid.

"Satisfied?"

I looked at him, frowning."I don't understand why you do it?"

"What am I doing?" He was surprised.

"You're so kind to me."

"We must integrate with Earthlings, and this is a great opportunity."

"And what are they mark for it?" I was starting to get mean, but probably only because I was trying to understand what makes him tick."

"Not yet, but it's not a bad idea. What are you doing tonight?"

What is he thinking?!-

"I play the guitar."

"And tomorrow?"

"I play too." I couldn't stand it. "What do you mean? Do you want to fix me up?"

"I'm not dating Earthlings," he said calmly, but after a while he added, "Neither with the Arisyan women."

"So?"

"I thought I could teach you how to drive a car."

"Okay, then tomorrow." Don't let him think I'm at his beck and call. "Today I have to sleep, because yesterday I maxed out and practiced the game a little too long."

"You don't have better things to do at night," he said, rolling back his eyes. "Sleep well, then. I'll come for you tomorrow, late afternoon."

"OK."

He waved goodbye at me and walked away, and as usual I couldn't take my eyes off his agile, athletic figure. I turned my head only when he disappeared behind the door of the school building and then I noticed a small group of students standing near the corner of my eye. Two girls and a boy. All three were watching me with interest. They came as soon as they saw that I was looking in their direction. One of the girls was short, plump, she had red dreadlocks on her head, five earrings in her left ear, and her face lit up with a radiant smile. Dressed in red pants and slightly worn boots, she looked like a real rebellious teenager. The other girl was her exact opposite. Tall and slim, and long, straight blond hair flowed down her thin shoulders. She was wearing a black, short dress revealing shapely and tanned legs. Looking at her, you could get complexes. The boy, however, did not stand out as anything special, such a common guy in goggles. Brown, short hair, a plaid shirt thrown on a dark T-shirt and faded jeans. In fact, he had the appearance of a classic nerd.

"I see that we have a new guitarist for the band," the first one with dreadlocks said, and despite the strange appearance she seemed nice. "I'm Ana, but call me Red, I don't always response to my name."

"Emily," I answered with a smile.

"This is Erica - bass, and this guy is Skinny, plays the skins," she introduced her friends briefly. "Me on electric."

"What do you have there?" She asked, pointing at my case.

"Acoustic Gibson."

"That's great." She looked delighted.

"Come on, Red, there is no point in talking to her." Erica pursed her lips contemptuously. "Haven't you seen that she is holding with orange boring guys?"

"They're not boring at all." I felt obliged to defend the Arisyans. "They are very nice."

"Nice?" She snorted. "Nobody made you realize that nice equals boring?"

"Then maybe you will enlighten me, rude is equal to what?" I was getting more and more pissed off. I tried not to rash against people, but in this case, I made an exception. I found that I just don't like girls and I don't think that this could ever change. I don't know how this quarrel would end if Skinny didn't interrupt:

"Erica, stop putting in an unhealthy atmosphere, it's not Emily's fault that Tom prefers to stick with orange than with you."

I looked at him curiously. Didn't Erica work out with Tom? And that's good. At this point, I gained more respect for the boy, concluding that he is a wise guy and was not fooled by a pretty face. Besides, it was hard for me to imagine Kori without Tom accompanying her forever. For me they were an inseparable whole.

"We'd better go now, because we won't have much time to play," Red cut off all conversations.

"Who teaches music?" I asked as if nothing had happened.

"No one. We play alone." Red's answer amazed me.

"How do you play alone?"

"There is only one teacher, so he deals with those who are just learning. Those who can play fairly, practice themselves. Once a month we are evaluated by Musician," she explained.

"I understand, although such classes are rather pointless."

"Why?" Skinny was surprised. "The band is doing quite well. We have some nice compositions.""How many people are on the team?"

"The three of us." He looked at me with a slight smile. "Well, now four."

"You'll see, it's quite fun," said Red. Erica was grimly silent.

We headed down the stairs leading to the basements. I shuddered a little because it reminded me of the years spent in the shelter. However, the decor of the large room was quite pleasant. The walls were covered with white mute, and the lighting was bright enough to not feel the lack of windows. There was a drum set in one corner and a piano in the other with an electric guitar leaning on its side.

"Play something, we'll see what you can do," Erica said with superiority.

"I had a break of a few years," I said, but without a word I took out my guitar, checked tuning and with the accompaniment of Gibson, I sang my composition from four years ago.

Monotony

Every breath slowly rises up,
every word is thought a thousand times,
and every thought builds a new image in your head,
and every day is a new challenge.

You are in all of this
absorbed in the monotony of the day,
you are open to everything,
with nothing to hide.

Around you are familiar faces
waiting for time to finally show something.
Still streets full of busy people,
staring at each other, they want to wake up finally.
You are in all of this
absorbed in the monotony of the day,
you are open to everything,
with nothing to hide.

Erica turned pale, while Red gave an enthusiastic shout:

Wow! In addition to the guitar we got the vocal. Good vocal. I would never have thought that such a small body could hide such a strong voice. Awesome. Who taught you to play?"

"I learned it myself."

"Respect, friend, I take my hat off to you," said Skinny, giving me a courtesy bow.

I smiled and breathed a sigh of relief. I was appreciated and accepted by the group, of course except Erica, who was the only one who did not share the general enthusiasm. She didn't even look my way. I didn't care too much about it, I was perfectly aware that even if I try so much, I wouldn't please everyone."

"Maybe we'll finally start this play," Erica said with a hint of voice.

"Let's go then," Skinny said, and began to beat with the sticks.

The play went quite well, although it took me a while before I fitted my guitar with the songs played by the band. We all zoned out, without exception, carried by a wave of sounds. Even Erica put aside all her claims to people and the world. She was clearly having fun. I've never played in a band before, but I liked it. If Korin could hear us now, he would think we are making a terrible noise and would be 100% right.

At some point the music stopped, I also stopped playing.

"Enough for today," Red ordered. "We have to get together because we will be late for history and we will get owned again."

"I also have a history now, followed by geography," I said.

"Great, it means that the band spends Tuesdays together," Red summed up.

Joint classes solved my problem of "getting into phobia", otherwise I would have to hang out alone in front of the classroom until someone persuaded me to cross the threshold.

Slowly, I also began to get used to Erica, who was always puffed up and stinging, treating her with a pinch of salt. Skinny apparently specialized in silencing the storms unleashed by the girl. He was so into the practice that he usually strangled them in the bud, not letting them wreak emotional havoc. Red, on the other hand, seemed totally conflict-free, and full of such positive energy that she infected everyone with good humor. Everyone except Erica.

Two hours passed almost imperceptibly and now I was waiting for a fairly long walk to the hospital, where medical training was to take place. After such an exciting day at school, I didn't mind going to walk and cool down a bit. It's good that it doesn't rain though. I could use a car, maybe not just today in nice weather, but certainly someday in the future, when the rain or cold wind will not encourage you to walk. This made me realize why Korin came up with the offer of driving lessons. In his own way, he cared for me, since he remembered to take care of such details of my life. I liked it.

I could not fathom why oranges arouse such aversion in ours people, after all they were good from my point of view. How can they be considered as boring? I was not bored, neither talking to Korin nor Kori. I wondered why both races could not make friends for so many years that they are so different? Admittedly, I noticed the subtle differences between us, but everything seemed to indicate that the others saw these differences more and were clearly unacceptable to them.

I jumped violently when the car passing by made a loud bang from the exhaust pipe, stopping abruptly at the curb, maybe half a meter away from me. Oh, it's broke, I thought. I wasn't sure if I should pass by the vehicle indifferently, or maybe ask the driver how I can help? Before I could decide anything, a familiar voice reached my ears:

"Get in, Emily, I'll drop you off.

"Red!" I recognized the person behind the wheel and hopped into the car without hesitation. "Thanks."

"Where to take you?" She asked before she started again.

"To the hospital, I have medical training there, but if I cause a lot of trouble, there is no problem, I will go on foot," I said uncertainly, seeing the expression on Red's face.

"Don't talk stupid, you could just say earlier, I will have training too. I could have taken you straight from the school," she said with a slight reproach. "I'm surprised you don't have a car."

"I can't drive, but my mother has a car."

"Pity, you should learn to drive as soon as possible."

"I know, I know," I admitted. "Tomorrow, Korin will start teaching me."

"Come on? Korin?" She looked surprised. "And yet you're friends with him? You like him? How is he?" She flooded me with questions.

"Gee, Red, how can I know such things? I don't know him well. We sit in one bench on math." I tried to make my explanation cool when I talk about Korin.

"Do you go to advanced math?" She was even more surprised. "And I thought you were artistically oriented."

"Well... I am too," I said hesitantly.

"All in all, a nice cutie from this Korin. It is a pity that he is so numb. Oranges are all numb. You probably get tired in his company. I remember trying to talk to him two years ago. Defeat. He wasn't too talkative. As he said, he only talked about science and the importance of acquiring knowledge in life," she shuddered. "A nightmare, just like I heard my grandmother, except that Korin is younger. You probably heard those bullshit too."

"We're not talking about science."

"So, what about?" She raised her eyebrows.

"Nothing important." I shrugged my shoulders.

139

I told the truth, we did not touch on any important topics. I did not understand why the Arisyans were considered inaccessible. I received them as terribly open people, and above all kind. I enjoyed spending time in the company of Korin. It was true that there was no slight malice, on my part the most aware of it, with less of it, but being with Kori and Korin was never unpleasant for me. I don't know, or because I liked Korin? Or maybe because I was perfectly aware that he was strange, and I got used to it. I even accepted and liked his otherness.

"So, what exactly?" Red all the time demanded an answer from me.

"It's difficult to say... lately about music, and even earlier about books." However, I missed a small detail that Korin considered music as noise and books as a pile of waste paper. I smiled to myself at the mention of these conversations.

"I'm shocked, I didn't manage to talk to him about any sensible topic. Something doesn't suit me." The girl became suspicious.

I decided to change the subject as soon as possible to avoid another hail of uncomfortable questions.

"Tell me about this medical training, what are you doing on it?" I asked.

"We learn how to recognize a disease by symptoms and how to treat it. In the last class, we practiced artificial respiration, and for today Sofie announced first aid in emergencies."

"Doctor Sofie?"

"Yes. Do you know her?"

"This is the first..." I hesitated for a moment,

because Korin was the first, "the first person I met after leaving the shelter."

"You didn't move from another town?" Again, my answer surprised her.

"Actually, yes and no."

"I don't understand," she said, stopping the car because we had just arrived at the hospital building.

I opened the car door and when I wanted to get out, Red grabbed my hand.

"Wait, we have fifteen minutes. Tell me about yourself, I'm very curious."

I didn't feel like confessions, but if I wanted to find myself in a new reality somehow, I should talk to people, even about matters that hurt me. I had to make myself known to other people. So, I briefly described her story. It didn't take me much time, because I didn't have much to tell. I barely mentioned Korin. I was afraid he would guess what I feel to him. Everything that began to connect me with the Arisyan had a very intimate dimension for me, it was only mine and I had the impression that it would remain mine as long as it was only my secret. I felt like I knew him forever, without knowing him at all. Recently, Korin dealt with almost all my thoughts and this was no longer normal, because he was slowly beginning to border on obsession.

"So, Korin found you?" Red drilled.

"Yes, he came across me near Creston."

"Now, I understand why you hang around so much," she said with conviction.

"Why?"

"It's his responsibility to look after whoever he saved."

"What this mean?" I frowned, trying to figure out what this was all about.

"You know, just like the Little Prince. The Arisyans act according to the principle: you have to take care of what you have tamed. They believe that their mission is to properly introduce you to a new earthly life, actually Earth-Arisyan.

I felt all the blood drain from my face and I felt weak. So, that's all he meant? And I stupid imagined God knows what. I'm an idiot, and my brain is devoured by killer, youthful hormones. Did I have to fall in love with him? What was the first specimen in my pants? In addition, I let go of the fantasy that he likes me, and maybe even something more? Meanwhile, here is such a prosaic explanation of his behavior - a standard procedure for dealing with the miracle of a surviving Earthling. I'm a moron, a big one. Red just deprived me of any illusions.

"Korin's sister offers Tom similar care," continued Red.

"How is that?" I asked automatically.

"She's the one who made him stay in the city. The family who took Tom in the shelter went north. The boy clearly did not want to go with them, but he also did not have the courage to stay. I don't know the details, but in the end, he chose Exira. He immediately made a hit with Erica, she impressed herself for a while, but he was extremely resistant to her charms. In fact, since then they have become almost inseparable with Kori."

After this explanation, I saw a light in the tunnel. I was convinced that Tom and Kori were not only bound by a duty of care, but something much stronger, maybe even love. What I have not been able to give me peace from yesterday finally said:

"Do you think Kori and Tom are a couple?"

"It's hard to tell, but I don't think so," she said after a moment's reflection. "Although they often hang out and Tom is apparently interested, unlike her. I think he really fell in love with the girl, he follows her like a dog. Embarrassment."

"Why are you convinced that Kori doesn't want him?" I drilled, trying to find more vulnerabilities in her explanations at all costs.

"It's obvious."

"Not for me." I had no idea what she was getting at.

"Didn't you know that the Arisyans are emotionally defective?" She asked surprised.

"I heard something," I said uncertainly. "But it's good that they got rid of the aggression and hatred?"

"All in all, good, but they also removed love. They can't love anyone."

I didn't expect that answer. I involuntarily opened my mouth and blinked nervously, trying not to cry. My reaction surprised me.

"You did not know?"

"I had no idea," I whispered, although I should have figured out earlier. After all that I learned from Korin, I should just link the facts. "Why did they do it?"

"I don't think this was entirely intentional. The same brain center is said to be responsible for feelings of hatred and love. By eliminating one, they accidentally deleted the other."

"Are you sure?" I slowly shook off my shock, trying to turn on logical thinking. Again, I didn't agree with too many things. "They have families and children, they look happy and connected with each other."

"Maybe they are nice, accommodating, kind, but nothing more. If any of the Arisyans suddenly lost their entire family, you can be sure that he wouldn't care." She thought for a moment. "Their relationships are strange."

The situation was even worse than I thought. The truth was cruel as usual. Korin deals with me only on duty, in addition he is not able to love even his parents, not mention about some feeling for me. Similarly, Kori couldn't love Tom. I felt like some nightmare. Although, right away, I couldn't go wrong. I saw how Kori looked at Tom yesterday, and it certainly wasn't a look of indifference. Maybe Red is wrong, maybe she heard something wrong or twisted something? I decided at the earliest opportunity to ask Kori how it really is.

As soon as something starts falling, I don't know why, but it must fall all the way. I mean all day today. First Erica's pout, then a conversation with Red, who managed me so badly that it couldn't be done any more, and in addition... I moaned, and I think I got green on my face. We just entered a spacious room, where on several massive metal tables lay dismembered human corpses. On each table a different part of the body, an odiousness. I felt weak, half bent and crouched so as not to fall.

"Emily, what is with you?" Red asked, surprised by my reaction.

What is with me? Is she blind or totally crazy? Doesn't it bother her?!

"I feel sick," I stammered with difficulty. "I have to get out of here. Now."

Unexpectedly, Sofie appeared beside us. She pushed Red away gently and leaned over me.

"Emily, did you feel bad?" She asked anxiously.

"Yhm..." That's all I could say to avoid vomiting.

Sofie embraced me tightly and set me upright. I forced myself to keep myself up on my feet.

"The point is this?" She gestured toward the tables with the corpses.

"Yhm..." I confirmed, pursing my lips and closing my eyes. I didn't want to look at it. If it hadn't weakened me so much the view of fragmented bodies, I would have probably run out of here and never returned. However, I was unable to move.

"These are training phantoms, they are artificial. I know they resemble human bodies, but they are puppets. You have to practice something," Sofie said calmly.

It took me a moment before I understood what she was saying to me. Phantoms, puppets ... I kept repeating my thoughts until the meaning of these words fully reached me. I swallowed loudly. I was starting to recover slowly.

"Is this not a corpse?" I just wanted to make sure.

"No, silly," she said gently. "Come with me, you'll find out for yourself. Where to begin?"

I looked around the room uncertainly. I didn't even notice that there was a crowd around me, everyone was staring at me. I looked at the phantoms. The knowledge that the body fragments are artificial did little to do, because they were still abhorrent to me and caused gagging. I sighed heavily.

"Maybe because of this hand," I said resignedly, pointing to the shoulder resting on the nearest counter. "Looks disgusting."

"Probably the best choice, at least for starters," Sofie said. "This is just a model of the hand for suturing, we have, among others, an injection arm, a special military simulation kit, a leg for..."

"Maybe it's enough," I interrupted her, wincing. "This hand is enough."

"Come on, Ana." Sofie nodded at Red. "You'll put the seams first, and Emily will watch."

Red, approaching, gave me a light blow to the side, saying:

"You can do it, baby."

"I don't know," I answered skeptically.

Then I turned to Sofie with hope:

"Can you unsubscribe me from it?"

"Unfortunately, not, medical training is compulsory."

"Oh well," I sighed in resignation. "I'll have to get used to it."

I watched in disgust as Red, with great skill, put stitches on an eight-centimeter wound. I tried to remember how she did it and in what order she performed all the activities.

"Finally, you need to compress," she said, pressing each seam with her index finger. "If they don't let go now, they should stick. This is the so-called knot seam."

"Arisyans seem to have such advanced technology, and I see that they can't do without a needle and thread," I said ironically.

"Apparently, they have, but on Earth they cannot apply everything. In addition, they believe that we should deal with certain situations using earthly means. All in all, it's right. In life, it's best to count only on yourself. Now you," she said, handing me the needle.

I went out of the hospital. My mother was already waiting in the car in the parking lot. She was surprised when I got in the car, slamming the door so hard that the windows shook.

"Emily, what is this behavior?!" She rebuked me. "Something happened?"

"Life is disgusting," I said.

"Emily, what's going on? You've never acted like that," she said anxiously.

I shrugged my shoulders and thoughtlessly stared at the side window, I wanted to scream.

"Will you finally tell me what happened that you almost broke the car door?"

I shook my head, pursing my mouth.

"I have to understand that I won't know..." she said calmly, but I sensed she was worried about me.

"Not now. At home... we'll talk at home," I finally said.

I wasn't in the mood to talk right now. I needed some time to sort things out. My whole life was getting more and more confusing, and I felt more and more lost, and I felt bad about it.

We entered the kitchen. I sat at the table and my mother put water in for tea. We were both silent. The silence was filled only by the sound of water in the kettle, but it soon died down. Mom put a cup of hot tea in front of me and sat down opposite me. She waited for me to speak first.

"I'm sorry..." I muttered.

"Don't apologize but explain to me what happened."

"Everything is not what I imagined. I've been living a normal life for less than a week and I'm sick of it."

"Nobody said normal life is simple. In this shelter it was easier in this respect, apart from the conditions in which we lived. Things can be really complicated here, but you have to face it," she said forcefully. "You are strong Emily, emotionally strong, much stronger and braver than me. You can do it. I didn't have enough courage to move into the unknown, and YOU had one. I should be the first to leave the shelter, but I didn't do it, YOU made the decision. Now, I don't have the courage to go to our old home and leave a message to your father just because apparently it is dangerous there. Of the two of us, YOU are strong and believe in me, there are worse things than a bad day at school."

"I suppose you're right," I answered without conviction.

"I certainly have," she confirmed. "Will you finally explain to me what upset you so much?"

"First Erica..." I told her all day today, starting with the band's play and ending with too realistic phantoms. I omitted the fact that most affected my gloomy mood,

i.e. the sphere of feelings or rather lack of feelings.

"As for Erica, you just have to get used to it and stop paying attention to her. Actually, you should be glad to have only one such person in your class. I didn't have so good, there were only kids like Erica at my school. As for the corpse, you made such a prophesy in the morning and that's also a reason to be satisfied, because it turned out not to be real, and you can get used to plastic-silicone."

Because I omitted the sad truth about the Arisyans in my conversation, my mother had a distorted picture of my feelings. Not surprisingly, my reasons for displeasure seemed extremely trivial to her. She probably thought that due to many years of isolation I was oversensitive and did not take my worries seriously. Maybe someday I will mature to confide in her on everything. But not yet, it's too early for that. Nevertheless, I needed this conversation, and even if we didn't touch on the key topic, I felt better. The future was in much brighter colors than an hour ago. Besides, I have a ride with Korin tomorrow and I came to the conclusion that it doesn't matter if he can feel something or not. It is important that I can, and I feel good in his company. I decided to behave as if I hadn't learned anything today and to follow my instincts. He has not let me down yet. The same instinct told me to leave the shelter and then directed me to the road where I met him for the first time. I could only believe that he would not disappoint me this time.

CHAPTER VII

The wave is still floating us, that's life. You can't understand or judge it, you must let the wave float you.
JEAN-PAUL SARTRE

Hope has wings, it sits down in your soul and sings a song without words that never stops, and its sweetest sounds are heard even during a gale.
EMILY DICKINSON

Well, we're in place," Red said when she gave me a lift home after school on Wednesday

"Thanks for the ride. This is the second time."

"No problem, I was going this way. Besides," she looked at me closely, "I feel like there is something wrong with you today. You seem to be distant."

"I could not sleep at night," I gave the first reasonable justification that occurred to me. I had to say something or anything to stop her from guessing. I was afraid she would guess the real reason. The reason is Korin. "By medical training. When I closed my eyes, I saw dismembered bodies. A nightmare," I added, to make it sound more credible.

Red shook her head disapprovingly.

"Oh mother, Emily, you care too much about bullshit. It's best to think of something pleasant before bed, at least I do it and I don't have nightmares."

"I'll try," I promised without conviction and when Red left, shooting goodbye from the exhaust pipe, I entered the house.

My mother had to stay longer at work, so if it wasn't for Red, I would have either a long walk or an additional three hours spent at school. I didn't want both of them, so when the girl offered a lift, I took the opportunity.

Red was right, I was distant today. I didn't even try to mask it somehow. I was too absorbed in thoughts about what I learned yesterday about the Arisyans, their feelings, about Korin... I was playing our conversations in my head. I tried to do it with the smallest details. I analyzed every word, every gesture, every look, finding hidden meanings in them. Meanings that maybe there wasn't at all.

Every moment I felt more and more deceived. This is probably the best term - deceived. By whom? By Korin, Almar, or maybe by Sofie? It's hard to blame them for my current state of mind. Again, life made me laugh, not the first time, and probably not the last. Can I still hope for more than friendship with the knowledge I have? Reason said no, but some small subconscious whispered something completely different. I intuitively sensed something special about Korin, but I couldn't define what exactly. A special bond, thin, uncertain, impermanent, but always... I sometimes saw it in his purple gaze, in a fleeting gesture, in the way he addressed me.

I came back to our first meeting. Rusted road, dead forest, bend and him. It was then that our fates intertwined. It was then that we marked each other

with our presence, each of us left a mark on other. Now I understood that I would carry a piece of Korin inside me forever. Perhaps he had similar feelings, or is it my wishful thinking? On the one hand, I should not delude myself, but on the other... Is it not that if we do not expect too much from life, if we are not too greedy, then life can surprise us positively, surprise us?

I looked nervously at the clock. Two hours separated me from the meeting with Korin. I opened the wardrobe in the hallway and, sighing heavily, sat in front of it on the floor. As usual, I had a problem, what to wear. I didn't want to dress too defiantly, but I didn't want to look too modest. Traditionally, I chose jeans, the blue ones, because they emphasized a slight roundness of the hips and covered a bit for too slim legs. I looked in the mirror, it's not bad, just... somehow too little feminine. I decided to make up with my blouse. I searched the shelf for a long time in search of the right one. I finally found it. Intensely green, airy, with short puffy sleeves and a large neckline. I dressed it and was a bit ashamed to see my reflection in the mirror, the neckline was really big. I glanced once more, actually... hmm... pretty, pretty, the blouse's green perfectly matched the color of my eyes. I tousled my hair with my hand, corrected my makeup and was ready.

I didn't know if my mother would be able to come back before I left, so I sketched a few words of explanation on the blackboard hanging by the fridge in case she'd forgotten my plans today.

"Mom, I'm learning to ride with Korin. I'll be back. E".

I began to get impatient. I looked out the kitchen window to the driveway. What if he forgot or gave up? Although he would have anticipated me if he changed his plans, I was sure of it. I wondered how it would be with us now. Now that I know about his inability to feel. Will this knowledge change anything? Besides, he doesn't know that I know. Should I tell him? Should I ask about something? I shook my head. No, I will leave everything as it is, I will simply try to observe Korin closely and interpret his behavior towards me accordingly.

I heard the sound of the engine. The sound increased until it became quite clear and after a while the green Land Rover stopped in our driveway. My heart beat faster. I immediately moved away from the window, trying to calm myself somehow, but it didn't work out. Meanwhile Korin got out of the car. He looked great as usual. His hair was unruly in all directions. He was wearing black jeans and a steel gray undershirt that gripped his muscular torso. Korin's orange skin contrasted nicely with the dark colors. I took one deep breath and went outside.

"Hi, Am I late?" He asked in greeting.

"I don't think so," I answered, struggling to be cool. "But you probably never be late."

"I rarely do," he confirmed and looked at me with interest, keeping his eyes on my breasts longer. "Nice blouse," he said a little confused, and immediately looked at my face.

"Thanks." I looked into his eyes. He had some overwhelming, magnetic force in them that drew me closer to him, day by day. Probably Korin didn't even

suspect that this was affecting me. However, today it was different than usual, I felt it, just as I felt the positive aura he had. I had the impression that now we were connected by something special, some invisible bond, but it lasted only a few seconds, because almost immediately it turned into something that I had never seen before. Lost? Mixing? Shame? It was hard for me to call it that, but a sudden change in his behavior was a fact, and it wasn't just me who realized it. Korin also, probably even at the same time, because he suddenly looked away, breaking this connection. He walked over to the car, and I still stood motionless, trying to figure out what I had just experienced.

"Emily, get in," he urged me.

Without a word I got in, slamming the door. I fastened my seat belt and only then I come back to my mind, and everything became so normal again.

"Where will you teach me?" I asked.

"On the outskirts of town, but first I'll show you something."

"What do you want to show me?" I asked, the tone of his voice intrigued me.

"Surprise."

"Not too many surprises lately?"

"You'll definitely like this one. Anyway, did you not like any of them?" He gave me a wide smile.

"All right, you have a unique sense for surprises," I said honestly.

He laughed.

"Because I finally figured you out."

"I don't think so," I said, but I myself had doubts about the truthfulness of these words. How much did he know about me and how much did he guess? Did he know me? Not likely, I was just starting to get to know myself. All I knew was my shelter. In the new world, new place and new life, my reactions were unpredictable, even to me.

We passed the dense town buildings, which slowly turned into individual buildings, most likely uninhabited. There was no need for anyone to live here, since there were still a lot of vacant houses in the center. After some time, even individual houses were left behind, and on both sides of the road there were only fields covered with some weeds.

Finally, Korin stopped the car. He got out, walked around it in front and opened the door on my side. He unceremoniously grabbed my hand. I guess I will never cease to be amazed at the exceptional softness of his skin.

Why is contact with me so easy for him? Why I can't do that? Why does his touch make my heart tremble and the whole world suddenly begins to spin?

Holding hands, we walked a few steps along the road and only then Korin stopped. He took my forearm in both hands and slowly moved it forward as if he wanted me to catch air with my fingers. I was surprised that my hand did not cut the free space as I expected but leaned on something. I felt an invisible obstacle under my open hand. It was only now that I noticed that the rest of the road, the one in front of me, was covered by a delicate mist. I looked at Korin questioningly. He was clearly amused by my face. I was annoyed, so I pushed the barrier with all my strength. With no effect. I hit it with my open palm a

few more times, but all the time I came across something that did not exist in a healthy mind. Resigned, I lowered my hands.

"It's not funny at all," I murmured when I heard Korin choking with laughter.

"Ehm, take it easy. Look." He lifted his right arm, then where my hand encountered resistance, his without difficulty passed through the invisible wall. "That's how the force field works," he explained.

I frowned. I remembered what he was saying a few days ago about his bracelet and I didn't like the thought that just dawned on my mind.

"And this is the key." I pointed to his wrist. "So, I'm a prisoner here? Nice surprise for me."

He did not answer. He reached into his left pants pocket and pulled out of it almost the same bracelet he had in his hand, but a little smaller.

"You are not a prisoner," he assured me. He took my hand and fastened the bracelet on my left wrist very efficiently. I don't know if it was his touch or the coldness of the bracelet, but suddenly I got goose bumps.

Of course, he noticed it.

"Are you cold?" He ran his finger slowly over my forearm, watching the short hair in my arms rise slightly. A pleasant shiver ran down my back.

Is he doing it on purpose?! Is that how it works out for him?

"Don't do that," I said softly.

"Are you cold from my touch?"

"I'm not cold, I just feel strange when you do that," I said irritably. Maybe he didn't do it on purpose?

Apparently, he didn't realize it was affecting me. "Do not worry about me. And this bracelet... How does it work?" I quickly changed the subject to distract my reaction to his touch.

"Come, I'll show you."

Squeezing my hand tightly, he pulled me towards the dam. This time I did not come across an invisible wall. We were both easily on the other side. Quite a peculiar experience.

"I feel like Alice on the other side of the mirror."

He looked at me, frowning.

"Who is Alice? Does she go to our school?"

I sighed. His ignorance defused me. I couldn't even get angry, I just got a bite of laughter.

"Should I know her?" He asked uncertainly.

I laughed even louder, and he stood looking grimly at my unusual reaction. Finally, I calmed down enough to be able to answer.

"Alice is a literary character."

"Oh. You are obsessed with your books."

"You're impossible. I just don't know..."

He didn't let me finish.

"Okay, I'm slowly getting used that this is your way."

"That's not what I mean. I don't know how you brought me to Exira, since I didn't have it." I touched the bracelet. "You set up another one for me?"

"You can't use another one. Each is linked to the owner's genetic code, each is unique."

"Then how did you bring me here?" I repeated the question.

"In exceptional cases, you have to ask for permission to cross the force field without a key," he explained calmly. "I did it too. Then the appropriate procedures are launched and under special supervision you can get to the city through one of four portals."

"What are these protections for? Are you afraid of something?"

"There are different people in the north, not everyone is bad, but not everyone is good."

"Why didn't they join you, actually... now to us?"

"I don't know, maybe they don't believe in our help. Not everyone trusts us, we are strangers here."

"Maybe you're right," I said without conviction.

I could not get rid of the impression that he did not give me all the reasons, and the important ones.

Or maybe he didn't know them himself?

"Do you have any more questions?"

I shook my head to say no.

"So, we can start learning," he said.

We returned to the car parked by the road. I sat uncertainly in the driver's seat. Korin put my hands on the steering wheel and then explained how to shift gears, when to push the clutch, when to release them, and when to add gas. I was completely lost in all this, I mistook my left leg and right, and the gearbox grinded unpleasantly a few times when I tried to shift into gear. I looked at him anxiously.

"I won't learn," I groaned.

"You can do it, Emily," he said confidently. "I will help you, I am here for this. First a clutch," he commanded.

I pressed the clutch.

"Put in first gear now."

I dutifully grabbed the gear stick and of course I started to struggle with it because the gear refused to enter. Korin put his hand on mine. I felt the pleasant warmth of his touch. He gently led my hand in the right direction.

"Now slowly release the clutch while adding gas," he instructed, still holding my hand in a light grip.

The car pulled forward and began to roll lazily along the way.

"Great, now the clutch again and we throw two." He took my hand again and headed down. He didn't release his grip for a while. He finally let go, but then I felt terribly insecure. He must have noticed, because he leaned towards me, saying:

"Both hands on the steering wheel."

I listened immediately, although I felt much better when he squeezed my hand. His touch, despite distracting me, gave me confidence. However, I realized that it was easier to control the vehicle with both hands. I tried to focus as much as possible on the road so that he had no reason to make fun of me, but I clearly saw that slow driving bored him.

"I think you can easily move three," he said after about an hour.

He helped me again, and I quivered again under his soft touch. I realized that my hand was waiting for this contact for that hour. The atmosphere in the car got extremely tense, and I don't think that only I felt it, but only I was aware of the reason. The car accelerated, and the role of the driver suited me more and more.

"I think I'm doing pretty good," I said with satisfaction.

"You are extremely clever for..."

"An Earthling?" No, it's starting again. Does he always have to ruin everything?

"That's not what I meant to say," he laughed. "Extremely clever for a woman."

Even better. Now I'm just pissed. I pressed the brake pedal angrily and gave him a warning look.

"And who do you think you are?! For a super-male?! First you gave me to understand that Earthlings are worse than Arisyans, now you say that women are worth little! Who gave you the right to make such judgments, and why?!"

He looked scared.

"You misunderstood me," he muttered.

"Do I look like a jerk?"

"Sorry, I said it wrong, and you misunderstood. Whenever I am in your company, I do or say something wrong. I only have such a problem with you."

"So, I'm a problem for you?"

"See, I did it again. I have no idea why this is happening. I don't want to hurt you, really, Emily. I like you and I like spending time with you, although you are so... explosive. Unpredictable. Sometimes I am afraid to speak, and when I say something, it turns out that I formulate my thoughts quite unfortunately."

I calmed down a bit.

"I intimidated you?" I asked surprised.

"Sometimes," he said, and I looked at him with genuine surprise.

"And you have always seemed so conceited and confident to me."

"See, you have another proof of the differences

between our races. I assure you that I do not exalt myself, at least I have never intended to."

"I'm sorry I rose my voice. I promise I'll be nice next time. There is no point in arguing about nonsense," I concluded.

He relaxed, and he was relieved. He apparently tried to avoid conflicts, probably only those that happened with me. It was only now that I realized that the fault lay more on my side than on his. I just picked on the little things. I guess because I was analyzing his every word too carefully. And he said he liked me, and it sounded honest. And what I enjoyed the most was the fact that he likes to be with me. I wanted to get to know him better, he fascinated me. And it was not only about his appearance, but also about the interior and the thin thread of understanding that has developed between us.

"What did you mean with those women?" I asked calmly.

He smiled softly.

"See... we don't have cars on Arisa. We use similar vehicles, but they work on a completely different principle. After arriving on Earth, we had to learn to drive. It wasn't difficult for me and my father, but Kori and my mother had a lot of trouble with that. Hence my belief that women are less talented in this field. I didn't think you would take it personally. Say you are not angry."

"I'm not angry, really," I assured him. "Why didn't you bring your vehicles here?"

"These are complicated devices. All our vehicles are part of a larger system. First of all, we don't have to

waste time managing them. Just tap the on-board computer's destination, the data is transferred to the main computer, which sets the detailed route. While driving, you can do something useful."

"So, our cars are annoying to you."

"Not completely. I really like to ride, especially on verses. This is my little earthly weakness," it sounded as if he was justifying himself.

"Good to hear you have some weaknesses."

"It's late," he said suddenly, looking at the car clock.

I looked around. I didn't even notice that the orange sun shields almost completely hid behind the horizon. It will get completely dark soon.

"Are we going to the center?" He asked.

"Do you think I can do it?"

"Sure, you're doing great. We'll wander around the city a bit, and then drive home."

I turned the key in the ignition and even managed to start the engine the first time. I do not hide, I was proud of myself. I headed for the hospital building visible from afar. After dark it looked even more impressive than during the day. Lights burned in many windows, creating a checkerboard of bright spots against the sapphire sky. In the warm light of street lamps, the whole town gained a peculiar charm. I was constantly surprised that the world can be so beautiful. I arrived quite efficiently near the hospital and stopped the car so violently that it jerked us forward. It's good that we had our seat belts fastened.

"Emily, what are you doing?!" Shouted Korin.

"Look over there," I said delightfully, turning my head to the left.

Korin followed my gaze and noticed the fountain that caught my attention.

"If some gushing water is the reason you almost broke my nose, you are deeply disturbed on some level." He was clearly annoyed...

But I didn't listen to him anymore, got out of the car and ran like on wings towards an illuminated fountain with six ballerinas. As I live I haven't seen anything more beautiful. Why didn't I notice it before? It seemed made of glass or glass-like material. The costumes of the dancers were woven from streams of water that gently flowed from their belt, forming delicate, ethereal ballet skirts. The gushing water created the illusion of movement and the ballerinas really seemed to be dancing. On a sudden impulse, I took off my shoes and jumped on the wall of white marble surrounding the fountain. I felt like joining them. I glanced toward the car.

"Korin, come on." I nodded at him.

He didn't move. He was leaning against the side of the car with his hands folded across his chest and looking as if he had seen me for the first time.

"Come on," I encouraged him again.

"Emily," he said resignedly, "you really are unbelievable."

However, he did not move. Now I got it. Stupid Arisyans. That's what people meant. Korin just didn't know what it meant to enjoy life, just for no good reason. The other Arisyans probably couldn't too. My mother always told me that life consists of small things and they mainly create our world, making everything around it shine. I felt sorry for him because of genetic interference he was deprived of it. His emotions were very impoverished. And if someone showed him, how wonderful life is... Maybe he could learn it?

I stopped thinking about it for a moment. Imitating the strange ballerina poses, I started dancing.

"You're wasting time on stupid things, Emily," he said impatiently as I danced two laps.

"Not for stupidity, but for real life," I laughed and at that moment I slipped on the marble wall of the fountain. I was still trying to keep my balance, waving my arms in disarray, but unnecessarily, because I only made matters worse. With even more impetus than if I hadn't fought, I fell into the water. Falling, I got under the skirt of one of the ballerinas, and the water gushing from her waist wet the parts of my body that were still dry.

Before I could bounce back, Korin was with me. He grabbed me firmly, lifted me up and set me in front of him. I felt the strength of his arms, the warmth and rapid heartbeat emanating from them, and most oddly - not just mine. Korin continued to embrace me. I didn't want him to stop. I clung to him tighter, breathing in his masculine scent and listening to the murmur of his breath, which seemed shallower, uneven, broken... I could stand like that for all eternity, dripping with water, chilled... important in his arms. I slowly raised my head and we looked at each other. His purple eyes expressed confusion and something else, something very difficult to define. The bond intuitively felt before us has now taken a real shape. I discovered that it wasn't just an illusion. I have found that it really is, that

it exists. Unexpectedly, a hot wave flooded me, spreading lazy tingling all over my body. I involuntarily parted my lips. I wanted to feel his lips on my own. I shuddered in silent anticipation, then he withdrew a strong move away from me. Confused, I looked at him reproachfully, I couldn't say a word. For the first time I saw him in such a state, as if he was not completely controlled, as if he were slightly dazed, as if he did not understand what was happening... It lasted perhaps a split second, because after a moment the lost expression disappeared from his face, and he was replaced by panic. He was looking at my wet, translucent blouse, breasts underneath it and protruding nipples with obvious fear. He pulled the shirt off and gave it to me in an outstretched hand.

"Change your clothes before I do some stupid thing," he said hoarsely, turning his back on me.

Before I do some stupid thing?

No, before you catch a cold?

What did he mean?

What did he mean by that?

Chattering my teeth - partly from cold, partly from nervousness - I treaded to the car. I took off my wet clothes and pulled on his shirt. It almost reached my knees. I felt warmer right away, but I still kept chattering my teeth. Korin kept his back to the car. The moment I looked at him, he turned away, as if he felt my eyes on his back. His face was exceptionally calm.

"Have you changed?" He asked calmly.

"Yhm," I murmured.

"You won't drive today, I'll drive."

I nodded my head. I was so embarrassed that I couldn't formulate any logical thought.

"Someone else should teach you," he said dryly as we drove. "I will ask Kori, she certainly won't mind. She likes you."

"And you don't like me anymore?" I asked in a barely audible whisper.

"Yes, of course I like you. But I understand less and less."

"You said you managed to decipher me."

"Maybe you, but..." he hesitated, then added more quietly, "I stopped understanding myself."

"Nobody knows each other completely," I said with conviction.

He shook his head.

"I know, at least until I met you, I thought I knew." From the tone of his voice one could read that he was worried.

I had the impression that he was moving away from me, that he was slipping away. I should say something now to prevent this and I didn't quite know what.

"I thought we were friends," I started shyly. "Don't you know friendship on Arisa?"

He thought for a long moment before answering.

"We know what duty and loyalty to another man are," he said. "I don't know, however, if it has something to do with friendship."

Finally, I had some point of reference.

"Of course, it does. They are almost the same," I assured. "Well, maybe not exactly the same, but duty, loyalty and friendship are closely related. Do you think we can be friends then?"

"I think we're already friends, at least from an

Arisyan point of view. However, I'm not sure I can provide you with worldly friendship. I have never had a closer relationship with any of you. Sometimes my mind doesn't always keep up with human reactions. And as for you, Emily... I'm totally confused."

"I actually know what you mean. I have never had any friends, except my mother, of course, and now I'm a bit lost."

In the distance, the shape of my house loomed. There was a light in the kitchen. I wonder what my mother will say when she sees me like this. I collected my wet things.

"Wait for me here," I said to Korin. "I'll bring you a shirt and I'll just change. You can't show up like this at home."

I rushed towards the porch and opened the front door with impetus. My mother gave a cry of terror at my view:

"For God's sake, Emily! What happened?!"

"I fell into the fountain."

"You were supposed to learn to ride, not swim," she said, amused.

"I know," I groaned. "It happened somehow."

I fell into the bedroom, pulled my shirt over my head, and hurriedly put on my bathrobe. I looked briefly at the mirror and shuddered. Nightmare. My makeup fell under my eyes, I looked like a character from some B class horror movie. The hair wasn't in the best condition either. With a cotton pad, I washed the black marks from under my eyes and ran my hand through my wet hair. Oh well, it won't be better. When he found me, I was in worse condition? I picked up a

gray T-shirt. I didn't feel like giving it back to its owner. I hid my face in it, imagining that I would hug Korin. I could smell his smell in my nostrils, a mixture of fresh air and mountain wind. Reluctant, I folded shirt and left the house.

He was waiting for me in the front seat of his car, with his elbow resting on the side window completely lowered.

"Thanks, Korin." I gave him the T-shirt.

"You're welcome." He gave me a disarming smile.

I watched him how he dresses, admire the play of muscles on his smooth chest and shoulders, he was so appealing, so male... I had to bite my lip so as not to moan with admiration. I think it's completely gone, but when he was close I didn't feel like myself. Today has only caused more confusion in my head.

"Get away because you will catch a cold. See you tomorrow," he said goodbye and drove away.

I dragged myself home. Suddenly I felt terribly tired. And nailed down. I knew that something had happened at the fountain, something important, something that neither I nor Korin completely understood. Is there any chance to teach him how to feel so that he would ever feel what I feel? Can you rebuild something that destroyed genetics?

"Emily, Kori called," my mother's voice broke me out of my thoughts.

"Kori?" I was surprised. "In what case?"

"She wanted to fix up with you. Apparently, you were supposed to write a joint work on literature."

"Oh, I completely forgot. I will talk to her at school tomorrow."

"Kori seems nice," my mother said. "You like her?"

"Yes, even very, though I don't know her well."

Mom looked at me thoughtfully.

"What?" I asked.

"In my time we used to do girls' parties with girls. You know, gossip till morning, confessions and stuff... Maybe Kori could spend the night with us from Saturday to Sunday? You would write a schoolwork and talk a bit. What do you think?"

"Great idea," I was happy. "I'll ask her tomorrow."

I think my mother has a sixth sense. On the one hand, I spend more time at school with Red, who is a very honest and open person, but on the other, I would prefer to make friends with Kori. I have the impression that she can understand me and that I can trust her. I no longer have the strength to choke my feelings for Korin. I need to talk to someone about this. But is telling his sister everything a good idea?

"Mom, I'll go to my place. I want to play some more."

"Sure, I'll call you for dinner."

Today, Korin and I freed a whole range of emotions under the fountain. I'm lost in them. I had to sort them out in my head. Understand. I picked up my guitar, sat down on the bed, and started strumming. I don't even know when my thoughts turned into words and feelings into melody. I composed a song for the first time in many years.

Voice

I love your voice, I love your warmth.
Please, keep me close to you.
I love your eyes; I love, when the time
seems to stop us for a while.
Tonight, it is raining, and the streets are empty,
so, come and walk with me.
Tonight, I feel more than ever
and it's like a dream.
Tonight, it is so cold and I'm falling in your arms now,
I like when the time seems to stop us for a while,
because there's nothing outside.
I hope that I'll never forget the way you taste.

CHAPTER VIII

I recognize friendship by the fact that nothing can disappoint it, and true love by the fact that nothing can destroy it.

ANTOINE DE SAINT-EXUPÉRY

Y our grandmother always made cakes when my friends were supposed to come to me," my mother said on Saturday morning. "Why don't we try to bake something together, Emily?"

"And you still remember how to do it?" I asked incredulously.

"Do you doubt my culinary skills? What kind of daughter are you?" She pretended to be sulking.

"I doubt my own. My previous performances in the kitchen ended in a total flop."

"Do not worry. You will only help me," she calmed me down. "Besides, I'll let you lick one of the mixer tips."

"Why one?" I was surprised.

"I'll leave the second for myself. It's the tastiest thing under the sun..."

She smiled dreamily. "Sometimes I think that this is the only reason for baking a cake."

I laughed.

"You convinced me. What should I do?"

"For now, nothing, I must first prepare all the ingredients. I will call when you are needed."

"Okay," I said. "I will make the bed at that time."

I went to my room. I automatically folded the sheets and fell into a reverie. It happens quite often recently, too often. I bet my mother noticed something, but her innate tenderness told her not to ask. Probably the idea of inviting Kori arose out of concern for me. She knew that something was bothering me, and she probably guessed what, but at the same time she realized that only a conversation with a peer could help me. With someone who has similar emotional problems during puberty.

I smiled sadly at the memory of Thursday's conversation with Kori and the eager comments of Erica and Skinny. We were standing in the corridor, that is the whole band together, waiting for some joint activities.

"How was driving lessons?" Red asked.

"It's all right," I said. "Korin claims to have a few more rides and I will be able to drive my own car."

"Mr. Boring teaches you how to ride?" Erica was surprised.

"Why not? This is not a crime," I was indignant.

"Maybe not, but they are already talking about you at school." Her voice was venomous. "You belong to our band and I would prefer not to be associated with your stupidity with orange."

"You know what I think. You are sick of hatred, it is strange that you tolerate your own company," I blurted out strongly pissed off. "I don't care, you can banish me from the band.

"Stop it," said the irreplaceable Skinny. "But by the way, Emily, you could cool your acquaintance with

oranges. It's really not well seen here."

I couldn't believe Skinny was holding Erica's side. Cool acquaintance? What are they all about? And anyway, it doesn't matter anymore, the acquaintance cooled down itself, I drowned it in the fountain yesterday. Korin began to avoid me. As he had clearly sought my company before, he was now trying to keep our contacts to a minimum. Sometimes, only when our eyes crossed, I could see some strange anxiety in his eyes. What did he realize at the fountain that it frightened him so much? Just what the hell did he promise we would be friends? According to him, should this be how friends behave? Why does the world have to be so complicated? I did not understand Korin, Erica, Skinny or Red, people and their characters were a growing mystery to me. I felt anger growing in me. I have to unload my emotions somewhere, because I'm about to explode! Then at the end of the corridor I saw the silhouette of Kori. Great, there is an opportunity to add oil to the fire.

"Kori!" I called and nodded to let her come over.

I ignored Erica's snort, Red's surprised look, and Skinny's significant grunt. Kori came to our group.

"Hello everyone," she said shyly.

"Hi." Only I answered the greeting. "I'd like to make an appointment with you to write a literature work."

"Sure." Her face lit up a smile.

"Maybe Saturday afternoon if you have no other plans," I suggested. "Besides, you could stay with us for a night. What do you think?"

"Nice, very happy," she said with a joyful surprise.

"I'll come on Saturday after dinner.'

"Then we have an appointment." I was relieved that she did not refuse with all those hostile looks. I would feel terribly humiliated. In addition, she seemed very pleased with my proposal.

"Now, you can kick me out with a clear conscience," I said aggressively, when Kori was far enough away not to hear what we were talking about.

"Nobody will kick anyone out," Reda said firmly. "I founded this band and I think I have the most to say in this matter. I suggest you cool your emotions and let everyone guard your nose. I will hear one more comment about who you can hang out with and who you can't, I will dissolve the band."

"But..." Skinny tried to say something, but she cut him off sharply.

"This is my last word and it's better to think Skinny, are you sure you want to add something?"

There was a gloomy silence. In that moment, which seemed to last infinitely long, Red was staring at everyone. None of us had the courage to speak.

"Well, I'm glad you got something there," Red finally said. "We close the topic and now we politely go to class."

"Emily!" My mother called from the kitchen. "Come and whip the foam!"

Yes, cake. I completely forgot.

I rushed into the kitchen.

"What should I do?" I asked.

"Whip the foam," she said, handing me the mixer and the red bowl.

I started to work eagerly, meanwhile my mother was grinding something in a second, much larger bowl. Suddenly I felt an overwhelming desire to talk about feelings. Someone has to explain some things to me, and she knows more about love than anyone around me. But will I not betray myself through the questions I want to ask? I don't think my fascination with Korin makes her happy. Fascination is an understatement. Although, she does not need to know that I am asking about certain matters because of him. I sighed softly.

"Mom..." I started hesitantly.

"What?" She gave me a surprised look.

Of course, she guessed that the conversation was serious. She read it from my face without trouble. She knew me too well. How on earth can I hide this miserable love from her?! I hope I don't cry. Oh well, it happens. As you said A, you must also say B.

"Tell me... tell me about love," I asked.

"What would you like to know?"

"Everything! What is it like falling in love? How do you know you're in love? How do you know that the other person is reciprocating it?" I said in one breath.

"Relax, Emily. Watch what you do!" She shouted, and only now I saw that I had splashed half the kitchen with foam.

"Oh, I'm sorry," I stared.

"Emily, I think we'll talk when the cake is in the oven," she said, handing me a damp cloth. "Wipe off before it dries. I will take care of this cake myself, in fact your work in kitchen ending in disaster. You did not exaggerate."

Fifteen minutes later we were sitting in the living

room on the couch. I was nervous. I didn't have the slightest idea what turn the conversation would take, but I knew I should be extremely vigilant. I knew that if something went wrong, my mother would definitely decide to leave. Take me as far as possible from this place. And I wouldn't stand it. Here is my home now and here is Korin.

"Did you ask for love?" She began shyly.

"Yeah."

"Between a woman and a man?"

"Yeah!"

"Between an earthly woman and an earthly man?" She continued. I swallowed hard. Damn, she guesses. I couldn't control panic.

"Of course," I lied. I never lied to her, so she probably shouldn't notice the slight difference in the tone of my voice.

"Do you like any boy?" She asked quietly.

"I'm not sure I like him. I have no experience when it comes to boys. I don't understand a lot of his behavior towards me. I was hoping that talking to you would explain a few things to me."

"Will you tell me who that is?"

"For now, I'd rather not," I said firmly. "It's nothing certain, so I don't want to speak too soon."

"Are you sure this boy's name is not Korin?"

"Why do you think so?" I tried that she will not hear the anxiety in my voice.

"It seemed to me that you dressed up for him on the first day of school. Besides..." She waved her hand. "Anyway, it does not matter."

"What besides?"

"I got the feeling you got along well."

My mother is percipient.

"We're friends, and nothing more," I reassured her with another lie, it was surprisingly easy lately. "You know very well that Arisyans are not capable to love. Which doesn't change the fact that I like him and his sister a lot. I can't understand one thing. At school, the Arisyans are not very liked. I thought about the cause for a long time, but I could not diagnose the reason for this reluctance. However, in the hospital, among adults, I did not observe any division between people and strangers."

"I think it's quite a normal reaction for young people. Anyone who does not match the generally accepted school and societal standards is a bit out of the way. It was the same in my time. They grow out later."

"Yes, that explains a lot." Her arguments seemed sensible. "But how is this love after all, because we departed from the subject?"

"It's not so simple." She smiled gently. "I would compare love to a complicated chemical reaction. Sometimes it is difficult to predict its effects. It can absorb both the mind and body. However, only unhappy love is dangerous and destructive. There is nothing more uplifting than loving each other. Then you have such strength that you can move mountains and destroy bridges, impossible things become possible."

"But how do I know that the other person is also showing interest?"

"It is the most difficult, but also the most exciting,

that drives the imagination. In general, both people send their signals, but you can have a lot of trouble reading them. They are often contrary to common sense. Some people show their feelings directly and then it is easier. Others, in turn, are afraid of rejection and, to hide their fascination with another person, they behave irrationally. They even push it away."

"But it doesn't make sense," I said.

"Love?" My mother was surprised.

"No, not love, pushing away," I corrected.

That's right, pushing away. Korin has been avoiding me over the past two days. Does this mean anything, or will I interpret his behavior? He's an Arisyan! Human reactions are not about him. But there must be some interplanetary norms in this matter? I realized now that I needlessly got into this conversation. She didn't make the slightest sense, only mother's vigilance increased. Everything that referred to human sensations ceased to have any meaning. Earthling-Arisyan relations were at stake, and I don't think Mother knew. Korin and I were like two opposite poles, like storm and silence after it, like fire and ice, like day and night. Despite this, I couldn't get rid of the impression that we can co-exist together, maintaining the necessary harmony. But now the more important thing was getting out of this pathetic conversation. What impressed me to raise the topic of feelings at all?

"And this boy?" She asked carefully. "How does he behave towards you?"

Good question. How does Korin behave? The point is that for two days now he did nothing. I felt an unpleasant burning sensation in my throat, I barely stopped my tears.

"He rather avoids me," I said resignedly.

My mother looked at me sadly and hugged me tightly.

"I don't think there will be something from it. Don't worry, it's probably just a crush. You won't even look back and you'll fall in love with the next one. This is normal at your age. You feel more like this because you have been isolated for many years. You've been living normally for less than a week, so I assume your sensations are slightly exaggerated. And remember, you can always count on me, I will always support you. No matter what, I will stand by your side."

"Thanks mum." I leaned tightly into her slim arms. "Do not worry. I think it will pass soon."

She kissed my head and went to look at the cake. I felt suddenly so lonely. I pulled my knees under my chin and wrapped my arms around my legs. What is happening with me? I have never been as unhappy as I am now. Even in the shelter, life seemed more bearable. I don't have the strength to deal with it alone anymore. I need to talk to someone, lose this burden. Maybe I made a mistake concealing my mother's truth? I looked towards the kitchen. Mom was just taking the baking tray out of the oven, humming merrily. No, initiating her would not be a good idea.

She is happy here. I don't want to take it from her, the more that she finally began to call this place home.

Kori is the last chance. Will she agree to help? She hardly knows me. Still, I had a vague feeling that Kori was also hiding something. And that it is burden to her. And that Tom plays a role in all this. The girl did not fit

into the pattern of a typical Arisyan woman. Although the feeling I have to her brother is a completely different matter.

Immediately after dinner I sat on the porch steps. I was waiting for Kori. I managed to control my sadness so much that a smile appeared on my face. Now I was only slightly nervous due to uncertainty and fear. For the first time, someone had to spend the weekend in our house, and I really wanted this visit to be the best.

Finally. A Mercedes drove around the corner and then stopped in our driveway.

"Mom, Kori has arrived!" I shouted and ran over to the car glad to help my friend unpack the things."

"Hi! I'm so glad you're here," I said, and the gloomy mood left me as if by magic. "You had to convince your parents to let you sleep with us?"

"Not really. They were a bit surprised, because it is a typical earthly custom. However, I explained that I have to submit a project from world literature for Monday and I can't do it without consulting a person. This argument was enough, in the end I won't waste time on stupid things but deepen my knowledge and develop my mind."

"Yeah, it's so Arisyan. Mind development. Apart from this literature, of course."

She smiled. She understood perfectly what I meant. Now I noticed how similar they were - Kori and Korin. The same smile, the same purple almond-shaped eyes, the same nose and lips, black straight hair. However, Kori's beauty was subtler and her girlish features were delicate. Korin, on the other hand, had a more

pronounced lower jaw, which made his face look incredibly masculine and appealing. Their height also differed. Kori was a little taller than me, while her brother was taller than us.

We entered the kitchen with her luggage.

"Mom, this is Kori," I introduced my friend.

"Good morning," Kori choked out shyly.

"Hello, call me Megan. And of course, feel welcome here."

"I will try to. What smells so beautiful?" She asked, sniffing the air.

"We baked a cake especially for you," said my mother.

"You rather baked it," I corrected. "I was just bothering you. It's good that it has grown at all."

"Well, Korin mentioned your kitchen activities," Kori said.

I blushed. Not because of the culinary failure that Korin witnessed, but because he was telling someone about me. I wonder what exactly he said and how? Or maybe he was making fun of me? I chased that thought away immediately. It's not his style. Definitely not. Although...?

"Come, I'll show you my room." I pulled Kori into my kingdom and closed the door carefully.

The girl stood in the middle of the rug and looked around the room in a bit shy manner. She kept her eyes on the guitar. She came closer and touched the instrument. Several strings made a soft metallic sound. She withdrew her hand, slightly scared.

"Do you play?" She asked.

"A little..."

"I like music. Literature and art too."

"It doesn't even surprise me. I immediately noticed that you were less Arisyan than the other Arisyans."

"Less Arisyan," she repeated, frowning. "You're probably right. But... I like the term."

"You know, Kori, I hardly know you, but I feel like I could talk to you all night."

"I have exactly the same feelings." She smiled.

"So, let's quickly get up with this paper, and the rest of the time we can devote to gossip," I suggested.

"Good idea, I just... I have to confess something to you," she said confused. "I've already written my own."

"To tell the truth, me too."

"And what now? It was supposed to be teamwork," Kori noticed.

"Fact, but I think I know how to get it out. We will read each other's papers and write the third one together. How about the title: 'Differences in the understanding of good by Earthlings and Arisyans'?"

"Great idea! My brother wasn't wrong in saying you were smart."

And yet. They talked about me, and Korin introduced me in a not-so-bad light. It's always a comfort.

We were just finishing our work when there was a soft knock on the door. Mother entered the room with a baking tray in her hands.

"I brought you coffee and cake."

"Thanks," I said. "Especially coffee will be good for us."

"How are you? Do you still have much to learn?" Asked my mother.

"We're about to finish," Kori said.

"In that case I do not bother." And she left the room with a mysterious expression.

"End," I said with relief, putting the tablet aside. "What are we doing now?"

I looked expectantly at Kori. She stared at me intensely, as if considering something, at the same time slowly and completely thoughtlessly stirring coffee with a spoon.

"What happened, Kori?" I asked carefully.

"I can trust you?" She finally choked out.

"I don't know what you're up to, but yes, you can trust me."

"This is serious thing, Emily. No one can find out."

It sounded quite disturbing.

"Maybe you better not say anything."

"It's about Tom." She hesitated, but briefly. "See, Tom is more than just a friend to me. We can say that we are a couple."

At the moment, Kori has shifted the line of familiarity in our relationship. All doubts, uncertainty and prejudices against the other person ceased to exist. Trusting me, she gave rise to sincere friendship."

"Seriously?! Great, I thought so." I almost clapped my hands in joy.

"Is it so visible?" The girl apparently scared my observation, curled up in herself. She looked like something the cat dragged in.

"I noticed," I confirmed truthfully.

"Not good," she moaned.

"Why?"

"I don't know how parents will react if they find out. They'll probably send me to Arisa."

"You can't pair with Earthlings? It's racism." I was indignant. Again, I couldn't get rid of the impression that they were treating us like a worse species.

"It's not like that," she began to explain quite chaotically. "We can't love, theoretically. Only something is wrong with me. Anyway, I've always been different. All my life I felt like an inexplicable emptiness. Only here on Earth something woke up in me. I felt like I was at my place. And when I met Tom... I became sure that my place was here. Emily, I love him. I know that for sure."

"I was firmly convinced that the Arisyans were not capable of love." I still couldn't believe what I heard from her. The spark of hope for a relationship with Korin returned to me. Unfortunately, just to go out in a moment.

"Because they are not. I think I'm the only case. Day by day my feelings are stronger. But not all are good, and that scares me. You don't even know how much. I often feel hatred. Especially in the company of Erica. I can hardly resist not to scratch her eyes."

"Erica probably raises negative emotions in everyone, I don't see anything abnormal in it. I don't understand what worries you? I don't think anything would happen if someone found out you have any human feelings. I think that's quite positive."

"Maybe positive for you, but the Arisyans have a different opinion on this subject. I can't even imagine how they will react. There has never been such a case. Everything was always right."

"And how should it be?" I was surprised. "Well,

how do you pair up? How did your parents get together?"

"Genetically," she said, as if it were something obvious. "We are genetically matched. This is how the life partner is selected. Then we have a guarantee that the offspring of these two will simply be perfect. This method makes subsequent generations more and more perfect. Mentally and physically."

"Terrible! Can't pick the person you want to spend the rest of your life with?"

"Unfortunately." She shook her head sadly.

"Wait, wait..." a thought began to dawn on me. "And you? Do you already have a life partner?"

"Yes, but I haven't met him yet. That's why Tom is so mad about these genes. He's afraid I'll choose that one."

"Why? You don't even know this "allocation"."

"Don't you understand, Emily? It does not matter. Apparently, when I meet him, I won't want to get involved with anyone else. This is what it is about. The genetic partner is supposed to be perfect for me in every respect. Perfect fit," she laughed sarcastically. "Tom is very nervous about this. He is afraid that he is not good enough for me and that he will lose in confrontation with that one. Emily, I'm afraid of that too."

Instinctively, I took her hands and squeezed tightly.

"You aren't sure about your feelings?" I asked quietly.

"I am," she assured. "But somewhere inside, I am terribly anxious that it may not be enough. I am especially afraid of the ideal traits of the genetic

partner and my reaction to them. I will face a difficult fight with myself, with tradition, with feelings, with his perfection... And I love Tom above all because not everything is perfect in him. It doesn't have to be perfect, I don't even want it to be perfect. I love him for his advantages, but also for his disadvantages. Especially for defects, because they prove that he is a real man."

"Do you know what I think, Kori? I think you're really in love. But how can you feel all this? You know, love, hate...?"

"I don't know, I think I'm defective."

"Do you think Korin is also defective?" I asked softly, hopefully.

"What do you mean by that?"

"Well..." I did not have to finish, because after a while she arranged everything herself, she figured out everything.

"Oh, no," she moaned, covering her mouth with her hand, and there was terror in her eyes. "You fell in love with my brother."

"That`s bad?"

"It's a disaster! He is not like you, nor like me. Korin can't love, he can't even learn it. He is a good brother, a good man, but nothing more. Don't make hope."

"Too late, I've already done it to myself," I said, shrugging.

"You're crazy! Nothing of this will happen, or at least nothing good."

"Why you are that confident?"

"Emily," her voice softened, "Korin is a true

Arisyan. He respects our civilization and will never go against the rules. I just don't understand what my brother did to make you hope? Or maybe you imagined something by misinterpreting his behavior? You shouldn't do that. Don't get me wrong, but you have worried me with this confession."

I could do nothing but tell her everything I did with some resistance. I have never confided in such personal experiences. I felt strange talking about the first night spent in a new home, about our conversations at school and outside of school. Kori listened intently, did not comment or was surprised. She accepted everything with stoic calm, thus letting me know that Korin had in no way crossed the line of ordinary Arisyan behavior. Nothing objected to her until I came to the incident at the fountain. She inhaled so violently that she almost choked it.

"He said: "change your clothes before I do something stupid"?" She asked in astonished voice. "Are you sure he used the exact words?"

"More than sure."

"So, his time has come earlier than expected."

"What time?"

What is this girl raving about?!

I didn't manage to gather my thoughts when Kori asked another question:

"Tell me, Emily, how is he behaving about you now?"

"Cold."

"Well, it's quite normal," she said.

"Defends himself? Before what? What time has come? You can finally make me aware of what you mean, what is it all about?!"

"He's defending against you. He physically desires you, that's the only explanation."

I was dumbfounded at her answer.

"But... it's probably good." Judging by the face of Kori, it wasn't good at all.

"Very bad! And it will be even worse, because his life partner will come to Earth in half a year. Korin will survive half a year of hell," she looked at me sadly, "and so do you."

"Sorry, Kori, I still don't understand much of this."

"Well... of course. How could you possibly know that?" She sighed heavily. "I'll try to explain something to you. Like all people, we also feel physical attraction. The first signs of puberty are a sign that it's time to match the genetic partner. It is very rare for someone to have a much greater sexual need than others. Then the genetic partner must be found extremely quickly. I think that's the way it is with Korin."

"Good, that's always a feeling," I murmured. "Although I don't understand why me. There are many prettier girls here."

"Emily, you're special and Korin noticed it. Man's beauty is not only reflected in the mirror. The interior is more important."

"I'm not special, I'm quite average, the most average of the average ones."

Kori shook her head.

"I don't think so, and he apparently too."

I sank deeper into the armchair, trying to make some sensible conclusions from the onslaught of new information, but my logic in contact with the Arisyan

perception of the world began to be bad. Out of all this mental chaos, a loose thought emerged that, without waiting for permission, evolved into a question spoken aloud:

"Is there any possibility that he would not pick a girl from the assignment, but me?"

Kori sighed loudly.

"Honestly, no. I assure you that she will attract him more," she said it with such force that it came to my consciousness that it was the end.

Something inside me broke, broke into small, sharp-edged pieces that hurt so badly that my emotional tears ran down my cheeks. Kori looked at me scared.

"I'm sorry, forgive me..." she whispered. "I shouldn't say that, not so directly."

I covered my face with my hands and at that moment I wanted to become invisible, just disappear. I imagined half a year of anguish and half a life of yearning for someone who might not even remember that I existed. So, it's over, after all... But I don't want it to be over and it doesn't have to be! After all, we largely decide about our fate and I can choose the ending. How many times my mother instilled in me that one should live for the moment, draw on handfuls of life, as long as possible, follow my dream. I straightened up and wiped the tears away with the back of my hand. I made my decision.

"I am happy with half a year with him," I said firmly. "It doesn't matter what happens later. I want it to be the most beautiful six months of my life. Will you help me?"

Kori stared at me for a moment, dumbfounded. Finally, she said:

"It's not so simple. Korin is obligatory, attached to tradition and devoid of higher feelings. Common sense already orders him to stay away from you."

"I don't want him to stay away."

"Are you sure about this, Emily?"

"I am."

There was a constant silence in the room. Kori silently turned the empty coffee cup in her hands. Finally, she put it on the table and looked at me. I saw hesitation in her eyes.

"I'll help you," she said without conviction. "I'll try to arrange something when we go out to field in a week," she promised in a more confident voice. "I just hope his power of will is weaker than desire."

CHAPTER IX

Speech is a source of confusion.
ANTOINE DE SAINT-EXUPÉRY

And Kori delivered. She made it seem impossible, and we spent most of our school time together: me, Kori, Tom and of course Korin. She was finding countless reasons why we should do different things together. Hmm, Arisyan woman and conspiracy? Quite an unusual combination, but Kori apparently didn't bother. Although Korin did not behave as freely towards me as in the first days of school, but at least he stopped avoiding me. Well, he had no choice.

Unfortunately, he gave up driving lessons for now, explaining the lack of time, but I already lived our trip in the field and just armed myself with patience. We agreed that we would leave as soon as dawn on Friday with two cars. Kori was supposed to go with Tom, and me with her brother.

I sat on the porch steps for a few minutes and was freezing. The morning was exceptionally cold, but I preferred to wait here than at home. The sharp air perfectly allowed to get rid of sleep remnants, in addition it effectively cooled emotions. I leaned my back harder on my equipment, i.e. a backpack, a bag with provisions and a guitar. Yes, a guitar. Kori insisted on taking it. I wonder what Korin thinks about that? I pulled my knees under my chin and looked up at the sky. The black of the night slowly disappeared, and the surroundings began to turn gray in the morning. Above the eastern horizon hung a band of clouds, behind which a pale sun shield shone through. It was going to be a fairly clear day. The question is, will it be cheerful also for me?

I didn't wait long. After a few minutes I noticed the characteristic Land Rover lights in the distance. I didn't have to look at my watch to see that Korin arrived on time. He was always on time.

"Hi, baby," he said cheerfully as he got out of the car. "Am I late?"

"No, I just woke up too early," I said, leaping to my feet.

"I thought I would have to wake you up."

"You're still not very good with thinking," I mocked.

"Fact," he laughed. "Where do you have things? I'll pack them in the car right away."

I pointed to the porch.

"Well, no..." he groaned at the sight of the guitar. "You have to be joking. Don't say you want to take this infernal instrument."

"Actually, the guitar wasn't my idea. Kori asked..." I stammered out frightened by his reaction. "She says that these trips to the field is boring and we will need some music for entertainment."

"I think my sister went completely loco."

"If you want, I can leave it." I shrugged my shoulders. "I play reluctantly to people."

"We'll take it," he decided. "It will be easier for me

to bear these noises than later Kori's claims. She can poison a man's life for a few weeks."

Grumbling something incomprehensible under his breath, he packed all my things into the car and we headed south.

"What about Tom and Kori?" I asked.

"We'll meet them there."

"Where are we going?"

"About one hundred and twenty kilometers south to Braddyville. There we have the first base, the second one is a few kilometers away, near Westboro, but we rarely use it. The first one has much better accommodation conditions, although quite Spartan. I hope you don't mind it?"

"After a dirty, smelly shelter, I don't think I find a reason to complain."

"Well, when I found you, you got stuck with dirt."

"Do not remind me." I grimaced offended. "Anyway, I did not stick with dirt, but with oil."

"Dirt is dirt," he said ruthlessly.

"I wonder what you would look like after a year without water!" I raised my voice because his silly pricks upset me.

"Okay, okay, I'm sorry," he said in a conciliatory tone. "I really don't know how you do it."

"What?"

"You will always provoke me to express myself incorrectly."

"Don't worry, I'm already used to it." I smiled. "Besides, I can't be mad at you for long."

"I noticed that. Your anger passes just as quickly as it appears."

We both fell silent because we have just crossed the force field of the town. Physically, it was impossible to feel it, but visually there was a clear change in the appearance of the area. We entered the brown-rust landscape from lush greenery surrounding us. I shuddered despite my will. It didn't take much time since I was wandering the road around the ruined world, but the neat and lively image of Arisyan's cities has already erased that memory. It was only outside of the cities that we could see how much work was ahead of us to bring everything to its original condition.

"There is awful here. Do you think that it will be possible to restore the former Earth?" I asked in horror.

"It will be hard, but maybe someday..." he sighed. "It takes many years, but it will not be as before. The biggest problem is keeping balance in nature. That is why we set up experimental plantations outside the cities. Anyway, the word plantation doesn't really fit here. More suitable is a nature reserve, because everything is left alone. You see, Emily, in the city the breeding of plants and animals is running smoothly, because we can always interfere when something is wrong. On the other hand, nature must do it by itself. If we want everything to live a life of its own without any help, nature must strike a balance, otherwise nothing will happen."

"So, what is our role in all this? Why are we going there? We shouldn't interfere."

"And we won't," he said. "We're just going to check how fast everything develops and grows, and whether it's functioning properly."

"So, we're going to learn from possible mistakes," I concluded.

"Exactly. Do you want to drive?" He asked unexpectedly.

"I do not know."

He stopped the car.

"Hop behind the wheel. Only without excesses, no sudden braking and bathing in fountains."

"I will try to." I gave him a forced smile.

We swapped places. Everything was almost the same as last time. Well, almost... Korin said what to do in turn, but clearly avoided physical contact. Of course, I had a lot of trouble with the gearbox, but this time he didn't help me. After several unsuccessful attempts to throw in first gear I gave up.

"It will not happen today," I said resignedly. "Unless you show me what these gears are all about again.

We looked at each other. A strange shadow flitted across his face, but immediately masked him with a smile. What was that? Panic? What is he afraid of? He grabbed my hand and, as on Wednesday, showed me how to throw more gears, then quickly withdrew his hand. Too fast.

In the end I could not bear it.

"Korin, what's the matter with you lately?"

"Nothing," he said without looking at me.

"You're so uptight. I did something wrong? You're mad at me? You've been behaving strangely for a week and I can't get rid of the impression it has to do with me."

"Don't turn this into something it's not. If something is wrong, it's all my fault. I have not felt

myself for some time. Anyway... it's not important," he replied resignedly.

"Important. Important for me. I would like to know what's going on."

"I do not want to talk about it."

"Maybe you should? Sometimes it's good to confide in someone."

"Certainly not you," he said, clearly impatient.

I turned my head and squeezed deeper into the car seat. I started feeling sad.

"Sorry, I didn't mean to offend you." He took my hand instinctively, but let go immediately, as if he had burnt himself. "Emily, you have to understand that my life is not easy here."

"I thought the Arisyans were quickly adapting to new situations, you said so once."

"Not to everyone, sometimes..." he did not finish. "It is beyond me. I think I will have to leave for some time, I will ask my father to move to another city."

I went pale.

"You can't move, you and Kori are my only friends."

"Kori will stay, and I'll be back in six months, I have to think about a few things calmly."

I understood exactly what he was aiming for. He wanted to isolate himself from me, keep his distance until the arrival of his life partner. That's how he figured it out. Over my dead body. He's supposed to be mine for the next six months. I don't want anything more. After this confession, I became certain that his sister had come to the right conclusion, Korin desires me and that scares him. At least I now knew what he intended. I decided not to drill anymore. It is not known what else he will declare, from which it will be difficult for him to get away. He also considered the conversation to be over.

"Let's change. It is better if I drive."

"Okay," I agreed.

And these were the last words spoken during our trip. We drove in silence, and the atmosphere in the car became more and more unbearable every minute. I cast a furtive glance at Korin. He clenched his steering wheel tightly and looked at the road with mock focus. He looked even more beautiful than usual in a black T-shirt with a grim expression. He wasn't the same cheerful and carefree boy I met a few weeks ago. Although it didn't matter. I just loved him for who he is and who he is not, who he will be and who he will not be, I loved him for everything and for nothing.

The landscape outside the window began to come alive slowly. Here and there appeared individual tufts of sharp, green grass, which is unknown when they turned into large clusters of lush greenery. Soon, we encountered short shrubs growing along the road and something else that amazed me more than the lush vegetation - animals.

We turned into a forest, weed road, which after several dozen meters expanded, suddenly turning into a large clearing. The initially visible delicate mist, indicating the presence of a force field, dispelled and we stopped in front of a small wooden log cabin. Korin parked right next to Tom's Jeep Cherokee. I got out of the car with relief, slamming the door.

"Took you long enough," Tom said with mock

resentment, standing in the doorway of the house.

"Emily tried to drive but didn't get far," Korin muttered in reply.

"It would be easier if you helped me with the gearbox," I replied.

"Maybe you, but not me," he grunted.

"Easy guys! What are you so militant about yourself?" Tom asked suspiciously.

Korin shrugged.

"You think so," he said.

Kori just left the hut. She looked once at me and once at Korin.

"Come on, Emily, help me in the kitchen, I'm preparing a second breakfast."

I will help you," Korin interjected and started toward the building. "Emily doesn't know much about cooking. You might as well let a tornado into the kitchen."

That was too much for me, why this boy insisted on making me sad at all costs. Earlier I thought that he did it unconsciously and that malice was not in his nature, but now I was not so sure. Tears stood in my eyes, I turned on my heel and walked blindly ahead, struggling to break through the lush vegetation here. Behind my back I heard Kori's indignant voice:

"I didn't think you were such an idiot. You behave like Erica or worse, because nobody expects such harsh comments from you."

I didn't hear any more because I left quickly. I defeated the thickets, reaching a small clearing. I sat on the moss rug by a thick, withered tree and rested my head on a rough trunk. After a while Korin appeared.

"I failed again," he said quietly in remorse. "Apologizing doesn't make sense, since I'm still doing the same, making you feel sad."

I didn't say a word, I turned my head the other way. I could barely hold back my tears. He crouched beside me and gently stroked my cheek.

"Will you say something?" He asked, running his thumb close to my ear.

I shook my head. With the other hand, he gently took my chin and turned my face toward him. I looked into his eyes, they were as sad as mine.

"Will we start from the beginning?" He suggested.

"Like what?"

"Friendship."

I thought friends didn't behave like that," I noted.

"You're right, they don't act like that." He brushed my hair back from my forehead. "Recently I have become nervous. I shouldn't take it out on you. This is not right on my part. Will you forgive me again?"

"I don't know..." I whispered.

"And if I promise you that I won't make you feel bad during this trip? I swear. I will be a real friend."

"And I have to believe it?" I asked doubtfully.

"You don't have to," he said. "I'll prove it to you, just give me a chance."

He grabbed my arms and pulled me up, putting me in front of him. I put my arms around his waist and hugged my head tightly against his muscular torso. I couldn't resist, the need was stronger than me. I waited for him to move me away, meanwhile with some hesitation he returned the embrace.

"I was bad," he said, releasing me after a moment.

"Fact."

"Come and have a snack." He put his arm around me and led me back to the cottage. "We've been away for a long time. Certainly, Kori and Tom have already prepared something to eat. We will prepare dinner together. I will even let you make a small fire or get cut in your finger. What do you think?"

I gave him a light prod. At least now I was sure he was really joking. Seemingly Korin regained his freedom and typical good humor, but I saw that it cost him a lot of effort.

We entered the cottage, which was really small. It had only one room, a large kitchen and a small bathroom. We didn't need anything better. An open fireplace occupied the center of the main room. It looked more like a hearth in an Indian hut, and if it wasn't for the thick pipe with a metal eaves coming out of the ceiling, one would think so.

Kori and Tom were eating sandwiches.

"I won't go into what you have been doing for so long in the bushes, but I can see that the storm passed," Tom said ironically. "Eat a sandwich and get to work before it gets dark."

"Don't overdo, it's only nine o'clock," Korin replied. "A few more hours until the evening."

I ate two slices, but Korin consumed six. Finally, we had a cup of coffee.

"Well, let's get to work. Guys bring some wood, it will be useful in the evening, and we will clean the dishes after breakfast," ordered Kori.

She gathered the plates in a pile and headed for the kitchen. Passing by me, she whispered conspiratorially:

"Come on, we need to talk."

Korin and Tom went outside, and we hid in the kitchen. Kori turned on the faucet and started washing the plates. I sat on the counter next to the sink.

"What's going on between you?" She asked directly.

"Do you think I know? It is your brother. You tell me."

She handed me a dish and plate. I started wiping vigorously.

"I don't know what's going on in his head," she said slowly. "I can't ask because he won't tell me. Anyway, you both behave strangely, there is a kind of tension between you that I can hardly name. For example, today when you arrive. What happened along the way? You were so upset that Tom even compared you to argumentative lovers."

"Ha... you can always dream." I smiled wryly. "So far it has the standard "let's be friends"."

"No..." She shook her head thoughtfully. "It's more than friendship. Korin has never behaved like this. You have to be alone, maybe then something will be explained. By the way, we and Tom will also have some time for ourselves." She winked at me knowingly.

"How do you want to organize it?"

"Don't worry, I have a plan," she said mysteriously.

"What plan?"

"You'll find out tonight, because you will blurt out."

"Oh, Kori. Say now..." I asked. "What is this plan?"

"Shhh..." She pressed a finger to her lips. "They came back."

The boys overwhelmed a pile of brown, dry wood. It looked gross. I was hoping that it would burn nicely at least.

The day passed quite nicely, though boring. Sample preparation and assay were not exciting activities. For me, admittedly, everything was new, so work in the base seemed more interesting to me than the others. We made a lot of notes that Korin intended to use later to make the expedition report. Unfortunately, I couldn't stay alone with Kori to get to know something. Curiosity consumed me, what is she up to?

The sun was low on the horizon when Korin approached me.

"Enough for today, we are coming back," he said.

He took the last sample from me and put it in the preparation bag. Kori and Tom were already packed, so we headed towards the cottage.

"You're preparing dinner with Korin," Kori reminded me.

"Sure, I remember," I replied, but I must have a blurred face because the girl asked:

"That bad? You know, with this cooking."

I couldn't answer because Korin interjected:

"Come on, sister, we can handle it."

It was dark inside the building because there was no electricity in the cottage. Therefore, Korin brought a bunch of tens of centimeters from the trunk, which he arranged in all rooms. The tubes turned out to be Arisyan field lamps, which did not give too bright light, but when turned on all in the house it became pleasantly

light. Tom started lighting the fireplace, while me and Korin went to the kitchen.

"What are we doing for dinner?" I asked.

The boy removed the cover from a large plastic container standing on the floor. The container contained about twenty different kinds of cans.

"I suggest you cook the soup. You can handle it," he said. "Just heat it up."

He set a large pot on the stove and set fire to the stove.

"Get to work," he encouraged. "I will catch up on the report during this time."

He took the thought recorder from the bag hanging on the back of the chair and unfolded it on the kitchen table. He put the headphones on his temple, but before he turned off the consciousness, I managed to ask:

"How many cans of these soup should I take?"

"Four are enough," he said, not looking my way. "And pour one and a half glass of water."

I poured the contents of four cans into the pot, added water, reduced the flame and sat down on the countertop, watching Korin at work with pleasure. While using the recorder, he seemed absent, as if he were in another dimension. All the time I remembered not to burn the soup. I jumped off the counter, leaned over the pot and stirred in it, vigorously scrubbing the spoon down the bottom. The longer I stirred, the paler my face became.

"Korin..." I said uncertainly, "there is something wrong with this soup."

I took some liquid on the spoon and carefully watched its contents under the light.

"She should be blue-brown?"

"What?" He immediately leaped up from the chair, put the headphones down and went to the stove."

Now we were both staring at the soup, or rather something that should have been soup, but apparently it wasn't.

"What did you put in there?" He asked vapidly."

"I've done what you told me to do." I pointed to the pile of empty cans abandoned on the counter.

He picked up one of them, turned it in his hand, looked carefully, sniffed and set it down. Later he looked the second and third and fourth one in the same way. When he put down the last one, he covered his mouth with his hand and started giggling.

"I don't believe, I don't believe..." he repeated.

"What's up?" I asked impatiently.

He didn't answer, he giggled louder. I looked at the empty cans until I realized what I had done. I just mixed together several types of soups with extremely different flavors.

"Yes, that's all me," I groaned, but I also started laughing.

When we finally managed to calm down, we leaned over the pot again.

"Do you think it tastes like it looks?" I asked grimly.

"I hope not," he murmured. "But at least we know it's not poisonous. After all, it contains only edible ingredients."

"Do we give them one or try to do something with it?"

"I will try to do something with it and YOU...

hmm... you will rest." He put his hands gently on my shoulders and led me to the chair. I dropped resigned to the seat.

I was fed up with this unfortunate soup, cuisine and all the confusion about food and cooking. Korin was writhing around the stove, adding and adding various things, which he tried every now and then, and I didn't care whether something came of it or not. Finally, he poured the soup into four bowls.

"Well, it won't be better," he said. "Let's hope they are very hungry."

"What is this soup?" Kori asked as we sat on the floor by the fireplace, each with his own bowl.

"I don't know, this is Emily's recipe," Korin said, barely suppressing laughter.

"But Korin was seasoning," I added quickly.

"Good," Tom said appreciatively, raising the bowl.

Korin and I looked at each other, but this time we fail not to laugh."

"I don't understand why you are laugh?" Kori was indignant, not knowing the reason for our cheerfulness. "But since the mood is great, maybe we'll set an action plan for tomorrow."

"What plan?" Korin asked anxiously, and I was all ears. Through this soup adventure, I completely forgot about our morning conversation.

"Good, of course. Tomorrow, Tom and I will go to the second base, take samples, spend the night there and return on Sunday morning. In the meantime, you will finish here. That way we'll be back home on Sunday afternoon instead of what we intended on

Monday morning."

This is the Kori plan, smart. I will kill two birds with one stone. She will leave me alone with Korin and spend the night with Tom. The question is, what does her brother say? I looked at Korin, he didn't look pleased.

"Kori is right," Tom came her with help. "Here we would work till the evening, we would have to go to the second base at night, and the road on this section is not very good. A night trip can be a little risky."

Korin looked for a moment as if he were considering something in his mind. Finally, he said with a heavy sigh:

"Okay, we'll stay here with Emily."

He stood up, added a few logs to the burning fireplace and moved the grate vigorously. Sparks popped up, and the wood began to lick lazy fires. A moment later the fire burst into a bright flame. Korin stood in front of the hearth all the time and stared thoughtfully at the flames. The vibrating light of the fireplace wandered his face, making it seem a little more orange than usual.

"Will you play something for us, Emily?" Kori said unexpectedly.

I looked at Korin questioningly. I knew perfectly well what his opinion about music was and I didn't want to risk being mocked again. The more that the day passed in an extremely pleasant atmosphere.

"I'll get the guitar from the car in a minute," Korin said with a smile.

He encountered a mute question in my eyes.

"I promised that I would be extremely kind and tolerant today," he explained.

"But you don't have to sacrifice yourself that much," I said.

"I don't sacrifice myself, I just like it when you are satisfied. Besides, I plug my ears."

After a minute he came back with a guitar. As I pulled it out of the cover, Korin sat down opposite me, pulled his knees under his chin and ostentatiously touched his hands to his ears.

"You can start, I'm already soundproof," he said, maybe a little too loud.

"What should I play?"

"Have you written something new lately?" Asked Kori.

I nodded but looked at Korin. He made a funny face, but his ears were still covered. Hope tightly. All in all, he wouldn't listen. I wrote this song for him and to him. The warmth of the dying fire, pleasant dusk and silence of expectation created an unusual atmosphere around me. I closed my eyes, letting myself be carried away by the moment. Emotions hidden for many days flowed from my inside, transforming into a melody:

Unbelievable
The wind is so cold here on the mountain,
the stars seem to shine a little bit brighter,
in the end of the road there are so many ways,
but there's only one we should follow.

He said I'm unbelievable.
He said I'm taking care,
of those things we should have known,
we are so unprepared.

I can feel anything except this cold,
the light seems to hide behind the walls,
take me, I need your hand.
And lead me to the everlasting end.

I opened my eyes and met Korin's eyes. He stared at me intensely, too intensely... I felt his persistent look not only on my face, but literally everywhere. In my mind, heart, soul, in the deepest recesses of myself.

"You were supposed to be soundproof," I said reproachfully.

"But it didn't work out," he said dryly, staring at the floor. "I have to walk," he said, rising suddenly from the floor. He grabbed the sweatshirt slung over the back of the chair and, without looking at anyone, went outside, not very gently slamming the door behind him.

We looked at each other.

"What's with him?" Tom asked in surprise.

I shrugged my shoulders.

"Probably his ears hurt," I murmured, wincing.

"This guy starting to freak out on my mind, this planet apparently doesn't serve him," Tom said.

"Stop, you're talking about my brother. I like him," Kori was indignant.

"I like him too, even very much, which doesn't change the fact that he is acting crazy lately. Although... maybe not so much crazy but behaving differently than usual."

"You're probably right," Kori admitted. "Nineteen years old is a stupid age, not only for Earthlings, but also for Arisyans. You know, hormones."

"Never mind." He waved a hand. "We're spreading sleep. Tomorrow is a harsh day."

We have been lying in our sleeping bag for a long time, but Korin still did not return. The wood in the fireplace has long burned out, and the only thing left in the hearth was the fire going out and giving virtually no light. The room sank in the impenetrable darkness of the night. As usual, darkness caused me an unpleasant shiver of fear, I associated it too much with a shelter. In addition, they made me worry about Korin.

However, I didn't want to reveal my anxiety first. Fortunately, Tom was thinking the same.

"He is gone for too long," he said. "Maybe I'll go get him."

"I think he wants to be alone," Kori said. "But go get him, you have to get up early tomorrow, so it's better for him to lie down."

I heard Tom pull his clothes on and grunting incomprehensibly under his breath, he left the hut.

"Everything is going well," Kori whispered.

"What do you mean?" I also asked in a whisper.

"That my brother freaked out on you. You turn him on."

"Don't make fun of me. If he freaked out, it was rather because of my noises."

"That, too," she giggled. "Pity you didn't see the look on his face as he listened to the song as you sang. This song... You wrote it for him, right?"

"He wasn't supposed to listen it," I groaned. "I could have sung something else."

"We're sleeping," she hissed suddenly.

I pulled the sleeping bag over my head. I heard the door creaking and footsteps. They returned. Although they tried to keep it as quiet as possible one of them hit the chair on the way.

"Sorry," the voice murmured in a muffled whisper. And yet Korin.

The rustle of nylon meant that they both had just slipped into their sleeping bags. I tried not to move and even my breathing. I didn't want him to know that I wasn't sleeping yet. I couldn't sleep for a long time, and probably not only me, because Korin's breathing was also uneven. In spite of the foam pads, I felt pressure on my hip against hard floor boards, which was also not conducive to falling asleep quickly. I do not know how much time I lay there with my eyes open, which despite the effort could not see any shape in the dark. Finally, my eyelids dropped from fatigue.

And again, I stood on an endless, dead plain. Vibrating from the heat, the unnaturally thick air smelled of loneliness, burning the lungs with every breath. The same place, the same dry tree and the same black crow as night, but now it seemed larger than before. He was still looking at me with a ghostly look in the empty eye sockets, but something changed in his attitude, something that awed me. This time he wanted to attack me, I felt it clearly and from second to second panic escalated in me. The only thing that came to my mind at that moment was escape. But I just thought I was running. Although I was changing my legs faster and faster, I couldn't move even by a millimeter. Unimaginable fatigue swept over me. I looked over my

shoulder anxiously at the tree. I shuddered, because at the same time the bird rose to flight. It wasn't until he spread his wings that I realized how huge he was. He was quilting towards me, and I couldn't do anything to save myself. I wanted to shield my face, but the attempt to raise my hand also failed. Right in front of my head, the crow suddenly stopped, hung for a moment in the air, then hit its wings in the face and landed on my shoulder, thrusting its pointed claws into it. A cry of despair escaped my throat. I opened my eyes in horror. Korin was leaning over me. He gently shook my arm with one hand and stroked my cheek tenderly with the other.

"Em, take it easy. It's just me."

My mouth was so dry that my tongue stuck to my palate, and my throat scratched as if I had eaten sand. I couldn't say a word. I raised my elbows and rubbed my eyes, trying to get back to reality. I looked around the room. Kori and Tom's bedding had already been cleared and a breakfast tray stood beside me. Korin handed me a cup of warm milk.

"Drink it," he commanded. "All."

I drank quickly, swallowing hard. The throat scratching subsided with every sip, and a pleasant warmth spread through the stomach. Nightmare fear was slowly leaving me. I emptied the cup.

"Thanks," I said, recovering a voice that sounded amazingly normal.

"What was that, Em?" Asked Korin with concern. "You screamed like somebody was skinning you."

I rubbed my forehead wearily.

"It's just a dream, a very bad dream," I said weakly.

"That crow again?"

"Yhm... but now he has attacked me."

Korin shook his head with a sigh and offered me the tray.

"Eat something," he said, finishing the topic. Maybe it's better that he didn't ask anything more. Telling with the details of my dream would be reliving this nightmare, and for that I had neither the strength nor the desire.

"What time is it?" I asked, taking breakfast.

"A few minutes past ten."

"And Kori and Tom?"

"They left about seven, they'll be back on Sunday morning."

So, it happened. We were alone.

CHAPTER X

It is said that love is blind. Believe me, it's a complete lie, there is nothing more visible than true love. Nothing. It is something that clearly sees under the sun. Sacrifice is blind, affection is blind, lust is blind but not true love. Make no mistake and do not call these feelings love.

ANTHONY DE MELLO

The day was completely normal. We did exactly what we did yesterday, except that we were just the two of us. Korin kept his word all the time and treated me extremely friendly. But nothing more. I don't know what I expected. I expected too much from that day. Meanwhile, Korin controlled himself perfectly, behaving with me with almost exaggerated reserve.

I just got out of the bathroom dressed in a sleeping shirt. While I was taking a cold shower, Korin spread his bed for us. With a twinge of regret, I found that the two foam pads are quite a distance away. The boy was lying on one of them on his back, covered with a sleeping bag. He was not wearing a shirt, and he put his bare strong shoulders under his head.

"Will you turn off the lamp?" He asked.

"Can't we leave it till morning? I will reduce the

light to a minimum." I said pleadingly.

"What are you afraid of? This raven?"

"That, too but mainly darkness. I am afraid that when I open my eyes at night, I will be consumed by darkness and I will never see the light again." I answered with shame, I did not want to pass as cowards in his eyes.

"If it's going to help you sleep, that's okay," he agreed.

I turned the knob at the end of the lamp so that the room was gently dim and slipped into the sleeping bag. I lay on my side and watched Korin from behind my closed eyelids. In the dim light I could see only the outline of his profile. He was still lying on his back, staring at the ceiling. One hand was still under his head, the other he dropped along the torso. I don't know how long we lay there, but at one point some familiar noise came from the court. I shuddered, feeling unspecified anxiety. I tried hard to remember what the sound was. I didn't associate it with anything pleasant. Only when it sounded the second time did I realize what it was - the murmurs of an approaching storm. Without thinking, I reached for the flashlight and turned on the light, then moved my sleeping pad near Korin. He turned his head slightly towards me.

"Emily, what are you doing?" He asked surprised.

"I'm getting rid of the fear of the storm."

"Yes," he sighed, resigned. "Don't shout in my ear at night if you're dreaming."

"I'll see what I can do."

"Sure," he laughed.

Encouraged by the return of his typical sense of humor, I went further. I gently took his hand. He shuddered, but he didn't release his hand, but neither he didn't return the embrace. I stroked the back of his hand. I still couldn't get over how Korin's skin was so smooth. I was ashamed that mine has a delicate, bright nap.

"What are you doing?" He asked quietly.

"Nothing, but you know... it's so weird, skin without hair. It's a pity that mine is not like that. I feel like a yeti with you."

He snorted in suppressed laughter.

"Your nap has a weird property," he said in an undertone.

"Property? What property?" I was surprised.

He rolled over and propped himself up on his elbow.

"Look."

The fingers of his free hand carefully touched my forearm. He moved his fingertips very slowly from the palm of my hand to the bend of the elbow and back again. This short, warm touch was enough to stimulate my already burning senses. A short, gentle shiver shook me, and goose bumps covered my skin, just like when he taught me how to ride.

"It always happens," he said. "I wonder why?"

He does it on purpose, does he accidentally get it?! What should I tell him? You turn me on when you do that? I want you? Would he like to hear it?

"You really don't know why this happens?" I asked doubtfully. Somehow, I did not want to believe that he does not even guess the real reasons for this, and no other reaction.

"Can you tell me?" He repeated the question.

"I don't think I can explain to you. But... I'll try to show, maybe it will work."

He looked at me in surprise.

"Show?"

"Yhm..." I nodded.

What am I doing?! It is impossible that he reacts to touch like me. Do the Arisyans have any erogenous zones at all? I have not heard of such a thing. I took a deep breath. Tough! If not, I'd be embarrassed.

I took his hand carefully and began to caress it gently. Hand first. I calmly traced the contours of each finger. Then, with a slow, sliding motion, the forearm, stopping longer at the bend of the elbow. I was unimaginably pleased to touch him, but Korin did not react. He seemed completely resistant to my touch. The room was full of silence broken only by the sounds of storm. I slowly headed higher, above his elbow. I fingered the shapely muscle of his arm. I felt it gently flex under the pressure of my hand. And when I was about to repeat the whole operation, Korin began to tremble. He didn't get goose bumps, of course, but his hands were shaking, and his breathing quickened. Startled, he quickly pulled his hand away from me.

"Enough," he choked out. "I understand."

I had no doubt that he understood. His eyes told me that. He looked at me surprised and a little confused for a moment. And yet he provoked me, apparently not realizing what it would lead us to.

"It's late," he said hoarsely. "We should be sleeping a long time ago. Good night," he murmured, avoiding my sight.

Then he lay down on the edge of his sleeping mat, his back to me. Well, that's it. I followed his example and lay down with my back to him. I closed my eyes. I tried to recall dream, but the storm raging outside and the closeness of Korin did not help me at all. I squirmed restlessly on my bed, rustling my sleeping bag.

"Can you stop squirming? Try to fall asleep," he said in resentment.

"It's easy for you to say, it's impossible in this noise, at least for me," I grunted.

"So, plug your ears up and don't talk that much."

"Your advice is priceless. Third rate genius," I said ironically, pulling my sleeping bag over my head.

I was furious. On myself that I fell in love. At Korin, he behaved like a moron. At Kori, that because of her intrigue I found myself alone with him. At the world that despite the disaster still exists. I was furious at everyone and everything.

This is not how it was supposed to look!

I heard a soft murmur behind me. After a while, I felt Korin carefully slipping the sleeping bag off my head. He leaned over me and whispered in my ear:

"You will suffocate to death. It's just a storm, it will pass in a few minutes."

"Give me a break," I snapped.

At first reflex I wanted to stick my elbow in his stomach, but I was disarmed by the soothing tenderness of his voice. If he wanted, he could be really loved.

"I was terrible again," he whispered apologetically.

I couldn't answer because there was a terrible bang

outside the window. I screamed and jumped in fear, and my heart started beating harder. The lightning must have hit somewhere really close. Unexpectedly, Korin embraced me and pulled me to his torso. I froze. I didn't want to frighten him, I didn't want him to leave. But he wasn't going anywhere. With a soothing gesture, he stroked my forehead, brushed individual strands from it and whispered soothingly in my ear:

"Don't be afraid... The force field perfectly protects against storms.

"I'm not afraid anymore," I said softly.

This was not entirely true. I was still scared, but it wasn't going to storm anymore. I was afraid that everything that is happening now is just a beautiful dream, and I did not want to wake up.

"Will you lie with me until the storm stops?" I asked shyly.

"I will lie down until you fall asleep," he promised.

He drove away my fears for some time. I relished the warmth of his body, his breath in my hair, the subtle touch of his fingers on my temple, I didn't have the courage to count on anything more. His closeness and awareness that he cared for me was enough.

"Close your eyes and try to sleep," he whispered gently. I barely stifled a laugh. Fall asleep? Now? When he hugs me? When he presses the bare torso against my back? Does he not realize that it is simply impossible? He stroked my head all the time. With a monotonous thumb motion, he caressed my forehead, skin on my cheek, and traced the shape of my ear. I bit my lower lip so as not to moan with pleasure. If he stopped now, I would feel physical pain.

Soon, something in this innocent caress changed, it ceased to be so innocent. His touch became more and more intense, even possessive. And finally... Korin kissed me. I wasn't sure he did it fully consciously. However, he did and did not interrupt, he continued to do so. His warm, shaky excitement lips wandered first on my temple to caress the delicate skin behind my ear. I held my breath as if it would help me stop time. I rolled over slowly on my back and tilted my head back, exposing my neck. Korin moved his lips into the hollow between his collarbones, subtly nipping skin with his lips. He moved his moist, warm lips up and down. Eagerly and more and more greedily.

I threw my arms around his neck, touched his thick, dark hair with my fingers, parting them tenderly. Our bodies were shaking more and more. I was gasping for breath. I put my hands on his neck. I massaged his arms and muscular back, still couldn't believe it was happening. Meanwhile, I was with Korin here and now, and it only mattered.

Wild lust overwhelmed us, and it was impossible to control it. Korin pulled my shirt up with a trembling hand. I felt his hand gently embrace my breast. He moved his lips over it. Carefully, the tip of the tongue began to outline the nipple. I felt a sudden spasm in my lower abdomen, and a muffled scream escaped my throat. Korin froze. My scream awakened consciousness in him. Restored to reality.

He looked at me. His face was full of terror with an admixture of fear and panic.

"I'm sorry... I got carried away..." he whispered, confused. "I shouldn't... I don't understand this... When you're close... Emily... I don't understand why..."

He jumped back, standing against the opposite wall, far away from me. I sat down slightly stunned. I felt dizzy and buzzing in my ears, my thoughts struggled to find my way into the brain. I didn't really realize what had happened and why he stopped so suddenly. I looked in his direction. He stood motionless against the wall, head bowed, hands curled into fists. Every now and then he stretched his fingers and after a while tightened them again. Finally, he looked up. He easily read the silent question from my face: why?

"I'm sorry..." he said in a barely audible whisper.

"Is this a bad joke?" I felt rage rising inside me. "I'm sorry?! Is this your favorite word? I'm sorry?! You're just pathetic! You tease me and then apologize, you piss me off with stupid texts and apologize again, ignite my senses so that I'm wet inside and just apologize?! You're crazy! I can't keep up with your mood changes. I do not understand what you mean?!" I said in a single breath, and fell silent, I ran out of air.

"I don't know what I mean, either," he admitted quietly.

He put a hand to his forehead, fingers tightly clenched on his hair, as if he suddenly wanted to rip all of them. His eyes burned with an unhealthy glow. I noticed that he puts a lot of effort into what he says. He was not used to talking about feelings, after all, feelings in his world did not exist.

"All I know is that my body responds to you, and it shouldn't," he finally managed.

I couldn't believe he said it out loud. I was

subconsciously waiting for this. But my joy did not last too long. It went out before it fully reached my consciousness. Because that wasn't all he had to say. And if the words could have spikes, then the ones he spoke now definitely had them. They hurt painfully, deeply, seemingly leaving no traces.

"I don't understand it," he continued. "You are neither particularly clever nor a beauty."

He has gone overwhelmed, at the sound of these words I was furious. I'm not very smart! I am not a beauty! These sentences echoed off the inside of my head. Awakened and brutally trampled hopes, disappointment, regret... All this made me turn off thinking. All I was feeling now was various emotions. I immediately rose to my feet. He looked at me in horror.

"I'm not particularly smart?! I am not a beauty!" I didn't even scream, I just gave up, and my rage seemed to have no limits.

If he thought that after a short burst it would pass, he was wrong. It was just the beginning.

"You dirty bastard, why are you doing this, why are you playing with me, why are you playing on my feelings?!"

I bent my shoes. Without hesitation, I threw one at him as hard as I could. He dodged. The shoe flew a few centimeters from his head and hit the wall with a deafening thump. Not thinking much, I swung to the other. This time he caught it with a swift move and threw it back. I was even more angry.

"Are you happy now?! Did you want that? Do you like me mad? Or maybe it excites you? I hate you!"

Yelling, I looked around the room nervously for something else I could throw and blow his nose. My eyes fell on the bookcase. Korin, however, was faster. Taking advantage of the fact that now I had nothing to bomb him with, he jumped at me and put his arms around me tightly. His hands wrapped around me so tightly that I couldn't move.

"Let me go, you bastard," I panted, trying to free myself.

Nothing of that. He was holding it tightly and he wasn't going to let go, but I wasn't thinking about giving up. After a long struggle I managed to free my hands. I gripped his arms firmly, just above the elbows, digging my nails into his orange skin with all my strength. He hissed in pain but didn't let go. He just pulled me closer to my chest and pressed my cheek against my head. I felt a warm breath in my hair and words that he tried to calm me down:

"Shhh... Calmly..."

I was gradually losing strength. I gave up. He sensed that anger was slowly leaving me. The more I calmed down, the more I loosened my grip. I stood motionless in his arms and I could stand like that forever. I relaxed, I took my fingers off his shoulders, and only now other stimuli came to me. I felt strange warmth under my fingers. I looked at my hands. A sticky red liquid flowed out from under the nails. Blood. His blood. It sobered me up and let me restrain my emotions completely. Now I was only ashamed.

I looked at Korin with remorse.

"Sorry," I groaned.

"Don't worry, it's my fault. Anyway... I deserved it."

"Undoubtedly," I admitted.

He grabbed my hand and pulled me toward a large plush chair in the corner.

"Sit down. I think we should clarify a few things. With conversation." He noted. "We don't need more blood."

Without a word, I settled into a chair. He stood in front of me. I felt a little uncomfortable when he towered above me.

"I acted like the last idiot today," he began. "I'm really sorry. This should not happen, but... when you're around, I don't know what's happening to me, I just don't think. It is getting harder and harder to control myself," he added quietly.

"Maybe I don't want you to control yourself," I said even more quietly.

He knelt, took my hands in his hands and gave me a questioning look.

"But you were angry."

Christ, he doesn't know anything.

"I wasn't mad at what you did, but what you said later. That's a big difference."

He frowned. I had the impression that it was only now that Korin got to what the whole row was about. The sadness that had previously appeared on his face replaced honest astonishment. I didn't wait for him to snap out of it. I had to act if I wanted to get something. I gathered the last courage in myself. Now or never.

"Korin, that's what we should talk about. You keep saying that something is happening to you in my presence, you are behaving strangely towards me. I think it's time you explained it to me."

"You're right. I will try, although I don't understand much of it."

He took a deep breath.

"I know one thing for sure and I have already told you this, I feel a physical attraction for you. I have less and less control over the sexual needs of my body and I'm afraid that in the end... you know..."

"I know," I said, taking advantage of the moment of hesitation. "And I want it."

"You want it?" He repeated incredulously. "Emily, this is not a good topic for jokes."

"Korin, I'm not kidding. I want this. For a long time. Because..." I swallowed loudly, "you are also attracting me, and probably in the same way as I attract you."

"Don't even say that." He squeezed my hands tighter. "Nothing good will come of it. Anyway... I just can't..."

"Why? Religion forbids you?" I snorted, and Korin smiled crookedly.

"Something like that," he muttered.

"A little clearly, Korin. You know that I AM NOT ESPECIALLY SMART. Still do not understand."

"Well... for centuries, to strengthen our species, we have been mating genetically."

"I know that," I said.

"You know?" He studied me carefully, concealing his surprise. "Well, since you know, so you probably know the concept: a genetic partner."

"I've heard about that too," I said impatiently. "I have also heard about the fact that your hmm... girl from the assignment will come here in half a year.

That's not what you were supposed to explain to me. I would like to know how you feel about me? Can you name it at all?"

He looked at me in silence for a moment. He wondered. However, I couldn't tell if he was thinking about how he felt or how to put in words what he wanted to say to me. I waited patiently for everything to sort out. Finally, he sighed in resignation."

"I can't... I can't name it or understand it." He suddenly got up from his knees and began circling the room nervously. "At first everything was so simple. I liked to spend time in your company, I liked to tease you, I was amused by your reactions. Sometimes they were funny. And it would still be like that, but then at the fountain... I still don't know what happened to me. When I saw you wet, slightly scared, I suddenly felt like I want to kiss you and I don't know if I would stop there. I barely resisted not to do it. This happened for the first time. I thought it was a one-time experience, but it got worse day by day. What happened today is a consequence of the tension that has been growing within me for several days. I shouldn't be in your company, I shouldn't agree to let us stay alone."

He stopped in front of the chair and stared at me seriously, he continued:

"We can't be friends, it will end badly for us. I will move to Harlan for half a year, there is a school there and research is underway. I think parents will not object."

"What are you going to tell them? Mom, Dad, I want to have sex with an Earth woman, so I have to move?" I asked ironically.

"Well... actually," he said a little uncertainly.

"Are you crazy?! Do you really want to tell your parents the true?!"

"What am I supposed to tell them? After all, the Arisyans don't lie, though - why would they!" He answered honestly surprised by my question.

I was about to say that there are those Arisyans who lie or at least don't tell the whole truth, but I bit my tongue in time. I didn't want Kori to be in trouble because of my indiscretion.

Although the situation seemed hopeless, I made a desperate attempt to fight for him. Although maybe not so much about him as about half a year with him. I didn't count on anything else.

"You don't have to leave. There is another solution," I said, blushing at the thought of the proposal that will soon fall from my lips.

"Other solution?" He asked, raising his eyebrows.

"I agree... for sex... without obligations," I finally choked.

Korin froze, staring only at me, and his face didn't express any feelings for a moment, as if he didn't understand a word of what he had just heard. The sense of my speech came to him with considerable delay, evoking open objection.

"Girl, you must be crazy! You don't know what you are saying. I can't use you just because I have to satisfy my desires. This is at odds with the idea in which I was brought up."

"What idea again?!"

"First of all, do not hurt anyone and respect the feelings of others."

"Very noble," I said with a mockery. "Only you supposedly don't have feelings."

"But you do," he said sadly. "I can't play with your feelings for my own benefit. You don't even know how embarrassed I am today. I behaved like a primitive, instinctual male. There is no excuse for me. What you just proposed would be a good solution if you were an Arisyan woman. The Arisyans do very well without love, but the Earthlings, unfortunately, don't. You fall in love too easily, often without so-called reciprocity, and then simple things can be extremely complicated. I'm afraid you won't stop at just sex.

"Are you suggesting I fall in love with you?" I asked with fake irony. "Don't flatter yourself, you're not a special one."

"I know I'm not, but apparently love is blind," he retorted.

"Not so much," I murmured. Slowly, this conversation started to piss me off. Such a slide on the topic and no declarations. "So, how will it end up with us?"

"Emily, this can only end in a catastrophe," he said gently. "In less than six months I will get married to my life partner. You know that I will choose her no matter what. This is called a perfect fit. This is the phenomenon of genetics. We have been using this method of partner selection for over three hundred years and believe me, there is no better one."

"Sure. I completely forgot that you found a pattern for the functioning of the universe," I said, pouting lips contemptuously. "Think about it anyway. Consider all the pros and cons. You don't have to make decisions

today. I just want you to know that I won't go with anything. I'll just leave before she arrives. I promise. You see... my body also has its needs and is increasingly demanding that they be met. I don't know anything about it, but it's probably nothing bad, just a natural process of puberty. We can try to help ourselves without expecting anything in return."

Korin stepped closer and sat on the heavily worn back of the chair.

"I promise I'll think about this... hmm... offer," he sighed heavily. "However, not now. It's the middle of the night. I think it's time to go to sleep. Hop in the sleeping bag."

He pushed me gently out of the chair. After a while I was lying on my sleeping pad, wondering if Korin would lie down next to me. He apparently had other plans. He leaned back in chair and closed his eyelids.

"Aren't you going to lay down?" I asked.

"No, I will take a nap here."

I didn't push. I closed my eyes, but I knew I couldn't sleep so easily. Before, the storm disturbed me, now the silence was heavy, broken only by our silent breaths. However, I had to be exhausted today because I soon fell into a shallow, broken dream. It was only in the morning that I dozed off for good. When I woke up, Korin, fully dressed, was sitting thoughtfully in the chair. I looked at his tired face, he also didn't have a good night. Or was he not sleeping at all? In any case, he looked like that.

"Hi!" I said yawning. "What time is it?"

"A few minutes past eleven."

I slowly got up from the pallet. Only now I looked

at him more closely. On his arms I saw marks of my nails and a stream of blood clotting. Why the hell didn't he wash it away?! It darted my eyes now, and a wave of remorse flooded over me. I got up quickly and approached him. I gently touched the bloody arms. He shuddered.

"Come on, you have to wash it."

He shook my hand violently and jumped up in confusion.

"Leave it, I'll do it myself," he said brusquely.

I backed away frightened. He has never been so unpleasant to me. His attitude scared me. He took a sterile gauze from his bag, walked over to the sink, and washed his arms in silence.

"I didn't want to hit them so hard. Excuse me."

"You have nothing to apologize for, it's a hell of my own making," he replied wearily.

For the first time I saw a Korin who was neither self-confident, carefree, or cheerful... And suddenly I realized why he was like that. At night he decided, perhaps the most difficult in his life. It was only a matter of time before I would hear "no" to my proposal.

"They should be back an hour ago," he said, looking anxiously at the window.

"They'll probably be here soon," I said calmly.

I didn't want to explain to him that it was normal after a hot night. No wonder Kori and Tom are late. But when they did not appear after another hour, I also began to feel anxiety.

"Can't you call them?" I asked.

"Telephones only work in cities, they are useless in the field. We have to drive towards that base, maybe I will make contact using the bracelet."

"Let's go then, I'm worried too. How far it is?"

"Not so far. About thirty kilometers to the southwest."

We packed extremely efficiently and quickly. After less than a quarter of an hour we were already sitting in the car on the way to the second base. Korin seemed restless. He drove at a much faster speed than the bumpy asphalt road allowed. The car was bouncing on the rough terrain every now and then and it cost me a lot of effort to stay on the seat. Fortunately, driving conditions were not conducive to conversation, so such a trip also had its good sides. At one-point Korin unexpectedly turned left and I was thrown at the door. Now we were driving at a dizzying side road. Big green weeds lay on the bonnet, rustling at the side windows. Finally, he stopped the car in the midst of the highest weed.

"Are you crazy?! What are you doing?" I choked out angrily, massaging my bruised arm.

"Kori and Tom are in trouble," he said shortly.

"How do you know?"

He moved the bracelet under my nose. One of the diodes pulsed intensely red light.

"They sent an emergency call," he explained, getting out of the car hastily.

He paled. I freed myself from the belt, jumped outside, and broke through the weed wet night rain to the back of the car. Korin fumbled fiercely in the trunk. When I approached, he handed me a bundle.

"Change into it. It protects well against moisture

and insects."

Without a word, I began to pull on a loose suit made of soft, thin khaki fabric. Korin put on a similar one, then reached into the trunk for two belts. Each of them had a holster with what looked like a pistol. He efficiently girded one and handed me the other. I hesitantly picked it up and shuddered.

"Will I have to kill someone?" I asked in a broken voice.

"It's an infra-paralyzer, to kill with it you have to try very hard. You would have to hit someone in the head with it," he explained. "I'll show you how it works. Just in case. You'll probably never use it."

He took a gun from my holster. It looked like a big gun. I took a step back instinctively.

"In infra-paralyzers, projectiles are sound waves of varying intensity and are not used to kill, but to temporarily stun an opponent. Look, there are two knobs. Red sets the radius of destruction. You can set the range from one to ten meters. Green, on the other hand, defines firepower. Time was assumed as the unit, i.e. how long the victim was to be unconscious. This model can be disposed of for a maximum of five hours."

"And how many hours did you deprive me of consciousness?"

"I needed three or so more to get you home. Do you remember anything about this?"

"Not really. The last thing I remembered was a strange whiz. And if it wasn't for the fear that accompanied me, it wouldn't be an unpleasant experience."

"You see that this is an extremely Earthlingtarian weapon. One more remark. All obstacles weaken the effects of infra-paralyzers, so it's best to use them with your opponent in sight."

"Alright, I understand."

"We must to go," he interrupted the conversation as soon as he noticed that I had overcome my moral resistance before using the infra-paralyzer.

He tossed me an empty backpack.

"Pack the water, first aid kit and several packs of biscuits. I need to check something before we leave."

While I was packing my backpack, Korin pushed back the lid at the bottom of the trunk. There was some complicated apparatus in the cache."

"What is it?" I asked surprised at this view.

"Satellite locator. The bracelets are sending a radio signal, I will try to track Kori and Tom via satellite," he explained, while entering some data.

Putting things into the backpack, I glanced at him with the corner of my eye.

"I don't understand," he muttered under his breath, frowning. "They're still at the base. Let's check thermo location."

"What's up?" I asked impatiently.

"There are four people in the base now," he said thoughtfully.

He closed the trunk, threw his backpack over his shoulder, and took my hand.

"We're going, time is pressing. I will explain to you along the way."

We started walking quickly. I looked at Korin with amazement and admiration. I found him out again. How

I was wrong to consider him weak and helpless before. Maybe Korin was a type of highbrow, but now he showed his other face. In a crisis he turned out to be a real man. He didn't lose his head. He didn't panic. He just acted. In his behavior, in his movements there were no unnecessary gestures, he made decisions almost automatically. He knew exactly what to do in what order. It made me feel no fear, though I should. I believed that Korin could handle everything.

CHAPTER XI

Waiting for danger is worse
than the moment when it falls on man.
ALFRED HITCHCOCK

Our love games have fallen into the background. It is true that we were holding hands, heading to the second base, but it had a completely different character. Now we were more like comrades-in-arms than like a boy and a girl. Korin had a task to do and consistently implemented it. Now, nothing could distract him. I was no longer in the amorous mood too. We were in danger and that was the most important thing for now.

"What do you think what could have happened?" I asked as we went for a while.

"I'm not sure," he said, helping me over the fallen, slippery trunk. "I have two hypotheses. First, that they found two people, maybe injured, and are waiting for our help. On the other hand, it doesn't stop them from joining us. Unless... some unforeseen circumstances have occurred. Maybe they had a car crash? The second possibility that they fell into the hands of rebels. However, there something does not suit me. First, the rebels never ventured south of our cities.

Secondly, without entering the appropriate code, no stranger would be able to cross the force field or get to the base."

I thought about what I had just heard. I found no weak points in these two theories. Maybe I would come up with a third option about a pair of lovers for whom both time and the universe ceased to exist, were it not for the presence of two additional people in the base. This completely excluded my version, so I preferred to keep it to myself. I felt a pang of anxiety in my chest and sped up involuntarily, and Korin with me.

"Both versions make sense," I finally said. "Which one seems more likely to you?"

"I don't want to worry you, but rather the second one. But only because I prefer to assume a worse option," he added quickly, which did not calm me down, quite the opposite.

"So, you think they're rebels?" I asked quietly, slowing down a bit. "Who are those? Anyone command them?"

"General's people," he snorted contemptuously. "His real name is John Smith, a great zero with dictatorial tendencies. Seemingly nice, charming, intelligent and trustworthy, in fact..." he hesitated for a moment, as if looking for the right words. "Emily, you wouldn't want to meet him. He is a bad man. Not just bad, but really bad, incarnate evil. In addition, the guy has a supernatural ability to manipulate others. In the earthly dictionary there is a term for sociopath or psychopath like him, there is no big difference."

For the first time I heard Korin talk about someone like that. As if with hatred, but not really. Unfortunately, I couldn't name it better. It wasn't just a description of the character, there was something more. Something that wasn't positive feelings.

"Hmm... you know a lot about him, I wonder how."

"He was one of us," he said bitterly."

"Was he an Arisyan who turned to the dark side?" The first thought that came to my mind, even though it was spoken aloud, sounded absurd."

"No. He was... he is an Earthling."

"What did he do or what did you do to become enemies?"

"We trusted him. It was our biggest mistake," he replied, wincing. "Paradoxically, this story has taught us a lot. We've become more careful. It was then that we introduced numerous safeguards, including a force field. And we choose people more carefully."

"How do you know that the General doesn't have his spies in Exira? It could be me or my mother, we came from nowhere."

"We checked you," he said. "Medical mind recorder, we're checking everyone," he said, seeing my face.

I didn't expect such an answer. It took me a while before I fully understood what that could mean. Indignation began to build up in me.

"Have you read my thoughts?! When?"

"In the hospital."

"You also listened to my thoughts?!" I didn't like the surveillance, which Korin immediately noticed. He knew me and my violent reactions more and more.

"Not me, just my father and Sofie. They said you were clean."

"Clean?" I raised an eyebrow threateningly.

"I mean, no bad intentions."

"Korin, it's sick... It's a breach of privacy."

"After what happened two years ago, we had no choice." His eyes dimmed, and a strange grimace appeared on his face. "Don't make me talk about it today. This is a difficult topic for me."

"You don't have to today..." I replied a little uncertainly.

I didn't push. I noticed that it was painful to talk about it for some reason. On the other hand, I was eager to see why Arisyans had enemies. And how is this even possible?!

"Someday you will learn this story, I promise, but maybe in more favorable circumstances."

"I took yours word for it." A thought did not leave me alone. "Korin, why did Sofie tell me to talk about herself then? She should read everything in my mind."

"It's also part of the test. She checked if you were honest with her," unexpectedly, he lowered his voice to a whisper. "Shhh... We're getting closer to the base."

We both fell silent. We took a few more steps and suddenly Korin dived into the bushes nearby, pulling me with him."

"What's up?" I asked in a whisper.

"The force field is not working. It was probably damaged by yesterday's storm, but it's better to be careful.

"And what now?"

"Nothing." He shrugged. "It doesn't change our situation anyway. We need to get closer to take a look at the hut. Can you crawl for several dozen meters?"

"Sure."

Korin moved first, and I followed him, trying to imitate his every move. At first, I was creeping awkwardly. The worst part was that we had to be careful not to make noise. In this forest, every murmur,

every rustle, even a small crackle was like beating an alarm. It wasn't until that moment that I realized how much danger we were in. My heart, driven by fear, began to pound so wildly that I heard its beats in my ears. I was surprised that Korin couldn't hear it. But he, despite everything, moving forward. I tried to keep up with him. After a few minutes gliding with the nose to the ground through the thickets he stopped. I crawled up to him. We lay in the wet grass, touching each other, and only one bush separated us from the hut in the middle of a large clearing. Korin nudged me lightly in the shoulder and pointed out that I have to prepare the infra-paralyzer. He was already ready.

When I pulled the gun from the holster, he gently opened the leaves to look more closely at the wooden hut. Hut... well, that's too much said, rather a large shed. Tom's jeep stood to the right of it, and two black motorcycles right next to it. We did not manage to look closely, because suddenly the front door opened with a bang. A heavy stood there with a shaved head that looked like he was attached directly to the torso - the guy had practically no neck. I suppressed a moan, because the worse scenario was just working out - rebels. We clung to the ground, forgot to breathe in fear.

"Where are you going, Dick?" A surly, hoarse voice came from inside the building."

"I'm going to pee," said Dick, spitting loudly.

There was a sweat on my forehead. I was afraid he would notice us soon. I was afraid that he would follow the need exactly in the bushes in which we hid. I closed my eyelids tightly. I was sure that it was over for us. After a while I felt Korin squeeze my hand and reassure

me with my thumb on the back of my hand. I opened my eyes and looked at him.

"He's behind the shed," I read his silent whisper from his lips.

After a few minutes, the guy returned to the cottage. He didn't close the door behind him, so we could listen to Dick and his companion's conversation.

"We're rolling up from here, Sam," Dick ordered. "Probably soon someone will start looking for them."

"Wait," Sam growled. "We can have some fun before boss takes them."

"Have fun." Dick snickered. "You have a brain. All in all... this orange bitch has pretty good tits."

"Get your hands off her, bastard!" I recognized Tom's angry voice.

We heard a loud rumor, sounds of struggle and a muffled blow, after which someone fell on the floor with a groan. And when Kori's sobbing reached my ears, I couldn't stand it. I forgot my fear, I had only one thought in my mind - save my friends.

"Not yet," Korin hissed, forcefully holding me in place.

Why not now?! So when? When they will be dead? What is this moron waiting for? Or maybe he is afraid? I looked at his face. It expressed maximum concentration, but not fear. I finally understood. He was waiting for the right moment, and his analytical mind apparently decided that he had not yet come.

"Your lover has a weak head," said Dick, turning to Kori. He laughed contemptuously. "Come on, babe, we'll have a little orgy."

"Wait a moment... Don't forget that it was my

idea," Sam shouted angrily. My turn first."

"You have to kidding me, if I did not decode this fucking field, you could only dream of it."

"Okay, okay..." Sam said in a conciliatory tone. "Do you have a quarter dollar, Dick?"

"What?" The other one was surprised.

"Twenty-five cents. We toss a coin. Let fate decide."

I tightened my arm tightly on my weapon, glancing at Korin again. He still didn't respond. I could not believe that. Two disgusting types are throwing a coin about who is the first to rape his sister and he does nothing. As if he didn't care, as if she were a completely stranger. I began to doubt who the bigger monster is - are those two inside or Korin? I elbowed him angrily. He didn't even look at me. He was still staring at the door with a stony expression on his face.

"Ha! I said I will be the first one," Sam laughed. "Look and learn."

"Just be quick," Dick growled. "I don't want to cum before you finish."

"Don't kick, bitch," Sam croaked with effort.

I didn't have to see this to know that the guy was forcibly trying to nail the girl down to the ground. I was hoping Korin knew that too. I was about to punch him with an infra-paralyzer to remind him that his sister is in the shed and it might be too late to change anything in a moment, but I didn't make it. This time he reacted correctly. He sprang up quickly.

"Stay here," he whispered.

In a few leaps he covered the distance separating him from the building and through the open door he fell inside.

The whole action took place so quickly that before I realized the situation, before I could react in any way, it was all over. The silence that now fell was preceded only by the sounds of bodies sliding to the wooden floor. I stood in front of the entrance, dumbfounded, legs shaking. I couldn't move or think, or even swallow. I stayed in this strange stillness until Korin exclaimed:

"Emily, come here, help me!"

I broke free from stupor and entered the hut on stiff legs. Korin was just shaking off the body of a bearded man lying on the floor at Kori. He gently touched the girl's neck, checking her pulse.

"She'll be fine," he said to calm me down. "Worse with Tom. Falling, he hit his head."

I looked in the direction he was looking. To the right of the door, Tom was on the side of the room in the corner. A thin trickle of blood dripped from his temple.

"What should I do?" I asked in a shaky voice.

"Wash the wound and give him a cold compress. It should be enough."

I put down my weapon, took a first-aid kit, a small towel and a bottle of water from my backpack. At that time Korin approached Tom and efficiently cut the ties on his legs and wrists. He turned him slowly on his back and carefully fingered his head.

"It's not serious," he assured, and returned to Kori to free her.

I washed Tom's face with blood. Fortunately, the wound just above the eyebrow turned out to be

superficial. A simple dressing bandage was enough to dress it. Finally, I put a wet towel on his forehead. Meanwhile, Korin was about to complete his sister's inspection.

"Some bruises, but all bones are unbroken," he said with relief.

"How long will they be unconscious?" I asked.

"About five hours."

"What?" I groaned in horror. "We will wait that long before we get back?"

"We won't wait. It is not known how many of these types are still around, so I would prefer not to risk. We should be at home as soon as possible. It is best that we leave immediately."

"What about your car? Will it stay in those thickets?"

"You will drive it," he said as if it were obvious.

"Are you crazy?!" I blurted out. "I can't do it. You can come back for it another time, no one will find it in this herb."

"I can't, we won't fit."

"There are four seats in Tom's jeep," my voice was more and more uncertain.

"We must take these two, too." He pointed at the rebels.

"Are you crazy? Should I go with them in one car?"

"Just a little. Later I will go with them and you will take Kori and Tom.

"That has to be a bad joke," I snorted. "Why should we drag them with us? Do you want to convert them?"

"I don't think we can," he murmured grimly. "I want to question them. I have a feeling that they are not here by accident. In addition, they broke the code for the force field and I'm afraid that this was also not the coincidence."

I capitulated, he was right. It was necessary to know what they were doing here and why, for the good of all of us.

Although Korin drove a Tom jeep to the door, it cost us a lot effort to stuff everyone in the car. We also hid both motors in the shed so that they would not be visible. It wasn't until we were finished that tiredness and nervousness came to light, and it was so bad that I felt sick.

"Get in, Em," Korin said."

"Wait a minute," I grunted incomprehensibly and ran behind the shed to vomit.

Emesis made me feel weak. Droplets of cold sweat appeared on my forehead. I had to lean my arm against the wooden wall of the hut, so as not to fall. I was shaking, and tears were flowing from my eyes. I was just feeling bad. When I tried to calm my stomach somehow, I felt Korin's warm hand on my neck.

"Go away, leave me..." I choked, sobbing.

I tried to push him away. I didn't want him to watch me in this condition, but he didn't pay the slightest attention to my pathetic protest.

"It's all over," he spoke gently, continuing to massage my neck and back between my shoulder blades. "You were very brave, really."

Under the influence of his soothing touch, I slowly recovered. I could still feel the unpleasant, acid taste of vomit on my tongue. Korin handed me a bottle of water. I rinsed my mouth several times, rinsed my face roughly, and took a few deep breaths. At last the blood began to circulate again in my veins.

"Your blushes are coming back," Korin said. "Can we go now? You can do it?"

I nodded to say yes. I didn't have the strength to answer him. I squeezed into the front seat between the unconscious Kori and Korin. The girl's head fell limp on my shoulder. I touched her cheek with my hand. Somehow, I couldn't get rid of the feeling that she wasn't breathing, but it was only fear that gave me such thoughts. Fear that did not leave me, even when we went on an empty asphalt road. It was lurking everywhere. In every shade and every corner. I moved my eyes nervously from one side to the other, looking for threats.

Korin, without taking his eyes from the road, found my hand, entwined his fingers in mine and shook it firmly. He wanted to calm me down somehow. He made it. I looked at his face. He noticed from the corner of his eye that I was looking at him, because he glanced at me, smiling warmly. The touch of his hand and that smile contained everything I needed now. All fear, uncertainty and terror evaporated, as if I was never afraid of anything. They were replaced by strength and courage and steadfast faith that I could manage, that I could, that I would drive a car and bring my friends home.

I really wanted to show him that I am, and I can be brave. Without hesitation I was left alone in the jeep when we got to the place where we left the car and Korin went to bring it off the side road. I didn't even blink when Kori and Tom had to be moved to the

second car. I started the engine without major problems and followed Korin.

When we arrived in the city, it was almost evening. I noticed quite a stir in front of the force field. We were expected. Apparently Korin started special procedures related to crossing the field. He had to do it, we finally carried an extra load. Three cars stood on each side of the road, and a row of people armed with infra-paralyzers stood in front of them. I should be scared because they looked really menacing, but all I felt was inexpressible relief.

A tall dark-haired man stepped out of the line, stood in the middle of the asphalt and raised his left hand. He was holding a gun in the right. Korin stopped a meter in front of him, I also pushed the brake.

"Hi, Will," he said in greeting.

"Hey. Did you somehow bring any survivors back?"

"Not exactly... they are rebels this time."

"Holy shit," Will hissed. "What a mess."

He walked around the car and looked in through the rear window.

"Well, well." He whistled under his breath. "Goody-goody. How much time do they have to wake up?"

"I think two hours," Korin replied matter-of-factly.

Brunet pulled his forehead from the window of the jeep. He became interested in the second vehicle now.

"Do you have any rebels there?" He asked, pointing towards me.

"No, there are only these two. Emily drives Kori and Tom, they are also unconscious."

There was a surprise on Will's face. He scratched his head with his free hand.

"It doesn't look so good," he said. "I think you've got yourself into a pretty big trouble."

"Yeah, I think so," Korin said grimly. "And I think it won't stop there."

In that second, Will understood a lot more than Korin wanted to tell him. He turned on his heel and walked quickly to his companions. I heard his voice give brief commands to them. After a while everyone jumped into the cars parked on the side of the road, three of them immediately headed towards the center. Will nodded to follow them. The convoy closed the remaining vehicles. It was only this sudden rush that made me realize that it was not a typical situation, that bringing unconscious rebels to the base is not on the agenda, that meeting them in the south is also not normal, and finally that we are not completely safe in the city.

I stopped automatically when the red stop lights of the vehicle ahead flashed. We just got to the hospital.

There was a lot of confusion. There were a lot of people in hospital coats. Someone was shouting, someone else opened the door, some people pulled Kori and then Tom out of the car. Everything came to me as if through a fog, as if a translucent curtain separated me from the world. I could not formulate any logical thought. Only single stimuli came to me. I felt someone's delicate hands release me from the belt, familiar breath wrapped my face and after a moment I touched the hard ground with my feet. Legs buckled under me, they were like cotton wool, but Korin's strong arms wrapped around my waist. I cuddled up into his chest and began to sob.

"You did great," he whispered, hugging me tightly. "I didn't think you would be such an excellent driver after one ride."

"I had a good teacher," I smiled through my tears.

"The fact, this is undoubtedly my merit."

He waited until I stopped whipping.

"Can you stand alone?"

"Yes, I guess," I confirmed.

He released me from his arms. Too fast. I staggered, barely keeping my balance. This time he didn't try to support me.

"You seem to be a little better now," he said, eyeing me for a moment. "Let's go then. I need to talk to my father," he added indifferently, and as he passed me he disappeared behind the hospital door.

I was hot under the collar. I clenched my fists and followed him. I had to run to catch up with him. He seemed as if he didn't care if I follow him or not. Again, his Arisyan self-control and sense of duty took over.

Halfway down the corridor we came across Almar. He pulled a cell phone out of pocket.

"Emily, I'll let your mother know you're here. She will take you home."

I didn't have to look in the mirror to know I looked miserable. I was still wearing overalls, which was now wet and muddy, my hair was full of weed, and cheeks covered with a crust of dried mud. Korin looked similar, so at least for that reason I didn't feel like a jerk. I could imagine how my mother would react to

my sight and I wanted to spare her that.

"I don't think that's the best idea, doctor. I look like something the cat dragged in. It is better if my mother does not see me in this state. She would still think that I was involved in some warfare, though... that won't be a big mistake. Actually, we were not going to come back until tomorrow, so..."

It seemed to me that only now Almar really looked at us. He looked from me to Korin and back again.

"Yeah, yeah," he finally said absently. "You don't look so good. You can, Emily, spend the night in the hospital."

"You too," he said to his son. He looked at his watch. "Come to my office in an hour. You will tell me in detail what happened. First you have to pull yourself together. I'll send Doris in a moment. She will take care of you."

He turned and walked away toward the room where Kori and Tom were brought."

"Doris..." I moaned weakly. I regretted my decision to stay in the hospital. Korin, seeing my face, smiled and rolled his eyes.

"Don't overdo it anymore, Em. Doris is not so scary. And compared to the types we brought, she is a real angel."

"I do not know..."

As if on cue, the massive figure of Doris loomed at the end of the corridor. She was moving towards us with certainty and we heard her complaining from afar.

"It's unheard of? A little bit more and they will convert this hospital into a hotel."

She came to us.

"Good morning, Doris," Korin bowed exaggeratedly.

"I wouldn't say good," she grumbled. "Don't even count on getting separate rooms. You have to settle in one, I'm not going to clean your both mess."

"Maybe a shared bed?" Korin suggested with an innocent expression. "It's always less cleaning..."

She glared at him. I also looked at him menacingly. Why did he say that? Who did he really want to annoy? Me or Doris? Or maybe he accidentally said it by accident?

"It's a hospital, not a brothel," Doris closed the subject and finally deigned to notice me.

"You again, Emily," she said, chuffed. "You look even worse than when Korin brought you. Do you always have to be so dirty?"

"Yes, growing dirt is my favorite occupation," I murmured, offended by her stupid and unnecessary attention.

Korin laughed. Doris turned abruptly toward him with her hands on her hips.

"I don't know why you look so happy, you look a little better than her."

Korin straightened up and suppressed a smile, but cheerful lights still played in his purple eyes.

"Doris, take it easy." He gave her a wicked smile. "It's just a little mud."

"A bit of mud." She raised her hands up, but it was obvious that he managed to calm her down somehow. "A bit of mud... End of the world."

"The end of the world has already been," Korin reminded matter-of-factly, "yet the world is not over,

so I do not know what all the hype?"

"Okay, it's okay." She waved her hand, walked over to the nearest glass door and opened it with a strong push. "Jump out of the dirt and in the shower! I have my hands full of work with all this confusion."

Doris went to set up in the corners of others, and we entered a brightly lit, two-person room.

"See, she's not so bad. She just likes order," said Korin, unbuttoning his dirty suit. Underneath, he was almost completely sweaty. The wet material adhered tightly to his torso and arms, emphasizing the shapely muscular outlines. I stood shocked by the scene, mouth open, not fully aware that the object of my sighs was just undressing in front of me. When he pulled off his shirt and threw it rolled to the floor, I felt my stomach clench, the blood in my veins began to circulate faster, and a rapid pulsing appeared in my temples. I had to look quite strange because he was still and he was watching me closely. Black jeans wrapped around his narrow hips. He has never been as disturbingly appealing as he is now. I felt a blush slowly pour over my cheeks. I could only count on it being invisible under the mud layer.

"Something's wrong?" He asked in mock surprise. He knew perfectly well that he   me. Maybe he even did it on purpose.

I swallowed hardly regaining my voice.

"Are you going to strip naked?" I asked directly.

"I didn't know you were shy," he said ironically.

"Now you know."

He bent to untie the shoelaces. He slowly pulled off both shoes and then socks. He removed a white towel from the back of the chair and threw it over his shoulder. He looked into my eyes seriously.

"Did you really think I would take my clothes off?" He asked.

"That's how it looked," I said.

He laughed.

"I had to take off the dirtiest. I'm going to the staff bathroom, it's down the hall. I may come across Doris, and I don't want to piss her off any more," he explained.

Of course, and I made an idiot of myself again.

He walked barefoot to the door and added:

"You'll probably go a little bit in the shower, so call me when you're done."

"How do you know it will take me a long time?"

"I have a sister." He winked at me and disappeared behind the door.

After a while, he opened it again, but only stuck his head.

"I wouldn't mind that you undress next to me," he said with amusement and disappeared back out the door.

"Get lost!" I shouted.

I heard him laugh out loud in the corridor.

He was right that taking a bath would take me some time. I spent over half an hour in the shower. For the first five minutes I tried to unravel the meaning of his last words, but I was so exhausted that I quickly gave it up. I only had the strength to stand still, letting warm water wash away not only dirt, but also fatigue, frustration, anxiety, fear, uncertainty and pain. When I finally turned the tap off, I felt much better. Even my mind was clearer now. And then it dawned on me. Was Korin sending me signals? But did he decide on this six-month relationship? I hurriedly pulled on clean clothes and stepped out into the corridor.

I was surprised by the peace here. The pale blue walls were lit by the dim light of ceiling lights. The corridor looked empty. It took me a moment to see Korin huddled behind a row of empty chairs along the left wall. He was sitting on the floor, knees pulled up to his chin. He was holding a cell phone in his left hand. I walked barefoot to him. He didn't move, I was sure he was asleep.

I sat next to him, gently touching his shoulder.

"Are you sleeping?" I asked in an undertone.

He squeezed my hand and slowly raised his head. There were dark bruises under his eyes.

"I'm awake, although I'm very close. I was waiting for you to finish." He smiled wanly.

"Something happened?" I pointed at the cell phone.

"Ah, that," he said absently, stuffing the phone into his pants pocket. "I called my father to talk to him tomorrow. I can't do it today, I'm tired. Yesterday for the first time in my life I took the night because of you. Until the morning I thought about what you said."

I swallowed hard. I felt uncomfortable. On the one hand, I was afraid of words that might come in a moment, but on the other I wanted to know. Anyway, I wasn't ready to know his decision.

"Let's go to the room, you should get dressed." I ran a hand over his bare shoulders. "You were cold."

He rose from the floor. Every muscle on the tense stomach was clearly outlined. I wonder if this is the result of intense exercise or genetic interference? I have to ask someday if the opportunity arises.

He let me through. We entered the room. Korin closed the door carefully. He didn't turn on the light, but the room was quite light. A lot of light came from the corridor through the glass door. I sat on the bed, meanwhile Korin went to the backpack and pulled out a clean T-shirt. I flexed my fingers nervously as he stoically dressed. He sat across from me on the next bed and focused his eyes on my nervously clenching hands. I immediately hid my hands behind my back, straightening.

"You're nervous," he said, but not in reproach or resentment. He just stated the fact.

"I'm not," I said quickly. I knew after a minute that he didn't believe me.

"I think it'll do us good if we finish yesterday's conversation. If you still want." He added.

No, I do not want to! - I should have shouted, but I just bit my lower lip and remained silent. I felt completely empty inside. Burned. I was waiting for a blow, for the word "no", which in a moment will hit me straight in the heart, stripping me of all illusions. But it not happened. Korin began to speak and his words surprised me.

"It's about these six months... you and me. What would it look like?" He was clearly confused. "How do you imagine it? This, um... relationship."

"How would you like?" I asked quietly.

"I have no idea." He shrugged helplessly. "I don't know what it's like for Earthlings. All I know is that I shouldn't decide. It's irresponsible."

"And you are always responsible and always do the right thing, right? Is this also in your genes?"

"I don't think genes play a role here. I just didn't have to think about such things once. It used to be simpler. Sometimes I feel that this planet has too much influence on us, it changes us."

He got up suddenly, sat down next to me, and brushed my cheek with his mouth. He slowly moved his lips toward my ear.

"I don't understand it, I can't control it, but... I want to touch you, I want to feel your touch on me," he whispered. "I'm not going to fight it for the next six months."

I held my breath, and my heart began to beat loudly, as if some crazy drummer was pounding the drum. I didn't think he would make up his mind. I was sure he made a different decision last night. Why did he change it?

"You didn't decide right away," I noticed. "When did you change your mind?"

He pulled away a little, now he ran his finger over my hand, drawing a complicated pattern on it.

"Today," he said in an undertone. "When I realized that the Earth was governed by other laws than Aris. Everything seemed so simple on my planet. The whole future was like an open book, and life planned out in detail. There I knew what I would be doing in a year, in two years, well... in ten years. Everything was predictable. Here, however, I'm not sure what awaits me tomorrow or even in an hour."

I relaxed when he said that. He seemed to have taken the earthly distance from life. The truth that my

mother had taught me came to him: enjoy the moment as long as it lasts.

"So, you want to say that you decided on this arrangement and you can say that from today we are a couple... at least for some time," I had to make sure.

"I think so," he confirmed. "Only you should enlighten me, which is what earthly couples usually do."

"They spend time together."

"Well, but how?" He inquired.

"They do everything together."

"What do you think everything means? You won't convince me to literature, music and other unnecessary earthly entertainment," he reserved. "I won't even mention the boogie around the fountain."

"Well, but we can learn together, discuss various topics and..." I blushed, "have sex. I think that's enough."

He took my chin in his hand, traced the outline of my mouth with his thumb, and looked at me partly with interest, partly with concern. When he spoke, there was hesitation in his voice:

"Are you sure you want this?"

I nodded my head.

"For sure."

For a split second I thought he would retreat at the last moment. In the meantime, he pulled me to him and kissed my lips for the first time. He just brushed my lips, but it was enough to make my body feel a little shaky. I put my hands in his hair and clung to him firmly. He sighed softly, and the kisses grew stronger.

He hugged me, kissed my hair, temple, neck, while

stroking my neck and back. At first, gently and gently, later intensely and possessively. He whispered my name every now and then. No one has ever said it like him... so tenderly, sensually, with such desire. I was also emotional. Without the slightest embarrassment, I caressed his strong, strained shoulders, slipped my hands under his shirt, stroking his back with subtle movements. Our caresses became stronger and sensations stronger. I have never felt like that, I have never been so emotional. I did not wonder what would happen in six months, the pain of separation will come later. Now we were both trembling with excitement. With a trembling hand, he unbuttoned my pants and slipped his warm hand into them, making circular motions. I had the impression that in a moment I would light a live fire. However, some impulse in my head made me stop it.

"Wait," I said, grabbing his hand abruptly.

He paused.

"Did I do something wrong?" He asked, breathing heavily.

"No, it's okay, it's my fault, I'm sorry," I pulled his hand away from me and huddled up. "It's a bit too fast for me."

He rolled over, covering his face with his hands.

"You're right, I'm sorry."

I moved cautiously and hugged my head to his chest.

"You see, maybe it's stupid, but... my first time... I would like it to be romantic. Not on a hospital bed. I don't know, maybe earlier a candlelit dinner. I would feel better later, you know, when I leave, there will be memories. I wish they were special."

He patted my head gently.

"I don't understand why it should look like this, but we'll do what you think, like you want. After all, we can first get to know our bodies better."

"You are not mad at me?" I asked.

"No. Arisyans rarely get angry." He said calmly. "Do you think we could sleep in one bed today? I will be polite, I swear, I will fall asleep right away."

"And if someone will nail us?" I asked anxiously.

"We'll say you had nightmares last night," he laughed softly at his own wit.

"No one will believe it."

"I would believe it. If you want, I'll tell them."

"You said the Arisyans didn't lie.

"Exactly," he said with satisfaction.

He embraced me and hugged me tenderly, burying my face in my hair. I sighed softly and sank into his arms. Every cell of my body felt its warmth, his smell, his taste... I couldn't understand why I stopped him? That's what I wanted, sex. He also only wanted sex. Meanwhile, I forced him to behave as if he loved me.

"Don't worry, Em," he murmured. "I'll wait until you're ready. It's important that you are close. That's enough, at least for now."

I got the impression that he was reading my mind. I wanted to say thank you, but words got stuck in my throat. None of us spoke anymore. There was no such need. I listened to the regular beating of our hearts. I heard my calm breathing and Korin's quiet breathing, which soon turned into a light snoring. Korin fell asleep, and I've never felt so happy.

CHAPTER XII

Jealousy of spiritual agreement between
two people can be just as violent
like jealousy for physical intimate.
ARTHUR CONAN DOYLE

I felt someone's look at me. The awareness that someone was watching me appeared somewhere inside the mind and was not related to sleep. Growing anxiety told me to open my eyes. It was dusk in the room. It was exactly the time when the night was over, but the day had not yet begun, just before sunrise. A figure was sitting on the next bed and had to sit here for a long time, because it was her persistent look that woke me up. I rubbed my eyelids to get a better look.

"Sofie?" I choked out.

I tried to sit up, but someone's strong hands pulled me back to a prone position. Oh no, I groaned in my thoughts. Korin. Not only that we were lying here together, but also in tender embraces, and the situation certainly could not be regarded as ambiguous. The more that both Korin's hands just stuck to my breasts. What was the official version supposed to be? Nightmares? Good one. If it wasn't for

Sofie's scolding look, I would surely laugh. I could always try to convince her that his hands on my breasts were nothing but a panacea to ward off bad dreams, well-known by the way. Only that besides promiscuity, she could accuse me of mental illness.

"I think you should move to the second bed before someone sees you," she said in an extremely serious tone.

"Sure," I moaned, trying to free myself from the arms wrapping around me, which turned out not so easy. I struggled to pull Korin's hands off my chest, finger by finger. Finally, I was able to put his hands on the quilt. I got up quickly so that he would not embrace me again. I did the right thing, because after a while his arms were where I was a moment ago. This time they went in a vacuum.

"Em..." he murmured, hugging a pillow and holding his face in it.

I glanced at the corner of my eye on the Sofie. I will never forget the look on her face. Astonishment mixed with something else. It is difficult to determine with what. With consternation? In disbelief? Well, Arisyans don't dream or speak in their sleep, and Korin just spoke my name, and not quite simply, but with affection.

"I hope you know what you're getting into?" Her voice softened visibly, now only concern was heard in it.

"Yes, I am aware of that," I said softly.

"And you are not scare that this will not end with nothing serious?" She continued.

"It scares..." I said grimly.

"So why you are doing this? Why are You doing this?" She corrected immediately. "Why does he allow this?!"

"I don't know." I shrugged my shoulders. I was supposed to tell her that I love him, that he wants me?

For what? Will this change anything?

Sofie sighed heavily.

"It's not my business and you are an adult. You can assume I haven't seen anything. Only one request. Try to have more discretion if you want to continue this. I have no idea what the consequences may be."

"Will they burn me at the stake?" I tried to joke.

"Don't tell stupid things, Emily," she said irritably. "It's not medieval. You will certainly be safe, at most they will send Korin home. I don't understand what this boy is guided by. But I know one thing. What apparently connects you is something completely different to him than you. The Arisyans have their own world and want to keep it only for themselves. You must remember that. Therefore, think carefully whether you really want to go on this, because it will not be a story with a happy ending."

"The ending doesn't matter," I whispered so softly that I was surprised she heard.

She shook her head disapprovingly, then shook my arm. I was sure she still didn't understand, but with this small gesture she wanted to comfort me. She stood up, smoothed down her apron, as if she had flapped it from invisible pollen.

"I must finally start my duty," she said calmly, going to the exit. She turned in the door to add:

"If you ever wanted to talk, you can count on me."

"Sofie, thank you," I muttered.

I stretched out on the empty bed, watching the morning light patches on the smooth ceiling. I was still tired, maybe even more than yesterday. It was intensified by the flood of thoughts in my head.

Is Sofie is right?

Should I give up?

I rolled over and leaned on my elbow, looking thoughtfully at Korin. He was still hugging the pillow. At one point he smiled blissfully and murmured my name again. It was enough. One short word "Em" in a dream was enough to dispel any doubts. Sofie was wrong. There is sense to it, even for moments like this. There was quite enough vegetation in my life, ten years is enough, now I just want to live. I prefer to go through the thorns and even slowly, but move forward rather than stand still, waiting for happiness that may never come. There probably is a bit of madness in it, but I have a vague conviction that it's worth it.

I didn't even realize I fell asleep again. In addition, I dreamed that I was not sleeping, which is why I was surprised when I suddenly saw my mother's face above me.

"Emily, honey, are you okay?" She asked, stroking my cheek carefully.

"Mom?" I was surprised. "You're here? How did you know?"

Before she answered, she tilted the blanket back, carefully examining me from head to toe. She calmed down only when, apart from a few scratches on my hands, she found no serious injuries.

"Relax, I'm fine," I assured, unnecessarily, she managed to know it. "Will you finally tell me how you knew I was here?"

"The whole school doesn't say anything else," she said. "Why didn't you call yesterday? I would take you home."

"I didn't mean to worry you." I made an apologetic face.

"Oh, Emily..." She shook her head and looked at me with such reproach that I felt ashamed.

At that moment the door opened. A tall, slim Arisyan woman entered the room. I did not have experience in determining the age of the Arisyan, but for my taste she could be about forty or so several years old.

"Good morning," she said in greeting. "I'm Ariana, Korin's mother."

"Megan Walker." Mom gave her a warm smile.

"And you're probably Emily?" She asked me, looking at me with moderate interest.

I nodded wordlessly, trying to smile. It didn't work out very well. I just imagined what my first meeting with Korin's mother would be like if Sofie hadn't chased me to the second bed earlier. Not much was missing, and our mothers would nail us together. Just like some cheap affair. Just a lover in the closet and we would have a set.

Meanwhile, Ariana approached Korin's bed, reflexively adjusting the quilt. There was nothing unnatural about it. And yet... I was struck by the chill of this gesture. Ariana's eyes lacked concern, warmth, love, fear, panic, there was none of the feelings that had just been on my mother's face when she tried to determine if I was in one piece. She looked at her son as if she were matter-of-factly assessing the situation regarding his condition. Without emotions. I guess I'll never get used to the fact that Arisyans are emotionally defective. Although Korin seemed different. He often

acted as if he had feelings, as if he did not fit into this Arisyan world, just as Kori did not. Or maybe I only see what I want to see?

"Emily, Kori was asking about you," Ariana said unexpectedly.

A sincere smile lit my face.

"Really?" I got up from bed. "Has she recovered? And Tom? What about Tom?"

"They're both awake now, but they'll be under observation until tomorrow."

"Do you want to visit them?" Asked my mother. As usual, she read my mind. "I will pick up your things at the time. We'll meet at the parking lot."

I nodded eagerly.

"Can I?" I looked at Ariana questioningly.

"Of course."

I ran out of the room almost immediately. After a while I was sitting on the edge of the bed in which Kori lay. Except for the swollen lower lip, dark bruises on her hands and the connected drip, she seemed in pretty good shape. Tom presented a worse picture. He seemed absent. He didn't even answer my greeting.

"Do you feel very bad?" I asked my friend.

"It could be worse."

"And mentally? You know... I heard what those nasty types wanted to do to you," I said carefully, I wasn't sure she wanted to talk about it.

Tom groaned and covered his face with his hands.

"What's with him?" I asked.

"A slight concussion, two bumps, a few bruises, a split eyebrow, and a giant sense of guilt," Kori recited in one breath.

"Tom, what's up?" I turned to him.

"Nothing," he growled.

"He thinks it's his fault," Kori explained. "He doesn't want to hear any arguments."

"Don't be so foolish, Tom, it's nobody's fault. Who supposed guys would decode the force field? That they can do it at all?!" I tried to talk some sense into him.

The boy rose abruptly on the bed. When he exposed his face, I was terrified. His blue eyes were now bloodshot and feverish, his mouth twisted into a desperate grimace.

"You don't understand anything, Emily," he said hoarsely. "I should be vigilant, but I was not, I should have a gun on hand, but I did not have, I should protect Kori, but I did not protect her. I should have done a lot of other things, but I didn't do them. I acted like the asshole. Do you still think I have done everything right?!"

I frowned.

"You know, Tom. I think we are only people, we can't predict everything," I said with the calmness I could afford. "Maybe it's good that you didn't have a gun on hand. It is not known how everything would end then. The rebels had real rifles that didn't put to sleep for a few hours, but forever. Did you even consider it?"

There was an unpleasant silence for a moment, which was broken by Kori's warm and gentle voice:

"Tom... The best thing was to send an alarm signal, and that's what you did. It didn't even occur to me, but it should. Besides..." she suspended her voice for a moment. "Korin could finally pay his debt."

Tom took a deep breath.

"Maybe you're right," he said finally. He jerked the tube up from a drip, slipped off the bed and staggered toward the bathroom. Before he locked himself in it, he said with a forced smile:

"I have to sort it out somehow."

We exchanged knowing looks with Kori.

"It'll be okay," I whispered, patting her lightly on the hand. "Do not worry."

"I know, but I don't want to talk about it anymore. Tell me better, did you get along with my brother?"

I nodded with a mysterious face.

"Really?!" With a joyful squeal, she threw her arms around my neck. "You have no idea how happy I am."

Immediately, however, she pulled away from me. She mumbled visibly.

"I shouldn't be happy, because nothing good will come of it. He will break your heart."

"Kori, it doesn't matter what happens. I prefer one day of life than a year of vegetation, believe me. Anyway, it's too late to retreat. Let's just not talk about it."

"As you wish."

"Explain something to me. What did you mean, Korin could finally pay his debt?" I changed the subject.

"Life for life."

"You mean...?" I raised my eyebrows, I still didn't understand.

"Two years ago, Tom saved my brother's life..." She interrupted. "I won't tell you about it. I think Korin should do it himself. Ask him, but don't press too hard.

It's a difficult topic for him.

At the same time, a memory flashed through my brain, more like a flash than a clear picture, but it made the pieces of information come together.

"Is it about the story with the General?" I asked.

"Did he tell you about it?" Kori couldn't hide her surprise.

"Just hinted. He did not go into details. We didn't have enough time," I explained.

Tom just left the bathroom. We stopped the conversation, looking in his direction. He obviously had to keep his head under the tap for those few minutes, because the matted hair was now dripping with water. Fortunately, the face regained a normal expression. Tom stopped just by Kori's bed. They stared at each other so intensely that I had the impression that they were communicating without words. I quickly realized that I shouldn't be here.

"I'll go now," I said, getting up.

Without looking at me, they simultaneously answered bye. Kori nodded at Tom with a recalling gesture, and he immediately took his place. I slipped out into the corridor, slamming the door quietly. I turned around to wave them, but I regretted it. I think Tom was sobbing. Nestled in her chest, he looked like a hurt big child. Kori stroked his wet hair and I could tell by her lips that she was talking to him. The scene was so intimate that I felt stupid. I should turn around, I shouldn't see it. It's like I'm peeping. I walked quickly down the hall. After all, I was glad that at least they had something real in common.

As I passed "our" room, I could not resist the

temptation not to look. Ariana was gone. Korin slept soundly on his back sprawling across the entire width of the hospital bed. I barely refrained from coming in and patting his cheek. I did not do it. I knew that I would not leave so soon.

Lack of faith
Wanting to get where you always wanted to go,you had hope.
When you walk, you turn around and suddenly you lose faith.
Coming back, you want to cover up all the traces behind you,
you go back with the conviction that there is no loss.
You deceive yourself, thinking that everything is lost.
Wars and constant fear do not allow you to hope.
You try not to think about what you want to do but you can't.
Lack of faith pushes you to the other side.
Wanting to get where you always wanted to go,you had hope.

When you walk, you turn around and suddenly you lose faith.
Coming back, you want to cover up all the traces behind you,
you go back with the conviction that there is no loss.
You deceive yourself, thinking that everything is lost.
You could live as you like, but you prefer to go astray.
You try not to think about what you want to do but you can't.
Lack of faith pushes you to the other side.
Wanting to get where you always wanted to go, you had hope.
When you walk, you turn around and suddenly you lose faith.
Coming back, you want to cover up all the traces behind you,
you go back with the conviction that there is no loss.
Wanting to get where you always wanted to go, you had hope.
When you walk, you turn around and suddenly you lose faith.
Coming back, you want to cover up all the traces behind you,
you go back with the conviction that there is no loss.

I had to relax last weekend. I spent the whole afternoon locked up in my room trying to create a song. And I think I succeeded. When the sun was going down and the last bars of the new composition sounded in my ears, there was a knock on the door. Mom came in with the phone in her hand.

"Emily, to you," she said softly, handing me the phone. She left immediately, carefully closing the door behind her.

"Halo," I said into the phone.

"Hi, baby. You weren't there when I woke up," Korin said with honest pretense. I didn't think he would ever think to call me. When I heard his voice, my mood immediately improved. I felt like I want a little tease him.

"You just woke up now?" I asked perversely.

"No... why?" He assumed a cautious tone. I sensed that he was thinking about the deeper meaning of my question.

"So, you didn't call right after waking up?" I continued with mock anger.

"You didn't ask why," he said.

"You didn't ask me anything either."

"Fact," he admitted. "But we can make up for it. So, you tell me why you weren't there?"

"I will consider it."

"Em..." he began to get impatient.

"Okay, where to start here? I know. Maybe from your idiotic idea of sleeping together."

"I liked it. I thought you too," he muttered, clearly confused.

"You can say that too, but later someone broke my mood."

"Did I do something stupid in my sleep?" He asked uncertainly, and I imagined sweating on the phone and I almost felt sorry for him. I gave up.

"Relax, it was okay," I reassured him. "Only in the morning Sofie appeared and turned into an affair. Of course, you slept like dead and there was no one who would sell her lies about nightmares."

"You could do it yourself."

"And act like an idiot?"

"What did you tell her?" He asked, but he didn't seem nervous.

"Truth. You should praise me, I acted like a real Arisyan woman. Sofie suggested that for the relationship with you, the Arisyans would burn me at the stake, but this is not an important detail. In any case, she finally took pity on me, but probably only because the burning bodies make her nauseous. Fortunately, she promised to keep the view of your lascivious hands on my firm breasts," I laughed softly.

"You have a sick sense of humor," he said. "Anyway, it does not matter. Sofie will have more serious things to do now."

The last sentence said in such a tone that I immediately guessed that something was wrong.

"Something happened?" I became serious immediately.

"We played records from thought recorders today. It has gone a bit wrong because the reading process is quite complicated."

"Have you fixed something up?" I asked and felt anxiety slowly building up in me.

"Even more than we expected. It turned out that the General persuaded the Professor to cooperate. It was the Professor who showed the rebels how to break the code for a force field. Therefore, our situation does not look very interesting. The father has already notified the members of the Great Council. They should start the

meeting tomorrow afternoon."

"Wait, wait," I interrupted him. "Slow down a bit. Professor, Great Council, General... Do you realize that I have no idea what you are talking about?!"

"Excuse me. I still forget that you have been here recently."

"Maybe one after another."

"It is too much. Maybe after school tomorrow?" He suggested. "You finish earlier because medical training has been canceled. Sofie will be busy with something else tomorrow, she is a member of the Great Council."

"Okay, let it be tomorrow," I sighed resignedly.

"Don't worry, we've got the situation under control for now."

"I'm not worried, you'll be fine. It only hurts me that they are like that, that they hurt each other. For those two, I'm ashamed to be an Earth woman."

"You are not like them and most people are not like that either," he tried to comfort me.

"I'm not sure," I said grimly.

There was a moment of silence.

"Em, are you there?" He asked when I didn't speak for a long time.

"I am."

"I still smell your fragrance on my shirt," he whispered into the phone.

I couldn't believe he said that. Maybe this way he wanted to soothe my troubled nerves or relieve tension? I do not know. In any case, he succeeded, and I felt extremely pleasant.

"You are perverted," I said softly.

He chuckled.

"See you tomorrow."

"Bye!" I answered.

I went to the kitchen to take phone back to my mother. She was sitting at the table, in her favorite place, with a sad melancholy expression on her face. Thoughtfully, she turned the yellowed photo in her hands. She realized too late that I had entered and was not trying very well to hide it under the sleeve of her sweater. I sat in the next chair. I pulled her hand away and looked at the picture. We were all three on it, smiling, average American family. I could have been five, maybe six years old. I didn't remember who made it and when. But I knew where it was made. We stood against the backdrop of our home in the suburbs of Fargo, Dakota and looked really happy. I wonder if the house is still standing? Does anyone live in it now? Did dad leave a message for us there?

"Do you think he survived?" I asked, meaning dad.

"I don't know," she said softly. "I used to believe that. I don't know now. I thought if your dad died I would feel something. Over there." She put her hand to her chest. "But I don't feel anything. I should go home. I should check. There is probably nothing worse than uncertainty."

"I know, but we won't find out soon," I said with resignation. Mom looked at me questioningly. "Rebels increased activity, in addition they gained a powerful ally. It got very dangerous, not only in the north, but also here. Apparently, the force field no longer protects as effectively as it should," I explained.

"Have you talked about it for so long?" She asked, looking at the phone.

"Actually, yes but Korin hasn't told me everything yet, so I'm a little lost in it. Tomorrow I will learn more details. I know something happened two years ago. It had a relationship with the General and in some sense with Korin."

"Looks like it will be something like a war," my mother said. "A senseless war. Do people always have to ruin everything?"

"I think so. We don't need a threat from space. We would take each other down," I murmured.

For the first time I was not happy that it was Tuesday, that lessons start with music, that we have another rehearsal of the band. I would rather spend this day in a completely different conversation with Korin. Sit with him alone, talk and just feel his presence. And when I came to terms with the fact that we would only see each other after class, I noticed a familiar figure on the stairs leading to the school parking lot. Korin sat in the middle of the upper step and played with the bracelet, mindlessly rotating it around the wrist. I don't know why, but I had no doubt that he was waiting there for me. I wondered if it would be today or would it always be like that. Although "always" is a relative concept, at least for me. My "always" is to last only half a year.

The sight of my person with a guitar in hand caused a slightly indulgent but warm smile on his face.

"Hey," I said hello, sitting down next to him. "Did you come to hear our play?"

"Sure," he laughed ironically. "First I will listen to

you and then I will create a song myself."

"You know, that's not a bad idea," I said. "To start with, try maybe write a text."

He rolled his eyes.

"Em, if I ever write something, you'll be able to consider me crazy with a clear conscience," he said with conviction.

I didn't have time to ask about Kori or other matters related to our last trip, because suddenly my band with Red, Skinny and Erica appeared next to us. I moaned in my head, yes, Erica. Damn, it's only eight o'clock in the morning, so what time do you have to get up to be able to get ready like her? In the middle of the night?! She looked like she had just stepped off the cover of some colorful women's magazine. Red sexy mini dress, perfect makeup and long blonde hair falling in waves on the shoulders. I must admit that I didn't like it. And the fact that she took the place next to Korin, I liked even less. The more that she almost sat on him, and the jerk didn't even step back, which he should have done. I want to hit my elbow between his ribs and pull her blonde shags, and to be honest I barely resisted.

Red, on the other hand, slapped next to me, spontaneously embracing me.

"Good to see you," she said sincerely. "Are you OK?"

"I'm fine." I brought a crooked smile to my face. But nothing was right. And the most unfair thing was that Erica suddenly began to notice Korin, as if in a few days from an orange bore he suddenly became an interesting guy.

"You are famous," Skinny said, standing in front of

us with his hands in his pockets. "The whole school has not spoken about anyone else since yesterday."

"Rather Korin is famous," Erica corrected, putting Korin's hand on his thigh. "He's a hero like Superman or Spiderman."

So, I know what's going on! She loves superheroes. Childishness. I leaned forward and threw redeye to her, mentally adding another minus to the collection to Korin, by her hand on his thigh, which he did not even try to knock off.

"You call me super what?" Korin asked unexpectedly, looking stunned at Erica. Red and Skinny exchanged glances. Although I wasn't laughing at all, I felt like laughing.

"Superman is a hero of comics, Spiderman also," I muttered, then added maliciously:

"You often have to speak in block letters to Korin, he is not very smart."

"What are you saying, man?" Skinny couldn't get it. "Haven't you heard of American pop culture icons? You know... Superman, Spiderman, Batman, Marilyn Monroe, Jim Morrison, Mickey Mouse..."

"Not really." Korin shook his head with a rather silly face.

"Oh, get off him," Red cut in. "The guy is from another planet, how is he supposed to know all this?"

"But he has lived here for four years, he should try harder," Skinny did not give up. "It's called assimilation."

He drew the last word through his teeth, and it seemed to me, that not just me was pissed.

"Get off, Skinny," Erica snapped. "I bet Korin has

better things to do than melt over our pop culture, which virtually doesn't exist anymore."

"Sure, he has unlimited knowledge of the universe and a computer instead of a brain," he said contemptuously.

"He also has a good body. And quite a lot of muscles," Erica added admiringly. Then she began to check the size of his biceps with her hand. I just don't know why she was touching them so much that their outline was clearly visible under the tight, long-sleeved navy-blue blouse he was wearing. My rage has almost entered the phase of throwing objects. I clenched my fists so hard that I almost pierced my skin with my nails.

The atmosphere thickened, and it got quite uncomfortable. Skinny and I barely restrained our anger, Red looked as if she didn't care, Erica stuck to Korin's shoulder spurted good humor, and he himself seemed confused. A great start of the day. Because Korin had some incredible gift of sensing moods, he quickly realized that something was wrong. He decided to leave. He stood up, grabbed his backpack and threw it on his shoulder. He looked at our faces, stopping a bit longer on mine.

"I have to go to class," he said. After a while he was gone.

Just that: "I have to go to class", nothing more. He didn't add: "we'll meet after school", "I'll see you later", "I'll take you home"... I couldn't help that I had a thought through my head "I had a boyfriend." In the clash with Erica my chances were close to zero.

"You saw, he was embarrassed. He seems to like

me," she said, brushing blonde hair away from her face and adjusting the neckline of the dress.

"No wonder, since you have everything on top in this dress. You still had to show him the panties, if you put any at all," Skinny grunted, and I finally realized that Skinny had a crush on Erica and was just jealous. "Who would have thought you would make goo-goo eyes to the orange."

"Jesus... shut up at last," said Red. "What's going on with you today?!"

"Spring and hormones, quite a nice explosive mix," I concluded.

Erica looked at me first, then at Red, then critically said:

"To really make it explosive, you still need to look something. Girls, I can give you some reliable ways to seduce a guy."

"Thanks, but I'm not going to seduce anyone," I answered bravely.

Exceptionally, Red also had to feel offended by Erica's comments, since she decided to take action.

"I think you should educate yourself in these matters. Somehow, I don't see a crowd of admirers around you," she retorted.

The atmosphere became unpleasant. Skinny saved the situation. The moment I thought we'd jump down each other's throats, he waved his arms violently.

"It's over, girls. Enough!" He screamed. "We're starting a rehearsal before I regret having three women in the band."

Without looking at us, he headed into the rehearsal room. We followed him without a word. He was right,

there was no point in arguing, we were a band. We should work together, whether someone likes it or not. And no guy, no orange, no other ointment can affect it. We played a few songs without much enthusiasm. Somehow, we did really feel flow to play or the conversations, but by the end of the class no one had argued. At least we could afford it.

I stopped counting on Korin waiting for me after school, even though a small spark of hope was in me somewhere. However, it went out as soon as I didn't find him outside the building.

"Drop you off at the hut?" Red asked.

"Thanks. I want to go for a walk." I had to be alone with myself and with my own thoughts. I hope Red understands and doesn't think I'm avoiding her. I smiled apologetically at her and headed for the house. Along the way, I just threw my guitar and backpack into the trunk of our Ford. As I approached the end of the parking lot, I heard a cry:

"Em, where are you going?"

I would have known this voice everywhere, I would have easily picked it out from a crowd of other voices, but I didn't stop. I kept walking at the same pace, pretending that Korin was not there at all. However, he caught up with me and grabbed my hand, repeating the question:

"Where are you going?"

"Home," I said dryly. I tore my hand free.

"We had a set up. We were supposed to talk... after school... did you forget?" He stared at me intensely.

I shrugged my shoulders.

"I thought it was out of date," I said, trying to be

indifferent. "I thought you were going with Erica somewhere."

"With Erica?" He seemed surprised. "Why did you think so? What came to your mind?"

He pretends or doesn't really know what's going on? I made a quick decision - he pretends.

"Do you think I'm a complete idiot?!" I almost screamed in his face.

He frowned. I saw that he was thinking hard about something.

"Is it in the morning? About your friends, I knew something was wrong. They were... strange. I mean, they were acting weird in my presence. They probably don't behave like this normally?"

What the hell is he trying to tell me? That my band is weird? He is somewhat right, but without exaggeration. He acted like he left his brain at home in the morning.

"Korin, everything was fine with them, maybe almost everything," I added after thought. "YOU didn't behave normally."

"What have I done?"

"Nothing, literally nothing, and that's the problem," I said with resignation. And then something broke inside me. All regret poured out of me in a stream of words. It's good that at least I didn't manage to cry.

"I thought we would be a couple, that we would create a relationship there, but I didn't foresee that I would have to share you with Erica. Not with her... I don't like it. You don't have to feel obliged to anything. Invite Erica to a date and give her a story of how superhero you are, she'll be delighted."

I finished my argument with sarcasm.

"What are you raving about?" Korin's eyes grew as big as two purple saucers.

"You know, Erica is beautiful. No wonder you like her. I can understand it," I tried to speak in a calm tone, but I don't think I worked very well.

"I do not believe." He smiled. "You are jealous... That's it. Why are you jealous and of Erica?"

"You liked how she cuddled up to you," I whispered reproachfully and looked down.

"I didn't even notice it.

"Who do you want to cheat?"

He grabbed my chin and lifted it so that our eyes could meet.

"Em, I'm just paying attention to you." It sounded extremely sincere, and my legs softened.

"Why should I believe you?" I didn't give up.

He didn't answer, but pulled my hand towards the school, and said in short:

"Come with me."

"Won't you answer me?"

"I will answer, but in a moment." He accelerated a bit.

"Where are you taking me?"

"In a place I like very much. I like to go there when I have to think about something or when I want to be alone."

"So?" I demanded an answer. I trod beside him, trying to keep up with him.

"To Eden."

He surprised me. Why should my question be answered to Eden? He intrigued me so much that I stopped sulking.

"Can we just go in there, since it is not the time of our classes?" I asked.

"Not really, but I have my ways." He winked at me.

We stopped in the school corridor at one of the blue metal cabinets. Korin took out two folded aprons from it.

"Our camouflage," he said, handing me one.

Dressed in the green clothes of Eden employees, we headed through the schoolyard towards the greenhouse. We tried to behave naturally, that is, Korin behaved naturally, and I tried to imitate him. Although I focused mainly on not tripping over my own legs. We did not arouse anyone's suspicions, without reaching the large greenhouse between two smaller ones. Korin carefully opened the door and peeked inside.

"Free way," he whispered. After a while, we found ourselves surrounded by several hundred species of fragrant, colorful flowers. The smell that was in the air until it disturbed the mind. I stood stunned at the door, soaking up the wonderful aroma and color of this place. I was about to say that it's beautiful here, but something didn't suit me. I noticed that Korin didn't even stop, but he was constantly breaking through the tangle of leaves and flowers. Finally, he realized that I wasn't following him. He turned to me.

"Em, come on," he urged me.

"You wanted me to see this."

"I didn't want to show you flowers," he said impatiently. "Come on, in a moment you will have enough of this smell, it is too intense, it may faint you."

I followed him with some reluctance. I only stopped once to smell the freesia. I love the smell of freesia. I took a deep breath and felt dizzy. Korin was right, the concentration of various scents was too high. I had the feeling that I would vomit in a moment. I stopped, and I tried to keep my breathing to a minimum.

"I hope we don't have classes here," I groaned.

"Ventilation works during classes," he replied, opening the brown glass door leading to the next room.

It was darker here than in a greenhouse with flowers. The scattered light filtered from above, as if reaching us through the dense foliage and tangled branches of the trees. I took one careful breath, then another. The smell of damp forest, soil and something else that I could not identify hit me in my nostrils. In any case, after a mixture of floral aromas, this fragrance carried relief. I looked around. I saw a few mossy boulders and a few fallen tree trunks, and between them patches of green, probably in all possible shades of green.

"Over a hundred species of mosses," Korin explained, and took my hand tightly.

We approached one of the fallen trunks.

"Look. Common cellulose, reticulum, mnium..." he pointed to further clusters of mosses.

"Are you going to give a lecture about mosses now?" I interrupted him. "You were supposed to answer the question, why me? Why did you choose me?"

He pointed to a large patch of green between a large boulder and a thick tree.

"Does this moss seem beautiful to you?"

"I do not know?" I hesitated, not really knowing where he was going. "It is so ordinary... but Korin, to the point."

He silenced me immediately, gently closing my mouth with his hand. He took a small remote control-like device from his pocket and pressed a button.

"And now?" He asked quietly.

And something happened that I once witnessed in Almar's office. The windows darkened, and everything was dark. Well, maybe almost everything. The moss Korin pointed to was glowing with a bright green light.

"Amazing," I whispered.

"Pennata schistostega, that is shining moss." He said. He embraced me around my waist and pulled me to him. "It's beautiful. Just like you."

"Are you comparing me to moss?" I stepped back a bit.

"I didn't mean to offend you," there was tension in his voice. "It was supposed to be a compliment."

"You didn't offend me. Only this... hmm... to put it mildly, unusual."

"I noticed an analogy a few days ago."

I still didn't understand what he meant and how this moss relates to me.

I gave up.

"Okay, I'm an analogous moss, that's all I could determine my limited earth brain," I said ironic. "And now in block letters, please."

Korin had to press the button on the remote control again because the dim, but quite bright light returned. I saw him smiling.

"I thought you only needed to speak in block

letters."

"There is a little difference. To you always and to me sometimes," I cut myself off. "Now it is sometimes."

"I understand you're still angry."

I did not answer. I sat up, pulling my legs up and resting my chin on my lap. After a while he joined me, taking the same pose. He reached out to touch me, but he quickly pulled it back. Apparently, he thought that I would reject him and he probably wasn't wrong.

"I came here in the evening, before leaving for the field," he began in an undertone, staring intently at me. I didn't interrupt him, I absorbed every word. "I was torn. For the first time in my life I didn't understand what was happening to me or how to behave. What I felt for you scared me because it should be reserved for my genetic partner. I was still asking myself why you? What is it about you that you took all my thoughts? Seemingly you didn't stand out, an average earthly girl, and yet you seemed extraordinary. I sat here for quite a long time thinking. It was almost dark outside. And then I really saw this moss. It showed a patch of green with his hand. "The association of it with you appeared on its own. It was like an impulse. Immediately everything became clear. I realized that this moss is not just ordinary moss, just like you are not an ordinary girl. You just need to be able to see it. I think you don't even realize the inner light that you have inside you. Especially when you laugh or when you sing and play your noisy songs, and even when you get angry and upset, mainly at me anyway."

As I listened to this monologue, my heart beat

faster and faster. Were it not for the fact that the Arisyans are not capable of love or of talking about it, I could swear that no one has ever heard a more beautiful love confession. Korin was romantic, although he was probably the last person I could have suspected. His romanticism may have been a bit strange, but it suited me the most.

I moved closer, hugged my cheek to his shoulder, but didn't say a word. I didn't know what I could say to make it not sound too banal. I was just hoping that I let him know that I have no regrets and that he means a lot to me. He turned his head towards me and buried his face in my hair.

"I know I'm taking advantage of you. I feel bad about it," he whispered. "In half a year I will hurt you and at least until then I would like to do everything as it should."

He tenderly kissed my head, pulled me back a bit and lifted my chin. Our eyes met. Korin's eyes were sad. He was worried about me and our parting, and I had no idea how to convince him that it would be okay, because I didn't believe it myself.

"You have to tell me what I'm doing wrong. How should I behave. What do you expect from me? Because, Em, I don't know that," he said softly. He was so disarmingly honest that he gave me a pale smile. "I don't know human reactions, I'm lost in them. And if I'm doing something wrong, it's completely unconscious."

"Just like with Erica today?" I asked, though I didn't have to ask, I knew. I should know at school too; stupid jealousy obscured my view.

"Like Erica today," he admitted. "You should have poked me then, I would understand."

"If I did that, you would be in the hospital now," I tried to joke, but it didn't work out. Korin didn't sense the joke, he just worried:

"Was it that bad?"

"Worse," I laughed. "Don't worry about it. At least now I know that you need to take corrections for your unusual behavior."

I reached into his apron and pulled out the pilot.

"Em, what are you doing?" He reflexively wanted to stop me, but I was faster.

"I want to look at my 'moss' again," I said, turning over to my stomach and pressing the buttons on the remote control at random. However, the greenhouse windows did not darken even a bit. In the end I gave up.

"How to turn the light off?" I murmured.

Korin stretched out on stomach next to me, took my hand and gently pressed my thumb against one of the keys, holding it for a while.

"You have to hold on longer," he explained calmly.

Almost immediately, we were enveloped in a dark with forest and moisture smelling, and the moss before me lit up green again. It seemed even more beautiful than the first time. Maybe because now it reminded me of Korin's confession and I knew that this moment would remain in me forever, it would always be a part of me. I reached out to touch the plant. Under my fingers I felt the amazing softness of the stem and delicate leaves. I ran my hand through the tufts of moss, enjoying the unique pleasure of it. At some point I noticed purple flashes between the lush greenery.

Intrigued, I moved closer and looked more closely.

"Korin, look, it glows purple in some places." I flicked away the green leaves, pointing to the few purple ones.

He examined the purple moss carefully.

"Looks like a mutation," he said. "I have to report it to Professor Spite, it will have to be removed."

I looked at him in surprise.

"You won't do it. So, what if this is the mutation? It's beautiful and... reminds me of your eyes."

"These are the procedures," he replied indifferently.

I sat down immediately. I was outraged. How can you just destroy something so beautiful? I understood that purple moss is not something completely natural, but hasn't nature created it for some purpose? You can't just liquidate something because it's a little different. Meanwhile Korin turned on his back and carefully eyed the feelings up on my face. He hesitated clearly. I leaned over him and kissed his cheek. Without lifting my lips from his face, I moved them toward the ear.

"And if I'd asked you in a nicer way?" I whispered.

He shuddered and hugged me tightly.

"I'd break the rules," he said, but there was a hint of indecision in his voice now.

I gently moved my nose from his ear, along the cheek line up to his lips, and before I pressed my lips to them, I whispered:

"You're breaking the rules anyway."

Even though I started this kiss, I didn't feel embarrassed. I think that for both me and Korin it was quite a natural need for intimacy, as strong as if it were a compulsion. Just like the urge to breathe, another element necessary to sustain existence.

Leaning over Korin, I kissed him slowly, sensual, passionately, making his warm lips tremble. He sighed and broke away from me for a short time, just to get a breath.

"You won."

He embraced me and turned me around. He hung above me for a moment and then stuck to my lips again. This time he kissed more intensely, greedily, even possessively, as if wild lust obscured everything else. He hung on my lips with hungry lips, ran his tongue over them, gently grasped his teeth, sucked. I greedily absorbed every taste of his taste, his smell, the warmth of his body, even with the smallest part of myself... Somewhere in the back of my head a quiet voice of reason whispered: "not here", "not like that", but fell silent as Korin's moan of pleasure escaped. And suddenly it didn't matter what to do and what not to do. Everything around ceased to matter. It was only us, me and him. Thirsty for themselves, connected by a common rhythm of breaths, accelerated heartbeat and synchronous movement of the lips. We've lost all control, both of us. And when it seemed that there was no strength to stop it, when our caresses became so insatiable that we almost ripped off our clothes, a strange sound reached our ears. As if in the greenhouse next door someone turned on a giant vacuum cleaner. We froze. For a moment only, our accelerated breaths were heard. Korin was the first to recover. He stood up, grabbed my hand and pulled me stunned.

"Let's roll," he said shortly.

CHAPTER XIII

Our past gives shape
to our future.
ANTONI KĘPIŃSKI

Who wants to take care of the future,
must accept past with humility and
the present with distrust.
JOSEPH JOUBERT

Korin, what the hell is going on?" I panted when we stopped at the door connecting both greenhouses. "What's that noise?!" I could hardly put my thoughts together. Another portion of excessively strong emotions. A broken kiss, a lump of fear in my throat, uncertainty of this moment and the next one... It's too much for me.

"Fan. In a moment the classes will start in the greenhouse next door. We have to get out of here before Spite appears," he replied calmly.

I already knew his apparent peace. There was not so much nervousness as a cold analysis of the situation.

"Great," I murmured angrily.

We're let ourselves in for something again. It could have been so beautiful. I have never thought that it is so difficult to find a solitary place these days that it is so difficult to be somewhere alone. In the greenhouse with mosses, there was a deceptively soothing peace, and I see that it has lulled both my alertness and

Korin's alertness. It was so easy to imagine that this place belongs only to us, our little world outside the world. But reality did not allow illusions. Now it's somehow disentangled.

Korin took a deep breath, as if in this way he wanted to gather all his courage and slowly opened the door. We slipped into the neighboring greenhouse. The floral scent was still in the air, but now that the ventilation was on it wasn't as overpowering and suffocating as before. Leaning, hiding behind the plants, we tried to sneak unnoticed - a side alley along the glass wall - towards the exit. From the central part of the room there was a buzz of conversations in low voices, and behind the tangle of greenery a few silhouettes of students flashed near me. Judging by the quiet conversations, Spite has not yet arrived. And when it seemed that everything was going extremely smoothly and that we were able to get out of here, a familiar screeching voice sounded behind me:

"Stand still!" The sharp tone left no illusions, we were noticed.

The thought never occurred to me to stop. Worse, the legs accelerated themselves, which was not very sensible, because I immediately ran into Korin, who, unlike me, obeyed the command and stand still. If he didn't squeeze my hand tightly, I'd probably fall over. We turned slowly. Spite stood in front of us furiously.

"What are the beings doing here?" He grinded out. "Are the beings aware that being here out of class is illegal?"

As usual in such situations, fear paralyzed me, I was not able to utter a word. It's good that although

Korin was hard to show disequilibrium, until now he was mostly successful.

"Sorry, sir. I was only showing the being... I mean Emily, mosses," he said calmly.

Being?! Did he want to say a being about me?! I do not believe. I stared at him in surprise. And yet, he got angry. Under the façade of self-control and peace, I could see maybe not panic but uncertainty.

"The being from Arisa wants to say that he showed earthly mosses to the being from Earth?" Asked Spite with a mockery.

"Well, yes," Korin replied.

"Doesn't the creature think it's a kind of paradox that it should be reversely?"

"That's a good point," Korin admitted.

"Beings saw something interesting?" He asked the question to both of us but looked at Korin. He obviously wanted him to answer. No wonder, after all, the Arisyans never lie, never.

I squeezed Korin's hand tighter to remind him to hold his tongue and not to mention the purple moss."

"Apart from mosses, we didn't see anything interesting," Korin replied, and, surprisingly, he didn't talk too much or lie. Smart, very smart.

Spite narrowed his eyes. Finally, he noticed our clasped hands, so he looked at us again, this time more closely. He didn't need much time to see the obvious. Tousled hair distracted looks and swollen lips from kisses. I thought we would be in trouble now, but no. I could even bet that on his usually gloomy face I saw something like a smile, crooked, but always.

"Interesting, interesting..." he repeated several

times, stroking his rare beard in a monotonous, strangely irritating movement.

I let go of Korin's hand and smoothed my tousled, unruly strands, but it didn't matter anymore. He saw what he wanted to see. However, the strangest thing was that he didn't get angry or threaten, he stopped nervous that we were illegally in a greenhouse with mosses. He looked pleased. What the hell is going on with this twisted brain?!

Finally, he said:

"This time I will overlooked to this, but good advice: stay out of the greenhouse outside the classroom."

"Of course," we muttered simultaneously.

"Oh, one more thing," he added, pointing a thin finger under Korin's nose. "If a being would like to become human sometime, I can help with one important point. The being will remember it."

"I will remember," Korin stammered.

"Beings can go away," he said and made a gesture as if to chase away an intrusive fly.

We went outside almost immediately. We preferred not to check whether he would change his mind or decide to pull the consequences out of our behavior. I didn't really understand why we were getting away with it. Certainly, Spite softened when he noticed that something connects us, indeed - I think he was even happy. Was he interested in mixing species? Has he decided to treat us like some sick biological-genetic experiment?

"What did he mean?" I asked Korin as we moved away from the greenhouse a safe distance.

"I have no idea, he's crazy," he said.

"He may be crazy, but what he said was strange, even very strange. Besides, Korin, he thinks you're not human!"

"I know." He shrugged.

"I know?" Is that all you have to say?!" I was indignant.

Korin stopped abruptly. He sank his purple eyes into me, which suddenly darkened so that they became almost black. Anger? I could not believe that.

"I've never made a secret of who I am. Did you need Spite's opinion to realize that I might not be human? Congratulations on reflexes. I thought you did not think in these categories." He said the last sentence regretfully, then added with resignation:

"You have to decide for yourself if you consider me a human."

So, being a human is good and not being a bad person? Worth remembering. What going on with him? Did I unknowingly touch a sore point? I didn't mean it at all! But what I heard was certainly food for thought. So, he cared what I think about him?! Hmm... that's probably good.

"I didn't mean that, you misunderstood me. All in all, it is good because we will clarify some issues," I said firmly. "First of all, in my opinion you are more human than many Earthlings and I have never had a problem with it, that's why your reaction surprised me. Secondly, I'm worried about Spite's attitude, because since he doesn't think Arisyan are people, maybe he works with the General, and I don't want him to hurt you."

Korin relaxed visibly.

"I'm sorry." He rubbed his neck with his hand. "Today's day got a little hard for me. All this made my mind crazy."

"No problem. So, what about this Spite?"

"We checked him, he's a weirdo, but harmless. For this he is an outstanding specialist in terrestrial biology. Were it not for him, we would not have managed to go that far in recreating the earthly nature. The guy really knows his job."

"If you think so," I said doubtfully.

We just arrived at the car.

"I'll take you home," he changed the subject unexpectedly.

I folded my arms and leaned my back against the mask.

"No, my dear." I made puffed face. "I won't leave until you explain a few things to me."

"What kind of things?!"

"Korin..." I snapped, poking his shoulder. "What's with you? General, Professor, Grand Council. You promised to say everything today."

"Sure, I forgot. What time does your mother return from work?"

"After three."

He glanced at his watch.

"We still have over an hour. We're going to you."

"Okay," I said and poked him again, this time gently."

"What for?" He asked in resentment.

"For thinking that I don't think you are human."

"Okay, okay." He raised his hands in surrender.

I punched him for the third time.

"And this one?" He groaned.

"For wanting to say a being about me." I grinned and jumped into the car.

I poured us a glass of iced tea and we went out onto the terrace.

"Where should I start?" Asked Korin, sitting down on a massive wooden bench.

"The General," I said without hesitation and deliberately took my place at the other end of the bench, as far away from him as possible. Korin raised an eyebrow in surprise but did not comment in any way. I think he understood that we should keep a distance. Mom could come back any moment, and I had enough screw-ups for one day. You will need to develop a strategy of greater discretion later, set certain rules, but now is not the time, now is the time to talk about the past.

"Korin," I said shyly. "Will you say something?"

For a moment he turned around the empty glass in his hands, ran his finger a few times over its edge, and without taking his eyes off it, he began to say:

"We landed on Earth almost four years ago, near this town. Your planet looked completely dead. The landscape was overwhelming, the grim impression was compounded by the ubiquitous brown dust, which due to moisture created a hard shell in some places. There was no oxygen in the air. And this unnatural silence. We were convinced that we were alone here, that none of you survived."

"That would be better for you," I interrupted him.

"What would be better?" He asked.

"Well... if none of us survived," I explained.

He looked at me. He was clearly surprised by the conclusion I reached, but I was probably more surprised by his direct answer:

"To be honest, we didn't care."

"Then?" I frowned. "And now?" Somehow, I couldn't resist asking this question.

"I do not know."

An honest, casual answer. At least he didn't try to lie to me, although I would prefer him to. I was sorry that the life of Earthlings, and therefore mine, is irrelevant to Korin, but I bravely did not show it. I didn't want to start another argument.

"I'm sorry, I shouldn't interrupt you. Keep talking."

He set the glass on the table and continued:

"Restoring adequate air composition has become a priority. It took us almost two months to assemble the filters and place them in the middle layers of the atmosphere. Another two, reconstruction of the skyscraper, which now houses a hospital."

"Wait a second. You said there was almost no oxygen in the air. Don't Arisyans need it to breathe?"

He laughed.

"Of course, we need it. Every living being need. All the time we used special masks with chemical filters."

"Oh. And filters, materials for the renovation and equipment of the skyscraper, bracelets...?"

"We brought it from Arisa. Any more questions?"

"Lots, but for now I will stop with one. How did you arrive here?" The question came to me now, although I should have asked it much, much earlier.

"We needed fifty space shuttles to bring the necessary equipment here."

I do not hide, it impressed me. Because I didn't speak anymore, Korin resumed his story.

"We waited for over a year for the atmosphere to return to its pre-disaster condition. A difficult year for all of us..." He paused for a moment, his face set. "We cleaned the area all this time. Under a layer of dust, we discovered dried human bodies, actually skeletons covered in wrinkled skin. They were everywhere, on the streets, at houses, in cars. Their number testified that either these people had nowhere to hide or they simply did not make it on time." He flinched, and a cold shiver ran down my back. Suddenly I felt like I was there, I could almost see these gruesome scenes through Korin's eyes. I felt strangely uncomfortable, I moved a little toward him.

He looked at me inquisitively.

"Fine?" He asked.

"Yes, don't worry about me."

"Among all this mess, we also found the remains of dead animals, which wasn't bad, because we could get the genetic material needed to reproduce species. You saw the effect in Eden."

"You did it well."

"Years of practice." He smiled slightly. "And when we were sure that the planet was completely depopulated, we came across the first people, and actually they came across us. The first group that arrived here was quite numerous. With them came the General, back then John Smith." Korin sighed heavily but did not interrupt. "Interestingly, Professor Spite was also in this group. The beginnings of cooperation were difficult, mainly due to the language barrier, but not only. The basic problem was people's lack of trust in us. It is John's merit that he urged Earthlings to work with us. The guy had all the qualities of a leader and people listened to him. Although now, when you think about it all, they just had to listen to him, they were afraid of him, but then we did not know it yet."

"When did you realize that John was not who you thought he was?" I asked.

"Far too late. There was no indication that something was wrong. We learned your language quite quickly. Every day new groups of Earthlings arrived. In short time our population was big as five towns. Side by side we fought to bring everything that was ever alive back to life, we fought for normality or at least to get closer to normality. My father trusted John almost completely. You can say that they made friends in their own way. We made a mistake because, without knowing your civilization, we had an incomplete picture of it. Aggression, violence, intrigue, jealousy, a struggle for power were completely foreign concepts for us. We thought that you are no different from us, except maybe less progress in a few areas, the differences were small."

"And what happened two years ago?" I asked uncertainly. I felt Korin revolving around the subject and apparently hesitating.

He leaned forward, put his elbows on his knees, and stared at something in front of him. He spoke very quietly, as if forcing himself to speak, but the most important thing was that he finally found it in his heart to do it.

"We ignored the first signals that John was not quite right. There were various rumors that he was plotting against us, that he no longer needed us, because he had pulled out all the information from us and would handle the reality himself, and that he was planning to take over. We didn't believe in a single word. And yet... It was the truth. He mainly wanted power. Not for the good of people, but for power, no matter at what cost. Even at the cost of human life, my life also, Em..."

He turned his head towards me and looked at me. His eyes turned dark purple, which made Korin, usually gentle for a split second, look really menacing. Anger, pain and barely concealed emotions completely overwhelmed him. He cleared his throat and restored himself. I don't know how it happened, but those few seconds when he was barely exposed, it was enough for me to feel the pain, his pain. What did the bastard General do to him?! I put my arm around Korin and kissed his neck gently.

"It's just me, Em," I whispered. "You can tell me."

He buried his face in his hands and, without looking at me, began to say:

"It was two years ago, in spring. One day my father sent me for some documents in his office. I found John there. It surprised me, but I did not suspect him of bad intentions, it did not even occur to me. I think that if he tried then he could convince me anything, I would believe everything. My sudden appearance disturbed him, he lost his head completely. He acted instinctively. He reached me. It wasn't until

the wild flash in his eyes made me realize that something was wrong here, but it was too late for any reaction. At the same time, I felt a strong blow to the stomach. I doubled over, trying to catch my breath to no avail. Another strong kick aimed at the face threw me back. I dropped onto the glass table with impetus. It fell apart below me, and fragments of the glass top dug deep into my back at waist height. The last thing I remember is unimaginable pain, and then I lost consciousness..."

He clenched his fists tightly, and I stared dumbfounded at the next wave of emotion sweeping over his face. I was not able to speak, I caressed his neck tenderly, reassuring him and myself.

"I woke up a few days later in the hospital."

"The most important thing is that you live. Nothing else matters."

"I was lucky." Korin smiled crookedly. "My father remembered something and sent Tom straight after me. It was pure fortune. Tom entered the office when Smith was just trying to cut my throat. He saved my life."

I closed my eyelids. The images themselves began to appear in my head: Korin in a pool of blood, Korin with a grimace of pain on his face, Korin unconscious among the shards of glass... I shuddered. It must have hurt a lot, there had to be a mark after the accident, and many more. I reached out unknowingly, wanted to touch his waist, feel the scar under my fingers, see if what he had just said really happened. He guessed what I wanted to do. He stopped me. He grabbed my hand firmly and shook his head.

"Not today, Em."

"Does it hurt?" I asked quietly.

"Not anymore, at least not physically," he added immediately.

What was I thinking about?

That I would heal his pain with my touch? That I turn back time?

But at least I found out that Korin is not completely devoid of feelings, he apparently suffered, so maybe he can also feel love? After all, I was still hoping for something more than a temporary relationship, the more that after everything he confessed to me today, I felt that I loved him more and more, crossing the border when you can stop.

He hugged my hand to his cheek.

"Since then, I haven't told anyone what exactly happened in my father's office," he confessed. "You can say that I put a blockade on my mind in this memory, I didn't want to go back to it. And you know, it's weird, but I felt relieved that I was spitting everything out. Thank you, Em..."

I kissed him gently on the lips. I wanted to say that I love him, but it was not a good time, and it probably will never be. The word "love" should not exist for me, at least when it comes to Korin.

The front door slammed. After a while, we heard my mother's voice:

"Emily, where are you?!"

"On the terrace," I shouted back, moving to the other end of the bench.

Mom stood on the threshold of the sliding door and gave us a quick look.

"Did I interrupt something?" She asked.

"No," I denied. "Korin was just talking about the arrival of Arisyans to Earth. He ended up with the General's betray."

"I'd love to find out, too," said my mother, looking at Korin. "Why don't you stay at dinner?"

He made long face.

"Don't worry," I laughed. "Unlike me, my mother cooks well."

"So, that's what this is all about?" Mom breathed a sigh of relief. "And I thought that the Arisyans do not like earthly cuisine."

"It's not so bad. It is true that earthly food is different from Arisyan, but it almost fully meets our needs," replied Korin. "I'm glad to eat something, to be honest, I'm hungry."

"Lasagna with spinach?" Asked my mother.

"Yes, of course." Korin gave her a sweet smile. "I can make béchamel sauce."

"I was supposed to ask Emily about that."

Korin glanced at me and shook his head.

"Better not if we're going to eat something today."

"You're right," said my mother, laughing. "Emily can even burn water for tea."

Great, first Korin, and now my mother is making fun of my culinary skills, or rather their lack. I grumbled.

"Em, are you offended?" Said Korin, seeing my face.

"No," I murmured.

"We were just kidding. Anyway, you started with this cooking."

"I know," I groaned. "I'm sorry, but... it's really not nice when the whole crowd is making fun of you."

"Crowd? Do you see any crowd here?"

"Well... you and mother," I muttered uncertainly.

"Indeed," he admitted seriously, then laughed and disarmed me as usual.

Mom shook her head.

"Eh, today's youth..." she sighed and went to the kitchen.

Before we joined her, Korin leaned forward and kissed my neck.

"Hey, behave yourself," I said in a whisper. "We supposed to do it discreetly."

"I did it discreetly, nobody saw," he whispered, tickling my ear with his breath.

I shivered. I wanted to cuddle into his arms and stay in them for the rest of the day. The knowledge that I couldn't do it almost made me crazy. I climbed my fingers and stuck to his cheek, teasing him lightly with my tongue.

"It was supposed to be discreet," he said, laughing softly.

I shrugged.

"And it was, nobody noticed."

Amused, we fell into the kitchen, meeting my mother's astonished look. She did not know me from this side - the mood swing was not my style. Meanwhile, the presence of Korin meant that I experienced many extreme emotions at once. Starting with real rage, stumbling along the way for love, and ending with euphoria. To tell the truth, my reactions surprised me too, although I was already getting used to their violence. It must have been related to growing

up and rediscovering yourself. I think my mother understood this, trying to intervene in the process as little as possible.

"Someone here supposedly knows the sauces well," she said, as if nothing had happened, looking at Korin eloquently.

"If I said so, it's probably true."

"We'll find out soon. Wash your hands and work," she urged him.

"Right away, boss," he replied, pulling up his sleeves.

He had beautiful hands, slender hands, long fingers and strong, muscular forearms. With a suppressed sigh, I sank into a nearby chair, still unable to take my eyes off Korin. How is it possible that he works on me? How can I feel that he fits here, this house, me and my small family, despite the fact that he is a stranger? And why are all the good things we encounter in life so fleeting? Why can't they just last?

"Stop staring at him like that," I scolded myself, closing my eyelids.

"Emily," I heard my mother's worried voice. I opened my eyes. "Are you okay?"

I forced myself to smile.

"I'm fine, except that I'm unemployed because of you and I'm dying of boredom," I joked, spreading my hands helplessly.

"I think tormenting me with a series of questions about the recent past would be a good way to kill this boredom," Korin said, thus hinting me that he didn't mind exploring the subject further.

"Well, sometimes you can say something with

sense," I said, leaning back in my kitchen chair. "So, what happened next with the General?"

Korin did not answer immediately. He turned his back and started making béchamel. I watched he put the saucepan on the stove and quickly added the necessary ingredients. Meanwhile, my mother dealt with stuffing. Finally, when the waiting silence began to get unbearable, he returned to the story interrupted before my mother returned.

"When it became obvious that the General had betrayed, we did not know how to behave. Especially since he was planning to murder us brutally. The question was born, what should we do with him in such a situation?"

"It would be wise to get rid of him," my mother said.

331

Korin stopped stirring the sauce and looked at her, frowning.

"On Arisa, violence is unacceptable... Actually, it is something unknown, completely incomprehensible."

"You're right, violence is not an option," she admitted. "Although sometimes there is no other way."

"There is always other way," he said softly and went back to mixing.

"You just didn't pick the best," I interjected. "From what I understood, the General lives, grows stronger and threatens you, and actually all of us. So, it didn't seem like a good idea that he saved his life. Arisa has own rules, but the Earth has its own and it's about time that it finally reaches you."

"Imagine that it has arrived... it has already arrived then," I recognized by his voice that he was annoyed.

"In the end, the Grand Council decided about the fate of the General."

Korin stirred again in the saucepan, turned off the stove, said to my mother "ready", then moved away from the stove. He was now leaning against the countertop, thumbs pressed into the front pockets of black, fitted jeans, and he looked extremely sexy. Again, I found myself just staring at him. It's good that at least my mouth was closed, otherwise I would make a complete idiot of myself. I wanted to ask about the Great Council when my mother stole thunder:

"Tell me more about this Great Council. What is it?"

"The originator of the Great Council was my father," he began. "Because he did not know how to solve the problem of the General, he said that it was necessary to create something like a government or rather a senate, so that difficult decisions were taken by majority."

"Fairly." Said my mother.

"The Council was composed of ten people, five Arisyans and five Earthlings."

"Well, and if the votes are even, what then?" I asked.

"Then it determines the voice of my father as the chairman of the Council."

"So, it was decided, I mean the General... hmm ... chase away?" I said looking gloomily at Korin.

"Exactly. Five people voted for banishment, three for the death penalty, and two abstained," he explained. "Fortunately, my father did not have to settle the matter. And that's good, because he probably wouldn't be too objective."

Fortunately, my mother did not ask why Almar would have a problem with objectivity. Maybe because she was busy pushing lasagna into the oven, or maybe this statement just escaped her attention. I didn't want Korin to be forced to tell her about the accident, and I don't think he wanted to. All he had to do was open to me.

"Shortly after the Council's decision, the General left, taking with him a fairly large group of his supporters.

The Great Council met for another week. It was then that numerous safeguards were introduced to protect against external attack, i.e. force fields around towns and around bases, as well as bracelets that act as keys."

"It turned out to be not enough, right?" I asked quietly.

"It's not enough," he admitted grimly.

"What really happened, why did everything fail now?"

"We are not sure…"

"But you read the rebels' thoughts," I said. "You had to find out something."

"Something like that… Just a little more complicated than you might think. The rebel's thoughts were helpful, but not enough, we lack some pieces of the puzzle."

"Can you tell us what you already know?" I asked uncertainly. "Unless it's a secret."

"No, it's not a secret," he laughed, looking into my eyes.

Mum pushed back a chair and sat at the kitchen table next to me. She rested her elbows on the table and stared at Korin, apparently curious about further revelations. He also sat down comfortably, but on the kitchen counter. He did not have to be encouraged to continue talking, he was well aware of the mood of silent waiting in the air. My mother and I had strange faces because before he spoke I saw a flash of amusement in his purple eyes.

"We were able to establish that in the south of Canada, a guy whom they call Professor created a center very similar to ours. Surrounded by a large group of scientists, he is working on bringing the planet back to life, and apparently, he does it well. It is not known why he agreed to cooperate with the General, because of what we know, the Professor does not have, or rather had no bad intentions."

"I don't understand what the problem is? Does it matter with whom the General comes into agreement?"

"Emily, move your head. The problem is not the General but the Professor. He is the brain, without his help the General will do nothing. Someone from the Professor's environment found a way to cross our force field. It is true that we have added additional security codes, but they are only an ad hoc measure, for a long time they will not be enough. Actually, we can expect an attack from outside at any time, and war is not in our nature. We may have to stop our mission on Earth."

"Interrupt the mission," I repeated flatly. "Will you have to leave?!" I almost shouted when the meaning of his speech reached me.

I didn't predict it. I assumed that half a year with Korin was a certainty, meanwhile the situation

unexpectedly got out of control and everything changed. I stared at Korin in horror and I could bet that I was as pale as a wall at the moment.

"We'll probably leave, but not right away," he said carefully, anxiously watching my reaction. "For now, we have an advantage because we know that something is being prepared and we can devise a strategy."

"So, how long are you planning to stay here?" I asked, putting a lot of effort into masking the trembling voice.

"Initially, we were to stay as long as needed, but we will stay as long as possible."

"How long can it be?" The question almost got stuck in my throat. If I wasn't sitting, my knees would certainly bend.

"I talked to my father about it yesterday. We came to the conclusion that probably no one will attack us before winter. Anyway, we've also received this information from one of the rebels. Apparently, the General is preparing to take over our cities in early spring."

"So, why did you say that the attack can occur anytime?!" I snapped.

"Because there is no guarantee that he will not attack sooner. Anyone can change their mind."

Mom, who until now only listened to the conversation, took the floor:

"So, you can also help the Professor change his mind."

"What do you mean?" I asked.

Korin frowned as if he understood immediately

what his mother meant. He slid off the countertop and began circling the kitchen. I could almost hear the cogs in his brain working at full speed.

"You have to somehow contact this Professor, talk to him," she continued her way of thinking, and finally I understood. It was brilliant!

"I know a little bit about scientists, after all I am, well... I was actually the wife of one of them. The desire for power and the pursuit of war are not their priorities. We don't know what made the Professor cooperate with the General, maybe some clever lie. The cause should be determined.

Korin stopped in the middle of the kitchen and ran a hand through his hair.

"All in all... This theory sounds quite logical," he admitted. "There is only a small problem. Nobody knows the Professor's whereabouts. The guy apparently never leaves his center, you can only contact him through some Mitch."

"At least it's a start," my mother muttered. "It's always an anchor point, this Mitch..."

"I will talk to my father today, he will definitely raise this matter at the Great Council meeting."

He went to the oven and opened it.

"This lasagna is probably already good," he said, glancing toward us.

Mom jumped to her feet, knocking over her chair.

"Shit. Of course, it's already good! I completely forgot."

Almost immediately after dinner, Korin gathered to leave. He couldn't wait to share my mother's suggestions with Almar. And if mother was right, there was even a good chance of avoiding armed conflict. I went outside with Korin. We were standing on the porch and only when we were alone I could vent my frustration. It was the vision of Arisyan leaving the Earth earlier that unnerved me.

"When did you plan to tell me that you were going to escape like a rat from a sinking ship?" I said reproachfully. I felt regret, rage and disappointment. I bit my lower lip, barely holding back my tears.

"I'd leave as the last, last ferry."

I laughed at the mockery.

"Good, last ferry, so when? An hour or a day after the others?"

"Damn it, Emily, what do you expect from me?! That I will stay here? Forever?!" He took a deep breath. "I don't belong here, Em," he added a little quieter.

"You said you didn't belong anywhere, that you didn't get attached to places."

"Because it's true, but that doesn't mean I belong here. Besides," he hesitated, "I wouldn't survive here."

I frowned, trying to read the last sentence correctly. I was certain of one thing, he wasn't afraid of the General, something else was a threat.

"Why would you not survive? Explain to me," I demanded.

"It doesn't matter. Forget what I said."

"So, this is a secret? Something like 'if I tell you I'll have to kill you'?"

"Kind of," he admitted.

"I'm not buying it." I crossed my arms. "Besides, we have a rather strange habit on Earth: you start to say

something, so you have to finish it regardless of the consequences."

"I don't buy it now. He smiled ironically and also crossed his arms over his chest. "I hear for the first time about such a habit. And believe me, I know all earthly customs, I had training in it."

Arrogant asshole. I was about to stamp my leg in anger.

"I'm not talking with aliens, with the big A, who make me an idiot. This is just my private custom, you can remember it."

I opened the door and wanted to slam it in front of his face, but at the last moment he grabbed my hand and pulled me to him.

"Okay. I don't know how you do it, but you won again," he sighed in resignation.

He was still holding me with one hand, although I wasn't going anywhere, and with the other one he put it in his jeans pocket and pulled out a small transparent vial. He handed it to me on an open hand. I took the bottle carefully and turned it over with my fingers and studied the contents carefully. At the slightest movement, small balls rattled softly against the walls of the vessel.

They resembled my mother's artificial pearls, which I used to play in my childhood, only that they were not white, but purple. I didn't have time to ask what that was. Korin, as if reading my mind, answered:

"Arisyanite," he said softly. "Mineral, which is not present on Earth, but on Arisa it is almost everywhere: in water, in soil, in food... We need it as you need oxygen to breathe. One inhale is enough to cover daily requirements."

"If you don't use it," I shook the vial, "will you die?"

"Exactly," he confirmed. "But not right away. First, the body gradually weakens, it lasts about a week. Later weakness progresses rapidly. Body temperature drops by several degrees, the iris loses purple color, visual disturbances appear, loss of consciousness... until after about two weeks all vital functions cease."

I turned pale. For some fucking Arisyanite now there is no physical chance for Korin to stay here permanently. He wouldn't have survived without this little purple shit in balls for up to three weeks.

"I worried you," he said, hugging a hand to my cheek.

"A little... You surprised me. When we were alone in the base, I didn't notice you taking a sip." I squeezed the vial in his hand and he immediately put it in his pocket.

"We have to be careful. It is better if too many people do not know how important it is."

"I'll keep it to myself, I promise. I don't want to hurt you."

"I know," he whispered, then leaned forward and skimmed my bottom lip.

I gave my kiss back and reluctantly moved away from him.

"Watch out, mother..." I said softly, looking at the closed door. "Go now."

"See you tomorrow." He took my face in his hands and kissed my forehead sensually.

When I felt his moist lips on the skin and warm

breath in my hair, I thought I would just melt away. I shouldn't get maudlin under his touch or just a kiss. From the very beginning, Korin acted on me like that, lit a fire in me, which I was getting more and more difficult to suppress. I was not alone in these emotions. The same heat was burning in his eyes when he gave me a wistful look before he flew off to the car. I smiled to myself at this thought and went back home.

I wanted to go straight to my place, but my mother called me from the kitchen:

"Wait, Emily, come here for a moment."

"Something happened?" I stopped in half a step.

"I don't know why you don't want to trust me, but... Emily... I'm not stupid, I see how you look at each other. How do you look at him. There is a spark between you and I would have to be blind, and not be your mother not to notice it."

"But..." I wanted to deny everything, but it didn't make sense, she knew better. If she had only guessed before, she could be sure now that we were connected by something more than mere friendship.

"Let me finish. I just want to tell you that I won't interfere if you don't want to, under one condition," she suspended her voice as if she was gathering courage. "You must promise me that you will protect yourself somehow when you do IT. I'd rather you have not a baby on the way in these uncertain times."

"Baby or an alien?" I looked at her menacingly under raised eyebrows.

"Honestly? Both. I'm worried."

At first, I was furious, but realizing that she was right. She is damn right. Her words worked like a cold

shower. On the one hand, I considered myself an adult and fully responsible, but on the other - I did not think of such a prosaic thing as protection against pregnancy. All anger left me immediately.

"You looked today like you really likes him," I said without a trace of anger.

"Because I like him, he's a good kid, but he's not the right boy for you."

"I know. I have everything under control. Nothing will happen, trust me," I lied.

"I'll try," she breathed a sigh of relief. She believed me.

I smiled.

"You did well," I said, trying to make it sound light.

"What?"

"Your first lecture on contraception," I explained and went to my room, feeling my mother's astonished look.

CHAPTER XIV

Feelings are the most incompetent form of reasoning,
imaginable.
COMTE DE LAUTRÉAMONT

The Grand Council met throughout this week and half of the next, and everything revolved around this. It has made us, to a greater or lesser extent, aware of how fragile and impermanent a sense of security can be. It was enough for two rebels equipped with a small device interfering with a signal emitting a force field to sow in us a seed of fear and uncertainty.

Korin became the most popular person at school overnight. Mainly because he participated in Council meetings. It was true that he was only an ordinary observer, but he was the only one who had access to current information. Therefore, at almost every step we were accompanied by a large group of curious students, and Korin with typical patience answered all questions.

I was slowly getting tired of it. The whole situation took me away from Korin, took him from me, and some egoistic part of me missed to have him only for myself. Each day looked similar. In the morning I went to school with my mother, I also came back with my mother or Red, and Korin rushed to the hospital after the classes for the Council meetings. I did not understand all this confusion, because the Council's decisions were too predictable, at least for me. First of all, a ban on leaving Arisyan cities was introduced, and thus all research in the field was suspended. Force tunnels were created connecting all locations, while the field was protected against interference from the outside. I did not go into technical details, what this additional protection consisted of. The only thing that surprised me a bit was to take seriously my mother's suggestion to make contact with the Professor. Some Will, commander of the unit overseeing our return to the city with rebels, volunteered for this mission. He was soon to head north, probably to Minnesota, to find Mitch, because it was only through this man that he could reach the Professor. In addition to security issues, a plan to evacuate the Arisyans from Earth was also developed, but in this case Korin did not provide any details, arguing that talks on this topic were secret and did not participate in them.

I was glad when this performance finally ended, and the emotions associated with recent events began to decline. So, everything has returned to normal since Thursday. And just on Thursday, during one of the breaks, Korin came to me with a proposal that I was subconsciously waiting for, but it was a pleasant surprise for me.

"Tomorrow... at my place... a romantic candle light dinner," he whispered in my ear, putting special emphasis on the word romantic.

I swallowed nervously. Dinner by candlelight. It could only mean one thing - sex. We will have sex. Together. I understood the hint, but still wanted to make sure.

"Do you mean what I think you have?" I asked teasingly.

A mysterious smile appeared on his face.

"I think so," he confirmed.

"And your parents? And Kori?"

"Father and mother leave for Manning, they will not be back until Sunday. And Kori will learn with Tom at his place."

Good one - "learn with Tom at his place". Does he really believe it or is he just pretending not to see what these two have in common? Anyway, I wasn't going to make him aware.

Well, his parents will not be there, but my mother... well, this is a separate problem. I frowned at the thought.

"Something's wrong?" Korin looked at me narrowly.

"I don't know what to tell my mother."

"You will figure this out."

"It's easy for you to say that. He won't believe a word if you come for me. She already suspects something, she has become very vigilant. Maybe I will ask Kori."

"I don't know if that's a good idea," he said skeptically.

"Do you have better?"

He denied shaking his head in silence. He stood there for a good minute, frowning and looking like he was analyzing something in his mind.

"Kori knows about us, right?" He finally asked. By the look on his face I knew that he had just come to this.

"Yhm..."

"She knew from the beginning," he no longer asked, but stated the fact.

"Yhm..."

"I suppose she has the same deal with Tom."

"You could say that," I agreed, though he wasn't quite right. Somehow I didn't want to explain the subtle difference to him, he wouldn't understand.

The class bell interrupted us. We waited until the corridor was empty.

"Settle the matter with Kori," he said, giving me a quick kiss on the cheek. "See you on Friday."

Then he started towards the stairs leading to the second floor.

"Korin, wait!"

He stopped and slowly turned toward me, giving a questioning look. I approached him.

"One more thing," I lowered my voice to a whisper, even though we were alone in the corridor. "We should protect ourselves somehow."

The corners of his mouth raised a slight smile.

"I know, I've already taken care of it."

In confirmation of his words, he rolled up the right sleeve of the shirt, indicating a slight lump on his shoulder.

"What is it?"

"Contraceptive chip," he explained.

Curious, I carefully moved my finger over the strange bulge on his arm, clearly sensing a tiny, hard foreign body under his skin. Unknowingly, I started running my hand over his biceps, which unexpectedly twitched and strained hard. Korin let out a loud breath, squeezed my fingers, pulled them away from his shoulder, but did not let go.

And it was a mistake.

Physical contact only ignited our senses, and the hunger for touch was so severe that neither of us wanted to stop it. Korin pressed his chest on my chest, pressing me hard against the cold wall. Our bodies adhered closely to the entire length. He was so close... too close. I could feel the warmth of his body through my blouse, I could hear the accelerated beating of our hearts and the taste of his lips on my lips when he kissed me with a heat I didn't even suspect him. He has completely overpowered me. Not only that he had practically immobilized me, the most overwhelming power of his lust was that it exploded suddenly, without warning, in the wrong place and time. A place, a school, a corridor... these words swirled in my head as faint flashes of reason in all this madness, but clear enough to make me think.

"Korin..." I muttered with difficulty between kisses. "We're in the school corridor."

He came to his senses immediately. He took his lips away from my lips, but didn't move away. He just touched his forehead to mine and continued until he calmed a little shivering breath.

"Damn, E... this is insane," he whispered and only then released me.

"I know." I pushed him gently. "Go to class, you are already late."

He looked at me a little blurry and ran a hand through my hair, ruffling it above forehead. I had the impression that he hesitated to stay. The sense of duty has finally won. He waved goodbye quickly, turned on

his heel and, not looking back, ran up the stairs.

When he was out of my sight, I slumped down the wall to the floor. I sat for so long trying to gather pieces of my brain into one.

Christ, what's wrong with me, what's wrong with him?!

Nobody reacts like that to normal touch, or at least shouldn't react like that.

It is abnormal.

We got carried away again, we lost control again.

I closed my eyes, thinking it would help me cool down. I was wrong. I could still smell his smell around me. He smelled like clean mountain air on a frosty, windy day.

I didn't move, I couldn't.

And... I didn't go to Arisyan.

Kori stopped on the side of the road, about halfway to her home. Before I could ask what was going on, she reached into the backseat for a plastic bag. She gave me it.

"Dress up, Emily."

I shook the contents of the bag on my knee.

"Blouse?" I was surprised.

White, airy blouse. So sexy, it should be added.

"Yes, blouse. You can't go on your first official date in a regular cotton T-shirt."

She was right. I knew that I had to leave the house in a normal outfit, so that my mother did not realize our intrigue, but the fact that I could change my clothes on the way, I just didn't think.

"Thanks, Kori, for everything." I looked at my friend gratefully.

"Don't be ridiculous, Emily, you have nothing to thank for."

"I do. If it weren't for you, I would sit in my room now and at best strum the guitar. You did great with my mother, really. She literally ate out of your hand. It is hard to believe that you are Arisyan. It turns out that lie is in your blood. In your case it's a compliment," I added.

She laughed.

"Here, on Earth, I become more and more human."

I changed quickly. I felt better immediately. Better, which doesn't mean comfortable. No wonder, since I had more than twenty-four hours for grim meditation. Twenty-four hours to realize all my flaws and imperfections. Twenty-four hours alone with my complexes. Is it possible that I am physically attracted to him so much that he will not pay attention to them? Or maybe, when we will be really close, he will realize that he was wrong and that he does not think I'm attractive at all?

"Emily, what's up?" Kori pulled me out of my thoughts. "You look like you're about to vomit."

"He won't find me attractive," I groaned.

She gave me a quick glance.

"With that long face for sure. Smile," saying that, she corrected my shirt, sliding one of the sleeves below to reveal my right arm. "Now good."

I didn't protest.

When we arrived, Korin was already waiting outside the house. He was leaning against the terrace railing and seemed relaxed, although I noticed

something strange in his attitude, something that made me think that this was not really the case. Was he nervous too? He looked great as usual. The rolled-up sleeves of the black T-shirt revealed muscular shoulders, and graphite fitted pants with a wide leather belt emphasized the narrow hips.

Before I got off, Korin had already approached the car from the passenger side. He took a backpack from me and helped me out.

"Have fun," Kori said and drove away. We didn't even manage to answer, we were too focused on ourselves.

I caught Korin's gentle smile as he glanced over the white blouse, keeping his gaze a second longer on my bare shoulder. He obviously liked what he saw. He put an arm around me and led me towards the house. From the spacious hall, we entered the large living room, where the surprise deprived me of my ability to move. I had a table in front of my eyes, beautifully set for two, on which several candles burned with a warm glow, creating a unique, romantic mood. I didn't think Korin would take the term "romantic dinner" so literally. For me, it was rather a synonym for what we have to do today. I felt a pleasant warmth inside, when I realized that he remembered my dream expressed aloud in the hospital and now he was trying to make it

352

happen, although he probably did not see much sense in it.

He looked at me uncertainly.

"You don't like it?" He asked.

"Of course, I like it," I assured with a smile. "But you didn't have to do that. For me," I added a little quieter.

"It's the only thing I can do not to feel bad about using you. We can still withdraw."

"You don't use me and I'm not going to back out," I said seriously. "What did you prepare to eat?" I quickly changed the subject. I didn't like that he suddenly started to hesitate.

I took a seat at one of the place settings, Korin served dinner, and I didn't feel the taste of the food at all because of stress. Well... if someone asked what I ate and what we were talking about, I would have a big problem with answering the question, as if this part of my life was consumed by a black hole.

We both carefully discussed the topic of what we will do after dinner. Apparently, not just me who felt uncomfortable. Finally, there was a strange, expectant silence that hung in the air like a thick, stormy cloud.

That's enough - I murmured in my mind. I couldn't sit still anymore.

I stood up and, with studied calm, began to collect dirty dishes from the table. Better than stupid staring at my plate for the rest of the evening.

"What are you doing?" Korin asked in a low voice, breaking the silence.

"You cooked, I clean up," I replied without looking at him.

He was right behind me in an instant. He clung to my back and murmured in my ear:

"Leave it."

He held my hand. He slowly took out the plates I had picked up a second ago to put them back on the table.

"Later, Em. I will take care of it," his voice became more and more sensual, while I unsuccessfully tried to deal with my own fear.

It wasn't Korin that I was afraid of. Nor what would happen soon. I was afraid of myself, that I would disappoint him, that he would not think that I'm attractive, that I would do something wrong...

Of course, he noticed it, he always noticed.

He could read all my moods flawlessly, although he wasn't always aware of its cause.

"Em, what's going on?"

"Nothing," I lied.

I closed my eyelids. In a moment it will pass, it's nothing, I repeated in my mind, trying to calm down.

"You're tense," he said, assessing my condition properly.

And what should I answer him? I have been waiting for this evening for weeks, dreaming about it at night,

354

and when it came - just chickened up? I barely admitted it to myself, so how to say it to him?

"Will you tell me what's going on before I completely go crazy?" He turned me over and hugged me.

He gently rubbed the skin around my lips.

"I'm scared," I whispered.

"Me?" He asked without interrupting his caress.

"No... maybe yes."

He pushed me away from him and put his head to one side to look into my eyes.

"You know I won't hurt you. I couldn't hurt anyone, especially not you. I thought you knew that."

"I know, but that's not the point. I'm afraid you

won't find me attractive, I'll disappoint you."

He laughed softly and hugged me tightly.

"I like you already, and if you take it off," he slightly raised my blouse, "I will like you even more."

My heart skipped a beat.

"Is something else bothering you?" He asked.

"Actually yes. I don't know anything about these things," I said, feeling myself blushing.

"I know, it should be enough."

Now I moved away. I looked at him in surprise. To be honest, I didn't like that answer. I think I was jealous.

Jealousy. A jealousy that I absolutely had no right to.

"I thought your first time was just to be with your genetic partner. I did not know that you already... But I do not mind." I added quickly, immediately regretting the words just said.

I knew what I signed up for. A relationship with no future and no obligations, there was no room for asking questions. Korin's reaction was surprising, he just laughed.

"It's not what you think. I know a lot, but in theory."

"Theoretically?"

"Hmm..." He scratched his head, clearly embarrassed.

"Korin, answer me."

"I had sex training, such a course."

"Are you kidding me?! Did you have sex to pass?"

"Not exactly."

"I cannot believe this. And what did you practice on each other or on special phantoms?!"

"We did not practice, the classes were purely theoretical, although they were very detailed."

"You know what? You are perverted," I said disgusted, but after a while I began to giggle and I could not calm down. I don't know if what he said was true, but at least he managed to release the tension.

"Don't laugh, I've learned something there. I'll show you what soon." He kissed my lips hard, then suddenly took my hands, threw me over his shoulder, and hurried up the stairs. After a while I landed softly on a large bed in his bedroom.

While Korin was lighting candles prepared earlier, I was looking around the room. Unbelievable. He took care of everything here and did it for me. Candles, wonderfully soft bedding in dark purple, which in low light seemed almost black and an exotic scent floating in the air, stimulating the senses, reminiscent of some original passion. I sat motionless in the middle of the large bed and waited. Korin approached slowly but said nothing. He just stood and watched as if he was assessing how much he could afford.

"I think you are wearing too much clothing," he said finally. "Do you want to get rid of it yourself or should I help you?"

"You first. Undress," I said, swallowing hard.

Without a word and without additional encouragement, he took off his black T-shirt, threw it on the floor, still not taking his eyes off my face.

I held my breath.

He had a beautifully sculpted body, slender muscles and smooth skin. I wasn't shy, but tonight, this

evening, the approaching night, just outgrown me. I felt like not me, as if I was just watching myself and Korin from behind a thick glass window, and everything I see was just an illusion.

"Em, now you," he said softly.

I pulled off my shirt with slight reluctance. I stayed in the bra itself. I wrapped my arms reflexively and lowered my eyes in embarrassment.

"You still have too much clothing," Korin murmured right next to my ear.

I shuddered at the sound of his erotic voice. He was so close that we almost touched our heads. He kissed me briefly on the shoulder, then reached into my back with his hand to unfasten the bra fastener. I disentangled myself from my straps and tossed my bra to the edge of the bed. I exposed my breasts and only then looked at him. The first thing I noticed was a flash of lust in his eyes.

He ran his hand lightly over my bare breasts, barely touching them. He didn't have to wait long for a response. The nipples hardened immediately, and a pleasant tingling spread throughout my body. He smiled slightly when he noticed it.

"Emily, lie down," he asked.

I made what he asked for.

He stretched out beside me, propping himself up on his elbow.

"Close your eyes."

"Why?" I asked quietly. I had no idea what he was getting at.

"Trust me, please."

And this is unlike me, but I made what he asked for again.

After a moment I felt the touch of his warm hand on my cheek. He caressed slowly with his slender fingers every, even the smallest detail of my face, eyelids, eyebrows, lips, nose, chin... He kept talking to me, or rather murmuring tenderly:

"You must open yourself to the reactions of your body, Em, learn to derive pleasure from it."

He moved his hand over my neck.

"At first you may not know what's going on with you. Excitement is something on the verge of pain, madness and loss of self-control. Turn off thinking, Emily. Let yourself be carried away."

His hand went down. Now he was contouring the exact shape of each rib to finally stop on my breast. I moaned quietly and began to breathe faster as he brushed my nipple with his thumb.

In his every move, in every caress, in every whisper of the word there was almost indefinable patience and some unimaginable heat that flowed in me in a stream, igniting from the inside. Korin did nothing special, just touched and whispered, but he slowly awakened my femininity. And I liked it, I liked it too much.

I wanted more. More caresses, more sensations, more Korin.

He sensed the moment when I opened up to him.

"If you want me to stop, tell me," he whispered, bringing his lips to my lips. "I won't do anything against your will."

I only nodded in the affirmative, because after a while he kissed me, but not like then in the greenhouse,

nor like yesterday at school. Those kisses were fervent and wild, but innocent, and there was hidden underlying indecent passion in today's kisses. Korin caressed my palate with his tongue, every now and then awakening my senses more and more, he led me to areas of sensations from which there was no turning back.

Past fears and uncertainty have given way to growing desire. I got lost in Korin, just like he got lost in me. But I didn't just want to take, I also wanted to give, and he didn't have to tell me what to do. I knew it myself. My body reacted instinctively. It responded with trembling to even the slightest caress.

I put my arms around his neck, entangled my fingers in thick, dark hair. I pulled him close to me. I could taste his tongue in my mouth, the smell of his skin pleasantly irritated my nostrils, and the heat of his hands ignited my senses. My body shook with gentle, single chills, and when I thought I was about to explode, Korin pulled away from my lips and with trembling lips followed kisses down.

He slowly, methodically went lower and lower. Now he caressed my neck with his tongue, and the whisper of his breath on my skin made me soft inside.

My breathing quickened.

I slid my hands over his strong arms, clutching my fingers with all my strength. In reply, Korin groaned softly and moved even lower, stopping for a long time in the hollow between my breasts. At the same time, he took one breast in his hand, massaging it gently. From time to time, he stabbed the skin around the nipple with his teeth. I crouched under it with pleasure, only by willpower refraining from screaming.Korin touched me exactly where I wanted to be touched, caressed me the way I wanted to be caressed, and each brush of his nimble fingers on my skin only intensified my excitement.

I still wanted more.

I squeezed his arms tighter. I gently pushed Korin down to feel him lower. Now he ran a warm tongue over my stomach, and his breath, excited with excitement, blew my skin, causing my whole body to shake. Korin was also trembling, and just as I was, he could hardly tame his emotions.

When his lips began to suck my navel, I lost control leftovers, and when he reached the edge of the jeans, I was ready, ready to take whatever Korin wanted to give me.

"Too much clothing," I gasped quietly.

"Far too much," he said, unbuttoning my pants.

I raised a little hip. Korin pulled off my jeans and briefs with one quick movement. Without taking his eyes off me, he hurriedly undresses his pants.

I saw him now, beautiful and shamelessly naked. He looked at me as if he saw nothing else, as if the world around had ceased to exist. He could read the same from my eyes - the same desire, the same heat and the same passion. None of us spoke. Words were superfluous, we both knew it.

He slowly parted my legs with his hand. He bent, sliding warm lips on the inside of my thigh. I shuddered and sighed softly. I have never experienced anything like this in my life, at the moment I needed his touch like air. He caressed the skin on my legs more intensively, with each kiss going higher, from the knees to the confluence of thighs. I felt hungry squeeze in the aching lower abdomen. A wave of wetness flooded me.

Everything I felt for Korin before seemed only a small stream of desire now, because what he was doing with my body turned it into a rushing river and I knew it would not end there. I knew that in a moment all the emotions that had unleashed in me would have the power of a waterfall. And this is also insufficient comparison. As if to confirm these thoughts, Korin moved over me, parted my lips with his tongue, and took possession of my mouth violently. At the same time, he pressed his right hand between my thighs and caressed my wet labia with gentle movements of nimble fingers.

A moan of pleasure died in my larynx.

I threw my arms around his neck and clung to him tightly. I wanted to feel him, everywhere, with whole body. He clearly wanted it too. He put a finger in me, then a second, he moved up and down, turned, slipped, teased, causing tremor. I felt myself tightening around his fingers. I screamed softly, more in pleasure than in pain. Korin was still at the sound. He took his lips from my lips and looked into my eyes uncertainly.

"Don't... don't stop," I moaned weakly.

"For sure?"

"Yes," I said softly, closing his mouth with a kiss.

He kissed me fervently, caressing my wet interior more and more intensively. I writhed in ecstasy, I wanted more. My body demanded more, even when my mind suggested otherwise.

"Korin, do something, please... I will explode in a moment," I whispered.

"Are you sure?"

"Yes. I want you... I want to feel you inside me."

"I want you too."

He put his hands at my shoulder height and slipped cautiously inside me. He hung above me, watching my face closely. He looked for signs of suffering, but apart from a subtle prick somewhere inside, I felt no pain. I didn't really know what I felt... Joy, love, excitement, fear, uncertainty. At that moment all sensations merged into one - boundless desire.

Reflexively, I wrapped my legs around his strong hips, arms around his wide back. We clung to each other greedily, two naked bodies entwined in a loving embrace. Hot, shameless and beautiful. Korin propped himself up on his elbows, buried his face in my neck, just below the ear, and began to move inside me. At first, slowly and gently, but when we found a common rhythm, his movements accelerated. I had the impression that in a moment I will go crazy from the overwhelming pleasure, I have never experienced anything like this before. I didn't breathe anymore, but I was panting as if after a crazy run. His breathing also got louder, uneven... Then he slowed down. Instead, he entered me deeper... harder... The trembling of his lips on my neck made the sensations even stronger. I screamed when I felt pleasant jerks inside me, as if some invisible force sucked me inside. Korin pushed a few more times, then fell on me with a low moan. We came almost simultaneously.

Without letting go of me, he turned on his back and pulled me on himself. We lay there until our breaths returned to normal rhythms. Then he asked quietly:

"How are you, Em?"

I raised my head slightly to look into those incredibly purple eyes.

"Awesome," I whispered dreamily. What else can you call sex with Arisyan?

"So, I didn't disappoint you?" He asked with a smile.

I straightened up and sat on his stomach. He put his hands on my hips and stroked affectionately.

"You didn't disappoint," I assured honestly, tracing my lower lip with my thumb. "They taught you a lot in this course."

"I didn't learn everything on the course," he replied.

"No...?" I frowned.

"I learned a lot from you."

"From me?" I was even more surprised.

Korin smiled with blissful hands over my bare thighs.

"Do you remember how in the base you showed me your skin's reaction to touch, while realizing that mine reacts exactly the same? Training did not include it, Em. This is not Arisyan caress."

"You don't touch each other?"

"We touch," he explained. "But in areas more obvious to Arisyan."

Without waiting for me to comment, he put his hand between my thighs.

"Here," he said.

Then he hugged me tightly and put me quickly on the bed next to him.

"Here," he murmured, taking my breast in his hand.

"And here..." He ended with a short kiss on my lips.

"Why didn't you follow the instructions, you know, those from the course?"

He brushed my hair back behind my ear.

"First of all, I have not once convinced myself that Arisyan instructions are not always about you. Secondly, I promised it would be special and I wanted to keep my word. Thirdly, I enjoyed it too. And fourthly, I felt your orgasm and it... it was amazing, Em."

I didn't speak, just stuck my cheek against his torso. Without a word, he pulled the blanket over us and put his arms around me. He knew I understood him. What we were doing that night was not just sex. Sex is an empty word, it doesn't matter. Korin did not have sex with me. He made love with me, tried in his own way to give me a substitute for something he did not fully understand, something that we call love here on Earth. And he succeeded. Now we both knew that.

The cold morning woke me up. I raised on my elbows slightly, only after a moment realizing where I was and why. Korin, who was sleeping on my stomach, embraced my waist. I looked around the room where the atmosphere of passion and sex could still be felt. The impression was intensified by the view of clothes scattered in disarray and bedding stacked at the foot of the bed.

I sat down and carefully slipped out from under his arm. I was happy, maybe a little sore inside, but happy... As if I woke up in paradise and got everything

I missed all my life. After a wonderful night in Korin's arms, it was easy to think that way. It is nothing that the reality is different, today I wanted to believe that I have it exclusively, that at the moment it belongs only to me and that it will always be so.

I looked fondly at Korin's face, deeply asleep in my direction, at his naked muscular body and felt a pleasant warmth spreading inside me. Despite his different skin color, he was no stranger, he was a flesh and blood guy, and now he was closer to me than ever before.

I sighed and reached for the quilt to cover his bare back. I froze with the quilt in my hand when I noticed the scar. At night I didn't even think about it, it completely occurred to me that it was on his back. Now, in the morning light, I saw it clearly. It was really nasty. Long, thick, torn. It stood out clearly against the darker skin.

I sat like as enchanted for a moment. I don't even know when I let go of the quilt and started running the scar with my fingertips. I felt its slippery surface under my fingers and, paradoxically, it seemed beautiful to me. Maybe because it belonged to him? Because it was associated with tragic, but earthly story? Because he trusted me and told me about it? Because it made Korin's perfect body not so perfect? It is difficult to determine which of these things stimulated the imagination more, but naked Korin, sleeping right next to me, suddenly seemed damn sexy to me. The scar, although not pretty, gave him some strange charm.

Korin shifted uneasily on the bed. I pulled my hand away in alarm.

Too late.

I looked at him confused, meeting the curious, purple gaze on me.

"I'm sorry, I know you didn't want me to touch it," I said quietly and had a grimace of pain in his face before my eyes when he told me about the accident.

"I didn't want to then, but now... I don't understand it... now it excites me when you do it."

As if to confirm his words he leaned aside, showing his manhood in full erection. He surprised me so much that I stopped breathing from the feeling. He laughed at my reaction.

I gave him slap in shoulder angrily.

"It's not funny at all."

He grabbed me halfway and pulled me. Torso clung to my back and wrapped his arms tightly so that I could not free myself.

"I can't help it that you affect me like that," he murmured, gently biting the lobe of my ear.

That sensual voice, the warmth of his breath in my hair and the touch of his smooth skin again made me shiver.

"You act on me in this same way, as if you didn't notice," I said weakly.

"I noticed," he whispered, and I felt on my skin that he was smiling.

He ran his tongue over my neck, again causing me a wave of delightful chills.

"I think we'll have to do something about it," he said, kissing my neck sensually.

With one hand he embraced my breast tenderly, and the other parted my thighs, lightly fingering my labia. I moaned when under the influence of this subtle

caress I felt pressure in my lower abdomen and an inflow of warm wetness flooding my interior. Korin immediately sensed it under his fingers. He clung tighter to my back, involuntarily flexing all his muscles.

"Are you very sore after yesterday?" He asked tenderly, lips sticking to my shoulder.

"A little bit, but it's nothing. I want it... I want to feel you."

"You'll feel me, but a little different... without penetration," he whispered.

At the same time, he slipped his swollen, throbbing penis between my hot with desire thighs so that he just touched the vaginal entrance. A touch of electricity ran through me and made me feel as wet as never before.

I bit my bottom lip with all my strength so as not to scream with pleasure.

Korin put his left hand to my womb, pulling me tightly to his hips, while his right clenched my breast and began to move. Slowly, carefully, but faster and faster with every second.

His penis silky smooth skin irritated my labia rhythmically, sliding over their warm wetness. His hand greedily embraced my breast, his thumb circled the nipple in a circular motion, his hungry lips fed my skin around my neck, his loud breathing almost took my senses away.

I didn't even moan anymore but wailed wildly.

I reached behind and clenched my fingers tightly on his hair. He murmured something incomprehensibly, squeezed me harder and accelerated. At the same moment, a wave of orgasm flowed over me, intense, overpowering and painful in its pleasure. And then one

more and the next one... Korin groaned for a long time, flexed a few times and came right after me. Sated and satisfied, we fell limp to the bed, panting heavily.

My body was still shivering, and Korin was still shivering. He didn't let me out of his arms. With a calming gesture, he stroked my hand, entwined his fingers with mine, and rested his cheek on my temple. He spoke tenderly all the time, at least I thought so, because he spoke in Arisyan. I didn't understand a word, but it was pleasant, and I didn't want him to stop.

He surprised me, not just now. He constantly surprised me, above all with his warmth and patience. This is not what I expected from Arisyan. I thought Korin would be cold, that he would only satisfy his needs without giving anything in return, while I received more than I could have imagined in my wildest dreams. I greedily remembered every touch, every gesture, every affectionately spoken word, as if the supply of these feelings would last me for my whole life. I don't know how many more moments like this there will be - we will soon have to stop this love game - but for now here and now is important, time has ceased to exist, and let it be so, at least today.

I sighed softly, snuggled closer into his strong arms, and the throaty sound of Arisyan whisper words made me sleepy.

CHAPTER XV

There are people who prefer to have nothing to hide, rather than being obliged to lie; people who prefer lying to having nothing to hide. And people who like both lying and hidden.

ALBERT CAMUS

I don't know what really woke me up: whether the sound of the conversation quite loud coming from below, or the rattling of dishes folded in a hurry, or the feeling of coldness and emptiness that enveloped me when I slept, but probably the last one. Definitely the lack of a soothing, warm touch of Korin woke me from sleep. I didn't have to open my eyes to know that he wasn't with me. His voice came from the kitchen, where he fiercely discussed something with his sister.

"Why didn't you answer the phone?"

"How many times do I have to tell you that I didn't hear my cell phone because it was on the kitchen table," Korin said impatiently. "Don't panic, we'll make it... You see, it's almost cleaned."

There was a silence for a moment, which was broken only by the clicks of closed kitchen cabinets and sliding drawers.

"What?" He asked. "Why are you looking like that?"

"Nothing," she laughed.

"What do you mean?"

"You look like a truck hit you. So, you haven't left the bedroom since yesterday?"

"Come on, Kori, it's not your business."

"Okay, you're right, I don't ask you anything anymore. Is Emily still sleeping?"

"In my room."

"I guess she is in your room, not our parents' room. I better wake her up, because if she is in the same condition as you, she will need some time to pull herself together."

I heard a quick patter of feet on the stairs and after a moment the door opened with impetus. Kori fell into the bedroom just when I sat on the bed slightly muddle-headed, unsuccessfully trying to find out what time of day it was.

"Hi, sleepyhead, get ready," she said, then pulled the quilt off me.

"What happened?" I asked, my voice still sleepy.

"A small change of plans, parents return the day before, they will be in an hour, so if you do not want them to get you out of bedding, you better hurry up."

"What time is it?"

"It's four pm."

"Oh my." I fell limp on the pillows. "We slept so long?"

"Slept?" Kori snorted. "I think you not only slept..."

"Hardly at all."

"And how was it?" She winked at me knowingly.

"Cosmically," I whispered dreamily, covering myself again with the quilt.

"I'm sorry to interrupt you, Emily." She sat next to me. "I tried to reach Korin, but hmm..." she smiled mockingly, "it looks like you were really busy."

She leaned over me and took a deep breath.

"It not my business, but you smell of Arisyan sperm and sex."

I blushed at the tip of my ears for this remark.

"Very funny," I snorted, though I knew she was right.

She jumped up abruptly.

"Don't sulk, just take a shower." She pulled my hand, raised me upright, and pushed me toward the bathroom. "In the meantime, I will try to clear up here somehow."

Then, grumbling something indistinctly, she began to tidy the room, first opening the window as if the concentration of erotic odors in the air disturbed her the most. I went into the bathroom quickly. I preferred not to be here when she began to collect parts of our wardrobe scattered across the floor. Certainly, it wouldn't be without some malicious comments.

I went to a warm shower. Washing the leftovers of the last night, I wondered how what had happened between me and Korin would affect our relationship. It was getting harder and harder to believe that it was just a game of love, but I no longer had the strength to stop playing it. That night changed something in me, made me passionate, exposed sexuality, causing even my body to react differently now. Just at the thought of Korin, I felt a pleasant throb inside my vagina. The newly discovered woman in me demanded fulfillment. At the same time, I was aware that I have no rights in

this relationship, and even if they are temporary rights. My choice, so I will have to deal with the consequences myself. Later. At the moment, I defined my mood as full of happiness and let it stay as long as possible.

I turned off the water, wrapped myself in a towel and left the bathroom. Korin was sitting on an evenly made bed. He was wearing yesterday's t-shirt, of course, back in front, and crumpled jeans, and his tousled hair stuck out in a different direction. He looked confused.

"Hi," I smiled shyly at him.

He stood up and slowly approached me.

"Hey," he said, embracing me tenderly.

He surprised me with this gesture. He did it just as if it resulted from some internal need, not from a sense of duty or decency. And if I was afraid before that his closeness would make me feel so bad after that night, then my fears would be dispelled. In a quite ordinary, natural impulse, we huddled together, lasting for a while without a word.

We only loosened the embrace when we heard Kori grunt significantly. She stood in the doorway and watched us with interest.

"I'm sorry to interrupt this idyll, but..." she didn't finish. She waved a hand in resignation. "And you have fifteen minutes. Emily, I'm waiting for you in the car."

She left, closing the door behind her.

"Korin, turn around, I have to get dressed."

He didn't move. He looked at me.

"Do not look at me like that."

He bit his lower lip as if he wants to say something but hesitated.

"How about I will dress you up?" He asked quietly.

"You're not serious," I said uncertainly.

"Let me do that, Em, please," he said and pulled the towel off me.

"Korin!" I growled, trying to grab the edge of the towel, but I did not make it, he threw it to the floor a meter from us.

I was standing completely naked in front of him and I didn't even try to hide myself. The intense gaze of his purple eyes immobilized me. It expressed everything: fire, desire, passion, worship, admiration, respect, promise... but not love. I don't know how I recognized that the latter was missing, it just wasn't there. Maybe if I did not know the truth about the defective set of unfortunate Arisyan genes, I would mistake all these

376

feelings for love, but I did not want to deceive myself. For now, it was enough for me that I felt special, special for him.

"One second. Don't move," he whispered, brushing my lips gently with a kiss.

He reached for the bra slung over the back of the chair, straightened up, and soon slipped thin straps onto my forearms. He did it slowly, sensuously, while caressing the skin on my hands with his fingertips. When he reached my arms, I felt hot, I couldn't catch my breath. The room swirled violently, and I felt it suddenly start to shrink.

Korin also lost himself in these sensations. I recognized this by the slight shaking of his hands that gripped my hips to gently but firmly turn me a hundred and eighty degrees. He managed the bra fastening very

well, then put his hands forward and touched my breasts. I shivered. I knew that one more touch and I would lose control over my body, and so would he. Contrary to myself, guided by a remnant of reason, I turned to face him, taking the opportunity to a safe distance, though in these circumstances probably no distance could not be considered safe.

"T-shirt now," I said weakly, trying to calm my breath. "You were supposed to dress me, not drive me crazy."

"Right." He ran his hand through my hair absentmindedly, tugging it even more. I liked his gesture and the uncertain expression he made.

He took a clean T-shirt from my backpack, and when he pulled it on me, I felt much more confident.

"Now is ok," I smiled. "This pace of dress is definitely safer."

"I'm not done yet," he said, grabbing me in his arms and sitting me on the edge of the bed.

I didn't even manage to protest. He immediately started putting on my black lace panties. Slowly and extremely sensual, he irritated the skin on my calves with his fingers, and showered my thighs with warm, passionate kisses. Every time he touched me using his lips, I felt a pleasant tingling build up in my body. At the moment, I didn't want him to dress me. I wanted to take everything off and then deprive him of his clothes. I felt hot and my thighs tightened when I felt the warm wetness between them. I dug my fingers into his arms, pushing him away with a firm gesture.

"Korin, you're torturing me again," I groaned.

"Not only you, me too," he admitted in a broken

voice. "Although this is quite a pleasant torture."

"Arisyan's inflicting pain through pleasure... Was that also in training?" I mocked, trying to extinguish the fire that he unleashed in me with his caresses.

"No, this is my original project."

"You just chose the wrong time for its implementation."

With a heavy sigh he rose from his knees and sat on the bed, keeping his distance.

"You're right, I think I exaggerated a little."

He handed me my pants and turned his head the other way.

"Finish it yourself, Em, I won't look."

"Next time I will dress you up," I joked to relieve somehow of the tension, but it turned out badly. The air around was so thick from our hardly concealed desires that no words, no matter how funny, could not change it.

We went outside. Korin embraced me at the waist with one hand and pressed hard against his hip, while in the other he carried my backpack. All over my skin I felt the burning heat of his touch, which made me want to go back to the bedroom with him and finish what we started, but in the reverse order. Therefore, as soon as we stood by the car, I slipped out of his embrace, jumped into the front seat and slammed the door to separate myself from him as soon as possible. I didn't look in his direction, I only heard him throw my luggage into the back seat. I didn't even turn to wave goodbye to him, I couldn't.

"Kori, move on," I said hoarsely.

She looked at me anxiously.

"What happened?"

"Nothing, just go now!"

She started off without a word but stopped the car on the side of the road around the next bend. She stared at me, repeating the question:

"What? Happened? Did you argue?"

"No."

"So, what did he do to you?!"

"Nothing."

"So, why are you so upset? It doesn't look like nothing."

"He dressed me," I finally choked.

"And...?" Kori looked as if waiting for the continuation.

"There is no 'and'... Your brother dressed me. The end. But he did it in such a sensual way that..." my voice broke, I did not finish. At the memory of what had just happened in the bedroom, I just lacked words. "It's getting harder. In addition, his behavior awakened my hope for something more."

Kori sighed and shook her head.

"Don't be fooled. He simply fulfills his duties and, as usual, does it perfectly. Don't imagine too much. I know he is trying very hard, which even amazed me, but he is not like me, don't forget about it, Emily."

"Why are you different?"

She shrugged.

"I don't know, it's always been like that. Maybe I have something wrong with my genes? Mutations do happen, rarely but they do happen. Arisyan woman with feelings. Strange right?" She laughed bitterly.

"Did you tell your parents?"

"No," she said quickly. "They can't find out because they'll send me home."

"You think they don't guess?"

Kori began nervously nibbling the edge of her blouse.

"Probably not. The only obvious anomaly is my fascination with literature, so they stated that I was simply suffering from a mild variation of Earth syndrome."

"Earth syndrome?" This is the first time I have come across such a concept. "What is that?"

"Some Arisyans began to show typical earthly features, especially when it comes to interests. For now, my father thinks that everything is under control and there is nothing to worry about. He is to take some precautionary measures only when he observes the manifestations of aggression in these people."

"Quite a sensible approach," I admitted. "That's what I like your father for. He knows how to do the right thing in every situation."

"Korin is like him in this respect. Although... She frowned, apparently wondering whether to finish her thought. "Ever since he got in touch with you, his rationality has deserted to Jupiter, and it doesn't seem like it'll be back soon."

I laughed at this unexpected statement, but soon became serious.

"Maybe Korin also suffers from Earth syndrome and maybe also feelings arise in him?" I asked hopefully.

Kori grabbed my arm tightly and looked into my

eyes seriously.

"Emily, come back down to earth. My brother has always been, is and will be a blood and bone Arisyan. Nothing will change that. And certainly not juvenile hormones, which now slightly obscured his logical thinking."

She moved away from me, adding a little quieter:

"I wish I had made it easier for you. It is dread to think about how you will react when his genetic partner arrives."

"In no way," I said, trying to be indifferent. "I won't be there."

"What does 'I won't be there' mean?" Kori asked anxiously. "I hope you don't plan to do some stupid thing."

"No worries."

"I don't think so," she murmured.

"I'll leave before she comes."

"Are you crazy?! And where will you go?"

"I will probably come home with my mother."

"To Fargo?" My answer clearly surprised her.

"Yes."

"Fargo is in the north! Don't you realize how dangerous it is?!" She raised her voice. She seemed terrified of my idea.

We were silent for a moment. Kori seemed to be thinking about something. She suspected that the trip plan was not born alone, it had to result from something.

"Wait, wait... Korin forced you to make such a declaration. Right?"

I rolled my eyes. This is not the content of the

question I expected.

"He didn't make me do anything, on the contrary, I forced him. I promised that I would disappear from his life as soon as this genetic bitch appears. Only then he decided to have a six-month relationship with me."

"I wonder now who is more affected. Him or you? It will end badly for you, and actually it will end badly above all for you. If I were you, I would withdraw from this deal," she said deadly seriously.

Of course, she was right. She was damn right, but some time ago I made a decision and I had no intention of changing it. Certainly not after last night. I answered equally seriously:

"Listen to me, Kori. I have practically been dead for the past ten years. So, it doesn't matter I breathed, ate, studied and functioned in all this. There were such moments that I just had enough. Now I have the possibility of a normal existence and I intend to use it. So, don't blame me I want to live as if there is no tomorrow. That's how I chose and no matter where it leads me. If you can't understand it, try to accept it though."

"You're right," she admitted, but very reluctantly. "It's not my business, but I can't help it that I care about you. Perhaps this is what earthly friendship is based on, among other things?"

I smiled warmly at her.

"Thanks for being with me... Kori."

"You're welcome," she murmured, but it seemed she had somehow calmed down. "We've been standing here for almost an hour and the windows in the car have fogged up. It's time to transport you home."

"Fact. I should still come up with another story for my mother, why I am the day before. She'll be a little surprised to see me."

"You'll be fine."

"Emily?" My mother looked up while she was reading the book, sitting comfortably in an armchair. "What are you doing here? You were not to return until tomorrow afternoon, unless something was wrong."

"You didn't make a mistake."

She looked at me closely.

"Something happened?"

"Kori's parents are back today. I felt a little embarrassed by their presence," I lied amazingly smoothly. "They are very nice and absolutely did not let me feel that I was interfering with them, but I felt a bit uncomfortable."

"I understand." She put the book on the back of the chair, stood up and hugged me tightly. "It is a pity that the weekend did not look like you planned."

If she would know at least ten percent of these plans, I wouldn't have had the chance to leave home for a month or more.

"The weekend was quite successful," I said with satisfaction. "Don't worry, it was very agreeably."

What am I saying 'agreeably'? What a terrible understatement. I found myself evacuating myself better before my mother, suggesting my statements, gains some suspicion. In addition, I exuded an extremely good mood and understood it would not escape her attention. I didn't want to lie more than necessary.

"Mom, I'll go to my place. I think I need to take a nap. We gossiped with Kori almost until morning, so you understand..."

"Sure, I know how it is." She tousled my hair affectionately. "I'll call you to dinner."

I stretched out on the bed, although I wasn't sleepy at all. I could still feel the smell and Korin's touch on my skin, and the taste of his kisses in my mouth, so it's no

385

wonder that contemplation of these fresh sensations made me think quite absurdly. In my mind's eye I saw a genetic shuttle falling into a black hole, colliding with a giant asteroid or looping through time for all eternity. No other cosmic catastrophe came to my mind at that moment. It is nothing that such things did not happen, but since I could not keep Korin for myself, I still had the right to dream.

Next four weeks were probably the happiest in my life so far, not counting my early childhood, when the world was not topsy-turvy. At school, Korin and I were almost inseparable, although we tried to behave decently - no hand-holding or even kisses. Even so, I had the impression that other students were guessing something. What worried me the most was Professor Spite, who watched us quite often, as if he were piercing us through, as if he wanted to read our thoughts, as if he knew... Whenever I encountered his appraising eyes, a cold shiver pierced me and prophylactically I moved some distance from Korin, which Spite acknowledged with a strange curving of lips that replaced his smile.

I liked school, but since the situation between me and Korin cleared up, I preferred moments spent with him after class. Most often we went to me or to him and we just were... We didn't do anything special, we talked a lot, we learned, although rarely the same things, but his presence was enough for me. When we want to have sex, we drove to the outskirts of the town and we made it in the car. Actually, we didn't have a specific place on earth, it didn't bother me. I fed on Korin and his presence while I could. We didn't have much time left, and the one we had at my disposal, I wanted to use to the maximum. Anyway, I didn't know at the time that there was much less of that time. After the rebel attack on the base, the world staggered again, and one should not take anything for granted.

Somewhere around mid-June Korin got a little sad. Like everything was as usual, he was smiling, joking, but I couldn't get rid of the impression that something was bothering him and, in some way, it has to do with me. It was Wednesday, it was raining, so we sat in my room. When we did all the lessons, Korin stretched out on my bed, stared thoughtlessly at the ceiling and sighed heavily. I couldn't stand it. I sat next to him and without further ado asked:

"Okay, now tell me what's wrong with you?"

He cleared his throat and rubbed his forehead thoughtfully.

"How to explain it to you..." he began uncertainly. "You have a special word for it on Earth... remorse."

"Do you feel guilty about your genetic partner?" I asked surprised.

I was surprised that suddenly Korin began to see the relationship with me in the category of betrayal.

Was he going to terminate our contract sooner?

I swallowed loudly. Seeing the expression on my face, he denied quickly.

"No, that's absolutely not the point." He sat up. "I promised you half a year together, but... I will have to go to the space shuttle pilot training for some time to Manning."

He calmed me down a bit, but I still didn't like what he said.

"Could you define the term 'sometime'?"

"Two weeks."

I breathed a sigh of relief. I thought he would say 'two months'. Meanwhile, two weeks without Korin did not seem so scary, after all, it was only fourteen days, I consoled myself in spirit.

"You are not angry at me?" He asked.

"It's not your fault," I said coldly.

"To be honest, I had no idea how you would react. Recently, when I said something wrong, you bombarded me with shoes."

"Ha, ha, ha... very funny." I grabbed a large bundle of foil lying on the edge of the bed and hit him in the head with it.

Before the next blow he covered himself with both hands.

"Well, that behavior is more like you," he said, laughing. "I know it makes no sense, but I think I like you the most for this unpredictability."

I put the foils aside and brought my face closer to his face so that we almost touched our noses.

"And I thought you liked my body and my green eyes," I murmured with feigned grudge.

He kissed my lips and hugged me.

"I think I should make a list of features that I particularly like in you."

"It could be interesting," I said with amusement.

At times like this, it was easy to believe that we would succeed, that I meant something to him, that we belonged to each other. What is love really? It's friendship, sex and mutual understanding... Theoretically, we met all the criteria, and yet what bound us together could not be called love. For the Arisyans, this concept was as foreign to our entire planet. This wasn't just about Kori and Tom. Although Korin did not notice the difference between their relationship and ours, but I did, and clearly. Meanwhile, I was aware that I did the stupidest thing in my life, I fell in love with the wrong person.

"Tell me about Arisa," I broke the prolonged silence.

"That's one of the things I like," he laughed softly.

"What?" I asked, a bit confused. I didn't quite know what he was talking about now.

"Your tendency to litter your brain with unnecessary information. You'll see, someday you will run out of disk space."

"Don't worry, I have more room there than many Arisyans," I bit back.

He embraced me tightly and kissed my forehead.

"So, what do you want to know?"

"Everything. Does your planet have a natural satellite, is the sky blue on a clear day, is the sun red when it sets, is the grass green and is there any grass growing on Arisa... I know these are stupid questions."

"If you think about it, they are not so stupid," he replied on second thought. "Did you know that Alpha Centauri has the G2V spectral type, just like your Sun?"

"Honestly? I had no idea," I said reluctantly.

I didn't like to admit to Korin that I don't know something. But I loved the look on his face when I surprised him with knowledge in some field. Although today it ceased to have any significance, today I could admit total ignorance on any subject, as long as he spoke to me, just to hear his voice.

Korin usually complained about my curiosity about the world, but when he was already explaining a problem, he did it with real passion. Therefore, I learned that the G2V spectral type means that both stars emit yellow light, which, when contacted with air particles, ice crystals, water droplets and pollen contained in the atmosphere, is dispersed in all directions. It is the sum of the scattered light in the entire visible spectrum that gives the sunny sky-blue color. If our planets had no atmosphere, the sky would simply be black, and the stars would be visible during the day.

Korin also tried to describe to me the fauna and flora of Aris. That's right, he tried. Nothing came of it. I don't know if he was guilty of not being able to use his word vividly, whether it was my imagination that fooled me. I had a problem illustrating something that does not exist in our world. Anyway, I was distracted that Korin had unknowingly put Arisyan words into his stories. Hearing them, I looked surprised and then we both burst out laughing. At that time, we were not yet aware that the last days before Korin left for training

are also the last days of our joyful carefree. After July 4, nothing will be as it was. My new, recently discovered world was slowly heading to the next catastrophe.

CHAPTER XVI

You better not narrate anything to anyone.
Because if you narrate - you will start to miss.
JEROME DAVID SALINGER

The next two weeks were simply nightmarish. Initially, I explained the bad mood to myself with the weather, but of course it wasn't the rainy weather that bothered me. I missed Korin. And until he left, I didn't even think I had become so attached to him. No wonder, since I found myself in this new Arisyan-Earth world, Korin has always been here. He actually appeared in it on the first day and from then on became its permanent element. Now I had a foretaste of what my life would be like without him, and I didn't like it at all.

And the worst thing was knowing that I'm nothing to him and he will not miss me because he just couldn't miss. In turn, I was getting more and more depressed day by day. It's good that after school my band had rehearsals lasting several hours before the Independence Day concert, otherwise I would be sitting in my room and sobbing at the pillow.

I think only Kori knew what was going on inside me. She watched me with growing concern. On Friday, July

1, she couldn't stand it and stopped me in the corridor before math. I expected to hear in a moment: "And I did not say that you and my brother are a bad idea" or other similar wisdom in life, but nothing was said.

"I'm taking you to the pub tonight," she said firmly.

"You have to have fun, or you'll go crazy. I'll come for you at 7pm."

"Kori, dispense with it. I'm not in the mood for fun."

"All the more you should go out somewhere," she argued unimpressed. "I think you need company and a portion of solid conversation. If you refuse, I will pull you out by force, even if you barricade yourself in your room."

"Agreed but promise we won't be there long. I really don't feel like going to parties. Besides, I don't know if my mother will let me go."

"She will, she will..." she smiled broadly at me. "Let me worry about that. Anyway, your mom likes me."

"She likes you," I admitted. "I don't understand why. Every time you fund her a lie." I laughed, because somehow Kori managed to improve my mood.

Kori and Tom picked me up by jeep at 7. Mom talked to Kori a moment and of course she didn't mind me going out to party somewhere. Apparently, she was also of the opinion that the company would do me good, because she didn't even give me the time to come back, thus depriving me of the excuse to leave earlier.

Tom stopped the car in front of the pub but did not get out.

"Call me when you want to come back," he said to Kori. "I'll come for you," he added, then waved goodbye and drove away.

"I thought he would come with us." I couldn't hide my surprise. On the other hand, I was glad that we were alone. I guess it would be hard for me to endure the company of a couple in love while I was in emotional disarray.

"We were supposed to talk, we don't need Tom here," Kori said, dragging me with her inside the bar.

It was the first time I was in such a place, maybe differently, it was the first time I was in any place. I looked around curiously at the dimly lit, smoky room. Mostly older youth sat at the tables, but I also noticed a lot of people my mother's age. We took a free table in the quiet corner of the room.

"I'll bring something to drink, keep an eye on the place," Kori ordered, and walked away toward the high bar, where the big bartender served crowded customers. The guy looked menacing, and through a thick dark beard, an earring and an anchor tattoo on his forearm, he looked like a captain of a pirate ship.

The room was filled with the buzz of conversations. In the middle of the tight dance floor - to the rhythm of the moody ballad flowing from the speakers - several pairs swayed. I found myself jealous of them. I wish it would be us. Me and Korin. Why can't it be us? I looked away so as not to think about it.

People were coming, every time the door opened, letting in more laughing groups. Sign 'Pool' glowed green between the entrance and the toilets, and some people were heading there instead of the bar.

Kori was back. She set two glasses on the table and sat down opposite me.

"Did you buy us drinks?" I was surprised.

"No, it's just a tonic for now, but..." She winked at me conspiratorially, pulling something out of the bag. I

couldn't see what, because she hid it under the counter.

"What are you hiding there?"

"Something illegal. Alcohol," she whispered. "Up to twenty-one years is not allowed in the States. Apparently, it was always like that, even before the disaster. When creating the new legal system, this provision was retained. Apparently, someone thought it was important. But... I have my ways to work around the system. Tom taught me." She laughed.

She grabbed her glass, poured something from a flat bottle, which she had previously removed from the bag, and put the drink back on the table. She repeated the same with my glass.

"Well, we now have a gin and tonic," she said with obvious satisfaction.

"Kori," I said softly, leaning over the counter. "I never drink alcohol."

"Does not matter. Believe me, today you need a drink."

She didn't convince me much.

I drank my first drink almost by force. I didn't like it, it was tart and extremely bitter. In the middle of the second, I stopped feeling bitterness, but my tongue loosened, and I finally felt like talking to someone.

"I thought I'd better bear this separation," I began. "He could call me at least."

"He won't call," she said with such conviction that I felt more depressed. "If you told him before leaving what exactly to do, he would."

"It wouldn't be the same. I just thought he would call of his own free will, that he would want to hear my voice," I said regretfully."Emily, it doesn't work that way. When he can't see you, he doesn't miss you. We are like that. I mean, Arisyans are like that, except me of course, but you know that there is something wrong with me in this respect," she explained. "Although... at some point I began to have doubts about Korin. After your first time, when I saw he make the effort. I didn't suspect him of such fantasy, you know, all the candles, dinner, flowers... almost like some cheap affair. I wonder how he figured that out, he doesn't read such things."

"It was my idea," I admitted reluctantly. "I asked him to be romantic and it was."

"Now everything is clear, so Korin acted as instructed. As usual, anyway. You wanted a candlelit dinner, so he gave it to you. Don't expect him to show initiative and call."

"I just want him to come to my first concert with the band on Monday, July 4th," I said, finishing my second drink.

"Call him and just ask him to come."

I shook my head.

"Not a chance. I am afraid that when I hear his voice, I will completely fall apart. I don't want him to know how much I experience our two-week breakup."

"Then send him a text invitation to the concert. Although in my opinion you will not make anything of it. He will not come. The training is to last until six, and my brother takes seriously the duties associated with Arisa." She rose. "I'll go get the tonic." She took both glasses and started for the bar.

I was pondering. What I heard a moment ago was not optimistic. Despite everything, I decided to take a chance. The idea with the SMS seemed pretty good.

Soon Kori returned and discreetly made the third drink for us. She barely managed to hide an empty gin bottle in her bag when Erica left the pool room. As usual, accompanied by Skinny. I cringed in my chair and turned my head, hoping that they would not notice me. I gave Kori a warning kick under the table to do the same. Too late.

"Erica and Skinny are coming towards us," she said without emotion.

"Great," I murmured.

I straightened up in my chair and looked in their direction. Erica with a nondescript smile was approaching our table, and Skinny followed her like a shadow.

"You are the last people I could have expected here," she said, sitting down uninvited next to me. Skinny hesitated a moment, but finally sat down on the last free seat next to Kori.

"Nice to see you too," I answered ironically. "It's a closed party, like you want to know. You weren't invited," I turned to Erica coldly.

"I only need ten minutes," she laughed.

"We're waiting for the pool table to be free," Skinny said apologetically.

"Don't worry about us. For ten minutes, we can just be silent," said Kori and began to play with a spice set, mindlessly rearranging the containers.

Erica looked at us closely for a few long seconds, then looked at the glasses in front of us and at us again. She finally frowned and before I could stop her she grabbed my glass and sniffed it."Gin... what do you know. Flawless, intelligent Emily and Dr. Almar's daughter are drinking alcohol at the bar," she said, smiling with a mockery. "If anyone found out, you would have super-trouble."

I looked uncertainly at Kori, who pierced Erica with her eyes and finally said angrily:

"You know what, every patience has its limits, even Arisyan. Mine has just ended. I suggest a duel. We will play pool, for everything. If I lose, you can tell what you want and who you want. You can even denounce me to the Great Council itself, if it is to please you. But..." she suspended her voice for a moment, "if I win, you will butt yourself out once and for all from Emily, my brother, Tom and me."

Erica was silent for a long time. I had the impression that the first duel now takes place in her head - a duel of thoughts. I was not wrong.

"That would be too easy," she said slowly. "Much too simple. We will play, provided it is a tournament, two on two, round-robin. She," pointed at me, "will also play, and of course there will be Skinny in my team."

"OK." Kori agreed without hesitation, and I came to the conclusion that she probably lost her mind, because about playing pool I had more or less the same idea as about the fauna and flora of Arisa. All I knew was that the balls should be hit into the holes using a wooden stick. This ended my knowledge and Erica was well aware of this because she smiled at me with undisguised satisfaction. She got up from the table, throwing up for the road:

"In ten minutes in the pool room."

"See you," Skinny muttered and followed her."I think you are crazy," I almost yelled at Kori when they were both out of sight. "I can't play it. I don't even know if I can get one ball into the hole, not mention to win."

"Don't panic, Emily, pool is not as complicated as you think. To win, you only need to know a few principles of physics and geometry, nothing more. And you know that very well. I'll explain the basics to you briefly. You can handle it," she said with conviction, then began a lecture on pool.

In just ten minutes I learned that the game uses fifteen numbered balls divided into two groups, i.e. solid balls and striped balls, that they are not hit into the holes, but into the pockets, and the player wins the game when all the balls in your group are in pockets, and finally - in a separate hit - the ball with the number eight. The last information seemed rather unnecessary to me, but I also assimilated it just in case. And also, that under no circumstances I can't hit the black ball before the others, because it means losing. After introducing me to the general rules of the game, Kori went on to explain technical matters, i.e. how to hold a stick, how to aim and what the bridge is and what it is used for. I was slowly getting lost in it all. Only when it came to the applications of geometry and physics in the game, I come to life a bit, because at least I knew all the concepts she mentioned, i.e. the principle of conservation of momentum and angular momentum, and that the reflection angle was equal to the angle of incidence. It will be worse with the practical application of these theories.

"Okay, it's time for us if we don't want to lose by forfeit," Kori ordered.

"We'll lose anyway, so what difference does it make?" I shrugged.

We entered the pool room. Erica was standing at the table, staring at Skinny, who was already arranging the balls in a triangle on it.

"Who starts?" She asked at the sight of us.

"I think you and I," Kori said.

Erica had no reservations. Later Skinny would play with Kori, then Erica with me, and finally me with Skinny. I was glad that during the first two games I would be just an observer. I was hoping that by watching the game I might learn something and if I lose, at least in style.

After just five minutes of the first match, despite my total ignorance in this field, I easily realized that Erica is a real pool champion. Licks in her performance were carefully thought out, and the accompanying fluidity of movements gave the illusion that the game is child's play. Kori's style was visually inferior, but also very effective, which meant that the game was even to the end, although Erica finally won, and I had to admit that it was fully deserved. Kori defeated Skinny, and I lost with Erica, which was hardly surprising. The last game was to be decisive one and to everyone's surprise, and probably my most, I hit the last black ball into the pocket, ending with a draw our team duel.

Disoriented, I looked uncertainly at Skinny, who winked at me discreetly and gave a sly smile. I knew he just let me win and I couldn't understand why?

"We have a tie, so what now?" Asked Kori.

"Nothing." Erica shrugged. "Deadlock. We will

have to repeat it someday. Maybe then it will be decided in favor of someone."

Skinny gathered the balls from the table.

"I'll take them to the bar," he said. "Emily, can you help me?"

"Sure. What should I do?"

"Take the cues."

I was surprised by Erica's complete lack of reaction to the fact that Skinny lost both parties. She wasn't even mad at him because of that. I thought she would react or at least say something malicious about his poor play, while she seemed not to care. Just then I discovered that if there is someone that Erica really likes, then that person is Skinny.

"Why did you let me win?" I asked when we gave all the equipment to the bartender.

"I saved Erica and you from trouble. Somehow, I could not imagine Erica denouncing the Great Council," he chuckled. "Contrary to appearances, she is not as bad as she seems. She also has been through so much and it's her defense mechanism. She doesn't let people to be close her. She is afraid that they will hurt her, so she overtakes them one step and hurts herself not to be hurt."

"Forgive me, but somehow it's hard for me to believe that there is at least a shadow of empathy under this outer shell in Erica," I said.

He did not answer. He stood motionlessly staring at one point in the room. I followed his gaze. Erica danced cuddled to a muscle man who unceremoniously squeezed her buttock with his right hand, while his left hand was wrapped around her waist. Only now I

noticed that Skinny looks at the girl completely differently than the other boys at school. They looked at her with lust, while he with unprecedented tenderness.

"She has no idea you care about her, does she?" I asked.

He shook his head sadly.

"Probably not. She treats me more like a brother than a man."

I felt sorry for him. I understood what it was like to do something you couldn't really have. We were both the same love derelicts.

I put a hand on Skinny's shoulder.

"Don't worry, she'll appreciate you someday." I tried to comfort him, though I didn't really believe in my own words.

"In fifty years, in a hundred...?" He asked grimly.

"I think earlier," I lied.

We bypassed the dancers and entered the pool room. Kori was sitting on the pool table with the telephone in her hand.

"I just called Tom, he's coming for us," she said at the sight of me.

"Drop you home?" I turned to Skinny.

"I'll stay," he replied. "Someone would need me." He looked eloquently toward the dance floor.

The night before the concert I had a dream again. The same as usual. A dead landscape, a huge, dry tree with ominously unfolded branches, a black crow and fear... My fear - squeezing the throat and crushing the lungs like a huge steel vise. I was afraid like never. I was afraid, despite the inexplicable certainty that this

time I was only an observer, that I was not really here, that what was happening here did not concern me, at least not physically, although it hurt similarly. Under the tree lay a dead, massacred, decaying body. The crow attacked it, pecking it eagerly, and I felt like it was ripping my guts to shreds. I should have run as far as possible from this tree, from the view of the torn corpse, from this awful place... But some invisible force forced me to come closer. I stood only a step away from the torturer and his victim. The stench of decay hits my nostrils. The pain inside became unbearable.

My eyes got fog and I sank down to the sunburnt, cracked earth.

I fainted.

I woke up just before dawn in my own bed, trembling and sweating in the cold sweat. I was panting heavily, and the echo of my heart beating against my ribs boomed in my head. I should get up, take a shower and change into a dry T-shirt. I could not. I crouched under the covers. Lying motionless, I tried to control my nightmare anxiety. After a while it weakened but did not disappear. It accompanied me at breakfast and while driving to the main square, the one with the fountain with ballerinas, where the Independence Day celebrations were to take place. Mum parked in one of the side streets from the main square. I threw my guitar case over my shoulder and we headed in the direction of the music. There was a mood of joyful rapture around. Nothing unusual. Independence Day was one of the few days of the year when we could pretend normality, although we were still far from true normality, such as before the comet's impact.

In order not to stand out from the crowd and to avoid uncomfortable questions, I brought a forced smile to my face. I wondered how many of these laughing people - just like me - pretend that everything was all right. Or maybe nobody pretends? After all, if it wasn't for this nightmarish dream and Korin's absence, my joy would also be sincere.

We stopped near the fountain surprised that... it is as it used to be. Colorful flags, balloons, popcorn, cotton candy and joyful families with children. Even my mood improved. Childhood memories came back, happy ones. I once celebrated this day with my parents. At the time, no one thought that it would take ten years for the next event.

"I noticed a colleague from work," my mother said unexpectedly and waved to a woman I knew only by sight. She clearly wanted to join her. "What time do you get on stage?" She asked.

"At 8 pm," I said. "Go to a friend," I encouraged her because I saw that she hesitated. She wasn't sure she should leave me alone. Today I wanted to be not so much alone as I didn't want to be with her. Faking a cheerful mood was becoming more and more onerous. I was afraid that this substitute of a smile stuck to my face would not be enough for a long time.

Despite my best efforts, I was unable to hide from my mother this strange fear which appeared immediately after waking up and, instead of slowly subsiding, increased. Fortunately, she considered it a kind of pre-concert stage fright.

"Don't worry, you'll be fine." She kissed my forehead. "Emily, I'm proud of you. Dad would also be," she added a little quieter and went away to a friend.

With a sigh of relief, I watched her and began to wade through the gathered crowd towards the stage. Red insisted on meeting a few hours earlier. We had to plug in the equipment, tune the instruments and reconcile the details of the performance once again, although we knew the order of the songs played for several days. We just didn't understand why Red, who is usually carefree, is very worried about this performance so much. After all, she always seemed like a person who cares only for good fun. Meanwhile, this concert was important to her.

She explained it to us on Friday during the band's rehearsal.

"I want to dedicate my performance to my grandmother. In thanks for raising me and for replacing me with my parents who died in the catastrophe," she said seriously. "Besides there will be her birthday on July 4, she is seventy years old. Granny, admittedly, has been deaf for several years, so theoretically no matter how we play, but she will definitely notice when we will be booed," she added, giggling, and we with her. Even Erica looked amused. Red would simply not be Red if she did not put similar comment.

In turn, I no longer care about the success of the concert, when on Sunday I became sure that Korin would not be there. Since he left for training, he has not called or answered my Saturday SMS invitation. I didn't sob in my pillow because of it, I felt only sadness and... disappointment. With my voice, lyrics and music, I wanted to convey to him my innermost feelings, whose existence he was not quite aware of and which I could not speak out loud. He would probably not be able to read them, could not name them or understand them more, but I did not completely lose faith that music can reach everywhere, move anyone, regardless of preferences, place of birth or a changed set of genes. Meanwhile, today, the only thing I have to convey to the recipients is a huge dose of sadness.

"Emily, where are you going so fast?" I heard Kori's voice behind me. I stopped abruptly and turned around. As usual, Tom was with her.

"Hello, guys," I said, and I don't know which one in a row I forced myself to smile.

Kori looked at me closely and then turned to Tom.

"Could you bring us a glass of lemonade?" She looked around. "From there." She pointed to the booth where the longest queue was.

"But..." he wanted to protest.

"They have the best there," Kori cut off the discussion.

Tom shrugged and, muttering something incomprehensibly under his breath, went to set himself in a tail.

"I don't think I have to ask where this face comes from?" She said. "You invited him, he didn't come, you're down. Right?"

"Almost," I admitted grimly. "I invited him, he did not answer, did not come, at night I had nightmares, I am full of bad feelings and they are not related to the performance, so do not be surprised that I am down," I recited on the one exhale.

"I warned it would be so," she said in an all-knowing tone.

I was nervous even though she was right. The peculiar arrangement I entered with Korin had no future, I knew it from the beginning. I don't know what I was hoping for. That I won't fall in love or that something will unlock with him and he will love me? For the past few months I have lived the illusion of a real relationship, forever, without time limits. The awareness that we had so little time left together frightened me more and more, although I did not regret any moment spent with Korin. If I could change my choice, it would be the same. I just didn't feel like listening to the comments, not now and not from Kori.

"I'm sorry, I will go to the stage, they are waiting for me. We will talk later."

I wanted to escape at all costs before I say something unpleasant with my gallows humor today. Something I will regret. "And Tom is coming back," I added, gesturing at the approaching boy.

I turned and wanted to leave.

"Wait!" Kori grabbed my wrist and held me in place. She looked into my eyes seriously. "Emily, the day after tomorrow Korin will be back, remember that. Play as if you were playing for him."

"I will try to." I smiled wanly, honestly this time. Though I didn't like the day after tomorrow. The day after tomorrow was very far away, even tomorrow it was too far away. And today? 'Today' I wanted to delete from the calendar, tear out a card with that day, crumble and throw it in the bin.

Tom came over, holding two plastic lemonade

cups. He gave one to Kori, the other was for me, but I said no. I didn't feel like drinking or eating, I didn't feel like anything.

"I have to go, we will meet after the concert," I said goodbye and quickly went towards the stage.

I found all band members behind the stage. They were sitting on a low bench discussing something stubbornly. They were so absorbed in conversation that I didn't even get owned for being late.

"What's happening?" I asked.

"We're trying to come up with the band's name, but nobody has a sensible idea," Red said with resignation.

"So, what are these senseless?"

"New Way, New Word, New Land, New Planet and Future of the Planet," Skinny recited.

"Too long," I said immediately. "The name must be catchy, preferably one word. Maybe just Planet or Future," I suggested.

Skinny looked at the faces of the girls, me too, but neither Reda nor Erica showed much enthusiasm.

410

"So, what do you think?" Asked the boy.

"I don't know..." Red hesitated. "Actually, both names sound bad. Although... Future suits me better. We won't think of anything better now. Erica, do you agree to Future?"

"I don't care, but all in all, it can be." She shrugged.

"So, then it's settled." Skinny rubbed his hands. "Four heads are better than three."

"I think two heads are better than one," I corrected automatically. Not necessary, because it sounded bad.

Anyway, Red rebuked me:

"Emily, what going on with you? Are you feeling

bad, do you have stage fright or did you have up on the wrong side of the bed?"

"The boy set her up," Erica said maliciously.

"I don't have a boyfriend," I snapped, struggling to keep myself from hitting her guitar. I did not do it only because of the sentiment for the instrument, because certainly not for fear of Erica's perfect hairstyle.

"Look at you... 'I don't have a boyfriend'," she repeated, drawing every word carefully. "You're lying, but you know what, I'll tell you something to improve your mood. Arisyans don't like such parties, so you should be happy that Korin is not here. If he listened to you twiddling, he would have dumped you, and you have the chance to stay in this sick relationship for a while."

"Erica, calm down," Skinny said quite sharply. "I don't understand what has gotten into you again. You girls too." He glared at me and Red.

There was a silent consternation.

I was grateful to Skinny for interrupting this sick discussion. And at the same time concerned. Erica deciphered me too easily. I suspect it's not just her. I think everyone at school was bringing me and Korin together. It is good that although they did not realize what exactly our relationship is about. Actually, I didn't really know myself. It was more than friendship, but less than love. A strange suspension condition between the two.

Erica was right about another matter. She said that the Arisyans do not like such events. Indeed. They considered it a waste of time, but they respected Earth's civilization enough not to interfere with our culture and

tradition. In turn, I respected Arisyan for this approach. They deprived us of a normal summer vacation. We have lost too much time after the disaster and we have too much to make up for. Nobody blamed, everyone understood that it was so necessary that only in this way we will recover the former Earth.

"When do we perform?" I asked, breaking this awkward silence.

"At the end," Reda replied. "First there will be a children's choir and two school theater groups, then a dance group. Boring. We are the only rock band here, so I hope we start the company somehow."

"For sure," I said with voice out of emotion. I can already see how I manage to start the company. Especially in the embrace of this grave mood, which squeezes my throat since the morning.

Fortunately, just before the performance I gave in to the atmosphere of general euphoria prevailing under and behind the stage. I also heard echoes of Kori's words: 'play as if you were playing for him'. And that's how I did it. When I stood in front of the audience and closed my eyelids, I played and sang only for him. Not for mother, not for Red's grandmother and not for myself. I sang for Korin, putting all myself in this performance and - judging by the reaction of the audience - with exceptionally good results. The last song differed from the others, perhaps because of the sorrow I had in its lyrics. I wrote it when I found out about his departure.

I know

I know it won't work

and don't think that I wish you bad.

I just know you are ruled by fear

instead of fighting, you prefer to stand still.

I know, it's hard,

when you want to get up

and somebody pushes you away.

413

Trust no one, be with yourself,
because somebody got you somewhere
even when he gives a hand.

I know it won't work
and don't think that I wish you bad.
I just know you rule fear
instead of fighting, you prefer to stand still.

I opened my eyes only when the last measures of the melody ceased. I felt awake from an hour of trance. At first, I was blinded by spotlights and apart from a sea of faceless heads, I saw nothing at all. I only received strong, positive vibrations from the enthusiastic crowd and it was a very pleasant impression. The moment all the lights went out on the stage, I regained my sight and began to recognize familiar faces among the audience. I looked around for my mother, but I couldn't find her. Instead, I saw someone who was not here today - Korin. He was standing in the front row, to the right of the stage, his hands pressed into the pockets of his jeans. He was

smiling at me. I thought I was under the illusion that he wasn't there at all, that I mistook him for someone else, but he waved at me and showed me that he was going on stage.

"Thank you on behalf of the Future band," I said into the microphone and went backstage with a lowered throat.

I wondered how long Korin stood there, how long he listened, how much he understood, and I didn't care if he liked it or if he became convinced of the music. All that mattered was that he came here for me.

I leaned my guitar on the amplifier and quickly went towards Korin, who was waiting under the stage. When he saw me, he gave me a cheerful smile, reached out his hands, firmly grabbed my hips, carried away me from the stage and put me in front of him. I snuggled into him without a word, pressed tightly to his chest, ignoring the people around us. Today, I didn't want to pretend that we didn't belong together. He probably didn't care too much about appearances because he hugged me tightly and buried his face in my hair. Only this closeness, warmth of breath and accelerated rhythm of his heart on my cheek made me realize how much I missed him during these two weeks. Hugging me with all his strength, he seemed to feel the same. When he released his grip and pulled me gently away, I asked:

"You missed me?" He hesitated for a moment. "A little...?" I added hopefully.

He was silent, and the worst part was that I knew what his silence meant.

"Korin, didn't you miss me even a bit?" I repeated the question that had been asked the second time just

415

sounded pathetic.

"Em, I was doing something else, I couldn't... I know what you want to hear, but I would have to lie to you and I don't want to do it," he said calmly.

He hurt me again. In the first impulse I wanted to push him away and just walk away, but I couldn't. It was not his fault and I should not blame him, but to myself. I got Korin along with a packet of unwanted Arisyan traits, but I knew the risk, I knew exactly what I was getting into. He didn't hide anything from me, he played open cards from the very beginning, and I should learn to take what he wants to give me and not demand anything in return, agree to everything, if only he was with me.

He read easily from my face that he hurt me.

"I'm sorry," he whispered in my ear, putting his arm around me. "I didn't miss you, but I'm glad to see you."

"It's alright now. Take me away," I said softly.

"Maybe under the west portal?" He asked.

"Sure," I said with a smile.

The uninhabited surroundings of the west portal were 'our place' in Exira, our little asylum. Before Korin left for training, we often went there when we wanted to be alone.

I disentangled myself from him.

"Wait here a moment for me, I'll be right back," I said and went to Red, who stood a few steps away from us in the company of Erica and Skinny.

"Ana," I first called her name. "I have a request. Will you take my guitar? I have to go somewhere now."

"No problem." She winked at me knowingly. "Have fun."

I was grateful that she kept all comments, even if she had them. Erica and Skinny also refrained from commenting. Although as I walked away, I noticed something strange in Erica's eyes, something I recognized as jealousy. Was she jealous of Korin? I wonder if she knew that our relationship was temporary, would she still be jealous or just laugh at me? How can she be such an idiot, how can she be so blind and not see the real feeling that is at her fingertips? She had nothing to envy me, I should rather envy her. I would like Korin to give me even a fraction of the unconditional love that Skinny bear to Erica.

Just when we approached the portal with Korin, fireworks lit up, creating an amazing riot of colors in the night sky. They ran down cascades of fountains to make room for more, probably even more impressive. Without looking at Korin, I jumped out of the car and stared at the sky with delight. He joined me after a while. He stood in the back, torso clung to my back and hugged tightly.

"You'll probably say that there's nothing to get excited about," I said.

He laughed.

"Actually, there is... although in a way it is a beautiful spectacle. It's a bit like a supernova explosion," he said.

I stood in his arms for some time and silently watched the sky burst with a whistle of colors. I was afraid to move. Somehow, I couldn't get rid of the

impression that it was just a wonderful dream, and I did not want to wake up. It wasn't until I felt his warm lips on my neck that trembled, wandered the skin, causing pleasant chills, and when his breath tangled in my hair, did I believe that I wasn't dreaming, that we were here and that now Korin is all my thoughts. I turned to face him, threw my arms around his neck and greedily clung to his lips. He groaned, parted my lips with his tongue and slowly deepened the kiss, taking almost complete control over my body, which no longer belonged to me, belonged to him.

Without breaking the kiss, he grabbed me in his arms and started toward the car. I didn't protest. I wanted to make love with him in the backseat, although his passion led me to such a state that I would not mind if he ever behaved like a barbarian and did it here on the ground.

He let me out of his arms only near his Land Rover. Before I got in, another series of fireworks flared up. In their light I noticed some movement behind the force field and a vague outline of the silhouette of a large car. I froze. Korin automatically followed my gaze. And when two powerful figures pulled a large, elongated package out of the trunk and threw it against the ground, a wave of paralyzing fear flooded me. I've never been so scared. It was like déja vu, it was my dream today, only in a slightly different scenery. I squeezed Korin's hand tightly. The unreal nightmare suddenly took on a real form and I didn't even have to check to make sure that someone's body had just been abandoned under the portal.

CHAPTER XVII

The only difference between me and the madman
it is a fact that I'm not a madman.
SALVADORE DALI

W hat the hell?" Korin muttered, and without hesitation moved towards the cargo abandoned by the newcomers. He didn't even wait for the rear red lights of the foreign vehicle to disappear for good.

Korin's violent reaction surprised me completely, he behaved strange. Until now, he first analyzed the situation thoroughly, and only then acted. This time, however, he did differently and for the first time I showed greater sense. At the last moment I ran to him and grabbed his arm before he could cross the force field.

"Wait! You can't go there without proper protection, you have to call for reinforcements," I shouted, pulling him away from the field border.

He looked at me in surprise, but I had the feeling that at least I was able to plant a seed of anxiety in him.

"Korin, there's a corpse there," I said with conviction, and when I said it out loud, the hair on my neck bristled with fear.

"Emily, we don't know what's in there. I don't want to start the alarm unnecessarily until I check."

"Believe me, this is a corpse," I repeated more emphatically.

He sighed in resignation.

"Okay, I'll be careful though you exaggerate as usual," he said, then returned to the car.

I followed him without saying a word, and seeing a serious focus on his face, I calmed down a bit. Finally, he began to behave as he should - with cold prudence. He opened the trunk of the Land Rover, took the infra-paralyzer out of it, and efficiently strapped the holster to the waistband. He handed me a second one. I did the same, though not so skillfully, because I had difficulty controlling my trembling hands. Meanwhile, Korin pulled out a bunch of Arisyan lanterns in the shape of sleeves, closed the trunk with a snap, then dug out his cell phone and dialed the number. He waited a long time for someone to answer, and as usual, I was surprised by his inexhaustible patience. I don't think I could wait for a connection with such calmness, at least not in a situation like today. I stood next to him, anxiously watching Korin, who was staring at me. Finally, someone picked up, a soft murmur came from the cellphone.

"I know, Dad, I woke you up, but we have a problem at the west portal. Send a ward here, special procedure," he explained briefly.

Almar apparently did not ask for any details, because Korin almost immediately hung up and unexpectedly pressed his phone into my hand.

"Why do you give it to me?" I asked surprised.

He put a hand on my shoulder.

"Listen to me carefully, Emily." I swallowed nervously, his voice was extremely serious. "On the other side of the field there is no communication, so one of us must be on the phone just in case. You will

wait here for security. In the meantime, I will go see what lies there." He pointed towards the town border.

I tried to protest, but he covered my mouth with his hand, preventing me from speaking."

You'll stay," he repeated. "We won't risk both. Do you remember that since the rebel scandals bracelets work only one way? You can leave, but return is only possible through an open portal, assisted by an armed unit."

"Korin, don't leave me alone here," I said plaintively. I completely fell apart, and I wasn't even ashamed of it. Maybe if it wasn't for the anxiety that accompanied me all day, I would be in a better shape now, but the current situation simply broke to dust my supposed innate courage.

He ran his fingers through my hair, studying me. He hesitated for only a few seconds.

"Okay, let's go together," he muttered, grabbed my hand and pulled me towards the force field.

After a while, we found ourselves on the other side of the light-fogged dam. Korin stopped at a distance from the package abandoned by the newcomers. Now we both had no doubt that the large plastic bag, judging by its shape and size, contains human corpse.

"Don't move," he said softly.

He scattered several lit Arisyan lamps around, walked over to the body and carefully ripped open the foil where we saw the head.

"Holy shit," he cursed, backing away sharply. "Em, don't look," he called warningly.

Too late, I saw it anyway. My head was spinning, my ears were buzzing, but I couldn't stop looking. The

same body from sleep, bloodied, profaned, dead... This time it was not impersonal. Even though I was standing some distance away, I recognized that face, frozen in a silent grimace. It belonged to Will, an emissary sent by the Grand Council to contact the Professor. The same one that was waiting for us at the portal, when we brought rebels from the base, and with whom I spoke not so long ago. My stomach came up my throat and I felt sick, I barely resisted vomiting.

I looked at Korin. He seemed unusually pale in the lights of the Arisyan lamps and looked no less moved than I was.

"Are you sure he's dead?" I asked in a broken voice. The question was meaningless, but it had not reached my consciousness that Will was dead. Maybe it's because I encountered death for the first time and I couldn't deal with it at all.

"For sure," Korin said seriously. "He can't be any more dead."

Saying this, he pulled off his shirt in one move, covered Will's face and proceeded to tear the rest of the foil, revealing to the end, as it turned out, a naked and terribly massacred body.

I took a few steps back, covering my nose with my hand as the stench of decaying corpse reached me along with the gust of wind. I felt a sudden rush of saliva into my mouth, half-bent and simply threw up. I wiped my mouth with the back of my hand and glanced at Korin. I felt stupid that this had happened for the second time in his presence, but he did not pay attention to me. Leaning over the body, he was just pulling out a crumpled roll of paper from between his

clenched fingers. After a moment, he straightened up and moved toward me, clutching what looked like... a letter?

"What is it?" I asked when he stopped right in front of me.

"I think there's a message," he said, turning a bloodstained envelope in his hands. "It is addressed to my father," he added and began to open the letter.

"You shouldn't read this," I said indignantly when he unfolded the paper that was inside.

"Why?" He was surprised, looking at me from under frowning eyebrows.

"The secrecy of correspondence, and this letter is not addressed to you."

He threw up his arms.

"There is no such thing as a secrecy of correspondence on Arisa, at least when it comes to common good," he murmured, bent down to find a flashlight on the ground and, ignoring me, started reading.

I watched his face anxiously, which changed from second to second, changing from cool composure to the expression of helpless anger.

"Read," he said curtly, handing me the letter. "Read and explain to me why... why is he like this, why are they like this, why must they be so cruel, why is it never enough for what they have, that they always have to have more..."

Without a word, I took the card from him. I stopped caring who the correct addressee of this letter was, now more important for me was the complainant of Korin - the reason for this regret and grudge against people.

Letters jumped in front of my eyes because my hands were shaking with nervousness, my sentences were a little blurred, because tears came to my eyelids, but despite that I tried to read the content as carefully as possible.

Almar, my friend.

So, you got a package? Forgive me for being a little damaged, but my boys sometimes like to have fun. I let them do like that. Subjects, like bread, need the games.

If you had a problem identifying this body, a little hint - it's Will, your spy. Did you think I wouldn't recognize him, that my human memory was so unreliable? Have you already forgotten that I have the intelligence of a genius? This is my greatest weapon, hidden in me, invincible. Don't underestimate it. Of course, you can send another spy, sorry, not a spy - an emissary, and then I will send you another corpse.

Apparently, you don't know what evil, aggression and violence are. I will tell you: evil is me, and on Earth evil should be locked in a cage, but you have let evil go outside, unknowingly opening Pandora's Box.

Do you think I'm crazy?

You're wrong.

I can't hear voices because I'm a Voice myself.

I have no vision, but I am a Visionary.

Nobody has won me because I'm a winner.

Nobody created me because I am the Creator.

I built my Little Empire on the ruins of a great civilization, but it is not enough for someone like me.

Earth has been and will be my battlefield. For as long as I can remember, I fought for life and then for survival. Now, I fight for world power, and I will win because no one has ever taught me to lose.

So, your time on this planet is coming to an end, but you have probably already realized that? You read it from the thoughts of my two people who were stupid enough to be caught. What did you do with them? Let me guess - nothing, they are still alive. You see how well I know you. But I'll tell you something, you can kill them, I don't need them, they are pawns.

April 20 - remember this date. Special day.

The day of my birth and the birth of the Lord of the World - Your Armageddon.

The day when the dichotomy of power becomes one, my world will devour yours - it will be the Absolute.

You will escape - you will pass the death sentence on all Earthlings who have trusted you.

You will stay - you can save them, but on my terms. How about the Giants' duel? Just you and me. The winner takes everything.

Life consists of opposites: day and night, birth and death, good and evil, happiness and unhappiness, courage and fear, struggle and escape.

You have a choice and you have time to decide.

General, John Smith in the past

I finished reading and I was just ashamed. I was ashamed not only of the General but of all humanity. So, I stood still, my head down, not knowing what to say, or even less, how to explain to Korin why such people are. However, I did not manage to speak, because six security cars had just arrived at the portal, a dozen or so armed men got out. I recognized Dr. Almar among them. Korin took a letter from me and

427

walked quickly towards his father. I didn't follow him. I watched from a distance as he handed the doctor a card with a message and, gesturing, explains something stubbornly. Meanwhile, the others approached the abandoned corpse. When one of them exposed Will's face, I turned my head away, I didn't want to watch it. All I could hear was a few men cursing loudly, someone spat, someone started vomiting as much as I did. I had enough. Enough of this place and this sick situation. All I wanted was to be at home as soon as possible and just to forget. Quite unknowingly, I started slowly approaching Korin and Almar. They were still talking. They only stopped when I approached them.

"Come on, Emily, I'll drive you home. Your mom is waiting for you. My father has already informed her of everything," he said.

I nodded my head. I couldn't say a word, something just got stuck in me.

"I will come to the hospital in a moment, then we will carefully analyze the situation," he turned to Almar, and then, without looking at me, started towards his car. I followed him.

During the ride Korin was stubbornly silent. He squeezed the steering wheel so tightly that under his skin the tense tendons and muscles of his arms were clearly visible. I had the impression that he was angry

at me, but not angry at Emily-person, but at Emily-human. The General's letter and Will's corpse apparently once again made him realize that our civilizations are very different, even by the level of unreasonable hatred. How was I to explain to him that most people are not bad, that I am not bad, and that the human inhabitants of Arisyan towns are not bad?

"Korin," I said in a low voice, and in the silence filled only with the monotonous murmur of the engine, it sounded like a scream. "Speak up at last, don't punish me for something that was not my involvement and which I could not control."

"Em, I know it's not your fault, but... what happened here today, this senseless death, then Smith's letter... I try to understand it somehow and I just can't. I can't find any logic in this."

"So, don't look up! You will not find sense in the fact that someone is overwhelmed by the morbid lust for power. And do not attribute this quality to the entire earthly race. Look around you. People in the towns are friendly, and they work with you not in gratitude that you have restored almost normal life on Earth, but mainly out of respect and sympathy for you. And they certainly do not treat Arisyans as a threat to our species. Like the General, individuals behave, and this should not affect the assessment of all humanity."

"Emily, don't forget that the General is not alone, he has a lot of followers, in your opinion they are also just individuals?" He asked with a note of bitterness in his voice.

The worst thing was that he was right in his own way. Despite this, I was outraged by his attitude.

"Korin, what the hell should I tell you? I'm sorry that people are like that? I'm sorry I'm a human?"

He only spoke after a long moment.

"I'm sorry, I just didn't expect such an end tonight."

I didn't either, but I didn't say it out loud, because we were just reaching my house and I noticed my mother in the dim light of street lamps. She was standing on the porch, wrapped in a thick wool scarf. She must have been very nervous since she was waiting for me outside. She went out into the driveway when she noticed a car approaching. She had to guess it was us. At this time there was not much traffic in the streets.

The sight of the waiting mum caused that the outer layer of apparent control fell off me, hiding feelings of fear and terror, which were creeping somewhere under the skin, releasing them in the form of tears, which began to flow down my cheeks with thick streams. When Korin braked, I immediately opened the car door and, sobbing, fell into my mother's arms. Safety. That's what I needed the most now, and no one can give us a greater sense of security than a person who loves us with unconditional love and who has never let us down.

She knew me, knew that now I did not need words but gestures. She hugged me tightly and stroked my hair soothingly. I closed my eyelids. I turned off. Only individual sounds came to me. Shreds of sentences.

"I don't understand... She was calm all the way... I didn't..."

"Korin, you don't have to explain."

"But..."

"She is shocked... Did she see the body?"

Silence - long, persistent, crushing into the skull, only a part of me, hidden deep inside, screamed: yes, she saw, she saw the body!

"Go now."

"For sure?"

I remember the rest as short flashes - snapshots of blurred slides.

Korin's car disappears around the corner.

We go home with my mother.

I'm taking off my clothes.

Bathroom. Bath. Heat.

I don't even know how long I've been taking a bath. In any case, it helped, restored the ability to think. Mom went into the bathroom a few times to see if I was all right. I was not. I don't know if I will ever be all right again. Repeatedly, I scrubbed my whole body with passion, as if I wanted to wash away the smell and touch of death.

I hardly talked to my mother. I lay down and she sat at my bed for a long time, waiting for me to fall asleep. In the end I pretended to fall asleep. I didn't want her to worry. She waited a moment and left, leaving the bedroom door ajar and the hall light on.

I lay still, and every murmur outside the window caused a cold shiver on my skin. I didn't want to be alone today, I couldn't...

I jumped out of bed, grabbed the quilt and pillow, and went to my mother's bedroom. She wasn't sleeping yet.

"I was just wondering when you stop pretending you are no longer a child and you will come here," she

said. She made room for me, moving to the edge of the mattress.

I forced a smile and lay down next to her, stuffing a pillow I had brought with me under my head. Only now was the tension caused by fear slowly escaping from me.

"Emily," she began cautiously. "I know it's probably the wrong time to ask, but I want to know why you and Korin went to the portal?"

I sensed that she would eventually ask about it. I used to dispose of similar questions in silence, but today I wanted to confess, or rather a little confession, because I did not want to reveal everything.

"We were supposed to make love in the car," I said, and until I said it out loud, I didn't think I could afford such directness. Judging by my mother's expression, she probably didn't think I would go with something like that.

She looked at me in silence, not quite sure how to behave, as if she was only now noticing me as a woman, not a little girl whom I had not been in for a long time, but somehow, she had escaped it before.

"Is what's happening between you serious?" She finally dared to ask.

"I don't think so," I said slowly.

"What you want to say by: I don't think so?"

"Not serious on my part, not serious on his part," I said in one breath. "Satisfied?!"

"And what do you think?" She tried to stay calm all the time, though it was hard for her. "Explain to me, I want to know what your relationship is, if you can call it a relationship at all."

I had to answer, but I increased my vigilance not to reveal too much.

"We're friends and having sex, that's all."

"Emily," she said reproachfully and looked at me chidingly.

"Do not look like this. I didn't plan it. Do you think I wanted to fall in love? In addition, in someone for whom there are no higher feelings because he has the wrong set of genes?"

She sighed in resignation.

"I have suspected for some time that this is how things are between you, I just did not allow this thought to myself. And I didn't think you got so emotionally involved. I don't like it," she said seriously. "I will ask you again, are you sure he doesn't feel what you do?"

"Mom, they do not feel, do not love, do not hate, do not enjoy each day as they should enjoy it, but they have everything planned, all their lives, from birth to death. And believe me, there is no place for love."

She looked at me intently, as if she wanted to read from my face if I was 100% sure what I was saying.

"Then you must end this relationship," she said firmly. "And as soon as possible."

I shook my head to say no.

"Emily, I'm worried. Your best friend is an Arisyan, your quasi boyfriend is an Arisyan... Maybe it doesn't reach you yet, but they are strangers here. They will leave Earth one day and you will be alone. You should be more with people, make new friends..."

"Great idea," I snorted. "Maybe you will tell me that I should tame Erica, and tell her all my secrets."

"Don't be snappy. You know that I don't mean that.

I just want to protect you from loneliness. You've experienced too much of it in your life."

These words cooled my agitation a bit - my mother was just worried and it was hard to blame her for that.

"I will finish this arrangement in due time." When his genetic partner arrives, I added in mind. Or rather a little earlier, because I have to leave before that one arrives. "I'll try to spend more time with Red. Does that sound good?"

"It must," she said.

"Mom, come on. I have enough for today," I groaned and covered my head with a quilt.

Of course, I overslept to school, or rather I didn't oversleep, only my mother didn't wake me up, probably concluding that after yesterday's traumatic experiences I should rest a bit. I got up around noon, fortunately in a much better mood than the previous day. Better, but still not very good, because my absence meant that I would not see Korin.

"I didn't go to school because of you," I said with rancor, entering the kitchen.

Mom stopped peeling mirepoix for a moment and looked at me with a smile.

"Me neither. I called that we would not be there. And really, you don't mean school, but meet with Korin, right?"

I poured myself a glass of cold tap water and sat down at the kitchen table.

"It's easy to decipher me, right?" I said, taking a sip of water.

"I'm your mother, so I know you well," she said

calmly and took the chair next to her. "Emily, Korin also did not go to school today. Yesterday he said he would not be there. Did you not hear."

435

"Yesterday my hearing was very selective."

"He said he would try to call you tonight."

That's a start - I thought - at least I would hear his voice, although I'd rather see him. After two weeks of separation, I missed him very much. At the moment I didn't even want to think about my promise to leave, it was beyond my strength. I had absolutely no idea where to go or how to tell my mother about it. Or maybe we should leave Exira together? I had the impression that I was sitting on a speeding train with the words TIME, which is accelerating more and more, heading for the CATASTROPHE station. Once I get there, it may turn out that Emily Walker is gone. So, who will I be and will I be able to put together some remnants of myself to function normally? I chased away intrusive thoughts.

"Red dropped your guitar in the morning." Mom pointed to the case leaning against the wall.

I looked towards the instrument and smiled to myself. Music. Only it was able to improve my mood, drown out the sounds of gloomy thoughts.

"Mom, I'll go play a little," I said, getting up.

I locked myself in a room with a guitar, sat on the floor with my back to the door, and began to hum. As usual, I zoned out, I don't even know for how long. I paused only when I felt someone's presence behind me. I thought my mother came to hear me play, sometimes she did it. I turned my head away. Behind me, leaning against the door, was Korin.

436

"Why you stopped?" he said softly. "I think I'm starting to like it."

"Don't make fun of me," I muttered confused, putting down my guitar. "How long have you been standing there?"

"A few minutes," he rose nimbly from the floor, came up to me and pulled me up.

We stood opposite each other now and for a long moment Korin studied my face closely.

"Apart from Will's death, something else bothers you, right?" He asked, frowning.

"I told my mother about us," I gave the most neutral reason for my vile mood, I did not want to reveal the more important ones.

"I figured it out after her cold welcome."

"Was she rude to you?" I was surprised that he noticed a change in my mother's behavior at all.

"That's not the point, just..." He chose the right words for a moment. "She was different, distant, not as outgoing as usual."

"She doesn't like our arrangement, but she somehow accepted it," I added quickly.

"Do you want to talk about it?"

"Not now. I would prefer to hear what you have established, or rather, what the Great Council has established."

I sat cross-legged on the bed, pulling Korin with me. He spread across the mattress, resting his head on his elbow next to my knee.

"We're going back to Arisa," he said at the beginning, and I felt the blood drain from my face.

"When?" I asked in a barely audible whisper.

"Spring," he said. I must admit that I was relieved.

I was afraid for a moment that their trip would come any day, and I was not prepared for such a version of events. Actually, I wasn't prepared for any version of events, but I hoped that for almost three months that left to us, I could somehow tame this thought.

"The first space shuttle will start in early April," he continued. "My father is wondering now how to save you because John Smith never make empty promises. Since he wrote that he intends to liquidate you, he will do so without hesitation, in addition with the greatest cruelty he can afford. That's why my father is now considering three options. Either we leave and leave you at the mercy of fate, which contradicts our ideals, but it is best for us, or my father will remain alone on Earth and will attempt to confront the General. The third possibility is that after our departure you will go to other cities and try to blend with the crowd, hoping that they will not find you."

"Can't you send another spy who will reach the Professor and somehow influence him not to help the rebels? After all, without this Professor, the General is a nobody."

Korin shook his head grimly.

"The General knows everyone here, lived with some of them in a shelter, and met the others here. Two years is a long time, and even if he can't remember the names, he'll definitely associate the face. And most of his people also lived here. That's why Will was exposed. So, you can see that we can't risk the next person's life."

"Can you risk the lives of everyone else?" I bridled. "Sometimes it is worth sacrificing something to achieve

more."

"The Great Council disagreed, it was almost a unanimous decision, so the discussion on this subject should be considered closed."

All I had to do was acknowledge it, though the powerlessness caused by this decision deepened my sadness. I didn't say anything. Korin sensed my mood almost immediately, in this respect he was like my mother, he read in me like in a book. With his free hand he took my hand and gently brushed the inside of it. In response, I patted his cheek with my thumb, then leaned forward and clung to each other greedily. I snuggled into him and let his lips be everywhere, his arms embrace me with all his strength, his hands wandering over my skin and if it wasn't for my mother presence behind the wall, we would probably make love quickly and violently, but in this situation only touch should be enough. I needed the closeness that

Korin was giving me now, and I had the impression that, despite those unfortunate genes that were deleting feelings, he also needed it, maybe even more than I did.

"Em, I'd like to talk to you about something," he said, abruptly stopping the caress, but he still held me in a firm grip.

"About what?" I asked anxiously.

I stepped back to see his face.

"You said you would leave when my genetic partner will arrive, so as not to create unnecessary tension and awkward situations."

"Yes," I said uncertainly, not knowing where he was going. "That was the deal, and I'm going to keep it,

you don't have to worry about it," I assured him.

"Then consider this point of the contract invalid," he said firmly.

I held my breath and my heart sped up.

Did he want to keep me here?

Did he care about me?

I looked into his eyes. They did not express anything that could be considered some hidden feelings for me, but I found something in them that I read as sadness. He didn't care, he just wanted to protect me, nothing more.

"Why shouldn't I leave?" I asked to be sure.

"First of all, it's dangerous and I don't want you to risk your life unnecessarily because of my momentary weakness, and secondly, I trust you and believe that when my partner shows up, you won't do anything wrong."

I sat up and stepped away from him. I was upset. I started breathing faster. How did he just describe me?! Momentary weakness? I knew I wasn't particularly important to him but naming it by this word hurt. It hurt a lot. I thought I was going to scratch his purple eyes that were now looking at me anxiously.

"Em," he said softly. "I said something wrong again, right?"

Just calm down, I kept thinking, it wasn't his fault. I clenched my teeth, trying to suppress my anger and control my emotions.

"Em?" He repeated.

I took a deep breath.

"Korin, it's not all about the promise, it's about me," I began to explain, trying to calm down. "I just have to

leave. I can't imagine going to school when your genetic partner arrives. I can't stand all the furtive glances and malicious comments on my address when you suddenly start walking around with your woman around the school. You've been associated with me so far. Do you know how awful I will feel? It's too humiliating for me. I don't want to, I prefer to get killed by rebels."

"That's no reason to be killed by anyone."

"You don't understand... You are different. You can't deliberately hurt anyone. And I do not mean wounds inflicted by weapons, but words."

"Words don't kill," he said coldly. "That's why you will stay here until we leave, you will endure somehow until April. You will have to, because the Grand Council made one more important decision today. The force field has been blocked and you cannot leave the city freely without a special code."

I got angry again.

"Wait a minute, you mean to say that we are your prisoners now?"

Korin groaned and run his fingers through his hair, always doing so when he felt helpless.

"Emily, it was a unanimous decision of the Great Council that is, Earthlings and Arisyans, so your accusation is unfounded. Well, almost... because this proposal came from my father. After reading the letter from the General, he became more cautious and distrustful, afraid of another betrayal."

Although I didn't like the field block, I agreed with Almar. Vigilance had to be increased. Recent events have shown that in the current world nothing can be

sure, so you should overtake your opponent at least a step so as not to be surprised. It didn't change the fact that my plans have turned into failure and now I had to find a sensible way to get out of here before the end of October.

"You're angry?" He asked as my silence continued.

"Rather scared," I said and curled up on the bed. "Korin, hug me," I asked.

He lay down and put his arm around me. I closed my eyelids. I tried to collect my thoughts. Meanwhile, he calmingly massaged my back. He caressed with a gentle touch, and I tried to plan to escape him, my feelings for him, and the sight of Korin and his girlfriend holding hands.

"I have to go," he said after an hour of silence, tenderly kissing my temple.

"Bye," I said, but didn't open my eyes. I didn't want to keep him, I needed a moment of loneliness to sort things out.

He left. Then I forced my brain to do more. I organized my thoughts, put together the facts I learned, and when my mother called me to dinner, I had a detailed action plan in mind, which I was going to start implementing tomorrow.

CHAPTER XVIII

Knowing that within a week
you will fall off the scaffolding,
perfectly concentrates the human mind.
SAMUEL JOHNSON

O n Wednesday, I skipped out of my last lesson to avoid embarrassing questions, why instead of going home after classes, I go to the hospital. I had a hard time today at school. I had had enough of telling everyone about Monday evening and about the corpse of Will abandoned by the General's people at the portal. Every time someone asked, and I had to answer, I felt like I was tearing open the wounds inside me.

As I headed toward the hospital, I had my first doubts. However, they did not concern the plan itself, which seemed quite good, but only the participation in the plan. I wasn't sure at all that I wanted to leave, although staying in Exira could only mean slow dying for me.

With mixed feelings, I crossed the automatic door of the hospital tower block, praying that I would not come across Doris. I'd rather go down the corridor leading to the elevators, leaning swaying against the wall, but common sense was to behave naturally. I did not look around or look into the eyes of people passing me so as not to attract attention unnecessarily. Without any obstacles, but all sweaty from nervousness, I got to

the corridor with elevators. I got into the middle one, breathing a sigh of relief as it started up with a quiet hum. For a moment I had the impression that I went back in time. It was like the first day when I went to talk with Almar to his office, with the only difference that at that time I was accompanied by fear of the unknown, and now pure determination.

I entered the office. Almar sat motionless behind his desk, his fingers to his temples, his lips moving in a noiseless rustle. He used the thought recorder. I waited a moment for him to notice me, but he was so focused on his affairs that he apparently did not know what was happening around him. I had to clear my throat to get his attention. He raised his head, took off his headphones, and smiled at me.

"Emily?" He asked in surprise. My presence surprised him.

"I'm sorry to disturb you, but..." I swallowed nervously. "I have a case for you, doctor."

"I'm listening." He showed me a chair.

I sat down and practically immediately began to speak, to get it over as soon as possible.

"I need to talk about something important, important for us that is, for Earthlings and Arisyans." And above all for me, I added in my mind.

He didn't speak, just looked at me closely. He waited for me to say more.

"I would like you to send me north instead of Will. I will try to contact Mitch and reach the Professor through him," I said without hesitation.

Almar frowned. I had the impression that he did not understand very well.

"I want to continue Will's mission," I explained again.

"Where does this ridiculous idea come from?" He asked sincerely, amazed at my suggestion.

"The idea is not ridiculous," I protested. "If I understand correctly, you don't send another spy for fear of being recognized and losing life as well. I came here two years after the General and his people left. None of them knows me, so I can easily finish Will's mission, or at least try to do it. If my plan is successful, first, I will save thousands of lives, and secondly, the Arisyans will be able to complete their research on Earth. Everyone will benefit."

Almar got up and started walking around the office. I followed him with my eyes, but remained silent, waiting for him to think about my offer. Finally, he stopped.

"And what does your mother think about it?" He asked.

I expected this question. Mum was one of the weak points of my plan, but I had the answer.

"I'm an adult, I do not have to ask my mother for her opinion, and besides, she does not know anything yet and I would prefer that she does not find out anything, that nobody finds out... This is my only condition."

There was a prolonged silence in the office. I was afraid that in a moment Almar would refuse, to laugh my plan, pointing out its weaknesses point by point, even though this morning it seemed quite logical to me.

"I have to analyze it carefully," he said in an

undertone. "Come after school tomorrow, I'll tell you what decision I made."

I nodded, said goodbye and left his office on trembling legs. Only in the elevator I breathed a sigh of relief. I was afraid of this conversation, and now it was over, paradoxically, I didn't care what answer Almar would give me tomorrow. It was enough for me that at least I tried to direct my life without waiting for destiny to decide for me. Although, if you think about it, trying to control your own destiny is also a sort of destiny. My mother always said that each of us' lives is programmed from the beginning to the end and it does not matter which paths we follow, because in the end they will lead us to the place where we were to find ourselves.

When I got off the elevator, I collided with Korin.

"Em? What are you doing here?"

I was speechless. I was looking at Korin with my eyes wide open, frantically trying to think of a credible-sounding lie, but nothing intelligent occurred to me.

"Did you go to my father?" He asked stubbornly, glancing over my shoulder towards the elevators.

Sure, the middle elevator, it's hard not to associate that I talked to Almar a moment ago.

"Yes, I was there to ask..." I started slowly, at the same time forcing the mind to intensify activity. "I wanted to ask if I could work after classes in the hospital," I spat out the first lie that came to my mind.

"You can't stand the sight of blood." He realized quickly that I was making up.

"That's why," I brazenly went on hoping that as a typical Arisyan, he would not recognize a lie, because in his understanding of the world something like this

did not exist. "I decided to fight my weaknesses, and at the same time do something useful," I said with such conviction in my voice that I almost believed it myself. Korin also believed.

"And he found you something?" He asked quite seriously.

"Not yet. He said he would think about it," I answered truthfully, though Almar's answer was not about that. I just hoped that the doctor would keep the discretion I asked for.

Korin stopped drilling and simply acknowledged the explanation. He reached into my shoulder and took the backpack from me. I gave him a questioning look.

"I'll take you home," he said.

"You didn't go to..."

He interrupted me.

"I went, but it doesn't matter, it can wait." He reached out to me. "Are we going?"

I gave him my hand. The vicinity of Korin, as usual, made all my problems smaller, went to the background. However, I did not want him to drive me home, today I felt like taking a walk. He didn't protest. We talked all the way nothing special, but when we got there, I felt like I used to, before he went to training. Everything between us returned to normal, at least for a while.

"Sit down, Emily. Before we decide together, I would like you to know more details," said Almar at the outset, when I arrived on Thursday after the school.

Obediently, I took my place on the brown sofa. The doctor sat down next to me and looked at me seriously.

"I will explain first what your mission would be. I will get you to the information that Will managed to get, although it is not much, but sometimes even the smallest thing can matter." He reached for the remote control I already knew. "Ready?"

I nodded my head.

Almar pressed a button on the remote control and the whole office sank into darkness, but only for a moment, because right from the cylindrical table, which I once considered a holographic planetarium, a beam of bright light shot up. I held my breath as the light began to disperse and in the form of shining fog covered the entire room, at the same time forming various shapes. Initially, the vision was very blurred, but it only took a few seconds to focus. I got up from the sofa and went to the center of the office. I was surrounded by an artificially generated image of an American town that was almost real. Houses, streets, sidewalks, cars, and even people walking by, everything seemed too real. I reached out to touch the car parked by the sidewalk, but it hit the vacuum, only the image in this place slightly waved.

"Alexandria, Minnesota." I heard the doctor's voice behind me. "Mitch is permanently in this town, Mitch Sullivan," he added, standing right next to me.

He pressed the button on the remote control again. The scenery has changed. A medium-sized, wooden building with a damaged facade, with blue paint peeling off, appeared in front of us, revealing a bottom layer of an undefined color. This house was definitely different from the neat buildings of Exira.

"Park Street 590," said Almar. "He lives there. Try to remember this building and the surrounding area. If

450

you leave, you will have to look for a home in this area."

He waited a moment for me to look carefully, then changed the picture again. The same house, but this time close. At one point, a well-built man left the building and he followed the narrow path straight on us. For fear of colliding with me, I jumped back, bumping into the desk with a bang.

"I'm sorry," I muttered.

"No problem." Almar smiled slightly. "I stopped broadcasting."

Before me was Mitch's figure frozen in half-step. I came closer to get a better look. He looked serious for about thirty years, though maybe he was fooled by the stern expression on his face and in fact he was younger. It was difficult to determine. His hair was short, cropped close to his skin, and the first association I had was a soldier. Dressed in cameo pants, a khaki T-shirt and military lace-up boots, Mitch resembled a marine member. My attention was caught by his eyes, very light, gray, but their color was not the strangest, but some silent threat contained in them. The cold look made this man seem dangerous.

"Can we continue?" The doctor's voice snapped me out of my thoughts.

"Yes of course."

Nothing has changed, only the figure of Mitch has disappeared, but a child, a girl, appeared on the porch.

"Elizabeth, Mitch's niece," Almar explained almost immediately. "He is taking care of her for some time.

The girl's mother died. Will couldn't find anything more."

I watched her play with the ball. She could have been five, maybe six. Something puzzled me.

"Why send spies when you can learn almost everything from observations?" I turned to the doctor, pointing at the girl.

Almar shook his head.

"This is not how it works, Emily, this is not a real picture, but a computer simulation developed by our IT specialists based on photos and information provided by Will. We do not have adequate equipment on Earth to conduct such observations."

"I see... that is watching something like a moving slide show."

"You could say that," he admitted. "Let's move on."

Another decoration changed.

"Douglas County Hospital," he said when a low, large building of red but heavily soiled brick appeared before us, in front of which an elderly man stood motionless. Two things occurred to me at the same time. The first that the simulation is designed to associate people with appropriate places and the second that the man who is just standing in front of the hospital is a doctor. He was very much like Almar,

452

not so much in appearance as in facial expression, which also showed gentle kindness.

"Doctor Grant," Almar confirmed my guess. "Mitch's friend," he added.

"I have to hmm... work him out too?" I was surprised.

"No, it's a little more complicated." He finished the projection, and it got bright again in the study. "Let's sit down." He pointed to the couch.

I sat on the edge. I didn't feel confident. Almar took the chair in front of me.

"Alexandria has its own rules," he began. "Only socially useful people can enter the city, i.e. those who have physical strength or at least some knowledge or skills."

He looked at me. I cringed. It couldn't be hidden that I didn't have an athlete's body.

"We'd have to put our knowledge to you, Emily."

"That means?"

"Will told us that they need a teacher in elementary school. I think you would find yourself in this role, but it is not known if the case will still be valid. So, we have to have plan B."

"So, what's the contingency plan?"

"Hospital." I heard a short answer. I barely resisted not to moan. I hated the sight of blood, and the hospital odors made me sick.

"What would I do there?" I asked, swallowing loudly.

"Anything. The hospital in Alexandria is a place where every pair of hands capable of work will be useful. There are periods that departments break at the seams. There is a lack of basic medicines, vaccines, dressings, equipment, medical personnel..." he interrupted.

Only now he noticed my face, obviously misinterpreting it.

"You have nothing to fear. You are safe. We vaccinated both you and your mother when you were brought to Exira."

I frowned. I did not like the vision of working in the hospital, but the fact that someone was in charge of my body, even for my own good, liked it even less. My thoughts were read, and a series of vaccinations were applied, the basic right to privacy was trampled on. I wonder what else I will find out? I was slowly beginning to see the flaws in the Arisyan system.

"I'm not afraid." I assured nonetheless. I didn't want Almar to notice that I had any doubts. "But I don't know medicine. I am not fit for this job."

"That's why you will undergo additional medical training from Sofie, as well as cryptography training with Lorena to be able to give us encrypted reports," he said.

"And that's it?"

"What 'that's it'?" He was surprised.

"It's about extracurricular activities. Do you think that all I need is a few extra lessons from medical training and mastering several encryption methods?"

"Why not?" He asked. "What else would you like to learn?"

I shrugged.

"I don't really know, but since I'm supposed to be something like a secret agent, I think I should master martial arts, how to use weapons, how to use all those spy gadgets..." I fell silent for a moment, because I noticed that Almar was trying hard not to laugh. "Well, at least James Bond could do it all," I finished uncertainly.

"James... who?"

"It does not matter. He is such a hero of action movies."

Almar couldn't stand it and just laughed. It took a moment before he calmed down, and I was ashamed of having egg on my face.

"I'm sorry," he cleared his throat, "but you made me laugh, someone rarely succeeds."

"I'm sorry. Sometimes I speak without thinking."

"Listen, Emily, if you go to Alexandria at all, it's not to kill someone there, but to contact Mitch and get information. You don't need advanced technologies for this. Most importantly, you have a trustworthy look. This is your biggest weapon. This and your sharp mind. I would like to hear now what your final decision regarding the trip is."

He stared at me. He waited. I folded my hands in my lap, but I didn't think long. I had no choice.

"When should I go?" I asked yet.

"When you will be ready, in any case before winter."

"Will the end of October be good?"

He nodded.

"I need to initiate Sofie and Lorena. Do not mind?"

"I do not have, but I thought we had already discussed this issue."

"I preferred to make sure."

"Fine."

"For security reasons, I would also like to ask for discretion."

"Of course."

For the next three months I tried not to think about the future, not to consider what would happen or what would happen if. I didn't always make it. I still had no idea how to say goodbye. How do I tell my mother that I'm disappearing? How not to reveal to Korin that I disappear? How to let him know that he is important to me and that he will always be important. I put it off for later. I focused on current issues. I filled the time tightly, dividing it between school, home, Korin, Kori, band and trainings with Sofie and Lorena. Just to not think, just have something to do.

The first training meeting with Sofie was not pleasant. On Monday, after classes, I entered her office. She stood still, staring at a point outside the window. It took her a moment to turn her face towards me. She didn't smile. She was serious. Too serious.

"Sit down," she said coldly. "Before we start any classes, we need to talk."

I didn't move. Sofie kept her eyes on me, and I felt more and more anxiety.

"Why?" She finally said. "Can you explain to me? Why are you doing this, to your mother? Why should I participate in this? I do not like it. I don't know how to behave. In the first impulse, I was to tell your mother everything, thus breaking the principle of confidentiality. I haven't done it... I haven't done it yet," she added threateningly. "You'll have to convince me not to do it."

I did not expect this to be the case. It seemed to me that Sofie agreed unquestionably with the Arisyan provisions. I was wrong. I sat in a nearby chair, buried my face in my hands, feeling tears welling up under my eyelids. I counted ten times back and forth in my mind. It helped, but only a little. I looked at her. She was still standing by the window, watching me.

"Sofie, I can't stay here," I whispered. "Soon Korin will replace me with his genetic partner. It hurts now that I think about it."

"I once warned you that this relationship is doomed to failure."

"I know."

"You replied that the future is irrelevant."

"That's right, because I knew then that I would leave. And after the last meeting of the Grand Council, it turned out to be impossible. I need to get a special code to leave the city. That's why I volunteered for this mission. This is the only chance, not only for me, but also for you."

Sofie went to her desk, pushed some documents aside and sat on the edge of the counter. She was silent for a long time.

"You stood up for yourself, Emily," she said with a heavy sigh. "But I'm acting against myself."

I breathed a sigh of relief.

"You can go now, we will start classes tomorrow."

At least the meeting with Lorena took place without unnecessary sensations. She treated me almost impersonally. For her, I was only a tool to achieve the intended goal. One day I might be outraged by this fact, but after the last conversation with Sofie I could only be glad that the Arisyans have a completely different system of values. Professor Lorena did not play any psychoanalysis with my participation, but almost immediately she began to introduce me to the secrets of cryptography. She told me to take a seat in front of a white glass board, and then wrote the whole alphabet on it with a black felt-tip pen, assigning each letter a number from 0 to 25.

A-0 B-1 C-2 D-3 E-4 F-5 G-6 H-7 I-8 J-9

K-10 L-11 M-12 N-13 O-14 P-15 Q-16 R-17

S-18 T-19 U-20 V-21 W-22 X-23 Y-24 Z-25

The quite ordinary letters and numbers written in this way did not look ordinary. They caused anxiety. They reminded us of the inevitable. They heralded danger. On one hand, I was uncomfortable, but on the other, I felt a thrill.

"I will now discuss the concept of an algorithm with a one-time encryption key, i.e. the so-called one-time-pad," Lorena began her lecture. "It is mainly used to encode short but very important information, often of strategic importance. Reading the cryptogram without knowing the right key is practically impossible. What you see on the board are numerical substitutes for letters. Encryption involves adding a modulo 26 one explicit character and the appropriate one-time character key..." she continued.

At some point, the meaning of individual words stopped reaching me. I'm confused. She might as well speak Chinese to me, it would have the same effect.

"Professor," I finally dared to interrupt. "Why don't you explain me on an example?" I asked in a very uncertain voice.

"You're right, I think it's better this way," she admitted.

She picked up a black marker.

"Let's define a key," she said, writing on the board:

key: Walker

"Numbers for this key:

22, 0, 11, 10, 4, 17

She gave me an enquiring look. I nodded as a sign that I understood.

"Now message. It should be remembered that it must be shorter than the key," she added, adding underneath:

message: Emily

"Corresponding numbers:

4, 12, 8, 11, 24"

"Now just add the appropriate key and message values, of course with modulo 26 operation. So, we have:

0, 12, 19, 21, 2"

"After assigning them the appropriate letters we get a cryptogram:

A M T V C"

At the end, with a sweeping movement of her hand, she underlined the string and turned towards me.

"Is everything clear now?" She asked, piercing me with her eyes.

I smiled.

"Now yes."

"We'll find out soon," she said skeptically. "It's your turn, Emily."

I coded the next message according to another key without major problems, then one more and then... until I got bored. Unexpectedly, something that at first seemed insanely interesting now became terribly boring. I yawned a few times without hiding it. After

an hour, my eyelids droop. Only when my eyes closed for a few seconds longer than they should have Lorena deigned to notice that I had enough.

"Enough for today, but you'll have to work on it at home. You should first learn the numbers that correspond to each letter. We'll devote the next class to decrypting cryptograms. You can try to develop the method yourself. I think it won't be difficult for you."

It wasn't difficult for me. I didn't need much time to determine how cipher-text decoding works. For this sleepless night spent a persistent thought: what about the keys to the codes? Could my next task be to learn them by heart?! I winced. Admittedly, my mind was quite roomy, but putting dozens of disordered strings of letters into my brain would be a big exaggeration.

I was supposed to ask about it in the next class, but I didn't have to. The problem was solved by itself. When I entered Lorena's office on Friday, my attention was caught by two tomes lying in the middle of her desk. I never thought I'd ever see books in her place. Curious, I looked more closely. They turned out to be slightly worn, identical editions of the Bible. She caught my astonished look. She picked up one of the copies, opening them on the first page with the text.

"I didn't think your literature could be of any use, and here, a surprise," she said. I didn't say anything without knowing what he was heading for. "The Bible will be your book of disposable keys," she explained.

"I don't think that's the best idea. I do not mean the Bible specifically, but any book. It seems to me that the key should not form logical sentences, because then it is easier to break the cipher." I said without thinking, realizing a bit too late that if Lorena would take my attention seriously, I would spend the rest of my time here on stringing chaotic characters.

"That's right," she admitted, "that's why the first letters of the next verses will be the keys. For the first message, the first page with the text, for the second the second one, for the third the third one..." explaining, she turned the pages and ran them with the index finger from top to bottom.

It made sense, and I should probably get used to the fact that everything the Arisyans do has sense and is quite deeply thought out. The choice of the Bible was not accidental either. This is a book that before the disaster could be found in almost every American home, not to mention hotels. If I accidentally misplaced my copy somewhere, I could easily get a second, identical one.

Everything was slowly beginning to clarify and form a logical whole, except for one thing that had been bothering me for some time. I was going to ask Almar about it, but Lorena might answer me as well.

"Professor, one more thing..." I hesitated, because she looked at me like an intrusive fly. "The doctor said my mission didn't require specialized equipment. So, when I have a cryptogram, what should I do with it? Shout the letters in the air, hoping that one of you will hear them, will I get some equipment so that I can convey the message in a more civilized way?"

"Of course, we will equip you with everything necessary," Lorena said indignantly. "But we'll deal with that later."

Seeing her harsh face, I could not ask which means 'later'. All I knew was that it did not mean the word 'now' and it had to be enough for me for now.

'Later' came somewhere after a month. Until then, I coded, coded and forced my mind to work at its best to do it all in memory. In any case, I was fed to the gills of ciphers, letters and numbers, which in the form of black, swirling stamps crept under the eyelids in the evenings, not allowing me to fall asleep peacefully. I didn't even think that sewing, drainage, fracture folding, bleeding control and other more or less complicated medical procedures that Sofie had tried to teach me would give me more pleasure. Apart from the fact that I almost didn't vomit at the sight of blood, I was doing quite well.

It wasn't until the end of August that Lorena took me to a large garage adjacent to the school building. There were three cars in it, among them a land rover - the same as Korin drove, but black.

"Once you asked about equipment," she said. "Here it is." She pointed at the car.

I came closer and frowned.

"Only means of transport? What about the rest?" I asked, walking around the vehicle and looking at it critically. It did not make a good impression. He looked like it was about to fall to pieces at the first corner.

Lorena looked at my indistinct face with real amusement, which did not suit the usual serious Arisyan woman.

"Are you sure this car can get to Alexandria?" I asked skeptically.

"Emily, don't look at its appearance. It's camouflage. The vehicles in the north all look like this.

If yours looked better, you would pay attention."

Sure, and I had egg on my face again.

"We've installed the necessary equipment inside," she said, opening the car door. "Come closer." She nodded at me.

I stood right next to her, watching her tilt the rear seat cushion with some effort. I pointed my foot and looked curiously over Lorena's shoulder. Under the seat there was a large cache like the one in Korin's trunk.

"Transmitter." She pointed to a small device equipped with a computer keyboard. "Simply enter the encrypted message and it will convert it into radio waves."

I listened carefully as she explained its work to me and lectured on the safety rules that I had to follow when sending reports. Because of the threat of rebel tracking, it was essential not to do it too often. I also had a well-stocked first aid kit. I didn't really understand why I needed some medications and medical supplies, but I preferred not to ask about it, not to say some foolishness again. I've already got used to the fact that the Arisyans are doing nothing without a goal. It's better to have too much than too little.

Finally, Lorena dug out a long, over two-meter-long rubber hose and a plastic container with some liquid from under the seat. I raised my eyebrows questioningly.

"Fuel now," she said.

Fuel. Why hadn't I thought about this before? I can't get to Alexandria in one tank, and I don't think gas stations in the north are working normally. At the

same time, I tried to remember if my mother had refueled since we were here, but to no avail. However, I refrained from asking a question that again might have been stupid. Lorena handed me an unmarked liquid bottle. For a moment I turned it uncertainly in my hands.

"Gasoline retarder," she said.

"How much, hmm... it retards?" I asked.

"Ten times."

"It's not much," I muttered under my breath.

"Emily! What did you expect Perpetuum Mobile?" She raised her voice a little. "One tank is enough to get there and back several times."

"All right, I'm just saying things. You are right," I admitted and immediately changed the subject. "What's that for?" I pointed to the rubber hose that was still clutching in her hand.

"Another camouflage."

Again, I didn't show that I didn't understand. I was just silent, so she continued:

"Used for transferring gasoline from one car to another. In the north, abandoned vehicles are the only available fuel sources. Rather, you will not have to use it, but you should have it somewhere on top, because everyone has it, and the basic principle is: do not stand out from the crowd."

"I know, I know, I will try not to stand out." I forced a faint smile.

I was beginning to realize that soon I would be alone, that I would be among strangers and that I would have to watch out for every word I spoke. It was not optimistic, although I was supposed to go to "my own",

but paradoxically Arisyans were closer to me than any other Earthling, except maybe my mother.

"That would be enough," Lorena interrupted my thoughts. "We'll meet again just before your departure."

"We won't have classes anymore?" I looked at her in amazement.

"I do not see such a need. You have already mastered all the necessary skills. My role is over."

I thought I would be happy, meanwhile I felt a bit pity. I liked Lorena, despite her cool attitude and exceptional, even for Arisyan, seriousness. On the other hand, it was the most difficult for me to keep cryptography secret from Korin and my mother. I had to put a lot of effort into inventing more and more new lies and lies so that none of them could guess the truth, because then they would easily guess the rest. Meetings with Sofie did not pose such a threat. Korin was firmly convinced that I did voluntary internships in the hospital, and I did not get him out of mistake. Mom was also deceived by this petty deception.

Lies, lies, lies... seemed to have no end, but they were the only way to calmly implement my plan. I hated myself for that. I've changed inside there. I had the impression that Korin sees it, the other me, the one who hides something, the one that is not completely honest, because I just can't be honest. Sometimes he looked at me thoughtfully, pierced me with his purple gaze, as if he saw much more than others. Or maybe already then, he sensed the presence of the Time Thief, who was approaching me relentlessly, to finally deprive him of all illusions at the end of September?

CHAPTER XIX

*It's weird, but when man is afraid of something
and give everything to slow down the passage of time,
the time has the terrible habit of speeding up its course.*
JOANNE KATHLEEN ROWLING

September 22, Thursday. Another date in my life that was to be deeply imprinted in my memory, despite the fact that it was not associated with someone's birthday, death or any significant holiday.

Red and I were standing in the school corridor, waiting for history classes when a breathless professor Holix approached us. He looked like he had just finished a marathon. Before he said anything, he wiped sweat from his forehead and breathed deeply a few times.

"Emily, I'm looking for you everywhere," he gasped out.

"Me?" I was surprised, but at the same time an alarm sounded in my head. "Did something happen to Mom?" I was worried.

"Absolutely not," he said quickly. "You need to go to the principal's office for an interlocution."

"Now or after classes?"

"Immediately. It's urgent," he added.

"All right, I'm going there."

I threw my backpack over my shoulder and walked down the hall toward Lorena's office. I didn't quite understand what an urgent matter could be, but it certainly had something to do with cryptography classes. Apparently this Arisyan reminded that I should still learn something. Maybe the Bible by heart?

I was joking about my thoughts, but I wasn't really laughing at all. I had a vague feeling that something was wrong. My anxiety worsened when I knocked on the principal's office door and heard a clear male voice:

"Come in."

I crossed the threshold and panicked at first. Lorena was gone, instead, Dr. Almar sat behind the massive desk. His grim expression only confirmed my belief that something had happened. I did not wait till he will ask me to sit down, I just sank limply into a nearby chair.

"There is a problem, right?" I asked directly.

Almar leaned back and sighed heavily.

"Unfortunately..." he admitted. "There was a small change in plans. You will have to leave at the latest on Sunday morning."

"This Sunday?" I asked to make sure I wasn't overheard.

He nodded affirmatively.

"But... it's already in three days!" I raised my voice. I was starting to panic. Thousands of chaotic thoughts flashed through my mind in an instant. What now? Will I make all the arrangements? Can I prepare mentally for the trip? Say goodbye to my mother so that she doesn't realize it's a goodbye? Enough to enjoy to the full of Korin?

"Emily," Almar said calmly. "If you want to

withdraw, just say. Nobody will blame you."

"Withdraw..." I repeated in a flat tone, slowly getting used to this information. "No, I don't want to withdraw," I said more vigorously. "Only... I would like to know the reason. Was the General going to attack Exira earlier?"

"I do not think so. I think he will stick to the date he gave. The reason is quite prosaic, namely: meteorological."

"So...?"

"At the beginning of next week, meteorologists announce heavy snowfall."

"Snow? In September?"

"Unfortunately." He spread his hands helplessly. "Weather on Earth will not stabilize until nature returns to normal. This process can take years. It's a shame to admit it, but when it comes to atmospheric phenomena, we are not good at predicting them. All because of insufficient data. Those before the disaster are unreliable. Our meteorologists are able to forecast only a week in advance. If you don't reach Alexandria, you'll have to cancel the mission before it covers all roads."

"I understand." Finally, I realized the seriousness of the situation.

"I talked to Sofie and Lorena, both claim that you are already properly prepared."

But damn, I am not saying like that - I wanted to shout, but I bit my tongue in time.

"I'll try not to disappoint expectations," I said, trying to calm down, as if the fact that someone had stolen a month of my life meant nothing to me.

I slowly got up from the chair. I wanted to get out

of here as soon as possible, hide in a quiet place, think calmly, sort everything out, though I wanted to cry most.

"Can I go now?" I asked.

"Yes."

I headed for the door.

"Emily, wait," I heard behind me when I was about to press the door handle.

I turned and looked questioningly at Almar.

"Think about changing your name and a new life story," he said. "Just in case, for safety."

"Well, I'll figure something out."

I don't even remember how I left the president's office. I felt completely broken. In an instant, the world collapsed on my head, not the first time and not the last, but each time it hurt the same. In addition, I learned that Emily Walker is about to disappear, and in her place some other Emily will appear who will not really be me anymore. I don't know if I'll ever be the same person again. I must leave here everything that is important to me, everything that I love and everyone I love...

I accelerated. My legs directed me towards Eden. I didn't even look sideways to see if anyone was watching by accident. I didn't care. I simply ran through the greenhouse with flowers, just remembering to hold my breath. I stopped only when the greenhouse door with mosses closed behind me with a soft click. The first gulp of air filled with the smell of earth restored my relative peace, and each subsequent seemed to clear my mind of unnecessary thoughts. I sat on the cover of mosses and closed my eyelids, from which thick drops of tears began to flow, monotonously rolling down my cheeks to finally crash into the ground. I stayed there for some time until I calmed down for good. I wiped the rest of my tears with the back of my hand and only then I could try to form a meaningful plan of action in my head. First, two letters - to my mother and Korin. This form of farewell came naturally and was probably the most appropriate in my situation.

I took out a supply of foil from my backpack. They were slippery, cold and uncomfortable to the touch. I shuddered. I regretted not having a piece of paper with me to write a traditional letter. One that, unlike foil, has a soul and, above all, can 'listen'. And absorb tears. Pouring the innermost feelings onto a cellophane sheet seemed to be stripped of all emotions.

I reluctantly picked up one of the 'cards' and a marker. I started writing, first to Korin. The first sentences of the letter unwittingly formed into the words of the song.

I don't know how to start, how to say it.

A million thoughts, zero words to tell you that:

I wanted to give you everything I have,

but one moment changed everything.

So, goodbye, I'm gone,

I disappear in the shadow of words...

Sorry to find out this way, but I couldn't find a better one. I had to leave before her arrival. I had to do it. For myself.

I couldn't watch you touch her, not me; how do you talk to her, although you have talked to me so far; how

your lips smile at her, and not long ago they belonged only to me; how do you hold her hand...

Something you can't see doesn't hurt. Or it hurts less.

You can try to believe that it is not there. Believe that you do not go to bed with her every night, that you do not fall asleep or wake up with her.

A perfect, genetic match mocked love. Because, Korin, it was love - at least on my part. You don't understand the meaning of the word and you never understood. I knew this. I knew before I decided to give you my whole self. I have no regrets, because if I had to decide again, it would be the same. I don't regret anything. You gave me everything you promised that you would give, and nobody would take it away from me.

But you know, sometimes I counted on a miracle. There were times when I thought you could beat genes and teach love. Naive fantasies, false hopes... Because how could I teach you something that does not exist in your world? How was I supposed to teach you something that is not there?

Do not worry about me, I will be fine, although I do not know if I will ever be the same person or if I will ever be able to smile as I smiled at You.

I just want you to miss me sometimes, even a little...

Forever yours,

Em

I put down the marker and returned to the letter to see if it didn't sound too pathetic. I did not want Korin's pity or compassion - I just had to tell him how much he meant to me. I wasn't sure he would understand anything, but it didn't matter anymore. I pushed the foil to the bottom of the backpack and took another clean one. Time for a letter to my mother. I looked at the blank page for a long time, afraid to start writing. I knew my words would hurt her, so I tried to shape my mind so that it would be less painful. Nothing of that. Their very sense touched so much. So,

I focused on performing Korin in the best light. I didn't want my mother to blame him for my trip.

Mum forgive me...

Forgive me for all my lies, secrets, little secrets and half-truths. From the moment we became a part of the Arisyan world, I surrounded myself with a veil woven from falsehood, but... I had no choice. I speak wrongly. There is always a choice, better or worse, but it is. The problem is that at the beginning it is difficult to determine which one is right. I still don't know it and I'm not convinced that I chose wrongly.

I loved the wrong person. I was caught up in a relationship that was based on friendship, lust and sex, but it lacked the most important thing - love. His love. But... you already know that, I told you recently. However, this is not the reason for my trip, there is something else... He has a genetic partner who will soon reach Earth. I don't want to watch them together.

You probably think that I only found out about his girlfriend now. Well, no. I knew from the beginning. Therefore, if you love me, do not blame Korin. He played open cards, did not hide anything, did not want a relationship with me, did not want to hurt me... You can say that I forced him, or maybe he wanted to be forced to? It doesn't matter. Something just connected us, the first night spent in new home when I woke up with my cheek pressed to his hand. Or maybe even earlier? Maybe at our first meeting, when his car emerged from around the corner?

I don't know about you, but I have never treated Arisyans as strangers. For me they have always been a part of this world, just as Korin will always be a part of me even though I lost my fight for him. I couldn't compete with the genes.

I wondered for a long time where to go, where to run... I chose Fargo. Yes, Mom, I want to go home. I'll try to find dad, or at least determine if he survived the catastrophe. I owe you this. For staying with me when I needed it most, but above all for the pain I must inflict on you when I will leave.

Forgive me.

I love you.

Emily

I thought I would fall in tears while writing this letter, but I didn't cry, I didn't have anything. I threw the foil into my backpack and got up from the ground. I spent almost three hours here, but it did me good. There was something difficult to define here that restored inner peace. No wonder Korin liked to hang out here when he wanted to gather his thoughts.

I went outside the greenhouse. I felt a cold breeze on my face, the sharp air reminded me of the prematurely approaching winter and the fact that in

three days I am to become something completely different. I still must choose a name for this new Emily. Moss - the first word that came to my mind.

"Emily Moss," I said softly. Sounds nice.

I ran towards the parking lot. Korin was already waiting. He stood leaning against his car, breathing warmed cold hands. I slowed down, wondering how to justify almost an hour late. Nothing sensible came to mind, nothing that would explain the slightly swollen eyes from crying. I knew he would notice.

"Em, something happened?" He asked, watching me closely. "I've been waiting for you for an hour. A moment more and all my limbs will fall off because the cold."

"You had to wait in the car," I murmured in mock anger. I didn't want to explain myself, so I chose attack as a form of defense. "I thought Arisyans are smart."

He raised his arms above his head.

"I'm fine, I don't say anything more. Hop in," he said, opening the passenger door.

After a while he started the engine.

"To you or to me?" He asked.

"To me," I said without hesitation. "Mom isn't home yet, she will come after three o'clock today."

He smiled under his breath and put the car in gear.

"Wait a second." I stopped his hand on the gear stick.

He gave me a questioning look.

"What's happening?"

"Nothing." I shrugged my shoulders. "I just want you to do something for me... Make love to me on Saturday evening, give me all night," I blurted out.

"And I already thought something had happened," he laughed.

It happened the hell! Everything happened! - I almost shouted.

"Will we go to the portal on Saturday?" He asked.

I shook my head, wincing.

"I do not want to go under the portal, I associate this place badly."

"So, where?"

"Greenhouse with mosses," I suggested.

He looked surprised at the choice of place but did not comment.

"When do you want to meet?" As usual, he had to set the details.

"At eight p.m."

"What do you tell your mother?" He inquired.

"Korin," I groaned, "don't ask too much, I'm tired. I'll make something up. And you, what do you say at home, because probably not the truth?"

"I'll think of something too."

"Are you lying for me?" I was surprised by his answer. "It would be the first time. Are you lying for me?"

"No, I can't lie, but..." he lowered his voice to a whisper, "sometimes I can hide the truth."

He leaned toward me and gave me a quick kiss on the cheek. A short kiss, just a brush, but it was enough for a wave of pleasant warmth to flood me. I squeezed deeper into the car seat, pushing the memory of today and all the problems associated with it to the bottom of my mind. I think I was the first time I heard Emily Moss, who, unlike Emily Walker, was able to keep her emotions under control. I wanted to go through those three 'normal' days I had the best and hiding the deep 'me' was the only way.

We spent quite a nice afternoon. Even my mother, after returning from work, stopped treating Korin with such a cool distance as she did a few weeks ago, when she learned about our specific, love arrangement. In an atmosphere of laughter, carefree jokes and relative normality, it was easy to forget about the expedition to the unknown.

It wasn't until I fell asleep that I returned to the events of the previous day, but I approached them quite pragmatically and with a clearer mind, you can say almost in Arisyan. I made a list of things to do before leaving. I found the most trouble finding a way to get out of the house on Saturday evening. I didn't want to involve Kori again, for fear of suspecting something. She was less Arisyan than Korin, so it was harder to cover eyes with a lie, even if it sounded likely. And I've already lied enough, I didn't want to do it anymore. That's why I decided to ask for a favor from Red.

Friday was ordinary school day, or rather - almost ordinary. In the morning I packed some of my things into my backpack and tossed into the trunk of the Land Rover prepared for me before classes. Later, I was supposed to talk to Red, but by the corridor, I accidentally ran into Lorena, who decided to do a short repetition of my cryptography, so I was stuck in her office for a good half hour.

I found Red only after the second lesson. As usual, she was standing with Skinny and Erica.

"Hi," I said, coming over.

"Hi, Emily," she said cheerfully. Skinny accompanied her, even Erica managed a forced smile.

"Ana, do you have a moment?" I asked right away. "I wanted to talk."

"Sure, I do. Speak."

I pulled her aside.

"Not here," I whispered, looking around nervously.

She became serious at the look on my face.

"Okay, let's go to me then," she made a quick decision. "Nobody will disturb us there."

"Do you want to get out of school?"

"Not the first time, not the last," she laughed. "What's the matter with you, Emily?"

"You're kidding me," I snorted. "I never break," I said confidently.

We sneaked out of the school building and after a while we got into the 'winter rat', as Red called her car, and it was difficult to disagree with this term. I was wondering why she hadn't exchanged the winter rat for something better, but she apparently felt a special fondness for the sounds of the exhausts.

"And your grandmother?" I asked when we arrived at her house. "Will she not be surprised that you came back so early, in addition with a friend?"

"Have you already forgotten that my grandmother is deaf? She will probably not notice at all that we have entered, and even if tomorrow she will not remember it. She's got sclerosis," she added.

I struggled with myself not to smile because it wasn't proper. Ana was able to turn even the biggest problem into a joke. I think I liked her the most for this character trait.

Grandma actually proved to be harmless.

"Are you back yet?" came to our ears from the depths of the apartment.

"Yes!" Red screamed with all her might.

"Lunch in an hour. I will call you."

"Just don't burn the soup again," she muttered under her breath and started up the stairs, and I followed her.

She opened the door to her room for me.

"Sorry for the mess," she said, letting me go first. "I hate cleaning, and grandma is not allowed here."

I looked around the room. It was not so much a mess as the artistic disorder that matched Red's personality perfectly. She made room for me in an armchair, picking up a pile of folded clothes from it and forcibly stuffing them in the closet.

She sprawled comfortably on an unmade bed.

"Sit down and tell me what's going on," she got straight to the point.

"I need help. Will you do something for me?" I asked carefully.

"It depends... what I get from it."

I was speechless. I didn't think she would put any conditions. I didn't know her from this side. There was an unpleasant silence in the room for a moment, which was broken by Anya's sincere laughter.

"Come on, Emily. I was just kidding, you don't think I could ask for a small favor."

"It wasn't funny at all," I said grimly.

She frowned.

"I don't understand what's happening to you lately?

At rehearsals you are also different, as if distracted. Will you finally tell me what's going on?"

"Could you come for me Saturday night? I will tell my mother that I stay at you."

"But... you won't stay at me. Right?" She said, watching me closely.

"No, I don't," I admitted.

"I should not ask, or do you want to tell me something more?"

I wanted to tell her. About Korin and I. Not everything, but she should know at least the truth I told my mother.

"I made an appointment with Korin at school in the greenhouse for the night."

"Ha! I knew you were flirting with him," she exclaimed contentedly.

"But Red, nobody can find out," I said, just in case.

"I'm not a gossip girl, you know."

"I know, thanks."

"How is he?" She asked, barely concealing her curiosity. "He's not boring, right?"

"Not for me, but it's a matter of taste."

Then I told her about the relationship with Korin, about the friendship that unites us; about how I feel when he touches me; about the chemistry that is being made between us then... Maybe I revealed too many personal details, but I finally needed to open myself to someone. I did not mention only the genes that divide us or his girlfriend, who will appear in school in a month. Maybe if she asked... But Red, despite her rather relaxed way of being, was not nosy and did not ask questions, as if she knew that I wanted to keep

some things only for myself. Without knowing when, it got late afternoon. Finally, Ana drove me home.

Mom was waiting in the kitchen. With her arms folded and a pout, she looked very annoyed.

"I'm sorry, it's so late," I muttered uncertainly. "But I talked too much with my friend."

"You haven't been to school today, I want to know why," she said sternly.

"I was there, but briefly.

She didn't say anything. She looked me over, apparently waiting for me to try to explain myself.

"Red wanted to talk, so we went to her," I added, bending the truth a little. "I'm sorry. Are you mad about this hooky?"

She let out a breath, and her face softened considerably.

"I actually pretend to be mad. I think I should be angry, but in fact I'm glad you're starting to explore the other benefits of the school. This is not pedagogical, what I will say now, but I also sometimes missed classes when I was your age."

I came and hugged her tightly.

"I'm sorry, I'll try not to do that again," I promised, although the apology was for a completely different reason. I was sorry that I won't be here soon.

I jumped out of bed at the crack of dawn, although the slob outside the window did not encourage me to get out from under the warm quilt, but today I could not afford to waste my time. I took a quick, hot shower, then jumped into jeans, a T-shirt and a pull-out hoodie, all black, as if the color of my clothes wanted to

emphasize my mourning mood. My mother, without much resistance, not only agreed to spend the night at Red's, but also very pleased with the fact that I was finally trying to make friends with someone outside the Arisyan circle.

I packed my backpack quite efficiently and, just in case, hid it at the bottom of the wardrobe if it happened to my mother somehow look into it. She would immediately suspect. Some things are unlikely to be taken to a friend's weekend. I also got a guitar ready. I could not imagine leaving without it, although she would painfully remind me of Korin, it was a gift from him after all.

It was almost eight when I tipped into the kitchen on my toes to prepare breakfast for us. My mother always made it, but all this day, all the time I have, I wanted to give her. I felt extremely bad because of leaving, and it was a kind of redemption guilt, a peculiar form of saying goodbye without saying aloud: goodbye.

I made some sandwiches and put them in a toaster. I realized too late that it was a bad idea because my culinary achievements never ended well. My memory was only refreshed by the deaf sound of an explosion in a socket, a hail of sparks and the smell of a burning cable. Before I could react in any way, a sleepy and panicked mother ran into the kitchen.

"Emily, what the hell are you doing again?!" She shouted, pulling the plug from the socket.

"It was not me. This time it wasn't me," I moaned. "Not my fault, these stupid kitchen appliances hate me. I hate them too!"

She laughed.

"In fact, you don't seem to like it much."

"It's not even funny anymore," I murmured, but then I smiled. "I should be banned from entering the kitchen for life."

"Relax, nothing happened," she said, reaching into the cabinet for two plates. She put on them sandwiches taken out of the toaster, which did not manage to be baked enough to be called toasts. She handed me a plate.

I grimaced slightly, because they resembled a pancake trampled by an elephant. Fortunately, they tasted quite good. My mother did not complain either, but she took care of the dinner herself, from beginning to end. She didn't even let me cut the vegetables, although I insisted. She claimed that with my skills I should not use a knife at all, because I would still cut my finger or even my whole hand, and I would only cause trouble to everyone. It boiled down to the statement that if the rebels did not kill me, I would finish myself in the preparation of a simple meal.

However, I didn't let to be driven out to my room, I did not want to be alone today. I sat at the kitchen table and looked at my mother for a while, trying to remember her. By the way, I was going to ask her a little about Dad. I checked the map yesterday. Alexandria was less than two hundred kilometers from Fargo, so maybe I could visit our old house and learn something about my father.

"Mom, you once said that if you or dad survive a disaster, you will leave a message at home. Can you tell me something more?"

She looked at me, but without a trace of suspicion. Apparently, she thought that I was asking out of curiosity.

"Do you remember the house a bit?"

"Not really," I admitted. "Like a blur."

"There was a fireplace in the living room."

"I remember the fireplace, although more Christmas socks with presents that hung on it."

I smiled to myself at the memory of family holidays. For a moment I even had the impression that I could smell a festive smell - a mixture of spices and resinous spruce twigs.

"To the right of the fireplace, right next to the wall, there was a loose board in the floor. We called it 'a board of contention' because your father always said he will fix it later, while I insisted that he should firmly fix it right away. In general, the problem of the board ended in a row, and dad, out of usual perversity, never nailed it. Just under it we were supposed to leave letters with information about our whereabouts."

"Do you think there's a message waiting for us there?" I asked.

Mom looked at me thoughtfully.

"I don't know, Emily," she sighed softly. "I don't even know if I'll ever be able to check."

But I'll check. For you and me - I promised in my thoughts.

CHAPTER XX

Sweetly, sweetly shake dust off shoes and walk away without leaving anything behind, no, not walk away but go...[...] Walk away by going, go by walk away and don't even feel the memories.

WITOLD GOMBROWICZ

Ana arrived on time and thankfully. My facial muscles ached from the sticky artificial smile I had served my mother for several hours. Pretending that everything is in perfect order, that this Saturday is no different from other Saturdays, was exhausting me mentally. Before Red entered the house, I was already wearing shoes and a warm jacket, and in my hands a cover with a guitar and a backpack. I was ready to leave.

"Just don't fall apart. Not now. Because you screw up everything. Say goodbye as usual: Bye, see you tomorrow. No kisses, hugs, throws around the neck... It has to be as always, it has to be as if you were to come back tomorrow"- I reminded myself in my thoughts.

"Mom, see you tomorrow". I heard my own voice in surprise. It sounded almost normal, maybe a bit like a learned matter, but thanks to that nobody realized that a real emotional hell had broken loose inside me.

"Have fun," my mother said with a smile and wrapping herself in a warm scarf, she went out onto the porch to wave goodbye.

I dropped my stuff in the trunk, trying hard not to look toward the house. There was a little rain. I pulled the hood deep over my eyes and got into the car, staring fixedly at the windshield. I would give a lot to erase this moment. Apparently, with will one can do anything, but not in this case. I knew that this view would haunt me for the rest of my life and I also knew that tomorrow a smile in my mother's eyes would replace tears of despair.

Red moved almost immediately, and I felt as if I was suddenly out of breath.

"Have you had an argument with your mother?" She asked as we drove a bit.

"No," I said quickly through my throat.

"Because... never mind, it's not my business."

"We didn't argue, but..." I suddenly fell silent, I almost said too much. "I will tell you tomorrow."

Another lie. She'll find out, but not from me. Tomorrow or Monday at school. Then everyone will know that I left Exira. Red did not ask anything more. We arrived at the school in silence. Korin's car was already at the verge of the parking lot, but it was not inside, apparently waiting for me in the greenhouse.

"Your boyfriend is punctual like a Swiss watch," she said, nudging me lightly.

"Not really, he arrived too early, but that's what he does." I managed a faint smile.

I said goodbye not too effusively to Red, and when she left, I breathed a sigh of relief, because for a moment I could stop pretending. I did not immediately go to the greenhouse, first I left my belongings in the school garage, taking only my shoulder bag. I hid a

letter to Korin in it. I had no idea how to hand it to him, but I would probably leave it with him while he will be sleep.

I walked quickly towards Eden, trying to remember the path layout in the greenhouse with fragrant flowers along the way. I will have to grope through it blindly, because of all this I did not think to take a flashlight. I arrived there after a while, carefully opened the door and went inside. At the same time, somebody grabbed my arms tightly. I let out a shout that was immediately suppressed by a passionate kiss. Someone's warm lips clung to mine with all my might. I recognized them immediately.

"Korin," I growled softly, pushing him away. "Are you crazy?!"

The dim glow of the Arisyan lamp lit up the darkness. Korin stood in front of me with a flashlight in his hand and smiled apologetically.

"I didn't mean to scare you, and you could have guessed it was me. Because who else?"

"Maybe Spite," I snorted angrily.

"Do you think he also likes to kiss girls entering the greenhouse?" He joked.

"Yes, I think this is his favorite pastime," I laughed honestly, and all anger at Korin immediately passed away.

He embraced me and hugged me, kissing the crown of my head.

"Let's get out of here, I've been breathing these flower vapors for a good ten minutes and I'm slowly getting dizzy," he said and led me down the main avenue. "I went for you because I figured you wouldn't

get a flashlight."

I did not answer. I just embraced his waist, hugged him tighter, and lengthened his step. I wanted to be there as soon as possible, lay naked on the moss cover and make love with Korin until the morning. Today, I needed him more than ever before. I wanted warmth, tenderness and his strong arms that I could cuddle in so that I could feel safe for the last time in my life. This night should be special, for me, for him, for us... that it cannot be compared to any other, that it cannot be forgotten, that every time he makes love with his genetic tramp, he regrets that he doesn't love with me. Therefore, it's time to separate the body from the mind.

We entered the greenhouse with mosses, I disentangled myself from his embrace and began to undress. I took off my clothes, thing after thing, throwing away aside the pieces of clothing, and with them shame, uncertainty and all moral inhibitions that my mother inculcated for years. Today, I was only a body that feel, desire and desire not only to give but to take. Korin stood unmoved and stared at me with such astonished eyes that I paused, remaining in my underwear.

I took a step forward, stuck my fingers into the belt of his pants and pulled violently. He dropped the flashlight he had been holding in his hand and blinked nervously.

"You don't want me?" I asked, slightly confused.

"I do, but... I didn't know you would want to do it right away."

"Now you know," I whispered.

He took my hands, putting them on his neck. He

leaned over and ran the tip of his tongue over my lower lip, slowly, sensually... I let out a low moan. I tightened his neck. He shivered. Under my fingertips, I felt his pulse speed up. For a moment we stroked our lips slightly, in absolute silence, broken only by the whisper of our breaths. Warm, feverish, thirsty.

Too slow, not enough, more... I lowered my hands, unfastened the belt buckle with one firm move, sliding pants off Korin. In response, he ripped my panties off, opened my legs with his knee and slipped his thigh between them. When he began to move it rhythmically, rubbing the skin against my skin, I could not stand it, I clung to his arms, digging in nails in him.

He hissed but didn't stop, just hugged me tighter. He was so close. I burned from the inside, I was breathless, my head was buzzing, and he didn't stop.

A wave of warm humidity flooded me. He felt it. He took his thigh and replaced it with his hand, slipping his fingers into me. Deep and then deeper.

"Korin... I'll..." I groaned, curling unconsciously in his arms.

I screamed. An orgasmic spasm shook my body. And again. And one more time... until everything calmed down. I closed my eyes. He stroked my hair. He whispered.

I don't know how long we stood there, I lost my sense of reality, but I gained inner solace. I was just fine. My breathing was getting even, but Korin's heart was still pounding, he was still aroused.

"We're not done yet," I murmured softly.

I took a step back and took off my bra. Korin's lips twitched, he quickly pulled off his T-shirt, gripped my hand tightly and pulled me to the ground with him. He lay down on his back. I fell on him, still burning. I squeezed his hips with my thighs to feel him slip inside me. Full anastomosis. One body instead of two. Perfect synchronization of movements. Up - down, up - down, up - down... The same rhythm, the same desire and feeling of heat exploding under the skin where he touched me. We're lost, both of us. For long. And finally, it exploded in me and vaginal contraction again, first, the second... and again the same bliss penetrating the mind and body.

He put his arms around me and pressed me to him. He didn't say a word, he didn't have to. It was enough that he was there. He ran his fingers through my hair, gently ran his hand over my skin, and I couldn't get rid of the impression that we are not only connected by sex and lust.

"Korin." I broke the silence. "Are you sure you don't feel anything for me?" I asked hopefully to regret it in a moment. I wasn't sure I wanted to hear the answer.

He was silent. I knew perfectly well what silence meant, just as he knew what my question meant. I Gave my feelings away unnecessarily.

"Korin, answer me." Still, I wanted to make sure.

"Em... I am who I am, I won't change it," he began cautiously.

I closed my eyelids. I would like to plug my ears so as not to listen to it, but I provoked this conversation myself. And every sentence he uttered deprived me of illusions.

"I like you, I like to be with you, I like to talk to you, I like to touch you and hold you in my arms, but... nothing more. It's not enough in my world. There is no stronger feeling than genetic attraction to another person, it obscures everything else. In nature, this is also the case, the female chooses the strongest male to survive the species. However, her choice is instinctive, but we act fully consciously."

I sighed softly. I couldn't blame him. From the beginning, the matter was clear, sex and pretending to be a relationship, in exchange for what? Well, for nothing.

"You don't even know how much I would love to be able to love you," he said softly, as if with a bit of regret.

I sat down and looked him in the face. I forced myself to a carefree smile.

"Hey... don't worry. We have a nice time, we had such a contract, right?"

"Because for a moment I thought you..." he paused. "No matter what I thought."

I leaned forward and bit his ear gently.

"Good, we didn't come here today to think," I whispered, biting again, harder this time.

He embraced me firmly, turned me over and overwhelmed me with his weight, clinging eagerly to my lips. We made love again. Bit by bit, we caressed our bodies, examined them by touch of lips, tasted... To then fall into a short nap, wake up and love again. I have lost count as many times, because the wild passion and uncontrollable emotions tearing me free me from this place, placing me somewhere beyond time.

After the last time I didn't fall asleep. It was getting

light. I knew that soon I would have to go. Sofie was supposed to wait at seven-thirty at the west portal to let me out of town. Carefully, I freed myself from Korin's arms and sat down. He didn't move. He lay on his back, naked and... just beautiful. That's how I wanted to remember him.

I reached out and gently patted his cheek. Last time. I could not resist.

"Em..." he murmured in his sleep.

I withdrew my hand in fear. He did not wake up, but I jumped from the ground anyway. I began to collect parts of my wardrobe scattered all over the greenhouse. After a while I was dressed and ready to go. I didn't just zip my jacket so that the sound of the zipper did not wake him up. And the last thing - a letter. I felt uncomfortable tightness in my stomach as I pulled it from the bottom of the bag. He was a silent symbol of the end, the closing of a chapter in my life, the beginning of a new one... I weighed the foil in my hand for a minute before I decided to put it next to Korin's head. I cast one last look at his face, then at the mosses, which glowed with a faint green-purple glow, turned and walked resolutely to the exit. If I hadn't done it now, no force would have forced me to leave the greenhouse.

I had the feeling that I was suffocating. It wasn't until I fell outside and felt a single drop of cold rain on my face that I regained my breath. I ran the way to the garage, focusing mainly on not to cry and not to turn back. I took off my jacket and threw it into the back seat. As if in a trance, I started the engine, surprisingly, succeeded the first time and headed towards the west portal.

Sofie was waiting for me in a car parked by the roadside. She had to see in the rearview mirror that I was coming because she got out, pulling the hood over her head. I stopped next to her, not switching off the engine. She opened the door and hopped into the passenger seat.

"Nasty weather for travel," she said in greeting.

"Honestly, I don't care," I said grimly.

She looked into my eyes seriously. I don't know what she read in them, but today it could have been everything, today I had no strength to pretend anything.

"Emily, you can go back yet," she said, looking at me.

I shook my head to say no.

"To tell you the truth, I was hoping you wouldn't come," she added.

"No, this is the only solution, it may seem wrong to you, but it is my life and my decision," I assured. "Although, I didn't think it would be so hard for me."

"What did you tell mom?"

"Nothing."

"You didn't tell her?!" She raised her voice.

"No."

"You said you would do it. Why didn't you tell her?" She asked.

"I couldn't..." I said softly. "I just couldn't, but... I did it differently." I reached behind the bag and took the folded foil out. I passed it to Sofie. "I wrote a letter to my mother, I would like you to give it to her."

"Don't mess me with it," she frowned, giving me the foil.

"You're already involved in that," I said.

Sofie sighed, took a letter from me, but I saw that she was reluctant to do so.

"Actually, according to the procedure, I should read it first to make sure that you did not reveal any details about the action." Before I could protest, she added, "I will not do it. I don't read someone else's correspondence. Your word is enough for me. What did you write to mom, where are you going?"

"I wrote I was going to Fargo, looking for my dad."

"Something more?"

"I gave the reason for the trip."

"Korin?" She asked.

"Yes, but not only. I don't want her to blame him, because the fault is mainly mine and these fucking genetics," I said angrily.

"I will not comment on this, because I would have to say: I told you so."

"I know."

Sofie folded the foil again in half and slipped it into the inside pocket of the jacket, taking out a small rectangular piece of plastic.

"Give me your hand."

I reached out my right hand. She shook her head.

"Not right, left. The one with the bracelet. I need to enter the code."

I gave her my other hand. She grabbed my wrist, bringing a small device closer to it. She pressed a button. The red LED on the bracelet blinked in response.

"Ready. You can move. I'll go with you. As soon as

we cross the field, stop," she ordered.

I nodded my head. I put the car in gear. The car began to roll slowly, entering a delicate fog that was constantly on the edge of the field. I braked right behind the portal.

"From now on, you're on your own," she said.

"I know, I can handle it."

"Oh, one more thing, you have to return the bracelet. It cannot fall into the wrong hands."

I didn't want to get rid of it. It was the last link connecting me with Korin and the past. Thanks to it I belonged somewhere. I looked at my wrist in silence for a long time.

"Emily...?"

"I'm sorry, I thought." I unfastened the bracelet and handed it over to Sofie reluctantly.

"Be careful." She hugged me tightly. "Don't get hurt and don't be exposed. Do not trust anyone but try to inspire confidence yourself."

"Thank you," that was all I could say before she got out.

I waved Sofie and drove away with a squeal of tires. All these goodbyes were beyond my strength. For the first miles I drove like crazy, as if I wanted to escape memories. I slowed down only when low rain clouds swirling over the horizon from the morning, a heavy rain fell, which soon turned into an intense downpour. The wipers worked at full speed, and still could not collect all the water from the windshield. I barely managed to keep my way. Finally, I pulled over. I decided to wait, it won't rain all day.

I was desperate and angry, and my eyes began to fog.

"Just don't fall apart, you moron, not now," I said to myself.

Did not help.

I got out of the car, leaned against the side door and tilted my head back, letting cold rain pour my face, quelling emotions. Slowly, self-control and common sense returned, which I will be guided from today.

When I got back in the car, I was another person, I was Emily Moss prepared for everything. I was wrong - not for everything, and certainly not for the intense smell of Korin, which in the warm, cramped interior of the vehicle freed from a completely soaked T-shirt. I pulled it over my head and threw it angrily through the side window. I watched it sink in a puddle of cold rain, taking with it memories, smells, flavors, thoughts... Taking everything that does not let to forget.

I reached into my backpack for a dry blouse. I pulled it on, pressed the clutch and put the car in gear.

"Time for me," I muttered under my breath. "I disappear."

EPILOGUE

I disappear
In this rain I stand waiting for a sign
and even when you are away, you are so close.
I don't know how to start, how to say it,
A million thoughts, zero words to tell you that:

I wanted to give you everything I have
but one moment changed everything,
so goodbye, I'm gone
I disappear in the shadow of words.

You must show what you have, to count in this
world
or stay in the shadows, counting on nothing more.
When you try with your heart, you can lose it.
Hope will lose you, so don't risk.

I wanted to give you everything I have
but one moment changed everything,
so goodbye, I'm gone.
I disappear in the shadow of words.

ARISYAN VIOLET COLD

VOLUME II

(teaser)

CHAPTER I

We are the times: Such as we are, such are the times.
AUGUSTINE OF HIPPO

Be a good person. Nice decision in dark times.
JOHN MAXWELL COETZEE

The class emptied in a few seconds when the school bell announced the start of the weekend. I was left alone. I guess only I didn't like going home. It was cold, unfriendly and... stranger.

I went to the window. Large snowflakes swirled behind the glass. It was snowing from the morning, but only now it was falling apart for good. If it doesn't stop by the evening, all roads leading to Alexandria will become impassable. Something that meant a big problem for adults, was great fun for children. A snowball battle was taking place in the courtyard, accompanied by joyful squeaks and laughter of a group of kids. If I was the old Emily Walker, I would probably join the fun, but Emily Moss could only afford a faint smile.

This is the second snow this year. The first one was exactly a month ago, on my arrival in the city, but did not last long. After a few hours, it turned into a disgusting brown slush flowing down the streets, which intensified the unpleasant first impression Alexandria had made on me.

I came back to that day. A few hours journey from Exira was not the most pleasant. I struggled to break through the wall of rain, at the same time straining my eyes not to fall off the route or break the wheel, falling into a tear in the asphalt. It had its good sides. Focusing on the road, at least I didn't have time to grimly think about the house, my mother, Korin, or that I had just left behind everything that I knew and that was important to me.

It was already dusk, and the downpour turned into sleet when the contours of the town loomed before me. I was approaching it from the south on route 29 and it was good that I wasn't driving too fast because suddenly I was blinded by the light of several powerful headlights. I braked abruptly, freezing with my hands on the steering wheel. Before I could gather my thoughts and make any decisions, a silhouette of a man emerged from a patch of bright light. I couldn't see the face exactly. A shadow fell on it. For this I clearly saw a rifle aimed at me.

The man stopped just by the side door and nodded to show me to get out of the car. I felt that if I did not follow the order - he would not hesitate - he would shoot.

I got out slowly and raised my arms above my head.

"Name, purpose," he said in a commanding tone.

"Emily... Emily Moss," I choked, teeth chattering in fear and cold.

"Purpose of arrival?" He repeated emphatically.

He didn't look like someone going to let me into town. The only thing I could count on was to make him pity.

"I don't know..." I said softly. "I think I would like to stay here for a while. an I...?" I looked at him pleadingly.

It worked out.

He lowered his weapon hesitantly.

He went around the car and took a seat for the passenger.

"What are you waiting for? Get in!" He shouted at me. "Cold as hell."

I jumped behind the wheel. I wanted to say thank you, but the words got stuck in my throat when he put the cool barrel to my neck.

"One false move," he growled. "And I'll shoot your head. Understand?"

I nodded carefully.

"Perfect." He pulled back his rifle, secured it, and rested it on his knees. "Where are you from?" He asked as if nothing had happened.

"From around Rochester," I said in a shaky voice where I lived. Located not too close to Arisyan cities and far enough from Alexandria that nobody would want to check if I really came from there.

"Thank you for not sending me to hell," I added and dared to finally look in his face. She belonged to an over fifty-year-old man experienced through his life. It was hard for me to judge this man by the very appearance and the way he treated me. However, I had a feeling that he was not bad. He just carried out his duties.

He did not answer. He murmured something indistinctly, then took a walkie-talkie out of the side pocket of a worn-out US Army uniform. He turned on. It gave out a few protracted whistles and unpleasant clicks.

"What do you got there, Steven?" A distinct male voice came from the device, drowning out the noise.

"It's just a kid," said my companion. "Girl. I had no conscience to give air to her in such weather."

"You should. You know the procedures."

"Fuck, don't say me now about the procedures! You'd better turn off those damn lights before I go completely blind and open the gate. That's an order."

"Okay, okay. I hope you know what you are doing."

"Moron," he muttered annoyed. He hung up and stuffed the walkie-talkie in the pocket of his military jacket.

At the same moment all headlights went out. The entrance to the city was lit only by a weak, single lamp.

Only now I noticed that the town is surrounded by a barbed wire fence over two meters high, probably under voltage. An overwhelming view. For the first time I doubted my decision to leave Exira.

"Go," he said. "Only slowly," he added. "Turn left at the first big crossway."

I gently pressed the accelerator. The car rolled towards the gate. We passed a slim, tall man and headed to the center. We wandered a bit through the dark streets, and finally Steven told me to park in front of a low, shabby building with the inscription: MAYOR - OFFICE.

"Let's go. Put on your jacket, it's cold," he said roughly as he got out of the car.

I turned off the engine, pulled on my jacket, and joined Steven, who was just shaking his keychain nervously, trying to match one of them with the lock. He let out a steak of curses before he could open it. He turned on the light. I followed him into the white, long corridor. We passed another door, and our footsteps echoed off the empty walls. I had no idea why we came here, but this man somehow made me trust him.

And unnecessarily.

And it was a mistake.

We stopped in front of a small barred room at the end of the corridor. Even then, I didn't feel anything bad. Maybe that's why he pushed me into the cell so easily, slammed the lattice and turned the key.

I stood still for a moment, trying to gather my thoughts, understand - why?

"What are you doing?" I said by my throat, which was squeezed with fear.

"I provide you with safe accommodation," he replied coldly.

"Do you call lock-up a safe accommodation?!" I shouted. I got claustrophobic fear. An unpleasant remnant of childhood spent in a dark shelter cut off from the world. "You have no right to keep me here!"

He dug his hands into his pants pockets and looked at me seriously.

"The problem is, kid," he said calmly, "that all I didn't have the right to do was let you into town. Now I'm trying to soften the effects of this decision, and you don't make it easy with your attitude. I will say so," he sighed heavily, "you have two options. I open the cell, but within five minutes you leave Alexandria and look for happiness somewhere else, which in the current weather conditions is, to put it mildly, unreasonable. Or... you are waiting politely here until the mayor's decision."

I frowned, weighing his words slowly. I think he was actually trying to help me, and I had no other choice but to take this help in the form in which he offered it. I couldn't afford any weakness, especially now that I had almost reached my destination. I will still have to convince the mayor. The only question is: how? I remembered the words of Almar, who once said that my greatest weapon is intelligence and trustworthy appearance. In the case of Steven, the latter probably worked, because I didn't really show off my intellect. Tomorrow, when talking to the mayor, I will have to strain my mind.

"So? What is the decision?" He asked, examining my face.

"I'm staying."

He pointed to two damaged blankets lying on a metal bunk.

"Nights are cold, cover yourself well," he said quietly, then turned and walked toward the exit.

I didn't thank him. I was too scared to spend a lonely night in this place. The terror turned into rage as he turned the light off as he left. Impenetrable darkness surrounded me. I hated dark, closed, musty rooms, and I even hated the feelings of fear that accompanied me then. I couldn't help feeling that Steven did it on purpose. Angrily, I kicked the metal grate with all my might. It shook loudly, drowning out the muffled scream I made because of the pain in my right foot.

To be continued...